The Time of Our Lives

By Lynda Page and available from Headline

Evie
Annie
Josie
Peggie
And One For Luck
Just By Chance
At The Toss Of A Sixpence
Any Old Iron
Now Or Never
In For A Penny
All Or Nothing
A Cut Above
Out With The Old
Against The Odds
No Going Back
Whatever It Takes
A Lucky Break
For What It's Worth
Onwards And Upwards
The Sooner The Better
A Mother's Sin
Time For A Change
No Way Out
Secrets To Keep
A Bitter Legacy
The Price To Pay
A Perfect Christmas
The Time Of Our Lives

headline

First published in 2013 by
HEADLINE PUBLISHING GROUP

1

Cataloguing in Publication Data is available from the British Library

ISBN 978 0 7553 9843 0

Typeset in Stempel Garamond by
Palimpsest Book Production Limited, Falkirk, Stirlingshire

Printed and bound in Great Britain by
Clays Ltd, St Ives plc

Headline's policy is to use papers that are natural, renewable and recyclable products and made from wood grown in sustainable forests. The logging and manufacturing processes are expected to conform to the environmental regulations of the country of origin.

HEADLINE PUBLISHING GROUP
An Hachette UK Company
338 Euston Road
London NW1 3BH

www.headline.co.uk
www.hachette.co.uk

To all the thousands of men and women who have worked tirelessly for long hours and little financial reward in holiday camps throughout the British Isles. Their efforts have enabled hard-working families to escape their normal, drudge-like existences for a short while in order to have a holiday of a lifetime. On their behalf, I thank you.

CHAPTER ONE

The brute force behind the unexpected slap across her face sent Rhonda Fleming reeling backwards, to land heavily against the wall several feet behind her. Before she could gather her wits a harsh voice was bellowing at her, 'Now you listen here, you bitch. I don't care how old or ugly yer are, while yer under my roof you'll do as I tell yer.'

Rubbing her throbbing cheek, where Rhonnie knew she was going to be left with an extremely colourful bruise, she looked directly into the malicious eyes of her attacker, whose face was now close to her own, and answered defiantly, 'I'll remind you that this is my father's house.'

Mavis Fleming issued a sardonic laugh as she gave Rhonnie a hefty jab in her shoulder. 'And I'll remind you, lady, that I'm married to yer dad so that makes what's his mine. When he ain't here, it's my rules we live by – and don't you forget that.'

Rhonnie's temper flared. 'And my father's not here because he's away risking life and limb driving lorries up and down the country, to keep this roof over your and your daughter's heads as well as funding your endless nights out.'

There was a wicked glint in Mavis's eyes when she shot back, 'For your information, you self-righteous cow, Artie knows I go out now and again for a bit of enjoyment while he's away.'

'Now and again! Staying in now and again is more like it.' Before Rhonnie could stop herself she blurted out, 'And don't think I don't know you're fraternising with other men behind my dad's back.' Fraternising was putting it mildly. Several neighbours had awkwardly confided in Rhonnie that they had seen Mavis with several different men in compromising situations, in places they had thought were secluded, and the only reason they weren't telling her father, the same reason as she herself hadn't, was from respect for him and his feelings. In Rhonnie's case, there was the added fear that he could lapse back into the depressed state he had fallen into when her mother had died, not just talk about ending his life but this time decide to do it. The worst thing was, though, that Mavis was well aware of this state of affairs so felt quite at liberty to carry on with her deceitful ways.

She looked suitably insulted by Rhonnie's comment and barked defensively, 'I like other men's company. There's n'ote wrong with having a laugh or two with a member of the opposite sex. Just 'cos I'm married and my husband works away it don't mean ter say I have to live like a hermit. Now I don't care what you've got planned for tonight, I've got plans . . . so like it or lump it, you're babysitting Tracy.' She gave a nasty smirk. 'If you go out and leave her on her own and summat happens to her . . . well . . . it'll be on your head, not to mention what yer father will think of his precious daughter, selfishly leaving her stepsister by herself while his caring wife has gone out to help a sick neighbour. 'Cos that's what I'll tell him, and I'll make sure he'll believe me over 'ote you tell him, yer can bank on that. I missed my calling, didn't I? I should have been on the stage.'

It was apparent that as far as Mavis was concerned this conversation was over. Dressed only in a shabby underslip, bra and knickers, she spun on her tatty mule-styled slippers and stepped over to the old oak gate-legged table, which was cluttered with the remains of their evening meal plus the contents of her make-up bag and hair paraphernalia. The rest of the small two-bedroomed terrace house in a working-class area just off the town centre of Leicester was equally scruffy and untidy. She plonked herself down on a shabby dining chair.

With utter contempt in her eyes, Rhonnie watched her stepmother pick up a mascara case, spit on to the block, rub a small brush over it, then begin darkening her sparse lashes.

How Rhonnie regretted the day her father had met this brassy blonde-haired, hard-faced gold-digging woman. The fault for this state of affairs lay entirely with Rhonnie herself, though. Artie had still been grieving after the untimely death of his beloved wife six months before. He'd felt desperately lost and saw a lonely future ahead for himself, especially when Rhonnie left home eventually. It had been she who had encouraged him to go out that night for a pint at his local, in the hope that being amongst his friends and neighbours again would help lift his depressed mood.

Her parents had been such a devoted couple, and equally devoted to herself, their only child, giving her a happy and secure upbringing. Her mother's sudden death from a blood clot travelling to her heart had totally shattered both Artie and Rhonnie. Dealing with her own grief was hard enough, but trying to shore up her father too was proving to be an impossible task for the girl – until he had utterly shocked her one evening by agreeing to pay a visit to the pub for an hour, if only to stop her nagging him. Unknown to Rhonnie, though, Artie secretly couldn't face the memories the place held for him of times he had taken Muriel there for a night out with their friends, and nor could he face the displays of sympathy that would come his way from the regulars, so instead he had gone to a pub a few streets away.

Rhonnie hadn't needed to be there at the time to know exactly what had happened to him that evening. A few types like Mavis lived in the streets roundabout and Rhonnie had always felt sorry for the naïve men they ensnared, never for a moment thinking her own precious father would be one of them. On the prowl for a meal ticket for herself and her daughter after her own husband had left her – according to Mavis for another woman, though Rhonnie suspected it was because he was fed up of being humiliated by her fornicating ways – her eager eyes had seen the potential in the new arrival. Artie, in his vulnerable state, hadn't stood a chance. Before many weeks had passed, Mavis had used her wily ways to cajole him into marrying her, and from the moment she and her nine-year-old daughter moved into the house, Rhonnie's home life had become a living hell.

Arthur Fleming was the gentle giant sort, and as long as the people he cared for were well and happy then so was he. His job took him away for several days at a time, sometimes over a week depending where his load needed to be dropped, then he'd be back at home for two days before his next trip commenced. When Artie was at home, Mavis would appear to be a proficient housewife and certainly the perfect bedmate, very affable towards Rhonnie and a devoted mother to her own daughter, Tracy, who in turn was very well mannered towards Artie, addressing him as 'Daddy' and constantly fawning over him. Consequently he believed all was well at home and considered himself a lucky man to have found love twice in his life when some men never found it once.

Nothing could have been further from the truth.

As soon as the back door shut after Artie departed for work, as quickly as a chameleon changes colour, the cloak of being a good wife dropped from Mavis and she became a person Artie would not have recognised: bone idle and foul-mouthed, sleeping with any man who would have her purely to quench her seemingly insatiable appetite for sex. Rhonnie knew without doubt that Mavis did not care in any way for her father bar liking the lifestyle he gave her, but she did care for her own daughter and would not consider going out at night unless she had someone to watch Tracy meantime. An old widow woman who lived a couple of streets away, who due to her profound deafness had not heard the gossip about Artie Fleming's new wife, usually obliged as she was mortally glad of the few coppers Mavis slipped her. But she was bed-ridden at the moment with a bad cold, so as far as Mavis was concerned Rhonnie would do instead.

One hand still cradling her smarting cheek, Rhonnie cast a look over at Tracy, lolling with her legs over the arm of the chair Artie always sat in when he was home, engrossed in a *Bunty* comic, carelessly drinking dandelion and burdock, heedless she was dripping it on the chair where the sticky liquid mixed with crumbs from the slice of slab cake she had just wolfed down. She was a petite, pretty girl with a shock of dark hair worn in a ponytail. In front of her stepfather and all outsiders she could appear willing and sweet-natured, the kind of child any parent would be proud to have, but Rhonnie knew at first hand that Tracy had inherited her mother's acting skills. Behind that façade she was a spiteful, manipulative minx.

Rhonnie surveyed the rest of the room. A feeling of deep distress overcame her at the sight of it. Her mother would be mortified if she could have seen how her beloved husband was being used and abused by his new wife and her daughter, not to mention deeply grieved by the way they treated the home Artie and she had so painstakingly saved for and had afterwards tended with great care. If it wasn't for Rhonnie doing her best to clean and tidy up after the slovenly pair, she dreaded to think how disgusting the house would look in a very short space of time.

The mantel-clock struck. Rhonnie's eyes darted towards the 1930s tiled fireplace. It was seven-thirty. Her heart lurched. She should be on her way by now to meet Ivan at eight outside British Home Stores in the town centre. Had in fact been about to leave when Mavis had dropped her bombshell. She was meant to be accompanying him to a lecture, she wasn't sure where, but the topic was Victorian architecture, a subject that wasn't of much interest to her but was very much so to Ivan. He worked as a quantity surveyor, and she was going along in order to show interest in his hobby. She felt so guilty, knowing Ivan would be standing waiting for her in vain, but she had no way of letting him know now. His parents were on the telephone. Had Mavis had the grace to spring this on Rhonnie earlier, then she could have run to the telephone box a couple of streets away to make her apologies, but it was too late now as he would already have left.

Her attention was caught by Mavis scraping back her chair and heading off towards the stairs accessed through a door at the back of the room, leaving behind the mess she had created on the table in the knowledge that Rhonnie would clear it up.

Immediately her mother was out of earshot, Tracy lifted her head from her comic, looked across at Rhonnie and said to her, 'Give us five bob and then you can go and meet that soppy boyfriend of yours. I promise I won't tell me mam.'

Rhonnie walked to the table where she collected together dirty plates and cutlery and shot Tracy a disparaging look before heading off into the kitchen with them. Her stepsister called after her, 'Well, half a crown then.'

CHAPTER TWO

'I'm so sorry to park myself on you at this time in the evening, Carol, but I just couldn't face going back. I feel it's not my home any more. I can't even escape to the privacy of my own room as I have to share it with Tracy. I know she rummages through my stuff and she's stolen money I thought I'd hidden away safely from her thieving little hands. That's why I never let my handbag out of my sight now, even sleep with it under my pillow as uncomfortable as that is.'

Rhonnie raked her hands despairingly through her hair. Her face the picture of misery, she went on: 'My life is such a damned mess, Carol. I hate my home life, my job . . . well, I get on well with everyone there, but it's just somewhere I go to earn money . . . and as for my so-called love life! I don't really know where I stand with Ivan. I don't think he's even speaking to me at the moment, and I can't say I blame him after I let him down last night. But there was no way for me to let him know. I called his office at dinnertime today, was told by the department secretary that he was out all day surveying a site with his boss, but I'm not sure whether that was just what he had told her to say if I called. Maybe he's avoiding me.' Rhonnie paused and stared sadly into the eyes of her best friend. 'I'm pathetic, aren't I? Here I am, a twenty-four-year-old woman who can't sort her own life out.'

Rhonnie had met Carol on the day they had both started as juniors in the offices of Kempton's Hosiery Company. They had become firm friends since then. Rhonnie had been with the eighteen-year-old Carol when she had first met her husband Rodney at the Palais de Danse, was honoured to have been one of her bridesmaids when the pair had married two years later, and again to have been asked to become godmother to their eldest child Garry, who was now three. A little sister for him had arrived eighteen months later.

The two women were seated at Carol's kitchen table, drinking cups of tea.

Carol immediately reassured her, 'You're not pathetic, Rhonnie. If I was in your position I would probably have cut my throat by now.' She leaned over and placed her hand on her friend's, giving it an affectionate squeeze. 'You can't go on like this, that's for certain.' She looked worriedly at Rhonnie for a moment, before she continued, 'That woman is taking you for a right mug . . . your dad too. You need to do something to put a stop to her shenanigans or this state of affairs will go on for ever.' She chuckled. 'I do think it's funny, though, that those two will be waiting for you to arrive home and cook their dinner. I wonder how long it will take them to realise that if they want a hot meal tonight, Mavis will have to get off her fat arse and make it herself.'

Rhonnie flashed her a wan smile. 'Yes, I must admit, that thought does give me a certain satisfaction.' Her morose mood returned then. 'But what can I do about Mavis always taking me for an idiot, Carol? If I told Dad what she was really like, she would only manipulate him into believing I was just trying to split them up because I don't like the fact she's taken my mam's place. Then that would cause bad feeling between me and Dad, and I couldn't bear that.'

Carol mused, 'Mmm, I suppose. I know you have no choice but to cook at home or you'd never get a hot meal, but you could stop cleaning up after them. Admittedly it would mean Artie coming home from work to find the place like a pig sty, and you living in one too, but it would at least show that trollop up for the lazy beggar she is, wouldn't it?' Anger blazed from Carol's eyes then. 'And I tell you something for nothing . . . if she had slapped me as hard as she obviously did you to leave that bruise, I wouldn't have been able to restrain myself. I'd have slapped her back just as hard as a warning that she'd better not use her fists on me again.'

'It took me all my strength not to, but if I had then it would only have given her further ammunition to blackmail me into babysitting for her whenever the old duck down the road can't oblige. She'd just tell my dad I attacked her, and get Tracy to back her up. I can spin a yarn when I have to, but I can't compete with those two in the lying stakes. Mavis would have a blind man believing he could see, and Tracy would kid anyone that she hadn't taken the last cake off the plate when she was holding it in her hand.'

Carol looked at her friend thoughtfully for several long moments before she said, 'I think there's only one answer to your situation, Rhonnie. You need to get out of there. It's the only way you're going to stop her treating you like Cinderella, and the only way Artie is going to see what a lazy so and so she really is. I hope that's enough for him to send her packing, as to be honest, like you, I don't want him to find out what else she's up to behind his back. What that could do to him, considering how he was after your mother died, doesn't bear thinking about.'

Rhonnie heaved another forlorn sigh. 'Don't you think I wish I could walk out, Carol? Not to leave my father, but certainly the other two. I wouldn't care if I never saw either of them again. I can't afford a place of my own, though . . . anywhere half decent, that is.'

Carol said in all sincerity, 'I wish I had room for you to come here, Rhonnie, I really do. But why don't you share a place with someone?'

'That's certainly worth a thought but there's a lot of risk involved, isn't there? You don't know what someone is really like until you live with them, do you? What if I find myself sharing with the housemate from hell and there's nothing I can do about it until they decide to leave? I'd be in the same situation I am now, wouldn't I?'

Before Carol could respond a baby's wail rent the air. Turning her head towards the door that led into the lounge of her two-bedroomed 1930s semi, she shouted, 'Garry, whatever you've taken off your little sister . . . give it her back now or I'll be through to tan your backside, you little monkey!' She turned her attention back to her friend. 'Those kids have driven me daft all day. Been a right grizzly pair, for some reason, and it wasn't like I could take them out as it's been hissing it down all day. The only breather I've had is when you came in and played with them for a while. Thank God their dad will be home soon. After dinner he can take over while I have a soak in the bath to ease my weary bones.' She eyed Rhonnie meaningfully. 'Bit of advice, though. I wouldn't be without my two, love them more than life itself, but you think twice before you have kids as they're a twenty-four-hour job for us women.'

Rhonnie issued a disdainful tut. 'Chance would be a fine thing. I've got to get married first.' She then mused, 'I've been courting with Ivan for five years now and the subject of marriage, or even getting engaged, has never been raised by him.'

Carol studied her friend. Ivan was a fool for not cementing his relationship with Rhonnie. Did he not realise that she was twenty-four, an age when most young woman were married and with a couple of children, like Carol herself had? If he didn't offer Rhonnie some commitment soon then he was risking her ending matters between them and finding someone else. And it wasn't like he couldn't afford to support a wife as he was a qualified quantity surveyor, had a decent job with a very reputable company and excellent prospects

Rhonnie wouldn't have any trouble finding someone else. She was a good-looking woman with her large midnight-blue eyes and narrow straight nose in a heart-shaped face. This was framed with thick honey-blonde hair that at the moment she was wearing in a pageboy flick. She was tall at five foot eight, with a willowy figure that any would-be model would give their eye teeth to possess. The latest styles designed by the likes of Mary Quant and Barbara Hulanicki were intended especially for women with a frame like Rhonnie's, the same sort as Carol herself had had before her pregnancies had changed her shape for ever, much to her chagrin.

At six foot two inches, with a muscular build and chiselled features topped off with a mop of dark blond curly hair, there was no denying that Ivan was the type of man many red-blooded females fantasised over landing themselves. To Carol, though, his looks and his job were all Ivan had going for him. To her way of thinking he had no charisma whatsoever, and neither was he a good conversationalist except on the subject of architecture when he would happily drone on for hours, boring his audience with trivia that was only of interest to the minority of people like him who found the subject fascinating. But Rhonnie obviously saw something in him that Carol herself didn't as she clearly loved and saw him as husband material. Ever a loyal friend, Carol realised she would have to support her friend in her choice, regardless of her own doubts about the match.

'Why don't you raise the subject then?' she suggested.

Rhonnie gawped at her. 'Me? Oh, but it's for a man to do that, isn't it? Ask a woman to marry him.'

'I don't mean you should propose to him. That's not the done thing at all. The only women who do that look desperate, in my opinion. What I meant was . . . well, if you bring up the subject somehow in general conversation it would give him an opening to ask you, if you understand me? Maybe he's been wanting to for a while but just can't find a way to do it. I don't mean to be unkind, Rhonnie, but he's not exactly good at expressing himself, is he?'

She shook her head. 'No, not really. Most times I haven't a clue what Ivan's really thinking, just have to guess and hope

I'm right.' She looked worried. 'Maybe he sees me as good enough to be a girlfriend but not to marry?'

'Don't be daft, Rhonnie. He's not right in the head if he doesn't see what a good wife you'd make him. Anyway, if he didn't see any future with you then he'd have walked away a long time ago, wouldn't he? I think he's just the sort who needs a hefty nudge, to push him in the right direction. Oh, but maybe he's worried that you don't want to settle down with him and is afraid that if he asks you, you'll end it with him.'

Rhonnie frowned. 'I hadn't thought of that.' There was a wistful look in her eyes when she continued, 'As you know, when I was younger I thought I'd be married and with a couple of kids by the age I am now, just like you are. At this rate I've visions of walking down the aisle on my Zimmer frame!'

Carol laughed at the idea. 'And me behind you as your chief bridesmaid, being pushed by Rod in my bath chair . . . Talking of bridesmaids, do you think you'll be expected to have Tracy as one when you do eventually get married?'

Rhonnie pulled a horrified expression at the thought. 'God forbid. I've no doubt that just as we were about to walk up the aisle that girl would be blackmailing me for yet more money before she followed behind.'

'Well, hopefully they'll both be long gone by the time that day comes.' Carol eyed Rhonnie earnestly. 'But even if Ivan proposes tonight, weddings take time to arrange so it's not the answer to sorting out your immediate problem, is it?'

Rhonnie shook her head. 'No. But I have been giving thought to something you suggested. I think you're right, I need to get out. I do need to find someone to share a place with. Whatever they turn out like, they could never be as bad to live with as Mavis and Tracy.' Her eyes suddenly sparkled as she recalled something. 'Come to think of it, Nadine at work was talking a few weeks ago about wanting to leave home. Her parents fight all the time and she says she can't stand it any more but can't afford a place on her own. She's a nice enough girl, a couple of years younger than me, the quiet sort who reads a lot. I get on well enough with her at work, so no reason why we wouldn't get on sharing a place together. I've just got to hope she hasn't already found someone to share with. I'll speak to her tomorrow.'

Carol smiled at her. 'That sounds promising. I know you've savings but probably not enough to buy all you'll need by way of household stuff. I'll start sorting some bits out for you. I can spare a pan or two, a couple of towels and some Bri-nylon sheets. Oh, and I tell you what you can have, and with the greatest of pleasure, that bloody awful vile-patterned dinner service my great-auntie Gladys bought me when Rod and I got engaged. She died not long after so I never had the worry of her popping in and asking why I wasn't using it. It's in the attic somewhere, covered in layers of dust and spiders' webs. I'll get Rod to dig it out. You hated it when you saw it, same as I did, but it'll do you a turn until you can afford something better.'

Her eyes twinkling, Rhonnie told her friend, 'Thanks, Carol. I shall guard it with my life and make sure I give you it back all in one piece.'

She snorted. 'That you won't! Either make sure you handle it carelessly or else find some other deserving case when the time comes to wave it goodbye.'

Rhonnie eyed her pensively. 'I still don't know what to do about Ivan. Do I go round after I leave here tonight? Or telephone him again, hope he's home, and try and make peace between us that way?'

Carol eyed her back knowingly. 'Well, if you don't sort it out with him you'll not sleep tonight. It's my guess you didn't sleep much last night either. Face to face is best. And while you're having your heart to heart, you could bring up the subject of marriage if you get the opportunity. You need to find out where you stand with him, Rhonnie. I'm sure he loves you enough to want to make an honest woman of you and it's just a case of him being given the nod by you that he'd not be making a fool of himself by asking you.'

'Yes, that's probably it. I hope you're right anyway and it's not *me* making a fool of *my*self.'

Before Carol could answer that the back door opened and a tall, well-made man came in, calling out, 'It's me, sweetheart. What a bloody day I've had! Gaffer was in a right bad mood . . . we all reckon he'd had a set to with his wife . . . anyway, I'm desperate for my dinner. What we having tonight? Smells good.' He spotted Rhonnie sitting with his wife at the kitchen table and a broad smile appeared on his handsome face. 'Hello, Rhonnie. Good to see you.' His grin broadened. 'Interrupted a good gossip, have I? Well, I'll go and play with the kids for a bit and let you get on with it.' Noticing the cups they were both cradling, as he stripped off his working donkey coat and hung his knapsack on the hook on the back door, he added, 'Any tea left in the pot for a poor hard-done-to working man?'

Carol scoffed. 'Hard-done-to! You have the life of Riley with me as your wife, Rodney Graves, and it's about time you counted your blessings.'

He responded in all seriousness, 'I do every night, my darlin' . . . when you're asleep and I'm getting some peace from your nagging.'

Carol grabbed a tea towel that lay on the table, rolled it up and flung it at him. 'Cheeky beggar,' she said, fighting to keep her face straight. 'There's tea in the pot, help yourself.' She got up from her chair. 'I'd better start dishing up dinner. You'll stay, won't you, Rhonnie? You can't face what you're planning to do later on an empty stomach. Liver, onions and mash, that suit you? And before you say it, no, you're not imposing. You could make yourself useful and set the table, though.'

CHAPTER THREE

Ivan was treating Rhonnie to a word-by-word account of the lecture he'd attended the previous evening, not bothering to enquire whether she was actually interested or not. Which she wasn't, though out of politeness she listened. Eventually, and much to her relief, he finished. 'Shame you missed it, Rhonnie. The man certainly knows his stuff on Victorian buildings. He's written a book on them. I bought a copy. Got it signed too. I know you'll take care of it, so I'll let you have it to read. There's a great chapter on . . .'

She cut in, 'Yes, give it to me and I'll read it when I have time.' She then took a deep breath before going on, 'Look, Ivan, I know I'm repeating myself, but I am very sorry I left you waiting for me last night. There really wasn't anything I could do about letting you know.'

They were sitting on comfortable chintz-covered fireside chairs next to one another before a roaring fire in the Coach and Horses. The public house was in a village called Anstey, a few miles out of Leicester, and they'd driven there in Ivan's red convertible Morgan Roadster sports car. It did have its advantages, having a boyfriend whose job afforded him the luxury of his own transport, as it meant he could take Rhonnie to places she would otherwise never have visited. The added bonus was that Ivan's car was an open-topped one and in good weather she did love the feeling of exhilaration that rushed through her while motoring at speed along the narrow, winding country lanes.

When she had called at his house earlier and his mother had shown her through, Rhonnie had found Ivan sitting in his parents' tastefully furnished living room. Their three-bedroomed, bay-fronted Victorian house was at the affluent end of Glenfield Road, on the outskirts of the city. Ivan was watching the *Tonight* news programme with his father. He had greeted Rhonnie in his normal affable manner, showing no outward sign whatsoever that he was upset in any way about her no show the night before. He asked her to join him on the sofa and watch the programme with him. His mother, who always treated her welcomingly, the same as his father did, offered her a cup of tea. It was Rhonnie who had suggested to Ivan they should go out for a drink so that she could get him on his own and talk to him in private. Without giving her any indication of whether he was in favour of that or would have preferred to stay in on such a bitter-cold March night, he'd gone to put on his thick outdoor clothing and off they went.

'As I told you earlier, it's no big deal you weren't there,' Ivan was saying. 'I met Charles from work. He'd come on his own so we sat together and went for a drink afterwards.'

This made Rhonnie feel relieved that he wasn't annoyed with her, or causing a fuss about it, but at the same time she would have liked him to have told her how disappointed he was that she wasn't with him.

Ivan was going on, 'It was good really that I met up with Charles socially. I've worked with the man for five years and never realised before that he enjoys camping like I do.'

Rhonnie looked at him in surprise. She had known Ivan for five years and he hadn't once mentioned this fact to her. 'I never knew that,' she said.

He looked surprised. 'Didn't you? Oh, well, I suppose the subject has never come up, that's why. I haven't been since I was young when my parents used to take me to the seaside. Mother and Father could easily have afforded to stay in a hotel, but they both enjoyed the outside life and I caught the bug too.

Anyway, Charles and I are planning something for next weekend. He usually goes with a few mates on their bikes. This time we'll travel together in my car. Hopefully we'll get everything into the boot but it'll be a tight squeeze. Charles knows a great place in Wales . . .'

Ivan rambled on about his plans for the weekend, but Rhonnie wasn't listening. She would really have liked a weekend camping with Ivan, savouring the fresh air of the countryside, the fun of cooking a meal on a small Primus stove by a campfire, sleeping under the stars, but he obviously hadn't given any consideration whatsoever to taking her along. She was about to say would he consider taking her along in future, but lost her chance when she heard him say something else.

'If this weekend goes well, I'm going to suggest to Charles that we make it a regular thing, maybe even go for a week in the summer.'

Rhonnie's heart sank. Ivan had never suggested going away with her for a few days. She felt hurt that he seemed eager to spend time with someone other than his own girlfriend. She said weakly, 'That will be nice for you,' and decided to take this opportunity to tell him about her decision to find a place of her own, hoping that his response would give her an opening to bring up the subject of marriage. 'I've decided to leave home, Ivan. I can't live any longer with my stepmother and sister,' she said. 'I won't be able to afford a place on my own on my wages so I've no choice but to find someone to share with.'

He looked at her thoughtfully. Rhonnie's heart thumped. Was he debating how to ask her to try and put up with her living conditions as they were for a while longer while they arranged their wedding and found a place to live in together?

Her hopes were to be cruelly dashed when he said, 'Well, I think you deserve a medal for living with them for this long. I can't imagine what your father was thinking of when he married that awful woman who's nothing like your mother in any way. Such a nice woman she was.' Then he eyed her warningly. 'Just be careful to make sure you check out carefully anyone you decide to share with, Rhonnie. I wouldn't want you to wake up one morning and find they'd robbed you blind and scarpered, leaving you with their share of the rent to pay.'

Rhonnie's disappointment at his response was very evidently written on her face, as he asked her in bewilderment, 'Have I said something to upset you?' Then, pre-empting the answer, 'Oh, of course I'll help you move in when you find a place, silly girl.'

She flashed him a wan smile and uttered, 'Thank you, Ivan. That will be much appreciated.' His response had left her aware that marriage was not on the agenda for him in the near future. But was that because he wasn't ready to settle down yet, or didn't he see Rhonnie as suitable wife material? She needed to know which it was, she decided.

Fixing his eyes with her own, she asked him, 'Ivan, do you see yourself settling down in the future . . . with me?'

He looked shocked for a moment by the unexpected question and took a long draught from his pint of lager before he finally told her, 'Yes . . . yes, of course I do. I thought you would have realised that, after all this time we've been going out together. My parents, of course, only got married when they were both thirty. Before that, neither of them was ready for the responsibility.' He downed the remains of his drink and got up, asking her, 'Another half of cider for you?'

She knew this was his way of telling her that he wouldn't be ready to take on the responsibility of marriage until he was at least thirty either. She was concerned that he didn't seem to be considering her feelings on such an important matter. She hadn't seen this selfish side of Ivan before and wasn't sure how she felt about this revelation. One thing she was certain about was that she didn't want to wait for another five years to walk up the aisle, then another while after that to start a family. By then she'd have reached the age when most women round here would be looking forward to becoming grandmothers. Rhonnie felt a great need then to be on her own so as to think seriously about her relationship with Ivan. It was obvious he was happy with the present informal basis whereas she was at a stage, had been in fact for a long time, where she wanted more.

'If you don't mind, Ivan, I'm tired. Would you take me home, please?' Rhonnie asked.

Whether he did mind or didn't, he smiled amenably and told her, 'I'll get our coats.'

A while later, Ivan pulled his car to a smooth halt outside Rhonnie's house. He leaned over, gave her a quick kiss on the lips then righted himself and said, 'I'll see you as usual on Saturday then. My house at four.'

The words 'as usual' seemed to reverberate inside her mind. It struck Rhonnie then that those two words seemed to sum up their entire relationship. Right from the beginning, they had met three times a week. On Monday they went for a drink in town. On Wednesday they usually went to the pictures or, as it turned out last night, to a talk Ivan wanted to attend. On Saturday they usually had tea with his parents then spent the evening playing cards with them. She couldn't ever remember seeing Ivan on a Thursday before in all the time they had been together, and was only doing so now so that she could smooth over any offence that her failure to meet him last night had caused. This arrangement had suited Rhonnie once; had freed her to make her own arrangements for nights when she wasn't seeing Ivan. Now and again, though, she would have been thrilled if he had arranged a surprise for her. But then, he wasn't the type of man to act spontaneously in any way. Now she wondered how marriage to him, when it eventually happened, would be with absolutely no surprises in it.

In a subdued voice she replied, 'Yes, I'll see you then.'

She got out of the car and stood on the pavement, shivering in the cold March wind as she watched the car pull away and head off down the street. Once the car had disappeared out of sight, she headed down the entry and let herself in at the back door. Having taken off her coat, which she hung on the back of the door, she made her way into the back room. Here she found old Mrs Trimble knitting in an armchair by the fire and Tracy lounging on the sofa watching the television. Neither of them had heard her come in, Mrs Trimble because she was deaf and Tracy because she was engrossed in a programme.

So as not to startle her, Rhonnie went over and laid a gentle hand on the old lady's shoulder to let her know she was there. Regardless, the old dear jumped and spun her head to look up at Rhonnie with alarmed eyes, staring at her for a second before it registered who she was. Relieved, she said, 'Oh, it's you, ducky,' and gave a yawn. 'Didn't expect you back for a while yet.'

'I came home early as I was tired, Mrs Trimble.'

'I'll get off home meself then, if yer don't mind, lovey? I'm ready for me bed,' she told Rhonnie, gathering together her knitting and putting it into a faded tapestry bag.

Rhonnie then helped her ease her aged body out of the armchair and, after offering to escort her safely home, which the old lady politely declined, saw her out of the house. In the back room again, Rhonnie went over to Tracy who as yet had not acknowledged her but still had her eyes glued to the television set. Rhonnie said firmly, 'You should be in bed, Tracy. It's nearly half-past nine.' When the young girl ignored her, Rhonnie repeated what she had said but louder.

This time Tracy did respond by looking up with a glint in her eyes. 'So?'

Rhonnie snapped back crossly, 'So, you are nine years old and shouldn't be watching adult programmes. You should be in bed sleeping. You've got school tomorrow.'

She defiantly responded, 'So what? I wanna see the end of this programme. I don't know who the murderer is yet. And you ain't me mam, so you can't tell me what to do.'

Rhonnie was normally easygoing, it took a lot to make her lose her temper, but tonight she wasn't in the mood for dealing with a bolshie nine year old. She strode across to the television set, switched it off and then pulled out the plug at the back. She turned to face a gawping Tracy, telling her, 'Your mam's not here. I am. You're the kid and I'm the adult. Don't give me any more of your nonsense, I'm not in the mood. Get to bed. Now.'

The young girl stared at her, flabbergasted. Her stepsister had never spoken to Tracy so harshly, even though at times she knew she had acted towards Rhonnie in a way that would have tried the patience of a saint. Uncharacteristically silent, Tracy scrambled off the sofa and darted towards the stairs. A second later Rhonnie heard their bedroom door slam shut. She was desperate to go to bed herself, to lie in the quiet darkness and think things through about her relationship with Ivan and how she would get herself out of this house, but she decided to let a few minutes pass so that Tracy would get to sleep first. Rhonnie busied herself with making a cup of tea and drinking it.

Since she had not been home earlier the kitchen and back room were both in a state of chaos. The remains of Mavis's efforts to make a meal, when she had finally realised Rhonnie wasn't coming home to cook for them that evening, littered the kitchen; dirty plates, cups, bottle of HP sauce, milk, teapot, sugar basin, salt and pepper pot stood on the dining table along with Mavis's make-up and hair paraphernalia. Tracy's school satchel, shoes, coat and several comics were scattered on the floor by the sofa and across it, along with a trail of crumbs from the food she had eaten. Normally Rhonnie would have gone around tidying it all up, but she decided to take Carol's advice. Her days of skivvying after Mavis and Tracy for the sake of her father were a thing of the past. It would be a hard lesson for him to learn, but Rhonnie felt she needed to be cruel to be kind to him.

A while later, Tracy snoring gently in the single bed a couple of feet away from hers in the small bedroom they shared, Rhonnie stared up at the cracked bedroom ceiling, thinking about Ivan. She'd had several boyfriends before she had met him, of all places, by literally bumping into him one dinnertime outside a greengrocer's shop where she had just been buying a couple of apples. After her profuse apologies to him for not looking where she was going, they fell into step together. He was an apprentice then, on his way to meet his boss at a site in the vicinity of Rhonnie's place of work. Before they parted company they had arranged to meet the following Friday to go to the pictures.

Ivan was nothing like the boys she had been out with before, who thought that buying a bag of chips and a bottle of pop was wining and dining their girlfriend and whose conversation had consisted predominantly of talk about football. Apart from the good looks that turned Rhonnie weak at the knees, Ivan was smart, well-mannered and intelligent. He didn't like football but was interested in the type of subjects that labelled him as boring to others, such as Egyptian history, Greek mythology, and in particular old buildings. Although not a natural conversationalist, he'd needed no persuasion to talk at length about the books he had read on these topics, which at the time Rhonnie had found a refreshing change from having to listen to the football league tables and then putting up with her boyfriend being moody all weekend when his team lost a game. Ivan's job prospects were of no consequence to Rhonnie when she'd first started dating him, but on finding her feelings for him were deepening after a while she had begun to hope he would see a future together with her, and the fact that he would be able to offer them a decent standard of living was an added bonus.

But discovering tonight that after five years with her he was in no rush to settle down, seeing the whole prospect of marriage as a huge responsibility, had worried Rhonnie. She perceived marriage as the union of two people who wanted to build a future together, to work alongside each other and weather the ups and downs. She thought about tonight's revelation long and hard, and reached a painful conclusion. Surely if Ivan truly loved her he wouldn't see marriage to her as a burden, and neither would he want to wait at least another five years to make her his wife? And what if, in another five years, he still wasn't ready to settle down?

She wept silently, the tears rolling down her face to soak into her pillow. Rhonnie was more than ready to become a wife and mother, and wasn't prepared to continue seeing Ivan while knowing he wasn't committed and there were no guarantees he ever would be. She did wonder now if she was still with him because their relationship had become a habit. Maybe what she'd thought was love was merely her own lack of experience and longing for security convincing her that she had found it, when really she had not. It seemed to Rhonnie that the only answer was for her to end their relationship now and hopefully give herself a chance to meet someone else who was ready for commitment. It might not be easy at her age when most eligible men were already taken, but she would sooner be on her own than with a man who after five years in her company preferred to go away camping with a male friend. She would do the deed when she met Ivan on Saturday afternoon, she decided.

Feeling that her world was disintegrating around her, Rhonnie turned over and tried to sleep. She wasn't sure at first what woke her and for a moment wondered if it was morning and time to get up for work until it struck her that it was still pitch dark. She turned over to look at her alarm clock on the floor at the side of the bed. The luminous hands told her it was a quarter to twelve. Rhonnie decided she must have heard some inconsiderate rowdy drunks making their way home from the pub. With upsetting thoughts of Ivan and her own decision coming back to mind, she turned over to try to get back to sleep again. Then the sound of an inebriated man laughing reached her and she realised it wasn't coming from outside but from downstairs in the house. Then she heard someone else laugh. This person's laughter she recognised. It had come from Mavis. A very drunk Mavis.

Rhonnie sat bolt upright, her eyes blazing with anger. It was bad enough that her stepmother was blatantly playing around with other men when she was out, but to bring them here . . . Her temper rose to boiling point. Rhonnie couldn't stop what the woman got up to when she went out, but she was damned sure she wasn't going to stand by and allow Mavis to carry on her despicable ways inside Rhonnie's family home.

Throwing back the bedclothes, she grabbed her dressing gown from the bottom of the bed, and hastily pulled it on. She slid her feet into her slippers, mindful not to rouse Tracy – though she didn't care for the young girl, Rhonnie didn't feel it was right she should actually witness her mother entertaining a strange man. Rhonnie felt her way over to the bedroom door, slipped through and pulled it quietly shut behind her.

She arrived in the back room and stopped short, gazing in horror at the sight that met her eyes. She had expected to find Mavis and her visitor drinking together at the worst, definitely not to find her stepmother sprawled on the sofa, the top half of her low-cut dress pulled down and a man lying on top of her, fondling one of her bare breasts while kissing her neck. Mavis had her head tilted back, eyes closed, a look of ecstasy on her face.

She had always vehemently insisted that her association with other men went no further than having a drink and a laugh with them, but she could hardly say that now Rhonnie had caught her red-handed in such a compromising situation. Outraged, she stepped into the room, declaring, 'You're nothing but a filthy whore, you despicable woman! How can you treat my father so diabolically? And your own daughter is upstairs. What if she'd come down and caught you . . . caught you . . . up to what you are?'

At the sound of Rhonnie's harsh tones, the man leaped up off Mavis to stand looking over at the young woman in guilty horror as he fumbled to do up the zip on his trousers. A drunken Mavis meanwhile sat bolt upright, yanking her bra back over her exposed breasts and her dress in place while glaring at her stepdaughter angrily.

She yelled, 'How dare you call me a whore, you self-righteous cow? Dare to call me 'ote like that again and I'll knock you into Kingdom Come! Now this is a private party and you weren't invited.'

Mavis's guest had straightened his clothes by now and was rushing for the door. She called to him, 'Oi, where you going, Nev?'

He stopped, spun around, flashed an awkward look at Rhonnie and then at Mavis, telling her, 'Best I get off. I'll be seeing yer, Mave.' With that he shot out and moments later the front door slammed shut.

Mavis fumed, '*Now* look what you've done! You've spoiled me fun.'

Rhonnie gawped at her incredulously. 'I can't believe you've no shame whatsoever for what I just caught you doing! Wait until my father hears about this. I'd start packing your bags now if I was you.'

Having fallen sideways in a drunken stupor, legs splayed to show the tops of her stockings held up by a dingy, frayed suspender belt, the older woman issued a wicked laugh and eyed her mockingly. 'You can tell that boring big fat oaf what the fuck you like 'cos like I told yer before . . . by the time I've finished, I'll have him believing that I'm a saint and you're nothing but a liar who doesn't like sharing her precious daddy. It'll be you who ends up out on yer arse. Now, I'm sick of telling you – either live here by my rules or get the fuck out and good riddance to yer! And while you're deciding, be a good little stepdaughter and get me a drink.' She pointed a shaking finger at the bottle of cheap sherry standing on the cluttered table.

Rhonnie stared at her while visions of her own beloved father filled her mind. At this time of night he'd be parked in a lay-by in the middle of nowhere on the long, lonely journey to deliver his load. He'd be huddled under a blanket, trying to catch some sleep on the uncomfortable bench seat in the cold cab of his lorry before setting off again in the early hours of the morning for the remainder of the drive back to Leicester. He'd be firmly of the belief that the three women back home were counting down the hours until he returned safely back to them, when in truth it was just one who was. The other two were only interested in the money he earned to pay for their new lifestyle. It was a far better one than they'd been living before Mavis spun her web of deceit to ensnare him.

It was one thing Rhonnie suspecting that Mavis was making a fool of Artie, but another one entirely having indisputable proof that she was. If she didn't tell him what she now knew then she would be failing him as his daughter, but if she did she risked Mavis turning him against her. It wasn't in Rhonnie's nature to act deceitfully. Little white lies to save someone's feelings she found easy to tell, but not blatant ones. Her father knew her better than anyone, even Carol, and immediately he came back he'd know something was wrong and demand to know what, wouldn't rest until he was convinced she was telling him the truth. She had decided earlier to leave this house for a place of her own but now she hadn't the luxury of time to find herself somewhere due to her father's imminent return. Rhonnie also knew that with everything that was on her mind going back to bed was a waste of her time, she would never sleep, and her desire to disassociate herself from Mavis was overwhelming, so she would go now.

As frightening as it was to her, Rhonnie knew that she had to leave Leicester, go somewhere far enough away that it wasn't easy for her father to visit her and ask awkward questions. Rhonnie decided she would write him a letter, which she would send to his firm so at least she knew he would get it, not trusting Mavis not to rip up anything that was left with her. She would use the excuse that she had gone away because she had broken up with Ivan and couldn't bear staying in Leicester and risking the chance of bumping into him. Then there was her job. Just leaving without notice wasn't the done thing, but Rhonnie felt she had no choice. Besides, she wouldn't be hard to replace, so she had no real qualms over that. There was Ivan too. He deserved to receive more than a letter ending their relationship, but better that than walking away with no explanation. Carol she would have liked to have gone and visited, to tell her dear friend face to face what she was doing, but at this time of night she would be in bed and it wouldn't be fair to disturb her. Rhonnie decided she would write to her also, but the letters could wait until she had reached her destination.

Thankfully she had enough money saved safely in her Post Office account, away from Tracy's thieving hands, along with what she had left from her last wage, to buy her a train ticket somewhere and to pay for accommodation in a cheap bed and breakfast place until she secured herself a job. She could decide where best to go once she was out of here and away from the vile woman waiting for Rhonnie to pour her a drink.

Giving Mavis a look of pure contempt, she spun on her heel and headed back up the stairs to collect her belongings, ignoring the cry of, 'Oi, I told yer to get me a drink!'

When Rhonnie returned back downstairs a while later, suitcase packed, all that remained was for her to collect her coat, hanging on the back door, and put on her shoes. Mavis was still in the same position as she had left her, slumped on the sofa, and had fallen into a drunken stupor, snoring like a pig. Rhonnie stood for a moment, looking at the woman whose selfishness was causing her to abandon the home she had been so happy in once. She vehemently hoped that, despite the pain it would cause him, her father would find the strength to kick Mavis and her daughter out, freeing himself to find another woman who would value his worth and treat him in the manner he deserved.

Rhonnie headed for the kitchen where she put on her coat and shoes and walked out of the house without a backward glance.

CHAPTER FOUR

As Rhonnie made her way through chilly streets that were deserted but for the odd drunk lying slumped in the gutter and the occasional copper on his beat, her emotions were in turmoil. She was very upset about the hurt and bewilderment her father would suffer at her abrupt departure, as well as fearful of heading off into the unknown while totally alone. There was no going back for her, though. Whatever she faced in the future could not be any worse than living in the same house as Mavis and being party to her deceit.

She had thought the train station would be as deserted as the streets were at one o'clock in the morning, apart maybe from a night porter keeping watch, but she was surprised to find the place a hive of activity. Several porters were loading sacks of mail and parcels, milk churns, livestock crates and other freight on to two trains. Steam was billowing from their funnels to swirl around the station in the cold night air. No one took any notice of Rhonnie as she went over to the waiting room where a timetable of train arrivals and departures was displayed. Putting down her heavy case by her feet, she stood before it wondering where best to go to build a new future for herself.

Wherever she chose she would be presented with the same problems and challenges. Her father's job covered the north of England and Scotland, so it would have to be somewhere down south, she decided. There seemed to be so many places listed for her to choose from, some of which she had never heard of. Then she noticed that trains to some of these places ran infrequently, maybe only once or twice a week, and to reach others she would have several changes to make, with lengthy waits in between. Wherever she chose, Rhonnie wanted to arrive there as soon as possible so she could start looking for work and a place to live. Then the name of one town glared out at her. Trains to that destination ran several times a day, and she'd have no changes to make. According to the timetable the next train left at six in the morning. Three hours after getting on the train she'd be on her way to building a future for herself in a city where most people headed to make their fortunes, although she'd settle just for making a reasonable living. That city was London.

Her decision made, there was nothing for her to do now but while away the next few hours until her train departed. Picking up her case, she went into the waiting room. It was quite a large space with wooden bench seats fixed to three sides of its dingy cream-painted walls. On the one at the far end was a large fireplace; unfortunately no fire was burning brightly inside it at this time of the night, and the room was cold. Above the fireplace hung a photograph of the Queen taken at her Coronation in 1953, twelve years before. On the wall opposite was a door leading into the buffet room, usually a hive of activity but now eerily deserted until it opened again at six-thirty in the morning. The waiting room was anything but welcoming but at least it offered some shelter from the chilly night air swirling around the platforms.

The room was dimly lit and at first Rhonnie thought she had the place to herself, not noticing the figure huddled asleep on a bench in the shadows by the fireplace until she made her way further inside, meaning to settle as far away from the draught coming under the door as possible. Her footsteps across the bare wooden floor obviously roused the slumbering person who sat bolt upright and opened its eyes to glance over fearfully at the new arrival. Startled herself by the unexpected presence, thinking it was someone lying in wait for no good reason, Rhonnie took a step back.

It was the stranger who regained control of their faculties first. 'Oh, thank God you're not what I thought you were!'

It was a woman's voice, Rhonnie realised with relief, and she crossed the room towards her, asking, 'Who did you think I was?'

'A robber, come to fleece me of my belongings.'

Rhonnie chuckled. 'Well, if it's any consolation, I thought the same of you.' She put her case down and took a seat on the bench nearby her new companion, taking the chance to look her over properly. She was about seventeen, Rhonnie guessed, stick-thin, average-looking, with a mop of bright ginger corkscrew curls, plus a splattering of freckles over her pale-skinned cheeks and button nose. Her eyes were bright blue and her pale eyebrows and eyelashes barely showed in the dim light. Considering the case and couple of bags that stood on the floor beside her, Rhonnie judged that this girl too was off somewhere for a lengthy period.

The young woman had noticed Rhonnie's case and said to her, 'Running away from home, are you?'

Rhonnie looked taken aback. 'What makes you ask that?'

'Well, who in their right mind chooses to spend the night in a freezing waiting room voluntarily?'

'You've got a point.' Rhonnie was flattered that the younger woman thought her young enough to be a runaway, but then she remembered the light wasn't very good in here. She flashed a glance at the young woman's belongings before meeting her blue eyes. 'Is that what you are doing, running away from home?'

The girl said matter-of-factly, 'No, I was waved off quite happily by my mam. She isn't what I'd call a motherly mother, isn't my mam. My dad left home just after I was born, and I have to say she did her best to look after us but made it clear right from when me and my brothers and sisters were all little . . . there's six of us in all and I'm the youngest . . . that she couldn't wait for us to grow up so she could be shot of the lot of us. I can't say as I blame her, I wouldn't like to be left on my own with six kids to look after either. Being the good kids we were, we granted her wish and all left home as soon as we could.

'I only came back for the winter. Believe me, today couldn't come quickly enough for me or me mam. But she wasn't in the best of moods tonight and I decided that spending it here was preferable to listening to any more gripes about how unfairly life has treated her. I'm not coming back home next year. I've made some friends now and we're all going to find ourselves a place we can share over the winter months and get temporary work in a shop or factory.' Rhonnie frowned quizzically at her, wondering what kind of job she did that gave her the whole of the winter off. Before she could ask, though, the girl was saying, 'So where are you heading to?'

Rhonnie told her, 'London.'

'Got family there, have you?'

'No.'

The young woman pulled a knowing face at her. 'Oh, I see, you think London's the place to make your fortune, do you? Well, let me tell you, it's a nice place to visit, but if you believe that the streets are paved with gold then you're in for a shock because they're the same dirty grey stone Leicester's streets are paved with.'

Rhonnie snapped back at her, 'I'm not so stupid as to believe that. I'm not after making a fortune. Just getting myself a job and a place to live will be enough for me.'

The other girl said matter-of-factly, 'That's all I was after too. When I first left home the year before last, London was where I headed. I was so excited at being where it all happened, so to speak. I saw meself living in a big flat, having parties every night that all the in crowd fought to come to, and buying all me clothes down Carnaby Street. But a fanciful dream is all it was. It's bloody expensive to live down there! The rent for a room in a slum of a house costs you nearly all your wage. It's easy enough to get a job, but the wages for ordinary workers like us ain't that much more than we get up here. And the food's much dearer too. If I hadn't met Jason and he'd told me about the job I'm doing now, I'd have ended up using the last of me money for my train ticket home and then have had to go back to me mam's, begging her to take me in. If I was you I'd think twice about heading down there, if you don't fancy joining the homeless.'

Rhonnie looked at her dumbstruck for a moment. This was not what she was wanting to hear. Living in a slum on the breadline was not at all the kind of future she wanted for herself. It seemed that the great city was not going to offer her what she was seeking after all. Before she went back out to look again at the train timetable and decide on another place to head to, out of curiosity she asked her companion, 'Just where is it you work that closes for the winter?'

'A holiday camp.'

Rhonnie looked impressed. 'Oh, Butlin's in Skegness? I know several people who've been there for a holiday. They said they had a fabulous time.'

'I wish. That's the camp everyone wants to work in as it's the best, but that means they can pick and choose their staff and to get a look in you have to have experience. I plan to work there eventually. But first I'm getting experience from Jolly's. It's a holiday camp further up the coast, just past Mablethorpe. It's similar to Butlin's but not as big.'

Rhonnie asked, 'Are you a redcoat there?'

The younger woman ruefully shook her head. 'I'm just a chalet maid. They don't have redcoats at Jolly's. The blazers the entertainment staff wear are striped yellow and green, so they're called stripeys. Even to be considered for a job as a stripey you have to be able to dance and sing and have a good smile. Unfortunately, I was born with two left feet, have a voice like a fog horn and me teeth are crooked, so I've no chance of ever becoming one of them. I want more than just being a glorified cleaner, though. I worked really hard last year, got no black marks against me, so I'm hoping I'll be promoted to a waitress in the restaurant this year. My aim is to work my way up to becoming a receptionist. I love helping people, you see.'

Rhonnie smiled at her and said encouragingly, 'I'm sure you'll get there.' Then she looked at her quizzically. 'The holiday season doesn't start until April, so why are you going there now?'

'You can imagine how rundown the place has got since it's been shut down over the winter, so all the cleaning, gardening and maintenance staff go in a month early to get the place ready.'

'Oh, I see. You must like working at Jolly's or you wouldn't be going back then?'

'Yeah, I do, even if the hours are long. We work from seven until six, and only get one day off a week. The money isn't that great either, but considering that I don't have to worry about paying rent or for food, and can eat as much as I like, I'm better off than I am at me mam's at any rate.'

Rhonnie's brows knotted in thought. Working at a holiday camp had never crossed her mind before, but if she could get a job at the likes of Jolly's then it would certainly solve her immediate problems all in one go, give her a useful breathing space while she made enquiries as to what town would suit her best to make a long-term future. She keenly asked her companion, 'Would there still be jobs going at the camp or is it too late to apply?'

'All the camps do a recruitment drive for the coming season in January in the national papers, but Jolly's might not have filled all their positions yet. Anyway, there are always some vacancies even during the season as some staff decide it's not for them and leave, especially those who work in the kitchens or cleaning like me.' She looked at Rhonnie quizzically. 'You thinking of coming to work there?'

She nodded. 'Yes, I am.'

The other girl said with conviction, 'Oh, then I'm sure you'll get set on.' Her eyes lit up. 'If you work as a chalet maid then hopefully you'll be on the same team as me and I can show you the ropes.' She gave a giggle. 'Prepare yerself, though. You'll never believe some of the things I've found down the back of the beds! Anyway, I can introduce you to the friends I made last year. Hopefully they're all coming back and haven't changed their minds. And you'd better like parties as most nights there's one going off in one of the staff's chalet.' She leaned down to pull a Thermos flask out of one of her bags, holding it aloft. 'Fancy a cuppa?'

Rhonnie's dismal mood was suddenly swept away by a feeling of excitement. She was about to step through a new door into an unknown world, but whatever challenges she faced, she would at least have a roof over her head, food in her stomach, and never be short of company. She smiled her appreciation. 'Thank you, I'd love one.'

CHAPTER FIVE

Rhonnie's eyes shot open as a rough hand gripped her shoulder and a stern voice spoke. 'Come on, miss. Wakey, wakey! If you don't want to end up back in Louth, you'd best get off. The train leaves in two minutes.'

Through bleary eyes she stared village idiot-like at the kindly middle-aged face looking down on her, wondering just where she was. Thankfully her memory returned and she said to him, 'Oh, we've arrived in Mablethorpe.' At long last, she thought gratefully.

The journey from Leicester had involved two changes of train, first at Peterborough, then at Louth for the Mablethorpe link. The waits in between had been lengthy. Her new friend, who Rhonnie now knew as Anita but was known by all as Ginger for obvious reasons, had kept her awake for the remainder of the night, through their breakfast of bacon and eggs in the station buffet when it had opened at six-thirty, until their train for Peterborough had arrived at seven-thirty for its departure at seven-forty-three, chattering non-stop about anything and everything, obviously too fired up in her excitement at returning to the camp and catching up with her friends for any sleep. A desperately tired Rhonnie, purely out of politeness, had forced herself at least to nod here and there as though she was taking in everything Ginger was telling her.

She had thought she'd be able to snatch some sleep on the train to Peterborough but their carriage had been packed and several noisy children had prevented her. Ginger hadn't lied, it seemed, she really did like to help people and offered her services to entertain the children, much to the relief of their harassed mothers, roping Rhonnie in to help. No sleep was afforded her either on the train to Louth. It wasn't because of noisy children but the booming voices of two middle-aged women who didn't seem to mind that the other travellers in their carriage were privy to their health problems and gripes about their husbands. By the time Rhonnie settled in her seat on the train to Mablethorpe she was so tired that nothing could prevent her from falling asleep. She still would be now had the guard not woken her.

Despite still being fuddled with sleep and wondering where Ginger was, and why she had seemingly been abandoned, Rhonnie hooked her handbag on her arm and jumped up to drag her case down from the luggage rack. Flashing a smile of appreciation to the guard for waking her, she stepped on to the platform, having to push her way through several frustrated passengers who'd been waiting for her to get out so they could get in.

Putting her heavy case down by her feet, Rhonnie took a look around. Several porters were loading the last of the freight on to the end carriage by the guard's van. Just visible through the swirl of white smoke by the engine stood the station master, whistle in his mouth ready to wave off the train as soon as the porters were finished. There was no sign of Ginger. Rhonnie vaguely remembered the girl telling her last night that they had to catch a bus from the station to the camp and so assumed that her new friend had gone ahead to ask the driver to wait for her. She'd better hurry as she couldn't expect him to hold up the bus for ever and she didn't relish the thought of having to wait around for the next to arrive, feeling she'd done enough waiting for transport for one day. To the sounds of carriage doors slamming shut and the station master blowing his whistle, Rhonnie picked up her case and started to make her way to the station entrance. She had hardly taken two steps when she heard the sound of pounding feet, and before she could look round something hard had clipped her shoulder, sending her suitcase flying from her hand. It took Rhonnie a big effort to keep her balance and not fall over. Next thing she knew a carriage door was slamming shut, a window was pulled down and a male voice was calling out to her, 'I'm sorry but I had to catch this train.' And as it chugged off she just managed to hear him add, 'Meeting my girlfriend to ask her to marry me!'

Rhonnie gave him a wave to show him his apology was accepted. With great sadness she watched the train disappearing off into the distance, thinking that this man's girlfriend was indeed a lucky woman that he was so keen to make her his wife.

She then remembered that hopefully Ginger was holding up the bus. With a feeling of urgency she flashed a look around for her suitcase and was embarrassed to spot it several yards further down the platform. It had burst open on hitting the hard ground and all Rhonnie's personal belongings, including her underwear, were scattered around for everyone to see. Thankfully, though, the station was now deserted. Dashing over, she gathered all her things together, ramming them unceremoniously back inside the case and having to sit on it to force it closed. Jumping up, she snatched the case and hurried out of the station as quickly as the heavy load she was carrying would allow.

Arriving outside Rhonnie gave a shiver as an unexpected gust of cold wind blowing in from the sea almost whipped her off her feet. Above her the sky was as grey as the buildings in the near-deserted street stretching out before her. This image of Mablethorpe was nothing at all like the inviting posters she had seen advertising it as the place to spend holidays basking in the sun on miles of golden sands. As she looked around, her shoulders sagged in worry to see no sign of either Ginger or a bus. Rhonnie wondered how long she'd have to wait for the next one to arrive. Stupidly, she realised now, she'd been banking on landing a job at the camp but what if they didn't have one they felt she was suitable for? It was coming up for three o'clock. By the time she eventually arrived there, enquired after work and possibly had to make her way back to town, it would be dark and the thought of traipsing alien streets looking for a place to stay for the night, considering it was out of season and few places would be taking in guests at this time of year, was not one she relished at all. Would it not be more sensible of her to find a place to stay for the night now and try her luck at the camp tomorrow?

As she stood debating the odds, the roar of a engine resounded and Rhonnie turned her head to see an old pre-war motor bike and sidecar heading at speed towards her before pulling to a screeching halt a foot or so away from her. As soon as he'd switched off the ignition the tall helmeted rider leaped off, dashing around the other side to lift up the top of the sidecar and help out his passenger. The squat elderly woman inside looked to be ninety if she was a day. After much pulling, the driver finally managed to heave her out.

Dressed in a long black woollen coat that almost reached the floor, a fox fur wrapped around her neck, black felt hat with a spray of plastic cherries on the brim rammed down over her head, as soon as the old lady had steadied herself on the pavement she started to hit the man with her bulging handbag, shouting angrily at him, 'Leisurely drive you said, our Melvin. I thought me end had come when we went around that corner so fast the sidecar wheels left the road. You was doing at least a hundred miles an hour. Wait 'til I tell yer dad what you put me through, he'll skin you alive so he will.'

Hands up in an effort to fend off the blows, Melvin shot back, 'The wheels left the road when we went around that bend 'cos the wind caught us, Gran, not 'cos I was going too fast. If I'd have gone any slower you'd have missed your train and there isn't another today so then you would have missed Great-auntie Mildred's birthday tea. And she's so looking forward to you staying the night with her.'

The ancient lady lowered her arm. Shooting him a dark scowl, she snorted, 'Well, if I wasn't white-haired before I got in the sidecar, I certainly am now.' Clutching her small overnight case, she turned and waddled off into the station, calling back in a cracked voice, 'Don't bother picking me up tomorrow, I'll catch the bus home.'

Shaking his head, the man watched his relative until she had disappeared inside the station. Having retaken his seat on the bike, he made to kick it into life when he spotted Rhonnie and said jocularly, 'Great-grandmothers, eh? Who'd have 'em?'

She had never known her great-grandparents, and both sets of her grandparents had died when she'd been very small. Rhonnie hardly remembered them but how she wished she had a kindly gran to go and stay with until her father saw sense over his choice of second wife. Then she'd not be in this strange town now, facing God knew what. Before he went off the young man might, though, be able to give her some information. Rhonnie called to him, 'You don't happen to know when the next bus is due to go to Jolly's camp, do you?'

He pulled a face. 'You've a bit of a wait for it, I'm afraid.'

'Oh! An hour? Two?'

'Try about eighteen. Out of season, there's only two buses a day that go to the camp. One at nine in the morning, and the one I assume you've just missed at ten to three. But I can give you a lift there, if you like? I go past the camp on me way home.' He saw her frown and added, chuckling, 'Don't take any notice of Gran. Any speed faster than a horse and cart goes is a hundred miles an hour to her. I was only doing thirty.'

She shot him a knowing look. 'Seemed faster than thirty to me when you drove up and skidded to a halt.'

He grinned sheepishly. 'Well, okay, thirty-five I was doing, but no more than that. I can see by your face that you're worried, but you've no need to be. I've been riding Bertha . . .' he patted the handlebars of the bike affectionately '. . . since I was eight and haven't had an accident yet. Well . . . except for when I landed in a ditch that time, but it wasn't my fault. Some idiot left the field gate open and let out the herd of cows. So do you want a lift or not? Only I need to get home and wash and change as I'm meeting my fiancée tonight to finalise the plans for our wedding. We're getting married in three weeks and the day can't come quickly enough for me. I can't wait to wake up every morning and find her beside me.'

It seemed to Rhonnie that she wasn't going to be allowed to come to terms easily with the fact that the man she had hoped to marry had been in no rush to make her his wife and wake up beside her every morning.

Squashed into the narrow sidecar, her knees touching her chin to allow room for her suitcase, Rhonnie clung on to the sides as Melvin drove the vehicle at a speed far in excess of the thirty-five he'd told her he would. Either his speedometer was wrong or he couldn't read it. Rhonnie was very relieved that the distance from Mablethorpe to the camp was no more than seven miles so lasted barely more than ten minutes. He skidded the bike to a halt before large iron gates with the name 'Jolly's Holiday Camp' in large iron letters incorporated into the arch which spanned them. The countryside around was flat and largely empty. After the motor-bike driver had helped her out and she'd thanked him for the lift Rhonnie watched as he sped off in his haste not to be late meeting his fiancée. It was only then that it struck her that should she not be lucky in her search for work at Jolly's, she faced a long walk back into town down narrow country lanes in the dark.

CHAPTER SIX

To Rhonnie's further dismay the large ornate iron gates, festooned with spiders' webs and dried leaves were chained and padlocked shut. For a moment Rhonnie feared that her trip out here had been in vain and she did face that long walk back into Mablethorpe, until with great relief she saw that a single gate set further down in the chain-link fence was ajar, and realised that was where the staff entered and exited during the winter months when the large gates the campers used were closed.

As she walked through the gate it felt to Rhonnie as though she'd stepped into a ghost town. She assumed the staff who had arrived today, Ginger amongst them, would be settling into the staff chalets, situated at the back of the camp somewhere away from the paying guests, ready to begin work tomorrow. The employees from last year would be reacquainting themselves with each other as well as introducing themselves to the new recruits, judging from what Ginger had told her.

Putting down her case, Rhonnie took a look around. Before her a wide tarmacked drive circled around a grubby white four-tiered fountain, adorned with statues of dolphins and mermaids from which water spouted when it was switched on. To her left, disappearing off into the distance, ran a long single-storey building sectioned off for various uses. There were signs above each entrance, announcing their functions during the season. To her right was a two-storey building which held the reception and administration office. The building joining it housed the cinema, the one next to that the ballroom, and what came next Rhonnie couldn't see, her view restricted by the fountain, but she assumed there would be other entertainment facilities. There was a large outdoor pool which was empty and filthy now, as was the sunbathing area surrounding it. Beyond the pool, the roofs of several rows of guest chalets were visible. Dead flower heads and foliage filled the flowerbeds; the grass on the lawned areas looked desperate for a cut. The gusting wind was swirling detritus all around.

It seemed inconceivable to Rhonnie that in four short weeks, through the efforts of the staff, the whole winter-weary camp would undergo a miraculous transformation, ready to receive the first holiday guests for the promised holiday of a lifetime.

Rhonnie imagined all those guests. She saw those faceless people growing ever more excited as the date for their stay here drew nearer. For them this would be a haven from their normal drudgery, especially the mothers who for one precious week would not be having to cook or clean. All they would need to worry about was filling the hours of leisure they wouldn't usually enjoy.

Rhonnie had been conceived in 1940 when her father had been on leave from fighting for his country. She had been five when he'd come home for good, thankfully unscathed but to no work, the family having to survive on what her mother had earned from working in a grocery shop until the beginning of the fifties when jobs for men became more plentiful and her father found work as a lorry driver for a company that carried all manner of goods up and down the country. Moving out of the tiny slum terrace her parents had lived in since getting married to somewhere better, then replacing their ancient furniture little by little, meant that family holidays didn't figure in their lives. By the time money was available for such luxuries, her mother was dead. Had she still been alive, Rhonnie knew without doubt that Muriel Fleming would have thought she'd arrived in heaven to be spending a week in a place like this.

Landing herself a job here suddenly became vital to Rhonnie. Apart from the fact that it would resolve her own immediate problems, she could do her best, along with the rest of the staff, to make sure all the work-weary mothers who came here received the carefree week her own never got to experience.

Assuming her best port of call to enquire after work would be the reception area, she heaved up her case and headed around the fountain towards it. On arrival she found Reception as deserted as the outside of the camp. The counter must have been manned earlier by someone checking in the staff and handing them their chalet keys, but now that the last bus had arrived they had gone off duty. There was a door to her left, a sign on the front announcing 'Radio Jolly', and through a glass window to the side of the door, in the tiny room beyond, hardly bigger than a cupboard, Rhonnie could see radio equipment. That room was empty too. She heaved a dispirited sigh. It seemed she was too late to enquire after work today.

Not at all looking forward to the long trek back into Mablethorpe, then the hunt for a bed for the night and somewhere to eat, she made to leave when the sound of voices coming from above reached her ears. Her spirits rose. Maybe she wasn't too late to seek work today after all.

A door to the right of her had a sign on it announcing 'Administration Offices'. She went over to it, opened it and peered through to see a set of stairs leading up. She stood still for a moment and listened. The talking had ceased, to be replaced by the sound of someone moving about. Hopefully that someone might consider her for a job. Leaving her suitcase at the bottom of the stairs, Rhonnie went up them.

The door at the top was ajar. Tapping on it to announce her presence, she pushed it fully open and went inside. The room she entered was large with white-painted walls, one of them filled with wide windows that looked out on to the entrance to the campsite below, making the room light and airy. There were two desks in the room. Obviously one belonged to the secretary, the other to her junior. As well as having a typewriter on it, on a small separate table butted up against the side of the junior's desk was a ten-line modern PBX switchboard. The room also contained several cupboards and at least a dozen filing cabinets. There was a door at the back which Rhonnie assumed led to other offices, possibly the accounts department among others.

An attractive, shapely, blonde-haired woman in her mid-forties, dressed very smartly in a navy fitted jacket and pencil-style skirt, with a crisp white blouse, stood behind one of the desks, taking items out of drawers and putting them into a shopping bag. On hearing Rhonnie arrive, she straightened up to look over enquiringly at her. Despite the fact that she looked extremely upset, angry even, she asked, 'May I help you?'

Smiling back at her, Rhonnie took several steps further into the room. 'I'm looking for a job.'

The woman appraised her for a moment before she asked, 'What line of work are you in?'

'Office. I'm a competent shorthand typist, can operate a switchboard, do filing . . . any office work really. I was my boss's right hand in my last job.'

'In that case, your timing is perfect.'

Leaving Rhonnie wondering what she meant, the woman picked up a photo frame from the desk and put it into the bulging shopping bag. She then took her coat from where it had been draped over the back of a chair, put it on and picked up her handbag. Walking over to Rhonnie by the door, she stopped long enough to tell her, 'You can have my job. Secretary to Mr Jolly and in charge of the general office.' She thrust a set of keys into Rhonnie's hand and said meaningfully, 'Good luck. Believe me, you'll need it with the likes of him as your boss.'

With that she disappeared through the door and went down the stairs.

Slipping the bunch of keys absently into her pocket, Rhonnie stared blindly after her for several moments, unable to comprehend what had just happened. The most she had hoped to land herself was a job cleaning chalets or in the kitchens, but secretary to the boss and in charge of the general office! Rhonnie possessed all the ability necessary to do the job as she had on many occasions stood in for her previous boss when she had taken time off work for any reason, and been praised for her competence. The workings of a busy hosiery factory office wouldn't be much different from those of a holiday camp. What troubled her, though, was why the woman who had previously held this position had just walked out of it? What had she meant by wishing Rhonnie good luck, telling her she would need it?

Just then the door to the stairs burst open and a young girl of about eighteen came rushing in, brandishing a bottle of Napoleon brandy. She was very pretty, of medium height and with a boyish figure. She was dressed in a bright yellow cap-sleeved mini-dress with black binding around the edges, black wedge-heeled slingback shoes, and with her thick dark hair styled in the same way as the singer Cilla Black. She blurted out, 'Sorry I took so long, Miss Hickson. I couldn't get the key to work in the door of the bar stores. It's really stiff but I got it to turn eventually. We should tell Dan it needs . . .' She stopped abruptly, realising that the woman she was addressing wasn't the one she'd thought it was. In a reproving tone she said to Rhonnie, 'Was that your case at the bottom of the stairs? I nearly broke my neck over it. You should be more careful where you leave things. You're here for a job, I take it? Miss Hickson seeing to you, is she?'

Rhonnie looked blankly at her for a moment, debating how to inform this young woman what had happened during her absence. She decided just to tell her straight. 'I apologise for leaving my case where I did. I'll be more careful in future.' Assuming Miss Hickson and the woman she had just encountered were one and the same, she then told the girl, 'Miss Hickson has dealt with me. I'm going to be working in the office with you. My name is Rhonda Fleming. Rhonnie.'

'Er . . . Jacqueline Sims. Jackie. I didn't know we had a vacancy in the office? Miss Hickson never said.'

'Well, actually, it's Miss Hickson's job I'll be doing.'

Jackie looked at her, stupefied. 'But if you're going to be doing Miss Hickson's job, what job will she be doing?'

'Well . . . none at the camp. Miss Hickson has left.'

Shocked, Jackie exclaimed, 'She's what! But this is sudden. Miss Hickson never mentioned a word to me about leaving. Mind you, no one tells me anything anyway.' She suddenly stopped her flow of words and stared at Rhonnie for several long seconds before she continued. 'It's to do with that row they were having, isn't it? I knew it was a bad 'un. I could hear him shouting at her even though the door to his office was shut. I couldn't hear what the row was about though. When Miss Hickson came out to ask me to fetch the brandy for him, her face was as black as thunder and she was angry. I've never seen her angry before.' Jackie looked sad when she added, 'She was a stickler to work for, liked everything done properly, but she wasn't a bad sort. I'll miss her.'

She lowered her voice before carrying on. 'We had no idea he was even coming. Miss Hickson has worked for Mr Jolly senior for ten years and there's no one knows more about how this place works than she does. Except Mr Jolly himself, of course. Miss Hickson tried to hide it but she was so upset when we first heard about him, she disappeared into his private washroom and was gone for ages. When she came out she'd tried to disguise it with her make-up, but I could see she'd been crying. Well, I suppose she would be upset, wouldn't she, having worked for him for all these years? Anyway Miss Hickson thought that the family would leave her to run the camp until he got better and came back, but obviously she was wrong.

'I didn't have a clue who the other one was when he came storming in here about two hours ago, demanding the keys to the drinks cabinet, and told Miss Hickson to come straight to his office even though we were up to our eyes checking off the staff and allocating them their chalets at the time. Miss Hickson knew who he was, though. I caught sight of her face when he first came in and . . . well . . . I can only say that she looked like she'd seen a ghost.'

Jackie paused for a moment, a touch of sadness glinting in her large green eyes, which were edged around in thick black liner and long false lashes resembling spiders' legs. 'It is awful about Mr Jolly Senior. One minute he's charging around as large as life, and now . . . well, he's lost the use of his left side and can't talk either. We're waiting for news on whether the doctors think he'll recover the use . . . Oh, dear, it really is so terrible.'

Rhonnie mouthed, 'Yes, it is. His family must be beside themselves.' Then she asked, 'Just who is this man Miss Hickson was arguing with?'

'Oh, I should have explained better. Mr Jolly Senior's son, Michael. I asked Miss Hickson who he was when she came out to ask me to fetch the brandy for him. I've worked here three years and I didn't even know Mr Jolly had a son.' Jackie pulled a face. 'From what I've seen of him and the way he spoke to Miss Hickson . . . well . . . I don't think I'm going to enjoy working for him. I suppose I've no choice, though, until Mr Jolly Senior is well enough to take over again?'

Rhonnie meanwhile was wondering about the cause of the bad feeling between the owner's son and his father's secretary. He obviously hadn't been working at the camp alongside his father, as Jackie hadn't known of his existence before, and Rhonnie wondered about that too.

Jackie was saying to her, 'Had you better take this to Mr Jolly as he's waiting for it?'

The girl was holding out the bottle of brandy for Rhonnie to take. She looked at it for a moment, wondering if in fact Miss Hickson had had the authority to hand over her job like that without even informing Michael Jolly himself. What if he didn't like Rhonnie and want her to be his secretary, overseeing the general office? More to the point, what if he was as awful as Jackie was claiming. Rhonnie certainly couldn't work for a man who treated her in the way he seemed to have treated Miss Hickson. She gave herself a mental shake. Young girls had a habit of exaggerating. Maybe Jackie was on the subject of Michael Jolly. There was really only one way to find out.

Rhonnie unhooked her handbag from her arm and put it on Miss Hickson's desk. She quickly took off her coat, draping that over the back of the chair, then took the bottle from Jackie, headed across to the door, took a deep breath before she tapped purposefully on it, then turned the knob and went inside.

She was surprised to see how big the boss's office was. Wall-to-wall windows ran the length of the side, looking over the outdoor swimming pool. There were numerous photographs on the wall showing a very handsome man at several periods of his life and posing with an assortment of very important-looking individuals. The floor was covered by an expensive woollen carpet in a Chinese design of red and gold, the pile so thick Rhonnie's feet sank into it. To the right side of her, in the corner of the room, were two comfortable-looking red velvet-covered sofas set around a low mahogany long John coffee table. Further down there was a door marked Private, which she assumed led into the boss's personal bathroom.

To her left a huge mahogany cabinet filled one entire wall, shelved in three bays and filled with books and expensive ornaments. In the middle was a huge drinks cabinet. The cupboard at the bottom was open, showing bottles full of every spirit imaginable plus spaces where a couple had been removed. The top half of this bay held glass shelves with an assortment of cut-glass drinking glasses. Across the room was a huge antique mahogany desk with a big silver inkstand, an ornate glass paperweight and a leather blotter pad arranged on it. To the side was a black Bakelite telephone. Behind the desk was a large, worn, brown leather wingback chair. Lounging in this, his cheaply shod feet planted firmly on top of the desk, was a big, flabby, florid-faced man in his mid-twenties, dressed in a shabby brown suit which strained over his huge paunch.

Michael Jolly looked at Rhonnie through piggy grey eyes and snapped, 'About time. Bring it over here,' he rudely demanded. Then he banged one fat fist on the desk. 'When I ask for something, I want it now, not when you feel like it. Got that?'

Distaste for this rude, arrogant man flooded Rhonnie. The thought of working for such an individual didn't hold any appeal for her. But she wasn't in any position to do what she would really have liked to and that was give him a piece of her mind for speaking to her as he had. It was now growing dark outside and from the sound of water running down the windows it was lashing down with rain. Not at all the time to be roaming the countryside, making her way back into town. That was aside from the fact that she was starting to feel the effects of having had so little sleep in the last eighteen hours. Whether she liked it or not she needed to hold her tongue and hang on to this job, at least until tomorrow.

Rhonnie walked over to the desk and put the bottle on it. Although the words stuck in her throat, she asked, 'Anything else I can do for you, Mr Jolly?'

'Yes. You can tell me if that Hickson woman has cleared her desk and gone?'

'Yes, she has, Mr Jolly.'

His glass now refilled with brandy, Michael Jolly took a deep gulp, then leaned back into the chair, cradling the glass almost lovingly between beefy hands, his thick rubbery-looking lips curling into a malicious grin. 'I've been dying to send that bitch packing for years, the slut that she is. So, you're one of her lackeys, I assume. I want the key to the safe. I know that Hickson woman had a copy. Go and get it, and be quick about it or else you'll find yourself out on your ear, the same as that bitch. As soon as you bring me the key, like the thoughtful boss I am, you and anyone else working in the office can go home for the night.'

Rhonnie didn't at all appreciate the way he was referring to

Miss Hickson. Albeit she had only been in the woman's company a few minutes, she had found the secretary pleasant enough. Rhonnie gave him a tight smile and through gritted teeeth said, 'Thank you, Mr Jolly, it is very considerate of you to let us finish early. I'll be as quick as I can.'

She walked out of the office, shutting the door behind her.

Sitting behind her own desk, Jackie looked up expectantly.

Rhonnie told her, 'Mr Jolly wants the key to the safe.'

'There's only two keys to the safe that I know of. Mr Jolly Senior had one, which he always kept in his pocket on a key ring along with all the others to this place. Miss Hickson had the other, which she kept in the petty cash box in the bottom drawer of her desk. She always keeps that box locked and the drawer it's in. Did she give you the office keys when she left?'

Rhonnie looked at the girl blankly for a moment until a memory returned of Miss Hickson handing her a bunch of keys as she'd issued her parting words. Rhonnie had slipped them into her coat pocket, hadn't she? 'Yes, she did.'

'The key to the drawer and the tin box will be amongst them. So hadn't you better get the safe key and give it to Mr Jolly?'

Rhonnie looked at the girl thoughtfully for a moment before saying, 'I don't know whether I should. This situation doesn't seem right to me.'

Jackie frowned. 'What do you mean?'

'Well, you told me you've worked at the camp for three years but have never seen Michael Jolly here before.'

'That's true, I haven't.'

Rhonnie heaved a worried sigh. 'That makes me think that father and son didn't get on for some reason. Don't you think it's odd that the first time you see Mr Jolly Junior here is after his father is taken ill? And why didn't he ask Miss Hickson for the safe key before she left?'

Jackie was frowning now. 'Is that because he knew Miss Hickson wouldn't give it to him?'

'Seems the only answer to me. He thinks he can bully her

minions into giving the key to him with the threat of the sack if we don't.' Rhonnie heaved a sigh. 'Maybe I've watched too many episodes of Frank Marker the private detective on television, but all my instincts are telling me that Michael Jolly is up to no good.'

Jackie enthused. 'Oh, I watch that programme. It's good, isn't it? I like *Z-Cars* too. My favourite is *Ready Steady Go*, though. I have to watch that on a Friday night before I go out.' Then something struck her. 'Oh! You think Michael Jolly is going to rifle the safe and scarper?'

Rhonnie nodded. 'That's what I suspect, yes. He told me that as soon as I give him the key we can leave for the night, but I very much doubt that is from the kindness of his heart. I believe he's planning to make his escape with the proceeds and be well away before anyone finds out what he's done.'

Jackie looked worried too. 'But what if you're wrong and he wants the key for a perfectly good reason?'

'Well, in that case, he won't mind waiting until tomorrow for it – after I've received the authority to hand it over to him. I do think it's a good idea if you go, though, Jackie. If you're not here, he can't sack you, can he?'

'He can sack you, though.'

'Makes no difference to me whether he does or not,' Rhonnie told her. 'I'm not prepared to work for a man like him anyway.'

Jackie looked sad. 'No, me neither. It would be a living hell with him for a boss.' She smiled at Rhonnie. 'Shame. I think I'd have liked working for you even better than for Miss Hickson. You're not so . . . proper, if you know what I mean?'

Rhonnie took that as a compliment and smiled back at her. 'Yes, I think I would have enjoyed working with you too. We'd have made a good team.' With a sense of urgency she added, 'Best you go off to your chalet before Mr Jolly comes to find out what's taking me so long.'

Jackie immediately jumped up from her chair and rushed over to collect a bright orange canvas zip-up mini-coat hanging on the stand near the door.

'Oh, I don't live in,' she told Rhonnie. 'I live with me mam and kid brother in Mablethorpe. Dad died a few years ago. I travel here and back on my moped. There's three of us office staff working full-time and living off camp. Miss Hickson . . . well, she doesn't work here any longer . . . lives in Mablethorpe too, and Mr Holder the accounts manager. The rest of the clerical staff are seasonal and will arrive a few days before the first campers do.' Jackie pulled a rainproof hooded cape out of her bag and proceeded to pull that on over her coat while continuing to explain. 'Even during the winter months people still telephone and write in to book their holidays, and we also see to all the ordering of supplies and take delivery of them ready for when the camp opens . . . check all the bedding, see what needs replacing, that sort of thing.'

'Oh, I see.' Rhonnie felt another pang of regret to hear it. So this job could have turned out to be the future she was looking for, not just have been a stopgap throughout the summer, but she would never find out now thanks to that odious man.

Ready for the off now and desperate to make herself scarce before Michael Jolly made an appearance, Jackie looked worriedly at Rhonnie. 'I don't like leaving you here on your own to deal with him.'

She didn't fancy being left here on her own either but regardless said to Jackie, 'I appreciate that, but I suspect your widowed mother relies on the money you give her so . . .'

Rhonnie was cut short by a loud roar from Mr Jolly's office next door. 'What the fuck is taking you so long? Find that bloody key!'

A look of pure terror flooded Jackie's face. She sprinted for the door and disappeared through it. As she heard Jackie's feet pounding down the stairs, Rhonnie thought furiously. She could do her best to convince Michael Jolly that she couldn't find the place where Miss Hickson had hidden the safe key, but then he could make a search himself, and locked drawers and a tin box would prove no deterrent. She needed to hide the tin box somewhere he wouldn't think to look for it. Rhonnie peered around the office. The filing cabinets and stationery cupboard were too obvious, as were the drawers in Jackie's desk. There was nowhere else. She mustn't give up though, Rhonnie decided. There must be somewhere in this room she could hide that key . . . Then her eyes settled on the very place and she had to stop herself from shouting out 'Eureka'.

By now highly anxious that Mr Jolly could come in at any moment, she fished in the pocket of her coat for the bunch of keys Miss Hickson had given her. After several nerve-racking failed attempts she finally found the key that unlocked the bottom drawer of the desk, pulled it open and revealed the tin box inside. Grabbing the box, she shut the drawer then put the box inside her handbag on the desk. She had just closed the metal clasp of the bag when the door to the boss's office burst open and Michael Jolly stood looming in the doorway, a glass of brandy clutched in a fat hand.

He bellowed across to her, 'What's taking so long?'

Determined not to allow him to see that his bullish behaviour was intimidating her in the slightest, she responded, 'I do apologise, Mr Jolly, I was just about to come in and explain that I can't find the safe key anywhere.'

His agitation was very apparent as he hurled at her, 'Go round with your eyes shut, do you? You worked for the woman, you must know where she kept it?'

This man was undoubtedly a bully but what worried Rhonnie most was whether he might turn violent if his verbal abuse didn't get him what he wanted. Still of the opinion that it was best not to let him see he was unnerving her, she calmly continued. 'Well, actually, Mr Jolly, I only started today and Miss Hickson never got around to showing me the security arrangements before she left.'

At this news, he gawped at her like a fish. Then he demanded, 'That other girl, the one who was sent to fetch the brandy, she'll know where Hickson kept the key.'

Now was Rhonnie's chance to see whether her intincts about him were right or not. 'Yes, she will, I'm sure, but she had to go home early as she's . . . an appointment with the doctor. She'll be back in the morning, though, and I can get it for you then.

Rhonnie knew then she'd been right. At her suggestion the veins on his thick neck bulged with fury until she feared they would burst. Lumbering over to stand before her, he fixed her eyes and said warningly, 'You'd better not be lying to me. I want that key and not tomorrow, now! That woman had to keep it in here somewhere so look again . . . and thoroughly this time. I'm going to be watching you to make sure you do.'

Taking a gulp of his drink, with his eyes still on her, he perched his backside on the desk and accidentally barged into her handbag, which sent it sliding towards the edge. Her heart hammering, knowing what the consequences could be if it fell off and hit the floor, Rhonnie made a dive to catch the handbag as it teetered on the edge of the desk. But she was too late. With a feeling of horror she saw the bag tip over the edge to smack down hard on the floor below. The impact caused the clasp to spring open and everything inside, including the tin box, came flying out.

Michael looked down, his eyes settling on the tin box. He looked at it for a moment then at her suspiciously. 'So just what are you doing with the petty cash tin in your handbag?'

Rhonnie froze, fearing he was going to attack her. With his face dark as thunder, Michael Jolly jumped off the desk, bent over and grabbed the petty cash box. With it clutched in his hands, he shouted threateningly at her, 'You fucking bitch! The key I want is in here, isn't it? Think you've been clever, do you? Well, I'll teach you what you get for crossing me . . .'

Her fear turned to horror as he lifted his hand to strike her. There was no escape for Rhonnie. He had her cornered behind the desk. All she could do was shut her eyes and steel herself for what was coming.

'Don't you dare hit that young woman, Michael. Don't you dare, you hear me?'

At the sound of a woman's voice, Rhonnie's eyes opened. She turned her head towards the door to the stairs.

Michael too was looking over at the door.

Standing there was a small, plump, homely-looking woman in her early fifties, dressed in a tweed skirt and pink twinset, a string of pearls around her neck. Her salt and pepper hair was cut short, and thanks to a perm curled around her pleasant face, which at the moment was staring fixedly at Michael Jolly. Rhonnie wanted to run over and hug her saviour tightly, thank her profusely for her timely arrival which had put a stop to the physical harm Michael Jolly had been about to inflict.

On recognising the new arrival, without showing a morsel of shame for what he had been about to do, Michael dropped his arm. With his face set tight, he said coldly, 'Well, how nice to see you after all these years, Mother. I was hoping the jungle drums would have taken a little longer to reach you.'

Drina Jolly answered quietly, 'Well, in that case, you shouldn't have drawn so much attention to yourself when you first arrived. I did suspect you'd show up once news of your father's illness got around, but I thought it would be at the hospital to see him. I was hoping you'd changed and would want him to see that. But from what I overheard just now, you haven't at all, have you? Still up to your old tricks. It is the safe key you're desperate to get your hands on, isn't it?' Her eyes settled on the glass in his hand. 'And you've wasted no time in helping yourself to your father's brandy, I see.'

Rhonnie was feeling mortally awkward at being privy to this exchange between mother and son and felt she ought to make a discreet exit. But to do that she would have to ask Mrs Jolly to excuse her as she was blocking the doorway. At the moment Rhonnie felt she had no choice but to remain where she was.

Michael was sneering openly at his mother. 'Yes, I'm having a drink . . . because I've something to celebrate.' A malicious glint sparked in his eyes. 'I thought I'd have to wait years yet before I got my hands on this place, but with a bit of luck this stroke will see him off and then I'll have the lot.' With a nasty smirk on his thick lips, he took great delight in telling his mother, 'I shall sell everything to the highest bidder, and believe me I will enjoy living on the proceeds.' He stabbed one podgy finger towards her. 'You'd better start looking for somewhere else to live too because as soon as I get my hands on my inheritance, you're out.'

The sadness in Drina's eyes deepened. Quietly she said, 'I think you'd better go, Michael.'

He downed the brandy, then wiped the back of one meaty hand over his mouth before telling her, 'I'm not leaving until I get what I came for.' Throwing the crystal tumbler forcefully across the room, sending it smashing into smithereens against the wall, he snatched up the set of office keys that was lying on the desk, frantically searching for the one that would open the cash box.

Drina turned to Rhonnie. 'My dear, would you be good enough to go down to Reception and ask Reg and Sid the security men to come up, please?'

Michael stopped what he was doing and angrily slammed the box and keys down on the desk. 'Might have known you'd have the cavalry waiting in the wings. All right, I'm going.' The look he gave his mother as he walked past her left no doubt at all of the hatred he harboured for her.

With tears of distress glinting in her eyes, Drina Jolly walked into her husband's office, closing the door behind her.

CHAPTER SEVEN

Rhonnie stared blindly after her. With Michael sent packing, Miss Hickson would no doubt be reinstated so the job Rhonnie had been given wouldn't now materialise. She was pleased for Miss Hickson but sorry for herself. She supposed she could still hope she'd be taken on as a chalet maid or some such job, but that wouldn't happen until Miss Hickson came back tomorrow. In the circumstances she knew she really ought to be embarking on the walk back into Mablethorpe or she risked arriving too late to secure herself a bed for the night. The only other option would be to spend another night on an uncomfortable bench in a draughty railway station waiting room. But setting aside her own predicament, Rhonnie felt she ought to show support to the woman who had just saved her from a beating.

She waited several minutes to allow Mrs Jolly some time on her own before going over to the door and pressing her ear against it. She could hear the muffled sounds of crying. Rhonnie tapped lightly on the door and opened it. Her heart immediately went out to the older woman. Mrs Jolly was sitting in the chair her son had not long vacated, bent across the desk, head cradled in her hands, quietly sobbing.

Rhonnie stepped over to the desk and said gently, 'I don't mean to intrude, Mrs Jolly, but can I get you anything?'

She wondered whether the woman had heard her and was about to repeat her question as a good minute passed before

Drina lifted her head. Finally she wiped her face with a handkerchief and gave Rhonnie a wan smile. 'Yes, you can, my dear, if you'd be so kind.' She inclined her head towards the bottle of brandy on the desk. 'You could pour me a large one of those, please. You will join me, won't you?'

Rhonnie didn't particularly like brandy but felt in this instance it would be rude to refuse. Collecting two tumblers from the cabinet, she poured out a good measure of brandy and a smaller one. Handing Drina the fuller glass, she took a seat in the chair before the desk, cradling her own glass of brandy between her hands. She took the opportunity to study Michael's mother as she did so. The woman was very well dressed and sounded like a typical middle-class matron, but from her olive skin and strong features it was clear that her origins were not English at all. Her ancestry was pure gypsy.

Drina Jolly took a long gulp from her tumbler, shuddering as the fiery liquid hit the back of her throat and sent warmth spreading through her veins. In a miserable voice she said to Rhonnie, 'I'd like to say that feels better, but nothing I could take would deaden the pain my own son causes me. It's something I have to live with constantly. I do apologise to you for his behaviour. I'm just so very glad I turned up when I did or I dread to think . . .' Her voice trailed off and she took another swallow of her drink, again shuddering at its effects on her before she leaned back in her chair. She stared blindly across the room before she began speaking distractedly.

'My people have a reputation for being thieves and vagabonds. I have no doubt many of them deserve such labels. I'm sure my own father helped himself to some potatoes out of a farmer's field or poached a pheasant or two where he shouldn't have, but only in desperate times in order to feed his family. Were he still alive he'd be mortified to see how his only grandson has turned out.'

She paused for a moment to take another sip of her drink, her eyes growing misty, the ghost of a smile playing around her lips, as she continued to speak. 'My ancestors came to

England in 1873 from Romania. Joe's – my husband's – arrived in the 1890s. They were all showmen. Travelled across the country along with similar families who owned fair rides, boxing booths and side shows. It wasn't easy to make money, the showmen competing with each other constantly to get a good pitch at a showground and to attract customers to that particular ride or stall. Fights often broke out between families, sometimes fatal ones, but at the same time showmen are a tight-knit community.

'My father had two stalls. A coconut shy and Pitch the Horseshoe. My mother had the "gift", inherited from my grandmother and her mother before her, and while my father was manning his stalls my mother would sit at the side of our caravan and read palms.'

She gave a distant smile. 'It sounds very romantic, doesn't it? Travelling from place to place, sitting upfront on a painted wagon on a hot summer's day, insects buzzing, birds singing, the hedgerows full of wild flowers. And that part of it was. I didn't realise until I looked back just how dangerous life on the road actually was for us travellers. Living conditions were basic . . . no doctors to call on when anyone fell ill, just hope our own traditional medicines did the trick . . . and besides that we had to deal constantly with the wrath of locals who enjoyed coming to our fairs and having a good time there but didn't want us camping near their villages. The menfolk, fuelled with drink, would come and pay us a visit by night, armed with their spades and pitchforks, and cause as much damage to our camp and our men as they could, as a warning for us to leave.

'As a child I was luckier than most as only three of us lived in our wagon, my parents and myself. In most of the rest there would be ten or twelve people, all sleeping top to tail, several of them crammed into one bunk, so at least I had a bed to myself. In late autumn we'd make our way down to Bristol, to hole up for the winter along with other members of our extended families and community. We'd stay in a place called Dorney's

Yard, all crammed in like sardines, and make repairs to our wagons, stalls and rides ready for next spring.

'We were wintering at Dorney's Yard when my mother caught a chill which turned into pneumonia. It was just so awful watching her fade away, with nothing we could do about it. We were very close and I still miss her dreadfully. I can picture her vividly. She used to wear colourful scarves wrapped around her head, with coins dangling from the edges; big jangling earrings and bracelets. I still have those in a special box in my dressing-table drawer. Neither I nor my father could bear to part with them, no matter how hard things were for us at times. I take them out now and again and put them on and it's like she's with me again, wrapping me in her arms, telling me I'm *pakvora* . . . that's Romany for beautiful.

'The day my mother died, something in my father did too. Overnight he seemed to shrink and age a good many years. He had many opportunities, the widows he knew saw him as a good catch, but my father never married again. As far as he was concerned no one could replace my mother and he mourned her loss until the day he himself died twelve years later.

'Before he did, though, my father decided he could no longer face life on the road. His ambition was to rent a small parcel of land where we could live without needing constantly to move on, and for me to go to school and get an education so that I could make something of myself. Hopefully the stalls would provide the means to fund our new life but in fact Father was willing to take on any work that he was capable of, labour all hours, to support us both. We would begin our new life as soon as spring came, he decided. The family and our friends gave him a very hard time, accusing him of abandoning his heritage, trying to persuade him that our kind would never be accepted and allowed to prosper outside our own community, but Father stuck firm to his plan no matter what was thrown at him.

'Mother had been hiding away odd coppers and silver from her fortune-telling, to help towards giving me a good send off when I came to be married. Father used that money, along with what he made by selling our wagon, horse and other large possessions. He took me along to a pawn shop where he bought clothes to make us both look as presentable as he could. Carrying what was left of our possessions in two small suitcases, plus the stalls – which were made of wood and colourful striped canvas that could be folded up and transported – we set off. Father had no idea where we were heading. It was a kindly lorry driver who decided that for us.

'We had walked quite a distance . . . well, it felt like that to me but maybe it was only a couple of miles . . . and were sitting on our suitcases, taking a rest in a lay-by on a country road, when a lorry pulled in. The driver jumped out of his cab and ran off into the woods at the back of us, obviously to relieve himself. When he returned he noticed us and came over to ask if we wanted a lift. He was heading to Lincoln to pick up a load. He must have read Father's face on receiving his offer . . . an Englishman extending a helping hand to gypsies was a rarity in our experience . . . and told us that as far as he was concerned people were people and he'd welcome our company as his job was a lonely one. I think Father was so overcome by his gesture that the man could have been heading to Timbuctoo and he'd have accepted.

'It took us two days to get to Lincoln. At night Father and I slept in the back of the lorry, while Mr Billings . . . isn't it strange that even after all these years I still remember his name? . . . slept in his cab. In exchange for him sharing his food with us, Father caught a couple of rabbits and cooked them over an open fire. Mr Billings said he'd never tasted as good. I think my father was very sad when we said our goodbyes as Mr Billings was the first Englishman to treat him as a fellow human being and not someone to automatically mistrust.

'We stayed in Lincoln for a couple of days, Father trying everything to get some work for himself and a place for us to stay, but even though he showed he had money to pay, doors were closed on us. Father decided we might stand a better chance at the coast. If there were funfairs there he might get a pitch for his stalls.

'The sky was grey and a stiff wind was blowing in off the sea when we first arrived in Mablethorpe. In 1927 it wasn't as built up as it is now, only a few thousand people lived there then, but my father was excited that we'd picked a good place to head to as there were stalls and cafés on the promanade, which showed promise of plenty of visitors. That March day there were only a couple of stalls open for business as the season hadn't started. Thankfully one was selling tea and, having bought a cup for us each, Father enquired of the stallholder how he went about getting a pitch for his own two stalls. It turned out that Mr Stone rented the parcel of land on which his hut stood from the council, along with a couple of pitches to the side which he sub-let. These just happened to be vacant at the moment. They haggled back and forth and finally struck an amicable deal. Mr Stone also told Father where he could find reasonable accommodation for us both with an old lady who took in lodgers not far away.

'She turned out to be a lovely old dear, Irish by birth. The rooms weren't up to much but she was welcoming and they were cheap. We stayed with Mrs Deveral for six months. It was strange to me, living in an actual house for the first time, sleeping in a proper bed, turning on a tap for water and not having to collect it, but Father couldn't adjust. He felt like a caged rat, and became obsessed with finding a place where the landowner would allow him to park a caravan. Despite the long hours he was working manning his stalls, any spare time we had was spent scouring the surrounding countryside.

'In the middle of October, when business on the stall was confined to weekends, I was out with him one day when he found the perfect place. I couldn't understand at first what had caught his attention. We'd crossed numerous fields like this before, the only difference with this one being that it edged sand dunes over the top of which the sea was just visible. I asked Father why he thought it would suit us and he told me to shush and to listen. All I could hear was the birds and insects and the babble of a brook nearby. It was the water that had caught Father's attention. Grabbing my hand, he ran me over the field and looked down at the fast-flowing stream for a minute or two. Then he turned and scanned his eyes around the field before excitedly telling me that this was the perfect spot for us, and I should pray that the owner would be more kindly disposed to the likes of us than others had proved to be. We went off in search of the farmer the field belonged to, so Father could talk business with him.

'Going back across the field, we took a path which disappeared off into the distance. We followed it until eventually we arrived at the gate leading into a rundown farmyard. The house, barns and outbuildings looked to me like they were about to fall down. Before we could open the gate a mangy dog came tearing out of the barn to bark furiously at us. Then next thing we knew a shrivelled old man appeared out of the farmhouse, pointing a shotgun at us, warning us to clear off. It took Father a while to coax him into lowering the gun and hearing him out. Eventually he agreed to listen as long as we stayed the other side of the gate.

'A week later we left Mrs Deveral, who was very upset to see us go, to move into an old caravan Father had bought and had towed by steam tractor to a spot in the field several yards from the brook and shielded the other side by trees. From our new home it was a good walk for me, three or more miles, to school and back, but I didn't mind even when the snow was higher than my wellingtons. On my way home from school, if Farmer Ackers happened to be in the yard as I passed by, I'd wave to him. After a while I found he'd be waiting for me at the gate and I would stop and tell him about my day at school. Even at my young age it was apparent to me that my chats with him had become the highlight of his otherwise solitary day.

'Now the season was over, during the day, weather permitting, Father would work on building two new stalls for himself under a canvas canopy he'd erected next to the caravan. I had told him how sorry I felt for Farmer Ackers, who was obviously lonely. So Father made it his business to make the trek up to the farm a couple of times a week on some pretext or other, and while he was there would chop some firewood for the old man, despite his protests that he was capable of managing for himself when actually he wasn't. When Father made a rabbit stew he'd always make sure he made enough for three and would take a dish up for the farmer. Soon, after making sure I was settled in bed, Father was going up to the farm a couple of evenings a week to give the old man some company.

'As the months passed, Father learned that Farmer Ackers was a widower trying to manage the farm by himself. His two sons were not interested in farming and had found work elsewhere, none of them seeming bothered about abandoning their father nor seeing him for years.

'It was early March of the next year when one Saturday evening, as Father and I had just sat down to eat dinner, there was a knock on the caravan door. We never had visitors and I could tell Father thought that Farmer Ackers had struggled his way down to us because something up at the farm was wrong. He was most surprised to find two young men enquiring if they could pitch their tent in the field overnight. Always keen to make more money, my father said it was fine with him for the price of thru'pence. The two men came back the next weekend but this time with several friends in tow. This time Father thought it only right he should check with Farmer Ackers before he agreed they could pitch their tents.

'Despite how desperate he himself was for money, which my father had offered to split with him, Farmer Ackers didn't at all like the idea of more people roaming his fields, but finally relented when Father assured him he would make sure the campers were aware that the farm was out of bounds.

'Before the summer was out, our field was full of campers during the week as well as at the weekend, and Father had had to dig latrines for them all to use. I had a wonderful summer playing with all the children who came to camp with their parents, exploring the beach and swimming in the brook. I was miserable when the season ended and I was on my own again, but then I had next year to look forward to.

'When Father totted up all the money he had made that summer, it got him thinking that it seemed a waste not to open up other fields that were otherwise doing nothing for campers to pitch on next year. Armed with a couple of bottles of beer and a bowl of rabbit stew, he went up to the farm to put his idea to Farmer Ackers.'

Drina paused in her narrative for a moment to swallow back the remains of her brandy and replenish her glass, Rhonnie signalling that she wasn't ready for more. It suddenly struck Drina that she was keeping the younger woman from her work. 'Oh, my dear, you must forgive me, boring you with my ramblings when I'm sure you have better things to be doing,' the other woman told her.

Rhonnie knew that the reminiscing was her way of dealing with the upset her son had just caused her. Although she really did need to be on her way, Rhonnie felt that listening to her was the kindest course. And in all honesty she was finding Mrs Jolly's story about the origins of the holiday camp fascinating and was keen to hear the rest.

'So what was Famer Ackers's reaction to your father's idea?' she prompted.

'Oh, well, Father had expected some resistance at first, but to his surprise Mr Ackers was all for it. The regular money he now had coming in meant no more sleepless nights spent worrying about the farm's survival.

'It was a few weeks later when I stopped off to talk to him myself on my way home from school. At the farm, Mr Ackers asked me to ask my father if he could see his way to loaning him a shilling – and to bring it up to the farm at six that night. Considering the money he had made from his share of the camping fees, Father couldn't understand why Farmer Ackers would be in need of a shilling, but regardless was only too happy to oblige. Father kept his money buried outside the back of the caravan and immediately went to fetch some. When he returned from taking it up to the farmer, he told me that he'd found two smartly dressed men at the farm also. Farmer Ackers didn't introduce them, just asked my father if he'd brought the money. Father handed the shilling over and was then asked to put his signature on a piece of paper which one of the men gave him, showing him where to sign. He was bewildered but did as he was asked without question. Farmer Ackers then thanked him for the money and Father took that to mean he was being asked to leave. Farmer Ackers never did pay Father the money back and Father never asked for it, believing that the old man had just forgotten about it. And anyway, to him their friendship was worth more than a shilling.

'Over the next few years, as word spread, the campsite expanded. Campers were by now coming from all over the Midlands and further afield. Some better off people were even bringing their own caravans. I lost count of the number of times I helped Father and other campers push cars and vans out of muddy holes when they got stuck. The locals were delighted about the influx of visitors to the town as they spent money in their shops, Farmer Ackers was very happy as he now had more money than he knew what to do with, and Father had the means to expand his empire, as he called it, by adding more stalls to the four he now had on the sea front. He could have more than afforded to move us both into a proper house by then but it never occurred to him, though he did buy us a bigger, more modern caravan, moving our old one across the field for holiday-makers to rent.

'One spring day in 1933, when I was thirteen, Father found Farmer Ackers dead in his rocking chair by the fire. His dog was by his feet, he'd a bottle of beer in his hand and a smile on his face. Him dying happy was no consolation to either me or Father, though. I'd only ever seen my father cry twice in my life, on the days my mother and Farmer Ackers died. We'd lost a good friend who'd become a big part of our daily lives, and had it not been for him Father wouldn't be prospering like he was by then. Of course, that meant the end of the campsite, Father decided. His old friend's two sons would sell up and split the proceeds. Father was very angry to see both of them arrive at the farm within hours of hearing of their father's death and start rummaging through his stuff to see what they could snatch. They called in a land agent to assess the farm's worth before they'd even begun to make funeral arrangements. The brothers both came down to tell my father – to put it in their words – that they wanted us "gyppos" off their land within five days. They even tried to make us feel they were being more than generous in not ordering us off straight away.

'Father found another farmer who was willing to let him rent a piece of land to park our caravan on. It was far from ideal but would do until Father could find us something better. It was very distressing to see the sons give Farmer Ackers the cheapest send off they could arrange, just a plain oak coffin and no flowers apart from the wild ones I had picked before we set off for church. The food at the wake was a few cheap ham sandwiches and no beer, just cups of tea for those who came. Father was most surprised when we were about to leave to be asked by Farmer Ackers's solicitor to stay for the reading of the will. But then, our old friend had always joked that he was leaving Father his rocking chair, so that he could sit in it while he was having a beer and remember good times they shared.

'We were all seated around the table, the two sons on one side, me and Father on the other, with Mr Brownlow, Farmer Ackers's solicitor, at the head. As he opened a long brown envelope and took out the will, I can still see the looks on the sons' faces. Both of them were smiling smugly, lolling back in their chairs, like cats who were just about to get a saucer of cream. After some formalities Mr Brownlow informed Father that Farmer Ackers had indeed left him his rocking chair. The old man also asked that all his animals be found good homes. Then Mr Brownlow told the sons that their father had left to them the contents of the money tin he kept on the Welsh dresser, and they should both help themselves to anything they wanted out of the house. Mr Brownlow then proceeded to fold up the will, replacing it in the envelope. Both sons were staring at him in surprise. It was the elder one who told the solicitor that he couldn't have read out all the terms of the will as he hadn't mentioned the farm and all its buildings being split between the two brothers. The solicitor looked at him in surprise then, telling him that it was because the farm hadn't been Mr Ackers's to leave to them. He'd sold it five years ago, with a clause in the contract of sale that the new owner wouldn't take possession until the time of Mr Ackers's death. The solicitor said it was an unusual situation but not the most unusual he had dealt with during his time in the law.

'My father was surprised by this news as his friend had never mentioned a word to him about selling the farm, no hint whatsoever, and he was intrigued as to who the mystery buyer was.

'Both sons sat shell-shocked while this unexpected news sank in. Then they erupted in fury, shouting and swearing like navvies that their father couldn't have been right in his mind when he'd sold the farm and they would contest the transaction. Besides, if the farm had been sold then where was the money? All they had found in the tin on the dresser was four pounds three shillings and sixpence three-farthings, and the farm was worth a couple of thousand at the very least. Mr Brownlow told the sons in no uncertain terms that their father's mind had been perfectly sound when the sale was agreed. The exchange of monies was legal and above board, and there was nothing to contest. What Mr Ackers had done with the proceeds of the sale was his business alone. He told the sons that he would be obliged if they would take what they wanted and vacate the house by the next day at the latest and hand the keys in to his office as he assumed the new owner would want to take possession as soon as possible.

'Father felt it best to go home and leave the sons to their obvious disappointment. He told the solicitor we'd take the chair and be on our way. We'd not gone far down the path when we heard Father's name being called and turned around to see Mr Brownlow hurrying after us. He held out a bulky brown envelope to Father, apologising for not giving it to him while the two sons were in the house. Father asked what was in it. Mr Brownlow said the contents would be self-explanatory. He then surprised Father by giving him his card in case he should need the services of a solicitor in future, and wished us good day.

'Father sat me down in the rocking chair, slit open the envelope and told me to read the contents to him. When I did, Father accused me of playing tricks, reminding me that today was no time for jokes. But I had read the letter properly the first time. Father really was the new owner of Mr Ackers's farm, all two hundred acres of it, along with the dilapidated farmhouse, barns and other outbuildings. The envelope contained the sale document with Father's own signature on it, the purchase price paid being one shilling, the deeds to the property and a letter from Farmer Ackers in his own hand, complete with spelling mistakes, thanking my father for making his final years a pleasure. He said he hoped that the interest being paid back on the shilling Father had "loaned" him would help towards building his empire further. There was a P.S. at the bottom telling Father that Mr Ackers had taken a leaf out of his book. He should look under the big stone by the ash tree at the back of the main barn, and he would see what was meant by this.

'That night Father took a bottle of whisky, sat down in the rocking chair and drank himself into oblivion. I covered him up before I went to bed and he was still there when I went off to school the next morning.

'When I returned that afternoon I was to find out what the cryptic message from our old friend had meant. Beneath the ash tree Father had found a rusting tin box. It was full of coins of all denominations, just as Father had handed them over, week by week. It looked as though very little had been spent, and like Father our friend had kept his savings buried where hopefully no would-be robber would find them. Farmer Ackers had obviously felt that this last legacy would be far more appreciated and put to productive use by my father than by his own greedy, thoughtless sons.

'The first thing Father did with the money was to have a large sign errected at the entrance to the farm, announcing 'Ackers Camp Site'. Then he had a marble headstone carved and put on Farmer Ackers's grave. With what was left, along with money of his own, he began to make improvements to the campsite. The house and buildings were desperate for attention but there was no question of us moving in there anyway. Father wasn't sure what to do with them so while he decided he made it clear to the campers that they were out of bounds. He still hadn't decided what to do with the place when he died in an accident five years later.'

There were tears glinting in Drina's eyes and a sob in her voice when she explained that her father had been accidentally run over while trying to help a camper whose car was bogged down in a field. After he and another man had helped to work it free, the car ran back and crushed her father under its rear wheels.

'Father left me with no worries over money,' she continued. 'The campsite and stalls were all flourishing. I was actually a wealthy woman and as long as the business carried on like it was I would never need to worry. If it failed, then there was always the land to sell. So I was sitting pretty, for want of a better expression. But I'd gladly have returned to the old days of living in a wagon if I could have had my father back.'

She paused again, seemed to give herself a mental shake, took a deep breath and said, with forced brightness, 'It was my husband's idea to develop the site into the camp it is today. During the war the fields had to be turned over to growing vegetables, but afterwards when we got it back Joe decided to follow in the footsteps of the new holiday camps that were springing up. He'd seen what Mr Butlin had done in Skegness, how successful his camp was, and insisted that was the way we should go. I had the pleasure of meeting Mr Butlin once at a Skegness civic function and what a charming man he is . . . genuinely nice. Anyway, we had the means to begin the development thanks to what my father had left me, along with the proceeds of the business since. I believed my father would have been very much in favour of Joe's plans so I didn't raise any objections. Besides, that was a busy time for me. I had found out I was pregnant and we had moved into a house Joe had found for us a mile or so nearer to Mablethorpe.'

There was a flash of bitterness in Drina's eyes and in her tone of voice when she said, 'Even had I been allowed a say, or to play a part even, in the development, all my time was soon taken up with caring for Michael as he wasn't an easy child at all.' The sadness in her eyes had given way to a look of dull despair. 'I'd been married for nearly seven years by the time I fell pregnant – had in fact begun to think I was never going to have children – so as you can imagine my first baby was very precious to me. Michael was a big baby, his birth a difficult one. I was in labour for over three days and relieved but absolutely exhausted by the time he arrived. He'd hardly taken his first breath before he was screaming to be fed. He was constantly hungry. It felt to me as though as soon as I'd finished one feed he was baying for another. He hardly slept for the first two years and during that time I felt like the walking dead myself. He didn't like being cuddled either . . . would lash out at me if I tried. He was also very destructive. Within a short time of being given a new toy he would have pulled it to pieces. He was very antisocial around other children and should any of them try to play with him or with anything that was his, Michael would lash out at them. Consequently invitations to friends' houses to play with other children dried up very quickly and any I extended were politely refused. I lived in hope that Michael would change his ways when he went to school. I was wasting my time.

'I was constantly being called in when my son got into trouble for fighting or stealing off other children. He also persistently played truant and would be found down on the sea front in Mablethorpe, relieving other kids of their pocket money with card and dice tricks he'd learned. He obviously thought I wouldn't notice the money he was taking from my purse also, and he denied it of course if I did challenge him so I had no choice but to keep it with me at all times and never leave money lying around or as soon as my back was turned it would be gone. No matter how much I tried to talk to Michael about his behaviour and light fingers, no matter what punishment I gave him, it was like water off a duck's back. Michael did what Michael wanted to.

'When he was old enough, Joe used to take him to the camp on weekends and school holidays, but that soon stopped and Michael was banned from going there completely because of his rude behaviour towards the campers and the staff. I prayed he would change his ways when it came to joining his father in the business on leaving school but Michael didn't think it at all right that he was expected to learn the ropes from the bottom up so he would be equipped to run it properly when the time came for him to take over. He felt he was entitled to all the glory of being the owner's son, swanning around the camp amongst the holidaymakers playing the big I am *and* being paid handsomely for it. Anyway, Joe stuck to his guns, putting him to work under the head gardener. Michael made the poor man's life a misery by deliberately, although innocently according to him, fouling up any job he was given, such as "accidentally" spraying all the bedding plants that were just about ready to go in the beds with weedkiller. Then he was sent to work in the kitchens. He lasted three days before Chef Brown gave Joe an ultimatum that either Michael was removed or he'd quit.

'So Michael was put under Mr Holder in the accounts department, with the warning that this was his last chance and if he fouled it up he'd have to seek work elsewhere. To our surprise he seemed to knuckle down and appeared to be enjoying himself. I was so happy! I finally believed he'd changed his ways. What a fool I was. A few weeks later it became apparent why Michael was happy to be working there when one morning Joe went into his office to find the safe door wide open, and all the cash that had been inside gone along with the company cheque book. At that time Mr Holder had a key to the safe which he kept inside his desk drawer. It was easy to work out that Michael had known about this, and used it to gain access to the money. Michael himself had disappeared. He'd managed to forge his father's signature on cheques amounting to nearly a thousand pounds before the bank could put a stop on them. The only reason Joe didn't call in the police was because of the damage it could cause the good name of the camp, which was of course his own too.

'Stealing from family was against everything I believed in, but I was beside myself to have no idea where Michael was. Despite everything, he was my son. The only comfort I had was that he was hardly penniless. I dearly hoped that he'd use the money he had stolen in a productive way . . . put it towards building a business for himself. Again, my hopes were futile. Michael turned up just over a year later at a time when he knew his father wouldn't be home. He was in a dreadful state, had obviously been sleeping rough for a while. He begged me to believe that he'd learned his lesson and changed and asked me to persuade his father to give him another chance. He was so convincing that I believed him. Joe wasn't easily persuaded but I eventually wore him down. He made it clear to Michael, though, that this was the last time. Our son promised us he was now prepared to learn the business from the bottom up. Joe put him to work under Victor Jones who then supervised the maintenance crew, not a man to stand any nonsense from anyone.

'A few weeks passed without any incident at all and Michael really did seem to have changed. But we were later to realise that all that time he was just lulling us into a false sense of security. When our guard was well and truly down, we got up one morning to discover Joe's wallet, safe key and car were gone. Michael had gone too . . . but not before once again clearing out the safe. He managed to get away with cashing cheques for over three thousand pounds before the bank could put a stop on them, money that we could ill afford to lose then as all our profits were being ploughed back into developing the campsite. Again Joe didn't have the police involved because of the damage this could do to our name, and again Michael returned two years later, the money having run out, begging us to take him back and give him another chance. But this time Joe was having none of it and turned him away with a stern warning never to darken our door again.'

Drina heaved a deep sigh. 'Every mother's deepest wish is for their children to grow up to be decent people who make good lives for themselves. After Michael's latest escapade there was no morsel of excuse I could find to exonerate him and I had no choice but to admit that he was born bad. His father was right, we should turn our backs on him before we risked losing everything through Michael's devious ways. Today is the first time I've seen him since the night before he disappeared five years ago. Judging by the state of him he hasn't changed and most likely never will.' Looking at Rhonnie earnestly, and in a voice that was a little slurred now due to the amount of brandy she had consumed, she added, 'I can only apologise again to you, my dear, for my son's appalling behaviour towards you. He didn't physically hurt you before I arrived, did he?'

Rhonnie had been riveted by the story of this woman's past, from her deprived roots to the privileged life of today, but felt sorry for the trauma she had endured while raising her obnoxious only child. What puzzled Rhonnie most, though, was that Drina had talked at great length and very emotionally about her life with her parents, particularly her time alone with her father, but she had hardly mentioned anything about her husband, except for the part he'd played in the camp's development. She just seemed to have passed over the story of how she'd met him, like it was a sore subject with her. And why had she implied that she'd had no say in the development of the holiday camp? Wasn't that a bit odd? According to what Mrs Jolly had said, the land the campsite was built on, along with the money used to fund its development, had been inherited from her father. She'd had every right to be involved in the business, surely?

Rhonnie had no time to ponder further on this as Mrs Jolly was waiting for her answer. Shaking her head, she told her, 'No, he didn't hurt me before you arrived.'

Drina looked mortally relieved to hear that. She then asked, 'Was it Miss Hickson who put you up to hiding the petty cash box so Michael wouldn't get his hands on it? Er . . . where is she, by the way?'

Rhonnie then told her the reason for the secretary's absence. 'I expect once she's informed Mr Jolly is not after all in charge while his father is ill, she'll be straight back.'

Drina Jolly stunned Rhonnie then by telling her with conviction, 'No, I think we'll leave things just as they are. If my husband wishes to reinstate Miss Hickson when he's in a position to take back the reins, then that will be his decision. At the moment the doctors cannot give any indication of how well he will recover or how long it will take. The hospital can do no more for him so he's being moved tomorrow to a convalescent home where the therapists will begin working with him. Anyway, you've shown yourself to me to be a very quick-thinking young woman. I know enough of Miss Hickson to realise you wouldn't be working here as her assistant had you not proved to her that you were very capable, so I'm sure you'll manage to keep things running here until decisions have to be made one way or another when the doctors can be more specific about my husband's prognosis.'

Rhonnie gulped as she fought with her conscience. The last thing she wanted to do was talk herself out of a job, one she felt she could do as well as anyone once she had had time to learn her way around it, but it wouldn't be right to leave Mrs Jolly under the impression she was experienced in acting as a senior secretary when in fact she wasn't. But she was thwarted in making her confession.

'You must have a mountain of things to do and I've selfishly taken up enough of your time,' said Mrs Jolly. 'I'm sorry we didn't meet under better circumstances. I'll come back tomorrow when I've seen Mr Jolly settled in the home and we'll take it from there.'

Before Rhonnie could stop her, a bleary-eyed Drina Jolly had skirted around the desk, stumbling slightly as she left the room.

CHAPTER EIGHT

Rhonnie made to run after Mrs Jolly and put her right about her assumptions but decided the woman had enough to cope with. Her confession could wait until tomorrow. Besides, Rhonnie's most pressing problem was to find a bed for the night. As an employee of Jolly's Holiday Camp, she was entitled to the use of a staff chalet. She hadn't a clue how to go about getting herself one but she did know of an employee who might be able to help her. Rhonnie just had to find her.

After double checking that everything in the office was securely locked, she went downstairs. She collected her suitcase at the bottom of the steps and walked out into Reception, locking that door behind her and putting the bunch of keys safely inside her handbag.

Thankfully the rain had stopped for the moment. Rhonnie stood and looked around to try to make a guess where the staff chalets would be located. Somewhere well away from the campers' accommodation, she felt certain of that. The main lamps that lit the camp at night hadn't been switched on yet. The only sounds she could hear were the roar of the wind and an owl hooting in the trees by the entrance gates. She had no idea how big the camp actually was and had a vision of herself wandering around aimlessly all night in search of the staff chalets. Suddenly the wind abated for a moment, allowing another sound to reach her. It was faint but she could definitely hear voices and felt positive they had been coming from behind her.

Her journey through territory she wasn't at all familiar with wasn't without its difficulties. The path she was painstakingly negotiating reached an opening in a high hedge. She emerged on the other side of this to see several rows of chalets across a small lawned area before her. Lights shone from a dozen or so windows and she could see people inside, busy emptying suitcases and pinning pictures and posters on walls. Others were coming and going between chalets. Someone had a transistor radio tuned to Radio Luxembourg, turned up loud enough for Rhonnie to recognise 'The Last Time' by the Rolling Stones. There was a buzz of excitement in the air which Rhonnie could feel even from a distance.

Keeping to the path that skirted the soggy lawn, she went to the first chalet in the front row and tapped lightly on the door. Inside was a young girl with bleached-blonde hair. She was wearing a mini-skirt and a crochet top which revealed the pink bra beneath. In the process of hanging clothes on a rail on the wall set between two single beds, she turned and looked across at Rhonnie, smiling broadly. It was apparent that she was expecting to see someone she knew. When she saw that it wasn't them and noticed the suitcase Rhonnie had temporarily put down by her feet, she said, 'What number?'

Rhonnie frowned at her, confused. 'Number?'

'What chalet were you allocated when you got took on, silly?'

'Oh, well, it's not a chalet number I'm after. It's a person. Anita her name is . . . or you might know her as Ginger. She's a chalet maid.'

'Oh, you've just missed her. She popped in here about ten minutes ago to say hello. She did tell me what chalet she's in this year.' The girl paused for a moment as she tried to recall. 'I'm sure she said she's in number fifteen. I think she's sharing with Bren, she's another chalet maid, same as they did last year. Anyway, you'll find it further down the row.' As she continued with her clothes hanging she said, 'I'm Shelly Stubbs, by the way. See you later when we have dinner in the canteen at six. Or at Terry's party later on.'

The thought of food was very welcome to Rhonnie, and normally she would have been excited at the prospect of a party, which would give her the chance to acquaint herself with the rest of the staff here. But after the eventful day she'd just had she didn't think she had it in her to party. Picking up her case, she went on her way.

She found Ginger in chalet number fifteen, on her knees by one bed, pushing her empty suitcase underneath. When she heard the tap on the door, she swivelled her head around to see who her caller was and looked at Rhonnie blankly for a moment before a broad grin appeared on her face.

She greeted her with a cry of, 'Oh, there you are, thank God! I've been really worried about you. I couldn't wake you up. I tried, honest, but you were dead to the world. So I asked a train chap to try while I went and held up the bus. The driver did wait but after five minutes past his leaving time he said he couldn't stay any longer as the other passengers were complaining. I wondered whether you'd been stuck in Mablethorpe for the night and wouldn't get out here until tomorrow. Anyway, you're here now so obviously you got set on. I've told Bren about you and she's looking forward to your joining us on the cleaning team. Did they tell you who you would be sharing a chalet with?' She looked worried for a moment. 'I hope for your sake it's not with Noreen Landers. She's a lovely girl, but apparently she snores like a pig and never stops talking, so no one likes sharing with her as they hardly get any sleep.'

Rhonnie told her, 'I didn't actually have a chalet allocated to me. Miss Hickson . . . well, she was on the way out when I arrived. She gave me a job but must have forgotten about my living quarters as she was in a rush to get off.' She eyed Ginger hopefully. 'I wondered if I'd be able to bunk in with you tonight until I can sort things out tomorrow, but obviously if you're already sharing you won't have any room for me.'

Ginger looked thoughtfully at her for a moment before she told Rhonnie, 'Hang on here and I'll go and see who ain't sharing with anyone yet until the rest of the staff arrive.' She darted off. While Rhonnie waited for her to return she took a look around the chalet. It was small, just big enough for two single beds set on opposite sides, with a pole spanning the narrow space in the middle for hanging clothes. This was covered by a curtain in a gaudy floral pattern that matched the pair at the windows. Two small chests of drawers stood side by side at the top of the beds, under the clothes-hanging pole. In the small space at the bottom on one side there was a sink fixed to the wall, with a mirrored cabinet at eye-level above it, and on the other side a small single cupboard. Ginger had stuck a couple of posters of pop groups on the wall beside her bed. One was of the Beatles, the other the Troggs.

Ginger arrived back to look at Rhonnie regretfully. 'Sorry, but the only person who isn't sharing with anyone yet is Noreen. Maybe she doesn't snore as loudly as is rumoured. You could always put cotton wool in your ears as a precaution. Anyway, once you've had a few drinks at Terry's party tonight you'll sleep through anything.'

Rhonnie was just too glad to have a bed for the night to be worried about her room mate's snoring and thanked Ginger for sorting it out for her. She decided not to mention her decision to give the party a miss until she'd thought of a plausible excuse. She didn't want to say she was far too tired, and risk getting herself the reputation of a staid old maid who would sooner go to bed than have a good time. After asking Ginger the number of Noreen's chalet, Rhonnie said she'd see her later for dinner and headed off.

A chubby girl with a moon face and a mop of curly brown hair, Noreen was waiting for her and enthusiastically welcomed her inside. As she stepped through the chalet door Rhonnie immediately knew that continuing to share this space was not an option for her. It wasn't the numerous pictures of cats and dogs Noreen had pinned to the wall next to her bed that Rhonnie couldn't live with, nor the fact that Noreen was obviously not the tidiest of people. It was the stuffed cat on top of the bedside chest, its glass eyes seemingly glaring at Rhonnie nastily, that convinced her she definitely couldn't put up with this arrangement for more than one night.

Noreen obviously saw her looking at it. Mistaking her look of disgust for admiration, she stepped over to give the stuffed animal a tender stroke on its back. 'This is Tibbles. I had her as a kitten. She was like my best friend. When she died it broke my heart and I couldn't bear life without her so Mum had her stuffed for me so I never had to be lonely. Come and say hello and give her a stroke.'

Rhonnie inwardly shuddered at the thought. 'Maybe later,' she told the other girl, though she had no intention whatsoever of touching a dead cat. She smiled kindly at Noreen. 'I appreciate you putting up with me tonight.' The girl opened her mouth to speak and Rhonnie feared she was going to suggest they made the arrangement permanent so she rushed on, 'Ginger mentioned dinner in the restaurant. I'd better get myself washed and changed.'

Noreen told her where to find the staff shower and toilet block. Not having thought when she had left home to pack such a thing as a towel, she had to borrow one of Noreen's. Instead of the shower refreshing Rhonnie, it only made her feel more tired. Noreen wasn't there when she returned to the chalet. Rhonnie looked longingly at the bed. Shelly had told her that dinner was at six. It was just coming up to five now. Maybe a nap might liven her up a bit. She lay down, pulling the thin flowery eiderdown up over her dressing gown, and closed her eyes.

About two miles away, curled up in a comfortable armchair by a blazing fire, Drina Jolly sniffed back desolate tears as she took a sip of scalding hot tea from the cup she was holding.

The brandy she'd swigged earlier had done nothing to dull the emotional pain of her encounter with Michael. But exacerbating that was the fact she was now feeling an utter fool for subjecting that poor young woman to her prolonged ramblings about the past. Despite the girl's display of interest, she must have been bored silly, willing Drina to hurry up and finish so she could get on with what she was paid to do. Drina's only consolation was that the young woman had seemed a very compassionate sort as well as intelligent. Hopefully she'd realise that the verbal outburst had been Drina's way of staving off the pain and shame her errant son had brought on her. She had so enjoyed reminiscing about her father, and in doing so had felt his presence close to her again. Although she still missed him dreadfully and always would, she was glad he hadn't lived to see what a disappointment his only grandson had turned out to be.

As she took another sip of tea Drina looked around the room. It was lovely, and all her own work with its antique furniture and lavish chintz furnishings. The same expense had been lavished on every room in the rambling five-bedroomed Victorian house, surrounded by an acre of landscaped gardens. It was a beautiful place but it didn't feel homely to her because the people living in it weren't happy together. The house had been Joe's choice; he'd bought it without even consulting her first. But then, from the moment they first married he had made it clear to her that he saw it as his job as her husband to relieve her of any worries about money or the business, leaving her free to look after him and the house and the children they planned to have. He had never given her a chance to voice any feelings she might have about this arrangement. Drina had wanted very much to be part of building a business on the legacy her father had left her, but in the aftermath of his death, while she was grieving, Joe had taken control and after that what he said went.

To bring some fulfilment to her otherwise mundane life she had worked hard at making a social circle for herself, but coffee mornings spent listening to the other women moaning about their lot in life and women's groups where talks on flower arranging and jam making were the highlight of the evening hadn't been for Drina. Besides, once most women had become aware of her Romany origins they had given her a wide berth, in their ignorance believing that should they unintentionally upset her in any way then she'd put a curse on them. This was in fact laughable as she had no more power to do such a thing than they had, her mother's gift for fortune-telling having passed her by. The arrival of Michael had come as a blessed relief at first, the role of motherhood bringing her temporary fulfilment.

But as Michael had grown and his need of her full-time care lessened, her feelings of loneliness and boredom returned with a vengeance. By then she knew that it would be a waste of her time appealing to Joe to give her a job at the camp. Now, though, an opportunity for her to work there had presented itself. Though she would not have wanted it to come about at the expense of Joe's health, and not necessarily at the level of responsibility it involved, she was excited at the prospect of filling the void in her life, even for the short time it would probably be until Joe was well enough to take back the reins. She knew she should take this opportunity; another might never come her way again. The trouble was, though, she hadn't a clue how the holiday camp was run or what Joe's role there entailed. But she felt sure that once she took the young woman she had met today aside and was honest with her about her total ignorance then the girl would teach her new boss what she needed to know.

CHAPTER NINE

Rhonnie woke with a start to look up fearfully into a pair of strange eyes looking down at her. 'What the . . .' she erupted.

'It's all right, Rhonnie, it's only me, Noreen. I don't like waking yer, but you really do need to get up.'

Her brain foggy with sleep, Rhonnie couldn't remember where she was or recognise this girl insisting she get up, although the name Noreen did seem familiar. As her brain began to clear, memories returned. Rhonnie rubbed sleep from her eyes and gave a yawn. Her empty stomach was growling loudly, announcing its desperate need to be filled. As she struggled to sit up she said, 'That nap has done me so much good, I feel I could run a marathon. I'd better hurry and get ready or I'll miss dinner.'

Noreen was now pulling on a work uniform over her clothes. 'You already have. I did try to wake you . . . I shook you, even pinched your arm, but you was dead to the world.'

Rhonnie looked back at her, dismayed. Her empty stomach issued yet another protest. 'Oh! Well, hopefully there'll be some snacks at the party then.'

'You've missed that as well. There weren't any snacks anyway, just drink.'

Rhonnie looked at her, astounded. 'You mean, I've slept through the whole night? No wonder I feel so rested.' And at least her deep sleep had spared her from being kept awake by Noreen's snoring, she thought, grateful for that mercy.

The girl grumbled, 'Well, I expect there'll be a few this morning who wish they'd took a leaf out of your book, me included, 'cos I feel terrible. The party was still in full swing when I left at two-thirty. Anyway, if you don't get up now, you'll miss breakfast too.'

Her last words had Rhonnie scambling out of bed and grabbing her suitcase to find clean clothes.

She was amazed by the size of the resturant. As she followed Noreen and several other members of staff through a side door, the main ones not being opened until the campers arrived, she gawped in shock. The huge space filled with tables and chairs seemed to stretch on for ever. Only a dozen or so tables were set out with cutlery and condiments, though. With just fifty or so staff on site at the moment, the place felt cavernous, every sound that was made echoing off the walls. It would be very different when the campers came, though.

Rhonnie took a seat next to Noreen at a table. Spotting her when she arrived, Ginger brought Shelly, Bren and another three girls to join them. As she introduced Rhonnie to the other girls, apart from Shelly whom she'd already met the previous evening, several waitresses arrived carrying plates laden with sausage, bacon, egg and beans, accompanied by plates of toast and pots of tea. Rhonnie was so hungry that she forgot to wait for the rest of the table to be served before she began on her food and was halfway through it before the last plate arrived. The breakfast was delicious and she savoured every mouthful.

As she pushed her empty plate away, Ginger said with a twinkle of amusement in her eyes, 'You ate that like there was no tomorrow. A bit peckish, I take it?'

Rhonnie grinned. 'Just a bit. That'll teach me for sleeping through dinner.'

'And a good party too,' said Shelly. 'It was still going on when I crawled back to my chalet at three-thirty.' She turned to Ginger and told her proudly, 'I got off with that new lad in maintenance, Roger his name is. Dead ringer for Paul McCartney.

Joan Mathers wasn't half jealous 'cos she had her eye on him. She should know, though, she doesn't stand a chance with any lad when I'm around.'

Ginger shot her a look. 'Ain't changed since last year, I see. Out to break last year's record for shagging as many men as possible before the season's out.'

Shelly gave a superior sniff. 'I can't help it if they find me irresistible. And there's nothing wrong with having a liking for sex, it's natural.'

Ginger shook her head and responded, 'Just make sure you remember to take your pill, is my advice, 'cos I dread to think what kind of mother you'd make. Anyway, that new chap looks nothing like Paul McCartney. You want yer eyes testing.' She gave a wicked laugh. 'If anyone, he looks like Brains in *Thunderbirds*.' Then she looked miffed and said forlornly, 'I was hoping Dan might show his face.'

Shelly scoffed, 'Why? It ain't like he's gonna look at you when he could have the likes of me.'

Ginger snapped back at her, 'You? Don't make me laugh! You've got no more chance with Dan than I have. He obviously ain't into blonde tarty types or he'd have asked you out before. Anyway, a girl can have her dreams, and I don't mind admitting I fantasize about him.'

A glazed look in her eyes, Noreen sighed dreamily and said, 'I do too.'

Shelly shot back at her, 'You drool over anything in trousers, Noreen Landers. Hark how you went on about that camper last year, making it sound to us like he was the double of Jess Conrad when he *did* look like Brains in *Thunderbirds* . . . but with acne.'

At her nasty remark, tears sparkled in Noreen's eyes.

Ginger snapped sharply, 'Eh, there was no need for that. Just 'cos that camper wasn't your cup of tea, doesn't mean he wasn't Noreen's.' Then, not considering that what she was about to say next was as cutting to the girl as Shelly's remark had been, she added, 'Noreen can't help not being pretty and slim like you. She can't afford to be too choosy, can she? Now just you apologise to her.'

A shamefaced Shelly eyed Noreen sheepishly and uttered, 'Sorry.'

The girl's moon face lit up. 'Oh, that's all right, Shelly. I know most blokes don't look at the likes of me twice. Anyway, he did have acne really bad *and* he used to pick it and make it bleed. It was disgusting. He was mad about the stars, they were all he talked about, so he was boring an' all. Anyway, when I met him that night for a stroll around the camp I was terrified of being seen with him and reported, 'cos us staff ain't supposed to fraternise with the campers, are we?'

Ginger said sardonically, 'There's lots of things the staff ain't supposed to get up to and could be sacked for if found out . . . but it doesn't stop 'em.' She turned her attention to Rhonnie. 'You wait until you clap eyes on Dan, Rhonnie. I'll bet you five bob you won't be able to stop yer legs turning to jelly. He's not just good-looking, though, he's nice with it too. Not at all conceited, like most good-looking men, who think they're God's gift.'

Rhonnie made to ask just who Dan was and what he did at the camp but was thwarted when Bren piped up, 'Like Terry Jones, he's full of himself.'

All the girls pulled a rueful face at the mention of the name. It was Shelly who said, 'Now that's one bloke who's well and truly up his own arse. He might be good at singing and dancing, and all the campers love him, but he's so oily he slides off a chair when he sits on it.' All the girls laughed at that. She went on, 'He tells everyone that the only reason he can't get a job as a redcoat with Butlin's is because the head redcoat put a block on when he applied for fear he'd be demoted 'cos Terry's better than him.'

She gave a smug smile and then announced, 'What he doesn't know is that I know he's got a criminal record. I kept it to myself in case I needed to use it against him for some reason. I found out because I had a bit of a fling with the lad he used to share a chalet with when he first came here. He's left now, didn't like being away from his mummy . . . right nancy he was. But anyway, Terry let slip to him that he got done when he was younger for shoplifting and only managed to get his job here because he convinced Mr Jolly that was all in the past and to give him a chance. To my mind, leopards don't change their spots. If he ain't up to anything now, then it's only a matter of time. But *that's* the real reason he wouldn't get a job with Butlin's . . . because they are very choosy who they take on as staff.'

They all looked at her agog when she relayed the information about Terry as it was news to them.

Ginger said to her sardonically, 'Is that the reason they wouldn't take you on then, Shelly? Because they don't want a slapper on their staff.' Having finished her food, Ginger then flashed a look at her Timex wristwatch, grimaced when she saw what it read, scraped back her chair and announced to the rest of them, 'Come on, work awaits. You know what Miss Walters is like if we're a second late for duty, and particularly on our first day back. Especially you, Rhonnie, it being yer first day. And don't look so worried. She might be a stickler for timekeeping, and if you leave a speck of dust in any chalet she'll spot it a mile off and haul you over the coals for it, but we could have a lot worse than Miss Walters for a supervisor. Treats us girls well and looks out for us. You and the other new starts will spend the morning with her, getting kitted out with yer uniform and being shown what's expected of you. After that, if you get stuck, just ask one of us. We'll keep you straight. That right, gels?'

They all nodded at Rhonnie.

She told them, 'Well, I haven't actually been set on as a chalet maid. I'm going to be working in the general office . . . for now, at any rate, depending on whether I'm up to the job or not.'

Ginger looked back at her jealously. 'Jammy bugger!' she grumbled, pouting her lips. 'It's going to take me years to work my way up to getting took on in the office, and you walked straight into it.' Then she added good-naturedly, 'Anyway, best of luck. I'm sure you'll do fine.'

Rhonnie let herself into Reception and went up into the office where she took off her coat, hanging it on the stand by the stair door. All she could do then was twiddle her thumbs until Jackie arrived and showed her round. Ten minutes later the girl's head appeared tentatively around the door. On seeing Rhonnie sitting at what had been Miss Hickson's desk, she issued a sigh of relief and came into the room, looking very fashionable under her coat in a short tartan pleated mini-skirt and tight red polo-necked jumper.

'Oh, I'm so glad to see you! I hardly slept a wink last night worrying over what had happened after I scarpered.' She then asked with a worried expression, 'He's not in yet, is he?'

Rhonnie shook her head. 'And he won't be either. Things did turn ugly after you went but thankfully the cavalry arrived in the form of Mrs Jolly, Michael's mother. She put a stop to his shenanigans and ordered him off the premises. I don't think we need worry about him showing his face again here in a hurry.'

Jackie heaved a relieved sigh. 'Thank God for that. I like my job and didn't want to leave. I've seen Mrs Jolly on the odd occasion when some bigwig has paid a visit to the camp, but I've never actually met her. What's she like?'

Rhonnie smiled. 'She's very nice.'

'So what's going to happen now? Will Miss Hickson be coming back since Michael Jolly's gone? Oh, but then what will happen about your job?'

Rhonnie told her, 'All I can say is that for the time being you're going to have to put up with me. But for how long, it depends.'

Jackie frowned at her, looking confused. 'What do you mean by that?'

'Well . . . Mrs Jolly is under the impression I've been working here as Miss Hickson's right hand for quite a while so I know what I'm doing. I never got the chance to tell her the truth. I intend to, though, as soon as I can. I understand she might come in later. In the hope that she'll give me a chance to prove myself to her, I want to show her I mean business. So I was hoping you'd give me an overview of how things are done here.'

''Course I will. Where do you want to start?'

'With the most important thing.'

Jackie said bewilderedly, 'But all the work is important.'

'And I totally agree with you but some things are more important than others and the one I'm referring to is top priority.' Jackie's brows were furrowed as she tried to work out which job her new boss meant. Rhonnie smiled and put her out of her misery. 'Where do we make tea and I'll mash us both a cup?'

Jackie's jaw dropped. The first task she had been shown on commencing work here was where and how to make tea and coffee and she had been the one to do the honours ever since, Miss Hickson obviously perceiving such a job as being beneath her. It seemed her new boss didn't. Jackie liked the thought of having a boss who took a share in the mundane tasks and vehemently hoped that Mrs Jolly saw fit to keep Rhonnie on. She'd do her best to help that happen.

Just after four that afternoon, Rhonnie's brain was reeling under the information that had been crammed into it during the day. Normally it would take several weeks to learn all this. Rhonnie was gratified to find that many things were handled in exactly the same way as they had been in her last job, but some things here were different and she had written herself notes on those tasks to help her remember when she came to do them, hoping that she would still be employed here after Mrs Jolly was told the truth about how she came to be here.

At the moment Rhonnie and Jackie were taking a much-needed break for another cup of tea and Rhonnie was laughing hysterically at a story Jackie had just told her about the early days of the camp in 1950. It seemed a very large lady had decided it would be a good idea to knit herself a bathing costume. The day she decided to give it its first airing, the area around the outdoor pool was packed with sunbathers and the water was full of people too. Waddling over to the pool, the large lady dipped in her toe to test the water and, finding it to her liking, lowered herself in – much to the horror of those around who had noticed her and what her costume was made of and realised exactly what was going to happen. She was in the pool, though, before anyone had a chance to warn her.

The garment immediately soaked up water like a sponge and the sheer weight of it caused it to sag down off the woman's body, exposing her nakedness to the rest of the gathering. Conscious of all eyes upon her, while desperately fighting to heave the heavy garment back up over herself, she screamed to her husband to bring a towel to cover her with then help her out of the pool. Apparently the mortified woman spent the rest of the holiday inside her chalet.

As Rhonnie wiped tears of mirth from her face with her handkerchief, to her horror she saw the door opening and Mrs Jolly walking in. The last thing she wanted was for her boss to think she was the type who would sit with her feet up, filing her nails or reading a magazine. To Jackie's bemusement since she wasn't aware of anyone coming in behind her, Rhonnie jumped up like a jack-in-the-box, exclaiming, 'Oh, good afternoon, Mrs Jolly. Would you like a cup of tea? Anything I can get you, in fact?'

The instant Jackie was aware just who had come in, she too jumped up from her chair, announcing, 'I'll make the tea.' And dashed off to see to it.

Drina said to Rhonnie, 'I hope you're not both going to jump to attention like that every time I come in? I'm not royalty, you know. Anyway, can you come into the office, dear, for a private chat? Oh, that's if you have time right now?'

'Yes I do, Mrs Jolly. And I'd . . . er . . . like a word with you too, please.'

When they were both seated, Drina took the lead by saying, 'It was very remiss of me but I never asked you what your name was yesterday when we first met. Far too busy making you listen to my family history.'

'Which I really did find very interesting,' Rhonnie sincerely assured her. 'My name is Rhonda Fleming. I like to be called Rhonnie.'

Drina smiled back at her. 'I'm very pleased to meet you, Rhonnie.' She took a deep breath, clasping her hands on the desk before her. 'I've settled Mr Jolly in to the convalescent home and he's starting his rehabilitation tomorrow. The doctor has warned me that it could be a long process. So in the meantime . . .'

Rhonnie felt sure she knew what was coming next. Wanting to get what she had to tell Mrs Jolly out in the open, she exclaimed, 'Excuse me for butting in but I can't let you carry on believing I worked closely with Miss Hickson so am ready to step straight into her shoes. The truth is, I only arrived here yesterday afternoon, looking for a job, just as Miss Hickson was packing up her personal things. She asked me what I did in my last job, I explained to her, then to my shock she said I could have *her* job because she was leaving.

'I might not have all the experience you need, but I am confident that the job is not beyond my capabilities. To show you I mean what I say, Jackie out there has been showing me everything she can today. I now know that the general day-to-day stuff is done in much the same way as it was in my last job. But I must just ask, Mrs Jolly, if you'll give me a little time to get to grips with whatever else you'll require of me, by showing me what to do?'

With a downcast expression on her face, Drina exclaimed, 'Oh . . . I see!' She gave a heavy sigh. 'Well, this is awkward . . . very awkward for me.'

A feeling of doom settled upon Rhonnie. Mrs Jolly obviously wanted someone as her right hand whom she wouldn't need to waste time with, plus she probably felt awkward about confiding in Rhonnie during their time together in the office yesterday evening. Expecting her to say at any minute that she wanted someone with more experience to run the office for an outfit like Jolly's, Rhonnie was shocked instead when Drina Jolly burst into laughter.

When she had controlled her mirth enough to speak coherently, she told Rhonnie, 'And I was hoping *you'd* be the one to show *me* the ropes because I have no more of a clue than you do. Well, it will be the blind leading the blind then, won't it?' While Rhonnie gawped at her astounded, Drina went on, 'I have no doubt that you're an intelligent girl and I'm not exactly brainless myself, so would you be willing to work alongside me while the pair of us muddle through it together?'

Rhonnie beamed at her in delight as the feeling of doom lifted. 'I'd be very happy to work alongside you, Mrs Jolly. Very happy indeed.' She did wonder, though, why Drina Jolly didn't want Miss Hickson back in the office? That she had a grievance against her was obvious to Rhonnie. But the grievance was proving to be Rhonnie's good fortune. She was in no doubt that she was going to enjoy immensely working for the woman before her. Between the three of them, Mrs Jolly, Jackie and herself, they would become a good team, she had no doubt about that.

There was a tap on the door then and Jackie, a hesitant expression on her face, walked in armed with a tray holding two cups and saucers, a pot of tea, milk jug and sugar basin, which she put down on the desk. Drina smiled at her and said, 'Thank you, dear.' Then, scanning her eyes over the contents of the tray, she told her, 'I think you've forgotten something.'

Jackie looked mortified, worried that Mrs Jolly would see her as incompetent for not even being able to set a tea tray properly. 'Oh, I'm so sorry, Mrs Jolly.' She looked at the tray, then at Drina, mystified at not being able to find anything missing as far as she could see.

Rhonnie couldn't find anything missing on the tray either.

Drina put them out of their misery. 'You forgot a cup for yourself, dear.'

Jackie's jaw dropped. 'Me! I'm to have tea with you? But you're the boss and I'm just the junior.'

'Senior in what you know about how this business runs compared to Rhonnie and myself. We need you to show us all you know. In fact, maybe we should be asking if we can join you for tea.'

Jackie's chest puffed out with importance and she responded in all seriousness, 'Of course you can. I'll be Mum then, shall I? Then I'm all yours. Ask me what you want.'

Both Rhonnie and Drina fought to keep a straight face as she did the honours.

CHAPTER TEN

A short while later the three women were taking a walk around the camp.

Drina had kept her distance from this place for the last few years for her own reasons, and tried to avoid questions from the two girls about why she didn't seem to know her way around as well as she should for the wife of the owner. Very keen herself to see just what improvements her husband had made during her period of absence, she used the excuse that Rhonnie hadn't yet had a tour of the camp and asked Jackie to do the honours. She made it appear that she'd decided to accompany them at the last moment for a blow of fresh air.

Drina hadn't yet realised just how astute Rhonnie was. In fact, she was now asking herself all the questions Drina had hoped wouldn't arise. Rhonnie could understand why Drina Jolly hadn't a clue how the business was run, but she couldn't understand why she didn't know her way around the camp. It was a source of great curiosity to her why Drina Jolly was a stranger to this place. If she herself were the wife of the owner then she would be up here all the time, taking a great interest in what was going on, she knew that much.

The air was certainly very fresh, a stiff wind blowing in from the sea, and all three women were glad they had wrapped up warmly for their tour.

Jackie was in her element playing tour guide. The first place she showed them around was the theatre-style cinema which adjoined the reception area and general offices. Three separate programmes were run daily. One was aimed at children at eleven in the morning, there was a matinee for the women at two in the afternoon, playing what Jackie termed 'sloppy, weepy films', and at eight in the evening a feature film. Next she took them to the dance hall which was decked out to give the illusion of being on a tropical island . . . hence its name, a big sign in the foyer saying 'Welcome to Paradise'. Dotted around the enormous room were plastic palm trees, paper flower garlands strung around the trunk and plastic tropical fruit hung from the leaves. Several huge tanks of brightly coloured fish were displayed in alcoves in the walls. The waiters and waitresses all wore grass skirts, the waitresses with vest tops and plastic flowers in their hair, the waiters wearing white tee-shirts and two hollowed out coconut shells strung together around their chests, which were always cause for amusement. Over the centre of the wooden dance floor hung a huge rotating glass ball. Dominating the back of the hall was a stage for the shows performed and the bands who played there. There were three bars, one a carousel; a quiet lounge for those who wanted to relax and talk over their drinks, a television room, and a games room with pool tables and dartboard.

Opposite the Paradise and the cinema, across a wide tarmacked area, was a long low building housing several shops selling souvenirs, beach equipment, Kiss Me Quick hats, cigarettes and tobacco, pop, ice creams, sweets and sticks of rock with lettering down the middle spelling out 'Jolly's'; there was a hairdresser's, barber's, penny arcade, camp photographer's, and at the very end a launderette. Next to the shops was the children's nursery where parents could pre-book a slot to leave children from a year to four years old, for up to four hours at a time, giving the parents time to themselves. It had its own kitchen where food for the children was specially prepared by a trained cook. Next door was the Nurses' Surgery where two qualified nurses were on duty twenty-four hours a day and also where the chalet night patrol staff would rest between their rounds. Then came the restaurant building where Rhonnie had eaten her breakfast that morning, through the back a huge kitchen where all the food was cooked by twenty or so staff overseen by a professional chef. For the benefit of the younger children, dotted here and there were huge colourful plastic cartoon-type models of animals, along with small playgrounds with swings, roundabouts and seesaws.

Across an expanse of grass which during the season held picnic tables and chairs was the swimming pool, with a children's pool adjoining it. Surrounding them both was a large grass area for sunbathers to lounge on. The pools were both empty now and in the process of being cleaned by two maintenance men, ready to be filled just before the first campers arrived. There was a dais at the back where pool competitions were hosted by the stripeys. After the pool area came the sports field, with putting and bowling greens, six tennis courts and a roller skating rink. Then came row after row of bright green-and-white chalets, each with a tiny garden at the front filled with shrubs and, when the gardeners had done their job, summer flowers. These chalets would accommodate the seven thousand campers who would descend on them each week in high season. There were also shower and toilet blocks. The doors of several chalets stood open as chalet maids were inside giving them a thorough clean out. At the back of this huge expanse of chalets was the boating lake, and down at the bottom of the camp a small funfair offering popular stalls and rides. By the side of the funfair a winding path led down to the beach which was accessed across the dunes by trails of duckboards. Running around the camp was a miniature railway.

Out of sight of the campers across the other side of the camp were the staff chalets, stables for the dozen donkeys for beach rides for the children, and several other buildings where supplies were delivered and stored, maintenance equipment was kept along with the picnic tables and chairs, parasol umbrellas and hundreds of stacked deckchairs ready to be taken out and placed in several huts around the grounds for the campers' use. A separate building housed the camp laundry. Everywhere loudspeakers were fixed on poles so no camper failed to hear the Radio Jolly broadcasts which, Jackie explained, kept the maintenance men busy reconnecting all the wires that disgruntled campers cut having been woken up by the first broadcast at seven-thirty in the morning.

The leisurely tour around had taken well over two hours and at the moment the three women were battling the wind, standing on a duckboard on the crest of a dune looking out over the wide expanse of golden beach towards the sea.

For Rhonnie this was a sight to behold. Having grown up in a city where the view in every direction had been of houses and factories, a trip a few miles into the countryside for the day, let alone to the seaside a hundred miles away, meant saving up and planning for. She couldn't believe her luck that she had been so fortunate as to land herself a job with this view on her doorstep, albeit at the expense of alienating herself from her father and friends. She was overwhelmed by the size of the camp and the facilities it offered in its aim to give the campers a holiday to remember and come back for, year after year.

As she stood watching the rolling waves crashing on the shore, Drina's thoughts were way back in the past. She was seeing the area behind her as it had been when her father had first brought her to live here in their tiny rusting caravan nearly forty years ago. A distracted smile curved her lips as in her mind's eye she saw him squatting by the outside fire, skinning a rabbit to go in the pot along with vegetables for their dinner while she played happily on the beach until it was ready. Then she remembered the first campers arriving, asking her father's permission to pitch their tent and he, never missing a money-making opportunity, taking advantage. Then her thoughts travelled forward to a few years later when she could have stood in the middle of Ackers's farm and in every direction she looked been met by a sea of tents. Then the tents began to be exchanged for caravans.

Drina wondered what her father would make of the campsite now? Joe had faults in his character that were extremely difficult to turn a blind eye to, but she couldn't find any in the way he had built on her father's legacy to her. By offering people some fun for a low price on his stalls her father had made a living. This camp was on a scale vastly larger than her father's stalls had been but the principle was the same. Giving people fun for an affordable price. So the answer to the question of whether her father would be happy at the way the campsite had developed from its humble origins was yes. He'd be very much so, and very proud.

The cold wind was whipping through Jackie's clothes to chill her to the bone but she wasn't aware of it because the warm glow burning inside her was counteracting the chill. She had always thought herself fortunate to have landed her varied and interesting job as junior to Miss Hickson, with prospects of advancement to greater heights should she prove herself worthy. Compared to what she saw as the mundane occupations some of her friends had got for themselves, in shops and factories, her job was a good one. Miss Hickson had been a decent boss to work for, very patient when teaching her new things, never failing to praise when she'd done a good job, but Jackie had always felt intimidated by her need for perfection. She'd made the girl feel inadequate if she failed to measure up to her high standards in any way. Jackie had felt it a real strain, having to be constantly vigilant of the way she conducted herself, to mind her Ps and Qs, to curb her youthful enthusiasm to put her own thoughts and ideas forward until she was asked to do so, which wasn't at all often as Miss Hickson was the type who thought young people were unlikely to be able to contribute anything worthwhile.

But Jackie had only experienced the company of the two women she was with now for a few hours and already she knew without doubt that neither of them saw her as just a young girl whose brain was filled with thoughts of pop groups, boys and going out enjoying herself. Neither of them would chastise her like a headmistress would a naughty schoolgirl should she forget herself for a second and say something she shouldn't, or unconsciously butt into a conversation to offer her opinion without it being sought. And they both very obviously had a sense of humour, whereas if Miss Hickson had, then Jackie had never been privy to it. She did feel sorry for Miss Hickson who, after years of loyal service to Jolly's, had been unceremoniously sacked. But then her misfortune was Jackie's lucky break. Under her new superiors she would prosper much faster than she ever would have under her last boss, but more importantly to Jackie they wouldn't be constantly monitoring her, ready to pounce if they thought she'd acted in any way they didn't approve of, and this made her feel far more relaxed.

It was Drina who broke into their thoughts by being the first to notice the darkening sky overhead. 'I think we should make our way back to the office as it looks to me like we might have a storm coming our way.' She gave a violent shudder. 'I always dread the possibility of a storm, after what happened in 1953.'

Looking grave, Jackie said, 'I was only young then but I remember it like it was yesterday.'

Rhonnie looked at them both in bewilderment. 'What happened in 1953?'

It was Drina who told her, 'The terrible flood, dear. January the thirty-first it was when the storm came. It devastated miles of the east coast. Places up to three miles inland were under several feet of water. The storm had been raging all day but to make matters worse we had a high tide. By the time the storm subsided the water along the coastline was up to roof-height and thousands of people had to be evacuated. Many lives were lost.'

Jackie chipped in quietly. 'My uncle drowned trying to help an old lady climb out of her window into his boat. We're not sure what exactly happened but the boat tipped up and my uncle and the old lady were swept away by the current. Her body was found washed up on the beach but my uncle's never was.'

Drina gave the young girl's arm a sympathetic pat before going on. 'We lost one of our maintenance men who lived on site during the winter, keeping an eye on it. We made sure he had a decent burial and that his wife and children were taken care of.' She told Rhonnie, 'The clean up afterwards was just awful. We couldn't do anything until the water subsided, which took days. The whole camp was covered in several feet of vile-smelling sludge which took weeks to clear along with the rest of the debris the sea had brought in, including the battered remains of three boats. One of them was discovered lodged in the fountain. We never thought we'd get cleaned up in time before the first campers of the season were due to arrive but thankfully we did, by the skin of our teeth. My house suffered just as badly and we had to find temporary accommodation further inland until it could be put right. We are prone to flooding in this area, the land being so flat. It's something we live with, but God forbid we ever experience the likes of that storm again.'

Rhonnie and Jackie nodded vehemently in agreement.

They all began to walk down the duckboard back towards the camp, Rhonnie following behind Drina and Jackie. She had just arrived at a bend in the path the other two were about to disappear round when she caught a stone in her shoe – it actually felt like a boulder to her – and stopped to remove it. Drina and Jackie had disappeared around a sand dune by the time Rhonnie had removed the tiny bit of grit and replaced her shoe. Hurrying after them, she rounded the bend in the path and to her surprise could see no sign of Jackie or Drina and was faced with three possible directions to take. At the side of her a wooden signpost would have aided her but the bad weather over the winter had faded the signage so badly it was no use to her. Her sense of direction had never been good, which didn't help her now, but her commonsense told her that whichever way she went she would eventually end up back at the front of the camp where the offices were. Deciding to take the path straight in front of her, she set off.

She hadn't gone far when it registered that the path she was taking was not the one she had come by. On that path the boating lake had been on their left; now it was still on her left, meaning she was on the other side of it and could be taking the long way back. At least the storm clouds seemed to be passing over without spilling their load and she hoped it remained that way until she was back in the office. Rhonnie carried on along the path as it would its way past a mini-maze and the roller skating rink, then a grassed picnic area and children's playground. One of the swings in the playground caught her attention, swinging back and forth, its chains squeaking. Obviously it was the wind causing its motion but for a moment Rhonnie saw herself as a child and revisited the exhilaration she had felt at flying through the air on a swing in a park in Leicester, being pushed by her father while her mother set out a picnic on the grass a few feet away.

A sudden overwhelming impulse to recapture that childhood moment consumed her. Flashing a look around to confirm that she was alone, she jumped over the small privet hedge edging the playground, went over to a swing and lowered herself on to the seat. Giving herself a push off with her feet, she swung her legs backwards and forwards, going higher and higher, the wind whipping her hair around her face as exhilaration flooded through her and she was a child again, with no cares in the world, and couldn't help herself calling out: 'Wheeee!'

She was as high as she could go when suddenly she sensed she wasn't on her own. Spinning her head round, to her utter surprise she saw a man sitting on the swing next to hers. He was grinning at her, a mischievous twinkle in his startlingly bright blue eyes. She didn't know how he'd managed it but he was swinging in time with her. As she locked eyes with him, Rhonnie's widened. If she had ever envisioned her ideal man, this was him: tall, dark, almost black-haired, with broad shoulders and narrow hips. He was devastatingly handsome. He had gypsy blood in him, that much she knew. And she knew without a doubt just who he was. Ginger had described him very accurately. Dan. Rhonnie wasn't at all surprised that the girls swooned over him. He was a sight for sore eyes.

How easy it would be to fall for this man . . . but Rhonnie stopped herself short. She had only a couple of days ago decided to end a long-term relationship with a man she'd thought she'd end up spending the rest of her life with, might have if he'd been willing to take the plunge. She still had feelings for Ivan and needed to give herself some time to get over him before contemplating embarking on another relationship. And there was the fact that whereas she might have found Dan overwhelmingly attractive, she may not be his type at all.

In a deep voice that was warm with amusement he shouted to her, 'You looked like you were having fun, so I thought I'd join you.'

Rhonnie shouted back, 'You were right, I am.'

They swung back and forth together for a moment before he shouted again, 'Shall we have a go on the seesaw next?'

Grinning, she nodded. Then thought to herself that not only did Dan possess all the physical attributes most women dream of in a man, he was fun too.

A few minutes later they were both travelling up and down on the seesaw, giggling hysterically. As she was much lighter than her companion, Rhonnie's backside lifted several inches off her seat each time his end banged down on the ground. They went on the roundabout next, Dan pushing it around as fast as it would go before jumping on, then both of them having to stand still for several moments after getting off, to allow the giddiness to subside.

Regaining her faculties first, Rhonnie suddenly became aware of the time and said, 'I'd best be off before the huskies are sent out to find me.'

'Yeah, work beckons for me too.' Dan looked at her for a moment longer before adding, 'We must do this again sometime?'

Rhonnie laughed. 'Yes, we must.' As she turned away from him to continue on her journey, she added, 'See you.'

'Yes, see you,' he responded to her back, and unbeknown to her watched her walking away until she disappeared from view behind an ice-cream hut.

Rhonnie was still laughing to herself, reliving the last ten minutes as she hurried back to the office. It had been a long time since she'd had such fun and especially with a member of the opposite sex. A sudden picture of Ivan filled her mind and her feeling of well-being was replaced with one of sadness. She really needed to write and tell him of her decision to end their relationship. She must write to her father too, and to Carol, let them both know she had found herself a job and somewhere to live and was happy. She would do it tonight and post the letters tomorrow.

Considering she hadn't actually got around to securing herself any accommodation yet and had only been on the camp for twenty-four hours, Rhonnie felt she belonged here already.

CHAPTER ELEVEN

Jackie spun around from the office window. Flapping her arms about like a fledgling duckling about to take its first swim, she excitedly announced, 'The first coach is just turning in to the gates.'

Drina was perched on the edge of a desk with Rhonnie sitting on her chair behind it, in the process of going through invoices due for payment.

The last four weeks had been hectic to say the least. At times Drina had been panicking that all that needed to be done to ready the place would not be finished in time for the first campers arriving. Although Rhonnie continued to assure her that it would, secretly she was doubtful. But thanks to the concerted efforts of the staff the place had been transformed and no longer looked like the eerie ghost town it had when Rhonnie first arrived. The chalets had all been thoroughly cleaned, repaired and repainted where necessary, and beds made up with fresh bedding. The paths had been swept, grassed areas neatly mowed and edged, plants coming into flower in the beds. The shops were filled with stock, the bars too, the kitchen stores and freezers filled with food; paddle boats bobbed on the boating lake, deckchairs were stacked in huts around the camp. The entertainment staff had all arrived the week before, new recruits been instructed on what was required of them, and old retainers put through their paces over and over. Considering how hard everyone had worked and the pace they would be operating at from now until the end of the season, Rhonnie couldn't get over the fact that some staff still found the energy to party into the small hours every night and yet still manage to look as fresh and alert the next morning as if they'd had ten hours' sleep.

She had written letters to her father, Ivan and Carol, the night she had promised herself she would, and posted them off the next day. It hadn't been the one to Ivan that had been the most difficult to write but the letter to her father. She'd hated the fact that the reason she'd given for leaving had been a lie; that she'd moved away to avoid bumping into Ivan now she had decided to end their relationship. She had decided it best not to tell either her father or Ivan where she was, not wanting either of them to turn up unexpectedly. Carol had responded to her, saying she was glad her friend was settled and happy; the rest of her letter had centred on her grumbles about her husband and children.

Rhonnie had seen Dan again on a couple of occasions since their escapade in the children's playground, but only from a distance as they'd been going about their work. He hadn't seen her, though, on these occasions . . . well, if he had, he hadn't tried to catch her attention. She never saw him in the canteen either so assumed he must be on the later sitting. She was aware that her eyes had lingered longer on him each time she had spotted him, liking more and more what she was seeing. She knew he couldn't live on site as he didn't share a chalet with any other member of staff so she assumed he lived off site with his parents, maybe in Mablethorpe, like Jackie and other office and permanent maintenance staff did. Out of curiosity she was itching to ask personal questions about him of Ginger and Jackie, but felt it best not to as if so she would be mercilessly ribbed that she had her eye on him and should it get back to him she'd be mortified. She had, though, taken a look through the personnel files while alone in the office but couldn't find his amongst the others. She did think she'd worked out just what his job was on the camp due to others passing comments she had overheard, like, 'We'll see Dan about it, he'll sort it out.' He had to be a sort of odd job man.

On Jackie's announcement, Drina and Rhonnie both rushed over to the window to watch the coach circle round the fountain, which was now in full flow. It came to a stop before Reception and the first campers started to disembark. Then another coach appeared through the gates, then another and another, until fifteen coaches were parked nose to tail, laden with passengers and luggage, all disembarking at the same time and heading into Reception.

The three women in the office stood looking down at the mayhem below in horror.

To avoid such a crush, the bus companies who brought the holidaymakers from whatever place they operated in to the camp were supposed to ring up and request an arrival time slot, and these were all co-ordinated to work around the train times too, so as not to overwhelm Reception and make the campers' collection of their keys, maps of the camp and booklets announcing that week's programme as smooth and quick for them as possible. At eight-thirty that morning five coaches were expected, certainly not fifteen, so somewhere along the line some bus operators had ignored their time slots and pleased themselves, more than likely the drivers of the coaches wanting to get back to their home towns for family dos or to attend a football match.

The three women looked at each other. Without even saying anything, they all knew what had to be done. Get themselves down into Reception and give the staff there a much-needed hand.

They arrived behind the counter in Reception to find themselves faced with a sea of travel-weary passengers, bickering children and screaming babies, the heads of these families all vying to be served first so they could unpack their belongings and start their much-coveted week's holiday. The six staff . . . three regular receptionists and three stripeys drafted in to help out . . . to their credit, were trying their best to deal with each booking as calmly and quickly as they could, with smiles on their faces and pleasant tones to their voices. Under normal circumstances booking in a camper would take a matter of three minutes at the most, unless there were unusual requirements, and on Saturday intake day, in the height of the season, there would be seven thousand people passing through the door in a steady stream. Thankfully today they were only expecting four thousand.

As Jackie and Drina joined the other staff, Rhonnie stood back for a moment, her thoughts whirling. She could see that amongst this crowd, and not forgetting the many more outside who were not able to get in as yet, tempers were beginning to fray. If something wasn't done quickly, fists would start to fly. Slipping out of the side door, she dashed off in search of stripeys who should have finished their morning briefing by now from the head stripey, Colin Grant, and be on their way to Reception to start escorting the campers to their chalets.

The first stripey she came across was the last one she wanted to meet: Terry Jones. He was leaning against the wall at the side of the campers' launderette, smoking a cigarette.

As Rhonnie breathlessly reached him, he flicked the butt end into a nearby flowerbed and grinned cockily at her, flicking back his head of fashionably shoulder-length blond hair. He was of medium height, slim build, and was boyishly good-looking. Shelly had described him perfectly. He was full of his own importance, believed he was better than all the other stripeys and that it should be him, not Colin Grant, who was in charge of the entertainment staff, that the camp would fall apart if he left for another job, but most of all that he was every woman's fantasy. Regardless of his big-headedness, the campers loved him, especially the young girls, and should he single one out to have a harmless flirtation with, then it made her holiday. Rhonnie did not like him at all, but as a professional she kept her feelings about her colleague to herself.

In a voice laden with innuendo, he said to her, 'Well, I knew it was only a matter of time before you couldn't resist me any longer. Not got time for you right now, babe, work calls, but I could fit you in tonight after I finish. Shall we say twoish down on the beach?'

She fought to hide her irritation. 'Shall we say now at Reception? But first I want you to round up several more stripeys to bring with you. We've a major crisis on. We were expecting five coaches first thing this morning and fifteen turned up all at the same time. It's mayhem there. The next lot of coaches are due in two hours.'

He pretended to inspect his fingernails. 'Oh, and of course you need Mr Fix It to deal with it. What would the place do without me, eh!'

She said dryly, 'I dread to think.' Rhonnie knew he would take little notice of her, but orders from the top had to be obeyed. 'This is what Mrs Jolly wants you to do, and as quick as you can, please.'

Having given him her instructions, she kicked up her heels and dashed back behind the counter in Reception. The noise was deafening as frustrated campers proclaimed they were here first and demanded to be dealt with. Squabbles were breaking out amongst children, fraught babies were crying even louder, and most of the women looked as if only a fine line was stopping them from dropping everything and walking away. The receptionists' calm manner was beginning to crack under the strain, Jackie was trying to assure a man that his chalet wasn't right next to a toilet block or playground or loudspeaker, which he was threatening to cut the wires of if it was. Drina was standing at the chalet keyboard, frantically searching for a key she couldn't locate. It was apparent from the worried look on her face that one of them must have snatched the wrong key off the hook and given it to another camper. If that was the case they'd be back any time complaining the key didn't fit the chalet lock, and there'd be more problems they didn't need.

Pulling a chair over to the counter, and much to the bemusement of Drina, Jackie and the four receptionists, Rhonnie clambered up on it. Facing the frustrated mob, she loudly clapped her hands together several times until she had managed to grab everyone's attention.

'Ladies and gentlemen, Jolly's would like to apologise for this situation. There has been a mix up with the coach arrival times.'

She paused for a moment and smiled broadly before she added, 'The main thing is that you're all here safely, ready to start your holiday with us. You can rest assured that we will do our best to get you settled into your chalets as soon as possible. There's tea on the way and cordial for the children.' Her smile then turned into a cheeky grin. 'And if you all behave yourselves you might even get a packet of crisps or biscuits, all courtesy of Jolly's.'

Much to the relief of everyone behind the counter the holidaymakers cheered and clapped. It was amazing to Rhonnie how the offer of something for nothing usually restored people's good humour, and thank God it seemed to have worked here. She was worried, though, that she hadn't cleared her benevolent gesture with Drina first and hoped her boss wouldn't be mad with her. She supposed she could offer to pay for the cost of the free handouts from her own wages, spreading it over several weeks.

A short while later peace had been restored. The coaches were all on their way back to wherever it was they had come from. The menfolk had formed an orderly queue in reception which snaked outside down the entrance drive and out through the gates. Females were seated in deckchairs around the pool, sleeping babies in arms, toddlers on knees, partaking of their tea and biscuits. The elder children were being entertained by stripeys on the sports field while they waited for their parents to collect them en route to their chalets.

They'd just managed to deal with the last campers when the next coaches starting rolling in. Thankfully this time it was only the expected number. Leaving the new arrivals in the safe hands of the reception staff, Drina, Rhonnie and Jackie returned back upstairs to the offices. Jackie immediately went off to make them a much-needed cup of tea.

As soon as she was out of earshot, Rhonnie began to apologise for acting on her own initiative earlier but Drina beat her to it with, 'Well, I dread to think what would have happened this morning without your quick thinking. You're showing how good you are in a crisis, my dear. Let's hope we don't get any more just yet, though, as I don't think my nerves could stand it.'

Rhonnie eyed her in relief. 'You're not annoyed with me then?'

Drina frowned, bemused. 'Why would I be annoyed with you?'

'Well, I should have checked with you first before I spent the company's money.'

'Every last halfpenny of it well spent in my eyes,' said her boss with conviction. 'I've worked with you long enough by now to give you my permission to act as you see fit in the best interests of the business, without having to consult me first. Oh, and that reminds me of something else I've been meaning to do. Ah, here's just the person I need to speak to about it,' she said, smiling over at Jackie as she arrived with the laden tray.

The girl only caught the last of their conversation and looked worried as she put down the tray, asking, 'Oh, have I done something wrong, Mrs Jolly? You need to tell me if I have.'

'On the contrary, dear. You've been a marvel, helping Rhonnie and myself while we've both got our heads around the way this office functions. I have to say, I'm still floundering a little and rely on both of you to keep me straight, but slowly I'm getting there. What I would have done without you both these past few weeks . . . Well, anyway, I don't think it at all appropriate that you should be called office junior any longer. From now on you're Rhonnie's assistant and your pay will be adjusted accordingly. How does a rise of a pound a week sound?'

Jackie gawped at her. 'Oh, Mrs Jolly, I don't know what to say.'

'That makes a change,' Drina chuckled. Then she addressed Rhonnie. 'And you, my dear, have more than earned the right to become our office manager, with all the authority that goes with it and an appropriate pay rise, of course.'

It was Rhonnie's turn to be struck speechless. She had never dreamed of receiving a promotion and pay rise so quickly and was absolutely delighted that Mrs Jolly was pleased enough with her work to respond in this way. Before she had a chance to express her feelings, however, the private telephone on Drina's desk shrilled out. As the call hadn't come via the switchboard, it was obvious it was a private call came directly through. Rhonnie silently motioned to Jackie that they should leave their boss to her conversation. They arrived back in the main office just as Beverley Wright, one of the receptionists, appeared through the door from the stairs, looking extremely frustrated.

Rhonnie took one look at her face and said, 'Don't tell me . . . it's the Major again. What is he complaining about this time? In fact, I don't think there's much left for him to pick fault with, is there?'

Bev pulled a face. 'Seems there is. He wouldn't tell me, though, as us receptionists aren't good enough to deal with him. As usual he's demanding to see management.'

Rhonnie sighed. 'I'll come down then.'

A small, wiry man with a completely bald head and a huge gingery walrus moustache, Major Reginald Baldock was standing straight-backed, tapping his fingers angrily on the counter top when Rhonnie arrived on the other side of it. His wife, a quiet, thin, mousy-haired woman, an inch or two taller than her husband, stood a foot or so behind him, looking both nervous and embarrassed.

The Baldocks had arrived on the first coach that morning and already he'd been back to Reception several times, demanding to move chalets as he didn't like what he termed his 'common, loud-mouthed neighbours and their boisterous snotty-nosed kids' to one side of him or the young honeymoon couple on the other. Rhonnie had only just managed to arrange a chalet change for them when they were back again, with the Major complaining that the water in the shower block was not hot enough for him. He wasn't at all happy about the fact that Rhonnie could do nothing about that as the thermostat was set not to heat it beyond a certain temperature. A while later he was back again, insisting that the second sitting for meals to which he and his wife were allocated was too late for them as his wife had a delicate digestive system, and must be changed to the earlier time.

Despite the fact she was getting thoroughly fed up with his unwarranted complaints, Rhonnie greeted the irritating little man with a smile. 'Good afternoon, Mr Baldock. What can I do for you?' She stopped herself from adding 'this time'.

'Major,' he snapped at her. 'Well, apart from the fact that your information booklet states lunch will be served at twelve prompt and it was two minutes past so I will be closely monitoring the situation tonight at dinner, it's so rowdy around the pool there's no place to sunbathe in peace and quiet. Trying to get the attention of one of those people in striped blazers who are supposed to be on hand to help all campers is a waste of time unless you're a pretty young girl, plastered in make-up and wearing clothes that hardly cover your modesty, or a handsome young man with hair down to your collar and dressed like a peacock! I've tested the mattress on my bed and it's lumpier than army porridge. I want it changed.'

His complaints seemed trumped up to Rhonnie. Was it really so important if the lunch service was a couple of minutes later than stated? It was the first day and there would be a perfectly good reason for it. Stripeys would certainly not ignore a camper of any age, it wasn't worth losing their job. What had more than likely happened was that the one he'd approached was already dealing with someone else and didn't break off immediately to deal with the Major, who'd had to wait and hadn't liked it. Of course it was lively around the pool with the competitions taking place there and people whooping it up in the water. What else did he expect? This was a holiday camp. As for the mattresses, well, Rhonnie agreed they weren't the most comfortable in the world but definitely not as uncomfortable as he was saying.

She really felt like giving him a piece of her mind and fought with herself not to. She'd just been promoted and didn't want to lose her job less than five minutes later over this obnoxious little man. 'I'll see about getting it done as soon as possible,' she told him through clenched teeth.

He gave a sniff, looking down his nose at her 'See that you do. I should also warn you that should I find anything else untoward,

I shall be writing to the national newspapers about your misleading promise of giving your patrons a fun-packed holiday to remember. I've had no fun whatsoever so far and neither has my wife.' He paused to look at Rhonnie meaningfully. 'Unless, of course, I can be persuaded otherwise?'

So that was this man's game. He was after a bribe not to do his best to discredit the camp. More than likely he'd not settle for anything less than all his money back, landing himself a free holiday. Before she could stop herself Rhonnie's temper flared. 'Major Baldock, Jolly's offers an all-inclusive holiday at an affordable price. If you wanted the luxury of a five-star resort then maybe that's where you should have gone for your holiday.' She then inwardly groaned, knowing she should not have spoken to him in such a way and was about to pay for it.

A smirk of satisfaction appeared on his face. 'Management rudeness to add to my list of complaints! You're going to be sorry you spoke to me like that, young lady. I am going to demand that you're sacked. I shall be back at four, tell the proprietor to be expecting me.'

With that he spun on his heel, gesturing to his wife to follow him. A mortified Rhonnie looked on, terrified that she'd just lost herself a job. As she scuttled after her husband out of the door, his wife turned her head and shot Rhonnie an apologetic glance before disappearing in his wake. Immediately a wave of pity for the woman rose within Rhonnie. She knew without a doubt that the poor woman's life was made utterly miserable by her dicatorial, freeloading husband.

Back upstairs, Jackie immediately accosted Rhonnie with, 'So what did that little Hitler have to complain about now?'

But Rhonnie hurried straight past her desk towards Drina's office, leaving Jackie wide-eyed in surprise as she snapped, 'Not now! I need to speak to Mrs Jolly urgently.'

Drina was just putting down the telephone receiver when she heard the tap on the door and lifted her head to see Rhonnie walk in. She was about to tell her what her call had been about but stopped short on seeing the mortified expression on Rhonnie's face. Instead she asked, 'What on earth has happened, dear?'

Wringing her hands, a shamefaced Rhonnie blurted out, 'I'm so sorry, Mrs Jolly, really I am. I should have known better but my temper got the better of me and I couldn't stop myself. I appreciate you'll want me to leave . . .'

Drina was looking astonished to hear it. 'Well, it would be good to be told just why I'd be wanting that?'

'Oh, yes, I'm sorry, I really ought to explain. You see, Major Baldock was complaining yet again in a totally unreasonable way. The only thing he hasn't mentioned yet is the colour of the curtains in his chalet, but I expect he will soon. This time it was the mattress, among other things. Anyway, I lost my temper with him. He wants to see you at four this afternoon, to demand that you sack me.'

Drina tutted disdainfully. 'Oh, does he indeed? I haven't yet had the misfortune of actually meeting the man, but from what I've heard from you, Jackie and the girls in Reception, I'm surprised no one else has lost their temper with him before now. I know his game. In his line of work my father met every type of con man in the book, and knew a good few cons himself come to that. I'd bet my life our Major Baldock makes a good few bob with his complaints scam, threatening hard-working people that he will discredit their businesses if they don't pay up.

'Well, he'll get no money from me. Let him do his worst. I trust the fact that the majority of the campers who come here go away happy and feeling they've had good value for money. I don't believe any adverse publicity will take away from that. I'm glad you lost your temper with the little weasel. I hope you gave him some home truths? In fact, I don't want his type in my camp. Do you want the pleasure of telling him to pack up and leave or shall I call security?'

Rhonnie was reeling in shock. She had thought it would be she who was sent packing. 'Oh, please allow me, Mrs Jolly.'

Drina smiled. 'As you wish. Tell him I want him gone within the hour or I'll get security to escort him out in front of all the other campers. That should teach him to be careful who he tries his tricks on in the future. Oh, and before you go, that was Butlin's head office on the telephone. They're fully booked until the end of the season and wanted to know if they should send on any enquiries for late bookings our way. We can't be doing so badly if the likes of the top camp in the country is recommending us to their clientele and risking their own reputation, can we? Off you go then and sort out the Major.'

Fifteen minutes later, Rhonnie took a deep breath before she knocked purposefully on Major Baldock's chalet door, hoping that he was in residence and she would not have to scour the camp for him. As she waited for a response her attention was drawn to a group of three middle-aged women, dressed in colourful summer frocks, sitting in deckchairs in front of a chalet several doors down, chatting together in the sunshine. One of them was looking Rhonnie's way and she smiled back, giving her a wave and calling out, 'Enjoying yourselves, ladies?'

The older woman grinned and responded, 'Pure heaven, lovey. Can't remember the last time I had a treat like this. I'm gonna save hard and come back for a fortnight next year.'

'And we'll look forward to seeing you,' Rhonnie told her.

Having received no response to her knock, Rhonnie went to peek through the chalet's curtains to confirm no one was home, but she couldn't see in as they were tightly drawn. She felt sure the light was on, though. They'd obviously gone out and left it on. With her thoughts on just where in the camp the Baldocks were likely to be, she turned and made to retrace her steps back down the path, then stopped and faced the chalet again. She was about to accuse Major Baldock of making false complaints and felt she really couldn't justify charging him with that without checking the mattress for herself. Since no one was in she'd do it now.

Thankfully she had the office keys on her, which held a set of skeleton keys for all the camp's locks. Fishing them out, she found the right key and opened the door, stepping over the threshold. The sight that met her made Rhonnie's eyes bulge in surprise and her mouth drop wide open in utter shock. Sitting on one of the beds, dressed in a red bra and pants and in the process of pulling on a pair of stockings to clip to the suspender belt around his waist was Major Baldock, gawping back at her in just as much surprise.

They stared at each other for what seemed like an age before Major Baldock yelled furiously, 'How dare you barge in here without permission? Get out! GET OUT!'

Still reeling in shock Rhonnie made to do just that, then thought better of it. What people got up to in privacy didn't matter to her as long as it didn't impact harmfully on others. But the successful running of the camp was very important to her, and she was damned if she would let an opportunity pass to put a stop to this odious man's wicked plan for extorting money out of Mrs Jolly. How she wished she had an Instamatic camera on her, but as she hadn't she hoped that threats would be enough to trounce him.

Keeping her face straight with an effort, she said to him, 'I've a pair of pants similar to those you're wearing. You look very nice in them, Major Baldock. Does your wife know about your . . . *little hobby*?'

He froze rigid, terror filling his eyes.

Rhonnie took his failure to reply to mean that she didn't. 'Well, maybe someone should tell her. Then the pair of you could dress up together and compare notes, couldn't you?'

He found his voice then and shrieked, 'No, no, you mustn't tell her! I beg you.'

'Well, that depends on whether you'll agree to forget your scheme to extort money from my boss?'

He nodded his head vehemently. 'Yes, yes, I promise.'

'Good. I'm sure you will appreciate why Mrs Jolly has instructed me to tell you she wants you to leave the camp, with immediate effect. I will return in an hour and if you haven't left by then I will get security to march you out in front of all the other campers. Oh, and Major Baldock, if we hear one bad word about the camp originating from you, I will make sure your wife learns of your little secret.'

Just then a small voice from behind Rhonnie asked, 'What little secret?'

She spun around to find Mrs Baldock looking at her quizzically. Oh, dear, thought Ronnie, it seems the secret is out. She stood aside to allow the timid little woman to see for herself, feeling mortally sorry for her.

On seeing her husband dressed as he was, the woman's hand flew to her mouth and she exclaimed in horror, 'Oh, my God! Whose underwear is that you've got on, Reginald?' When she received no reply, she seemed to change before Rhonnie's eyes. The timidness was forgotten, to be replaced by an angry woman demanding answers to her questions. 'Reginald, you'd better damned well answer me.'

His shoulders slumping in despair as his world crumbled around him, he sighed in defeat and admitted, 'Mine, dear.'

'Yours!' Her face filled with a look of utter disgust and loathing, she told him, 'Don't you dare "dear" me again. You disgust me. Now I know why you were always encouraging me to visit neighbours and friends . . . not to give me some much-needed enjoyment but so you could have the house to yourself for a while to do what you are now. *That's* why you insisted I go to the cinema this afternoon . . . so you could be alone in the chalet. If it hadn't been for the three women in front of me acting so annoyingly, talking between themselves so that I couldn't hear the film and constantly rustling their sweet papers, I might have gone to my grave never knowing what you get up to behind my back.

'Since the day we married thirty years ago I've put up with your pernickety, overbearing ways, with not having the children I so desperately wanted, with watching you preen yourself for being so clever when you went about lining your own pockets at the expense of hard-working people. I was always fearful of where I'd go if I left you. Well, now I don't care. I'd sooner live on the streets than with you any longer.'

She turned to look at Rhonnie. 'I arrived just in time to hear you say that Mrs Jolly wants *him* off the premises. I don't blame her. But does that include me too?'

Rhonnie told her, 'As far as I am aware you had no involvement in your husband's scam, so we wouldn't have any objection to your enjoying the remainder of your holiday with us, Mrs Baldock.'

'Good. That will give me time to make some plans for what I'm going to do once I leave here. I've always dreamed of working in a little café on the sea front. Maybe it's time to make that dream come true.' She shot her husband a disparaging glare. 'Goodbye, Reginald.'

With that she spun on her heel and walked away.

Rhonnie said to the pale-faced man, 'An hour, Major Baldock, or I call security.'

After she'd heard what had happened, Drina shook her head in disbelief. 'Well, you never know what goes on behind closed doors, do you? That poor woman . . . I do feel so sorry for her, finding out her husband's secret like she did.'

Jackie piped up, 'I'd have loved to have been there. I've never seen a man in women's underwear before.'

Drina giggled like a schoolgirl. 'Neither have I!'

'Well, I hope you never will as it wasn't a pretty sight,' Rhonnie told them both. Wanting to put the experience behind her, she offered to make them all a brew.

CHAPTER TWELVE

Several weeks passed and the season was progressing without any major mishaps. It was just after five-thirty on a June evening, Jackie had left for home and Rhonnie was clearing her desk when Drina came out of her office and asked, 'Have you any particular plans for this evening, dear?'

Rhonnie certainly had. After a day like today, she was going to have her dinner with the girls, then shower and have an early night, so tired she didn't even think the comings and goings of her chalet mate, Val Greenwood, a lively twenty-year-old stripey, would disturb her sleep. Regardless, if her lovely boss wanted her to do something then Rhonnie's own plans would be set aside. She shook her head. 'Did you want me to come back after I've had dinner and do something for you? I'd be only too pleased to.'

'I appreciate that. But I think you've done enough work for one day. I'm going to eat in the restaurant tonight. Not to check that the food is up to standard and the staff are doing their jobs properly, I'm happy with your daily update to me on that, but to save myself from cooking. Then I'm going to go over to the Paradise and have a drink, see for myself that everything there is as it should be and the campers are happy with the entertainment we're providing. I just wondered if you'd like to join me?'

Rhonnie said in all sincerity, 'I'd love to. Thank you.'

The noise in the restaurant at first sitting was deafening as over five and a half thousand campers clattered cutlery against plates, chatted and laughed about their day and plans for the evening with their fellow campers. The faces of Ginger, Shelly, Bren and the other girls were a picture when Rhonnie joined them with Drina in tow. The chalet maids felt they were honoured enough to have a member of the office in their circle, but the arrival of Mrs Jolly herself was an entirely different matter. They'd no alternative but to respond appropriately when Drina politely asked them if they minded her joining them at their table, but in fact they would sooner she hadn't. Not only would they now be the butt of the other staff's jibes about hobnobbing with the boss after this, but mealtimes were the only chance they got to air their gripes to one another, and they couldn't very well do that with the boss present.

The atmosphere in the restaurant as a whole might have been lively and good-humoured, apart from the odd po-faced camper whose day had not been as enjoyable as they had hoped, but around the table where Rhonnie was sitting it was very subdued. As she tucked into her bowl of minestrone soup she racked her brains for the right thing to say as an ice breaker. Drina meanwhile was feeling mortally uncomfortable, realising that she'd stupidly not considered how their difference in status might cause such awkwardness. She too was racking her brains to find something to say that would put them at their ease.

Rhonnie nearly choked on her soup, stifling laughter, when Drina in desperation came out with the one topic the British were famous for talking about in order to break the silence. 'Such a beautiful day today, wasn't it, girls?'

All but Rhonnie mumbled their agreement. She, though, made a response, in the hope it might be taken up by others. 'Be good if the weather is like this tomorrow for the Miss Bathing Belle and Glamorous Grandmother contests. There's a few women I've seen around the camp who should leave the other contestants standing.'

Rhonnie got a response but not quite the one she was hoping for. It was Ginger who matter-of-factly said, without thinking, 'It ain't the ones as should win who do, though.'

Frowning quizzically, Rhonnie asked her, 'What do you mean?'

Drina added, 'Yes, dear, I don't understand either.'

Ginger turned pale and spluttered, 'Oh, nothing. I didn't mean nothing by that.'

Silence reigned for a moment while the waitress cleared away their empty soup bowls and their main course of roast pork was put down before them. As soon as the waitress had departed, Rhonnie addressed Ginger. 'Come on, out with it. You did mean something.'

Ginger shifted awkwardly in her chair, conscious that all eyes were up on her. Drina and Rhonnie were looking quizzical, while the rest looked horrified that their friend's thoughtless comment was about to land her in the mire. She gulped and said stiltedly, 'Well . . . it's . . . er . . . I just happened to overhear a mother and daughter talking outside when I was cleaning their chalet. The daughter was crying, telling her mam what a fool she had looked in front of the other girls because she had bragged to them that she was going to win the Miss Teenage competition they were all entering. In the end she didn't even come third and she was blaming her mother for that, saying her mam had promised to fix it so that she won. The mother told her that she had kept her promise by paying a backhander to one of the judges, and it wasn't her fault if he went back on the deal. She said that she had challenged the judge afterwards but he'd denied all knowledge of a bribe so there was nothing she could do about it.'

Rhonnie looked shocked and said, 'Well, now it makes sense to me why that . . . well, unkind of me to say it or not, it was an ugly child who came first in the Bonny Baby Contest last week. The runners up were far prettier. This is not an isolated incident, is it?' she guessed.

Drina, too, was shocked to hear such a practice was going on in her camp and said with conviction, 'I won't have any underhand goings on here.' She asked Ginger, 'Did the woman you overheard mention the particular judge's name?'

She shook her head.

Shelly piped up, 'Well, my money's on Terry Jones. I told you he's got a criminal record. And I also told you leopards don't change their spots.'

Drina looked even more shocked to hear that a member of staff had a dubious past. 'Has he? Well, this is most awkward. We can't accuse Terry with no evidence, but I can certainly do something to put a stop to this little scam, whoever is behind it. All contests should be conducted fair and square or what's the point in having them? I appreciate your bringing this to my attention . . . er . . .'

'Gin . . . Anita Palmer,' Rhonnie told her.

'Thank you, Anita. And don't worry. Rhonnie and I will make sure that you're not suspected of informing us about this dreadful situation. I expect you other girls to keep this conversation to yourselves as we don't want the guilty party to be made aware we are on to them.'

Ginger looked mortally relieved to hear that she wasn't going to be thought of as a grass by the other staff. The girls nodded to let the boss know they wouldn't say a word.

Drina added, 'I would like you girls to know . . . and please do pass this around . . . that you are always welcome to raise any such concerns with me, or with Rhonnie if I'm not there. Positive suggestions too, for how we can make improvements to the camp. My door is always open.' Then she added hurriedly, 'And please rest assured that whatever you come to say will be kept confidential. After all, we aren't the only holiday camp in business, are we? We want our campers to come back year after year and say good things about us, to encourage their friends and family to spend their holidays at Jolly's too, and not with our competitors. It's just as important to me that you staff are happy here and enjoying your jobs.'

The girls all looked gratified to hear this.

Shelly said, 'Well, Mrs Jolly, it would be good if you could have a word with some of the campers about not leaving the showers in such a mucky state after they've used them. And if they'd stop pinching the sink plugs too that'd make our lives much easier. We're always running backwards and forwards to the stores to fetch new ones.'

Drina smiled. 'Well, if all the campers cleaned up after themselves, you wouldn't have a job, would you?'

'Oh, I suppose not,' Shelly said, obviously feeling silly for not thinking of that.

'As for the sink plugs, Rhonnie and I noticed the other day when we were checking invoices that we seem to go through a lot of them. Why anyone would want to steal a plug is beyond me, but unless someone comes up with a miraculous way to stop it from happening then it's just something we have to grin and bear.'

Taking Drina's cleared plate, the waitress replaced it with a pudding of spotted dick and custard, kept hot as all the food that left the kitchen was in 'Jackson' containers on trolleys, expertly wheeled through the row after row of tables. She looked down into her dish. 'Mmm, this looks good.'

Drina turned her head to look at the campers surrounding them, then observed to Rhonnie, 'They look happy enough with their meals except for the odd one or two, but you'll never please everyone. Before we leave I'd like to take the opportunity of paying a visit to Chef Brown, to check there's nothing he wants to speak to me about while I'm here.'

The rest of the meal passed pleasantly now that the girls realised their boss was not someone to be feared, but was in fact a very approachable woman. Regardless, they did weigh their words before contributing to the conversation. Ginger's slip was enough for one night.

Chef Brown, a stocky middle-aged man who'd perfected his craft in the army for twenty years before retiring and landing himself the job at the camp, was delighted to see Mrs Jolly enter his kitchen. Despite the fact they were busy preparing food for the second sitting, he insisted that she and Rhonnie take a seat in his small office and sample a couple of new puddings he was considing putting on the menu. They found both dishes delicious and he certainly got the approval he was seeking.

It was coming up for eight by the time the pair of them arrived in the foyer of the Paradise, to be greeted by the noise of a couple of thousand people already inside enjoying themselves. The resident band, the Paradise Boys, were playing a lively jive. Drina informed Rhonnie she needed to powder her nose, and Rhonnie said she would try to find a table meantime and would get them a drink. She knew Mrs Jolly liked a brandy.

Inside the ballroom it appeared all the tables were already occupied. She noticed that there were a couple of empty stools at the bar and rushed over to grab them before anyone else did. Seated on one, with her handbag resting on the other by way of securing it, she was looking along the array of drinks behind the counter, deciding what to have herself, when a voice she recognised said to her, 'Well, hello, playmate.'

She turned her head to find Dan grinning at her, having just arrived behind the bar carrying a crate of Schweppes fruit juices. He was dressed in a pair of tight black jeans and a black short-sleeved tee-shirt, his muscular arms taut under the weight he was carrying. Rhonnie was suddenly conscious that she was still wearing her work clothes and wished she had taken the time to change into something more flattering for the evening. Was Dan a barman then rather than an odd job man? And if so why wasn't he dressed in smart black trousers and white shirt the same as the other barmen were? She was surprised to find how delighted she was to see him again, face to face, though she hoped she was hiding the fact from him.

'Hello to you too,' she responded lightly.

Rhonnie noticed she wasn't the only one delighted to see him. A group of teenagers in mini-skirts and skimpy tops had suddenly appeared at the bar and were all gazing at him adoringly. 'You've quite a fan club it seems,' said Rhonnie with a chuckle.

Putting the crate down on the floor, Dan straightened up. He ignored her last comment, asking, 'Been on any swings lately?'

She shook her head. 'No. Too busy.'

His deep blue eyes were fixed on hers. 'Well, the office obviously hasn't kept you working late tonight, so when I've finished here we could put that right. Or better still, pay a visit to the funfair.'

So he had made it his business to find out she worked in the office! But Rhonnie liked the sound of his suggestion. She'd only had a brief walk around the funfair when Jackie had been guiding her and Drina around on the first day. Rhonnie had been to fairs when they had come to Leicester, accompanied by Carol, but that sort of activity had ceased on her friend's marriage. Ivan had thought such venues were for kids, not intelligent adults. It would be good to have some fun at the fair. But she knew it closed at ten, whereas the Paradise was open until twelve o'clock, so unless he was planning to walk off the job then it wouldn't be possible for them to go to the fair tonight. She was about to point this out to him when she was interrupted by the arrival of Drina.

Rhonnie said to her, 'Sorry, I couldn't get us a table. These stools were the only seats I could find.'

Drina looked at the high stool, the seat of which came up to her waist, and laughed as she replied, 'You'll have to help me on, dear. These things were made for people with long legs like you have, not short fat ones like mine.' The next thing Drina knew she felt an arm slide around her waist and heard a voice close beside her, saying, 'Let me give you a hand, Mrs J.'

'Oh, hello, Dan. Thank you, I'd appreciate that.' The words were no sooner out of her mouth than he had lifted her up in his strong arms and deposited her on the stool, like a featherweight rather than the substantial woman she was. After making sure she was comfortable he returned behind the bar. Rhonnie's attention was then taken by a barman who asked what they would both like. Rhonnie settled for a Woodpecker cider, Drina a brandy with a splash of water, telling Rhonnie in an aside that the water was to ensure she didn't end up in the same drunken state she'd got herself into the afternoon they first met.

Dan had disappeared while they were being served their drinks and now reappeared carrying a crate of bottled Double Diamond. Drina said to him, 'Your own job not keeping you busy enough?'

'I'm just helping out, Mrs J. I came in for a drink and saw how busy the bar staff were and that they were running low on some things, so I thought I'd fetch them up.'

'We're lucky to have you,' she said.

Rhonnie was still wondering what Dan's official job was if he wasn't a barman.

He had gone off to fetch another crate by now and Drina was saying, 'I'm glad to see this place is packed. People do seem to be thoroughly enjoying themselves, don't they?'

Rhonnie swivelled around on her stool, smiling in acknowledgement at one of the night patrol nurses as she passed by on her way to put a chalet number on the message board, to alert the child's parents that they were needed. She swivelled back to face Drina. 'Yes, they do, but I hope you won't mind my pointing out that the teenagers look bored. The band is good but they're not playing any chart stuff for the youngsters to dance to, except for a brief medley of Beatles hits.'

Drina swivelled around to check what Rhonnie had noticed. She frowned, bothered. 'Mmm, you're right, Rhonnie. I could speak to Jack Vardy, the band leader, and ask him to include more music for teenagers.' She saw the expression on Rhonnie's face then and said, 'You don't think that would be sufficient? Well, maybe we could rearrange the entertainment programme to give them a night in here to themselves, with the band playing only the sort of music they like to dance to.' Once again she saw the look on Rhonnie's face and said, 'You don't think that would do either?'

Rhonnie shook her head. 'No. Kids like to dance to the chart records played by a DJ.'

Drina looked taken aback. 'What on earth is a DJ?' Rhonnie

explained and her boss gave a small laugh. 'Oh, goodness me, I am sorely out of touch with the younger generation. So we drop the band for the evening and get a DJ in? That's all well and good but what entertainment do we provide for their mums and dads meanwhile?'

'Well, I feel we really should have a separate place like a discotheque for the teenagers to go to at night, where they can mix and dance together. They have the funfair but that's out of bounds for the under-eighteens at night as it's too far away for their parents to keep an eye on them. I'm sure without their moody teenagers around the parents would enjoy themselves better, and if we give the kids what they want they'll encourage their parents to come back next year.'

'Mmm, you've got a point. I can't fault my husband for providing entertainment for the young children, their mums and dads, uncles, aunts and grandparents, but he seems to have passed over the ones in between. We'll do something about it, though. First we need a place to have this . . . what did you call it? A dis something?'

'Discotheque. They call records "discs" now, and that's where the name comes from.'

Drina was looking thoughtful. 'All our buildings are fully occupied and the season is no time to have workmen on the camp doing major building works. But now you've pointed this out to me, I feel we need to do something for the teenagers straight away. And it has to be somewhere nearby so their parents can pop back and forth, keeping an eye on them.' She fell silent for a moment and then exclaimed, 'Oh, I think I might have an idea. Come along with me and tell me what you think.' She looked over the bar and, spotting the person she was looking for, called over, 'Leave that, please, Dan. I'd like you to come with us.'

As Drina slipped precipitately off her stool, Rhonnie wondered why her boss had invited Dan along. Not that she minded.

Drina led them out into the foyer towards a set of wooden double doors. Rhonnie had wondered where these led to; now it seemed she was about to find out. Dan knew where Drina was taking them, although he had no idea why. Fishing for her camp keys in her handbag, after several attempts Drina found the right one and opened one of the doors, the other being bolted from the inside. A set of wide stairs led down. Dan went in first to put on the lights which were on a panel on the wall at the bottom of the stairs. Rhonnie stared at what the lights revealed. They were in a large room, half as big as the ballroom above. It was extremely dusty, ribbons of cobwebs festooning it, and smelled musty. It had obviously been shut up for years.

Drina said, 'If my memory serves me right, when designing this building in the very early days, my husband's intention was to have a cocktail bar down here, but then he decided it wasn't a practical idea, like several others he had, so that's why it's empty.' She looked at them both. 'Do you think it's got potential?'

Dan held up his hands. 'Be good if you told me what you had it in mind to do with this place, Mrs J?'

Drina laughed. 'Sorry, Dan. Turn it into a discotheque for the teenagers.'

He immediately responded, 'That's a great idea.'

'I can't take the credit. It was Rhonnie's suggestion.'

He looked impressed.

She blushed in embarrassment.

'So, do you think you can turn this into a place the teenagers would like to come?' Drina asked him.

Rhonnie looked at Dan. If Drina was putting this project in his hands then his position at the camp was far more important than she had believed.

He answered, 'I'll have a think about it and come and see you tomorrow with some ideas.'

She looked pleased and said to Rhonnie, 'Let's go and finish our drinks.'

Back at the bar, unfortunately their seats were now taken so they stood together downing the rest of their drinks while Dan went back behind the bar to finish replenishing the shelves.

As she sipped her cider, Rhonnie noticed several fed-up teenagers, milling around by a palm tree, looking on in embarrassment as their parents smooched to the band's rendition of Pat Boone's 'April Love'. She felt so sorry for them. The management might have plans to give them somewhere of their own to go and enjoy the kind of music they preferred, but unfortunately these things didn't happen overnight.

She realised Drina was speaking to her, and turned to face her, saying, 'Sorry, Mrs Jolly, I missed that?'

She was replacing her empty glass on the bar. 'I just said I'm going to make my way home and leave you two love birds to it. See you tomorrow, dear.'

Rhonnie was struck speechless by Drina's remark, embarrassed that her boss had obviously noticed she had a fancy for Dan, which she had thought she'd kept hidden. But she had said 'love birds', so hopefully she had detected a similar feeling in Dan for Rhonnie.

Next thing she knew he was by her side, saying, 'Ready for some fun?'

Rhonnie smiled up at him and nodded.

Together they weaved their way down the path towards the sea where the small funfair was situated. They preserved the silence of two people not yet acquainted enough with each other to fall into general chit-chat. Yet Rhonnie felt no awkwardness. It was a comfortable silence. Rhonnie enjoyed being in the company of this tall, dark, handsome man. She only hoped Ginger was right when she'd said once that he wasn't currently attached.

They had passed several couples and groups of people laughing and joking on their way back from the fair. As they drew nearer to it and could hear the strains of the fairground music playing, Rhonnie's excitement mounted. She broke the silence by saying to Dan, 'It's a long time since I've been to a fair. I'm looking forward to this.'

His response was to show her his devastating smile and then cup her elbow as they reached the tall, colourfully painted wooden fence that surrounded the fair, guiding her through the metal entrance gates between other campers coming and going. Her realisation that Dan's job at the camp was more important than she had at first assumed was confirmed by the two stripeys standing guard at the gates, making sure no one they felt was unduly inebriated, or under the age of eighteen and unaccompanied by an adult, entered. They both nodded respectfully to Dan as he and Rhonnie went through the gates.

This observation, though, was swept aside by the electric atmosphere of the fair. Feeling almost schoolgirlishly thrilled, Rhonnie gazed around the array of stalls and rides. The fair was the only place in the camp where money was required. Dan, though, made it clear that Rhonnie wasn't paying for anything, and not wanting to dent his pride she went along with that. They had a go on the hoopla stall first, neither of them winning anything. Dan was luckier on the rifle range, showing her what a crack shot he was and proudly presenting her with a teddy bear. Then it was Rhonnie's turn to repay the compliment by presenting him with a rag doll from the Hook a Duck stall. Armed with their prizes they then had goes on the rides, she squealing and laughing as loudly as the other female riders on the Waltzer, Meteorite, Carousel and Big Wheel.

As they made their way back to camp later they laughed and joked together about the fun they'd had. Arriving back at the fountain, Rhonnie really hoped that Dan would ask to see her again, but to her disappointment all he said was that they must do this again sometime and then, satisfying himself she was all right to see herself back to her chalet, he walked off in the direction of the maintenance buildings.

Back in her own chalet, Rhonnie propped the teddy bear up on top of the cupboard at the end of her bed, thinking that if nothing else she still had a reminder of her lovely evening with Dan.

CHAPTER THIRTEEN

As soon as she joined Ginger, Shelly, Noreen and the other chalet maids for breakfast the next morning, Ginger immediately accosted her with, 'Sounds like you had some fun last night then, Rhonnie?'

She felt astonished for a moment at just how quickly the camp grapevine worked. Conscious that all eyes around the table were on her, she replied evenly, 'Yes, I did, thank you.'

A miffed Ginger snorted, 'Lucky bugger. That's my dreams shattered.'

'Told you before, Ginger, your dreams are hopeless ones as far as the likes of Dan are concerned. I had more chance with him than you ever had, but I made it clear to him I wasn't interested,' Shelly told her smugly.

Ginger snapped back, 'Liar! He's no more made a play for you than he has for me. Why would be want to be seen with the camp bike? The question with you is, who haven't you shagged, not who have you?'

Shelly snarled back, 'You're just jealous because you're still a virgin. And that's 'cos no one except a blind man would want to do it with you . . . even if you was the last woman on earth!'

Over the weeks Rhonnie had been sharing mealtimes with Ginger and her group of mates, plus the occasional social outing with them into Mablethorpe when off duty, she felt she had grown to know them quite well. For all her bravado, Ginger was actually a very considerate young woman who went out of her way to help people, friends or campers, regardless of whether it was her job or not. It was apparent to Rhonnie that she was very serious about working her way up, and she wanted to help Ginger if the opportunity arose.

Shelly, on the other hand, was from the same mould as Terry Jones: full of her own importance and only out for herself. Rhonnie felt they'd make a good pair if they ever got together. She had also observed Shelly out and about in the camp, and her reaction to the campers was entirely different from Ginger's. Anyone approaching her for help as she was a member of staff was immediately pointed in the direction of a stripey. As for her so-called friends, she would not hesitate to stab them in the back to get herself out of trouble. If she didn't change her ways then she would not go any further in this camp, assuming she had ambitions to. Noreen's only ambition was to find someone to love her. Rhonnie liked the girl despite her oddities and sincerely hoped that she would meet a kind man who would treat her well.

Despite Ginger giving Shelly just about as good as she got, it was apparent by Ginger's expression that the remark about her virginity had cut her deeply. Rhonnie was unable to stop herself from scolding Shelly for her thoughtlessness. 'That was uncalled for, Shelly. One of these days your nasty mouth is going to get you into serious trouble. You ought to apologise to Ginger if you value her friendship.'

That was the last thing Shelly felt like doing, but at the same time she knew that Rhonnie was talking sense and if she didn't apologise for her nastiness she would find herself looking for a new set of friends to pal about with. She was fully aware that she wasn't the most popular member of staff, under the mistaken illusion it was because other females saw her as a threat as she was so good-looking. It wouldn't be easy to change their attitude to her. She looked at Ginger and said grudgingly, 'Sorry. Are we still friends?'

Rhonnie got the impression that Ginger wasn't too keen to

agree but was also aware that should she refuse that could leave Shelly without any friends for the rest of the season. 'Only if you promise to watch your mouth in future,' the girl said.

Again the response was grudging. 'Yeah, all right.'

Wanting to put the incident behind them, Ginger turned her full attention to Rhonnie and eagerly asked, 'So what does he kiss like?'

She frowned. 'Who?'

'Who!' said Ginger sardonically. 'How many men were you with last night? Dan, of course.'

Rhonnie waited to respond while the waitress finished putting their breakfasts before them. Picking up her knife and fork, she announced, 'I have no idea.'

Already forgetting her promise to watch her mouth, Shelly piped up, 'Pull the other one, Rhonnie. I bet you was both down the sand dunes shagging like rabbits.' At the looks all the others around the table shot her, she declared, 'I was only having a joke!' Then said to Rhonnie, 'So are you saying you never kissed?'

By the girl's tone Rhonnie knew Shelly thought she was lying. 'It wasn't a date I was on with Dan. He just asked me to the fair as he didn't want to go on his own. We had some fun and he walked me back to the fountain, then he went his way and I mine. That's it, girls. Sorry if I'm disapointing you.'

Ginger grinned and put her tongue in her cheek, just to rile Shelly. 'You haven't disappointed me,' she said. ''Cos that means I still have a chance with him.'

Rhonnie arrived in Reception to find two girls already busy dealing with campers' queries. On spotting her, Julie Bradshaw, the head receptionist, called her over. Excusing herself temporarily from the campers she was dealing with, she said to Rhonnie, 'I need your help. Janice has a stonking headache. Between you and me, I suspect she was up late drinking with some of her mates, has had hardly had any sleep and that's the cause of it. Anyway I've sent her over to the nurse for some

Aspro. As you can see, I can't get away from here and it's nearly time for the morning announcements on Radio Jolly. Janice just managed the early-morning wake up call before her headache got the better of her. Normally in cases like this we'd be able to cover, but we can't abandon all the campers needing our help.' Just then the door opened and a woman with a crying child entered, making straight for the counter. Julie groaned. 'I can see it's going to be one of those days. Anyway, it doesn't look like Janice will be back in time, so will you do the honours for us?'

Rhonnie gawped at her. 'Make the announcements on Radio Jolly?'

Julie nodded. 'There's nothing to it. All the equipment is set up ready so there's nothing to do there. Just press the mic button and speak clearly into it. Say, "Good morning, this is Rhonnie on Radio Jolly with today's events." Then read out what the list on the desk by the mic says. End up by wishing the campers a morning of fun. And make sure you start the announcement at eight-thirty on the dot. Look, I need to get back and you've got two minutes to get yourself ready. Thanks, Rhonnie.'

Rhonnie's heart was pounding. She did not want to do this, terrified she'd make a complete mess of it, but it appeared she had no choice. She went over to the tiny radio room and sat down in the seat. She looked at the console with all its dials and switches and thanked God she hadn't got to attempt to master that before she did anything else. She glanced down at the list of events for the day. It was all clearly typed out, nothing on it that should cause her any problems. She glanced up at the clock on the wall to one side of her. The second hand was ticking at three times its usual speed, it seemed to Rhonnie, towards the appointed time. Fighting to quell her anxiety, she took several deep breaths and, as the minute hand reached the number six, pressed down the mic button and spoke into it.

'Good morning . . . er . . . ladies and gentleman. This is . . . er . . . Radio Jolly with a reminder of today's activities.' So far so good, she thought. Her heart still pounding anxiously, she then began to read from the list. 'At nine-thirty we have . . . er . . . oh, yes . . . the Children's Donkey Derby on the beach. Volley ball in the pool for the adults. At ten-thirty on the sports field . . .' To her horror she realised her finger had slipped and hurriedly corrected herself. 'Oh, no, sorry, the activities on the sports field are at two this afternoon! At ten-thirty the first heat for the Miss Swimsuit competition is being held at the pool, and the final for the Glamorous Grandmother contest and the Knobbly Knees . . . er, no, sorry. That's this afternoon at three o'clock. Oh, sorry again . . . there is an event at ten-thirty on the sports field – the Father and Son's race. This afternoon at two-thirty in the Paradise lounge there is Bingo, and in the ballroom old-time dancing until four. Tonight's theme in the Paradise is Elvis Night, for those of you who'd like to dress up for the occasion. Now . . . er . . . today's showings at the cinema . . .'

Before she could go any further, Julie appeared, yanked her out of the seat and sat herself down in it, saying into the mic, 'At two o'oclock . . .' She then proceeded to read out the list of that day's programme, making amusing little comments in between the film titles, and at the end wished everyone a good day and signed off. Heaving a sigh, she turned to Rhonnie and said, 'No disrespect, but next time we have a crisis, we won't be asking you to help us.'

'That bad?'

Julie nodded. 'In fairness, you were thrown in at the deep end.'

As she made her way upstairs to the office, Rhonnie was well aware that she was in for another ribbing at dinnertime from Ginger, Shelly and the rest, but sincerely hoped that her boss and Jackie hadn't heard her miserable attempt at radio announcing too. Her hopes were in vain as she arrived to find Drina and Jackie both wiping tears of laughter from their eyes.

Drina spluttered, 'Oh, Rhonnie, that was just so terrible, it was hilarious.'

Jackie agreed. 'Yes, it was.'

Rhonnie said dryly, 'Well, they won't be asking me to do it again in a hurry.'

'I shouldn't think so,' agreed Drina, heading back into her office. 'I've to telephone the convalescent home to check how my husband is today, then I've a few more calls to make. At ten-twenty, I'd like you to hold the fort, Jackie, because I want Rhonnie to come with me.' In her office by now, she shut the door behind herself.

Jackie looked quizzically at Rhonnie. 'Where does Mrs Jolly want you to go with her?'

She shugged. 'No idea.'

A while later, Drina came out of her office. Seeing the girls were both busy, she said she'd make a cup of tea for them all. She returned with a laden tray, which she put down in front of Rhonnie on her desk.

'How is Mr Jolly today? Any improvement?' Rhonnie asked.

Drina nodded. 'Yes, a slight one, thank you. He seems to be regaining the use of his left arm. His speech has improved too. I can just about understand him now.'

Jackie said, 'He'll soon be running around like a spring chicken, Mrs Jolly.'

'Mmm,' was the only response.

Rhonnie eyed her boss thoughtfully. Did she detect that Drina wasn't entirely happy with that state of affairs? Rhonnie supposed she could understand why. It wasn't that she didn't want her husband to recover from his stroke, but when that did happen he would obviously want to take back his position in the business. And where would that leave Drina? From what Rhonnie had gleaned from Jackie, Joe Jolly's style of leadership had been nothing like his wife's. Rhonnie knew she'd not enjoy working for him as much, and secretly hoped his recovery came later rather than sooner.

Having finished her tea, Drina looked at the clock, saw it was just after a quarter-past ten and said to Rhonnie, 'Right, drink up, we need to be off.'

'Where are we going?' she asked curiously.

Drina gave a mischievous smile. 'You'll see.'

Minutes later they arrived at the crowded poolside as the contestants for the first heats of Miss Swimsuit were giving themselves a last-minute preen before they took their place in the queue at the steps leading on to the platform. Behind a long trestle table covered with a red satin cloth Colin Grant, Terry Jones, and four other senior stripeys were already in place, to begin the judging. Catching sight of Drina Jolly, Colin immediately got up and hurried over to join her and Rhonnie.

He was a tall gangling man in his late twenties who had started with the camp as a barman ten years before and worked his way up to head stripey two years ago, replacing the then head stripey who was leaving the company to take up what his wife called a 'proper job' once she was expecting their first child. Rhonnie really liked Colin. He came across to her as very much like her father, happy-go-lucky, and she had never seen him with anything but a smile on his face. As boss of the stripeys his whole manner and attitude had to set an excellent example for the rest of them to follow. Colin bore a strong resemblance to Bruce Forsyth, the former compère on *Sunday Night at the London Palladium*, and, aware of this, Colin would mimic him, using his catchphrases at every given opportunity, much to the campers' delight. Some of them actually addressed him as 'Brucie'.

Having first greeted Rhonnie, he said to Drina, 'How nice to see you, Mrs Jolly. Come to watch the contests? As you can see we have a packed house today so I'll send someone to get a couple of chairs for you and Rhonnie. Make sure you've a good view.'

She told him, 'We have come for the contests but not to watch, Colin. We want to be on the judging panel.' Drina leaned closer to him and, keeping her voice low, told him, 'Not that I believe it for a moment, Colin, as I know you wouldn't allow such things to go on, but I've had a camper come to me saying that the contests are rigged. That some people are giving a judge, or judges, backhanders to make sure the vote goes in their favour. I'm appalled at that accusation. If it's true then the person or persons involved will be immediately sacked. But I don't think it will come to that. I'm fully convinced the camper who made this accusation was just doing so after they'd seen a family member not do as well as they'd hoped. Regardless, I have to be seen to be taking the accusation seriously and so, for the next two contests, Rhonnie and I will be taking your place and Terry's on the judging panel.'

Colin looked absolutely horrified by what Drina had told him. 'I can't believe one of my team would be up to such a thing. It's outrageous.' He flashed a look over towards the panel, looking at one person in particular, before turning back to tell Drina, 'I'll call an emergency stripey meeting as soon as the contest is over. Warn them that if this practice is going on then we will find out who the culprit is or are, and they'll be dealt with severely. If such a thing has been going on then you have my assurance it won't any longer.'

Drina patted his arm. 'Thank you, Colin. I knew I could count on you to deal with this. Why don't you go and break the news to Terry?'

Rhonnie mused aloud, 'I've never seen Colin so angry. He always prides himself on running a tight ship. Did you see the way he looked over at Terry? Colin suspects him of being the guilty one, I'm sure. It's got to be Terry, hasn't it? I mean, he's the only other stripey, apart from Colin, who's a regular on the panel and with the clout to rig a contest. And we mustn't forget about his criminal record.'

Grave-faced, Drina murmured, 'Yes, I agree. My husband must have been aware of it when he first look the lad on. It's a pity he decided to give him the chance to prove himself if this is the result. Terry obviously thinks he's clever enough to make money for himself like this without anyone being able to prove it. Well, hopefully this will see an end to his sneaky scheme. But all the same, I shall be keeping a beady eye on Mr Jones in the future, and I want you and Jackie to do the same. I'd hate to lose him, he's so good at his job, but one hint of any further misdeameanour and he's out. I can't risk the good reputation of the camp.' She smiled at Rhonnie then and said, 'Right, let's take our places on the panel and make sure that this contest is won fair and square.'

Both Drina and Rhonnie enjoyed their stints on the judging panel, and going by the reaction of the crowd when the winners were announced they agreed with the panel's choices. They arrived back in the office just before first sitting for lunch where Drina immediately fetched her belongings, announcing she'd be away for a couple of hours visiting her husband. She was driven there, as she was to and from work, by one of the security guards, always kept on hand to ferry her wherever she needed to go, in the company car.

As soon as she had left, Jackie quizzed Rhonnie about where they had been. When she heard, Jackie was appalled to hear that the contests were fixed. She then brightened at the thought that this was why she hadn't been placed in the top three in the staff's own Most Popular Employee contest at the end-of-season party last year. Terry had been on that judging panel too and now Jackie wasn't surprised that Shelly Stubbs had won, although she doubted very much the girl had bribed him with money!

Jackie then remembered, 'Oh, Dan came in not long after you'd left, wanted to see Mrs Jolly with some plans he'd sketched for the proposed discotheque for teenagers under the Paradise ballroom. First I'd heard of it but it sounds a great idea. Anyway, I put the sketches on Mrs Jolly's desk for her to look at and told Dan she'd get back to him when she had. I've got some ideas for it myself. Do you think Mrs Jolly would like to hear them, Rhonnie?'

'I'm sure she would. I've got a couple too.' She was desperate to ask if Dan had enquired after her, but decided it wasn't a good idea to quiz Jackie. But she did feel that this was the ideal opportunity to ask what exactly Dan's job was.

Jackie told her, 'Oh, he hasn't really got a job title as such. He's Mr Jolly's right hand man, so to speak. If there are any new projects, Dan's the one to oversee the works. He checks the maintenance men have done what they should, and generally keeps everything in working order. If it's not, he organises men to deal with it or does it himself. There's nothing Dan can't handle.' She then mused, 'Wish I was older as I think he's gorgeous, but then so do all the other female staff. And that motor bike he rides to and from work on, well, I understand he built it himself. I'd love to ride pillion sometime, but I doubt I'll ever get the chance. Anyway, Mr Jolly sets great store by him.'

Having had this explained to her, it made sense to Rhonnie now why Mrs Jolly had called on Dan to join them in the disco project. 'He lives nearby then, does he?' she asked.

'Not sure where, but I understand he has a cottage where he used to live with his mother until she died a few years back.' Jackie suddenly stopped talking and looked at Rhonnie knowingly. 'You fancy him, don't you?'

Embarrassed, she shot back, 'No. Not at all.'

Jackie grinned. 'Pull the other one, Rhonnie! You've got to be blind not to. He's gorgeous. Anyway, you're not bad yourself. He'd have to be blind not to look twice at you. Eh, and I'm not trying to butter you up 'cos you're my boss, I speak the truth.'

Rhonnie smiled at the compliment. 'Well, thank you, kind lady. You're a very pretty girl yourself.'

Jackie sighed, 'Well, I wish you'd tell that to Gavin Airely. He doesn't seem to notice me whenever I see him at the dancing in Mablethorpe or out and about. I've fancied him for ages. It's maddening because I know he likes me, I'm positive he does. His friend told me he does.'

Rhonnie looked at the very attractive eighteen year old before her, pretty enough to grace the cover of any of the young women's popular magazines in her blue and white mini-skirt, sleeveless fitted polo-neck and white plastic knee-length boots. Surely any modern young man would be proud to have Jackie hanging on his arm. 'Is he the shy type?' she asked.

Jackie scoffed, 'What, Gavin? Definitely not.'

'Then he's playing silly boys' games. He's let his friend tell you he likes you and now he's keeping you dangling. More than likely just trying to impress his mates. So turn the tables on him. When you see him next, pretend you haven't noticed him but make sure he sees you're enjoying yourself. It's a sure fire way to find out if he really likes you. If he thinks you've gone off him and there's a chance he could lose you, he'll come running. If not, then you know you're wasting your time and can find someone else who'll appreciate you. Plenty more fish in the sea, so it's said.'

Jackie wasn't being big-headed, just telling it like it was when she said to Rhonnie, 'I do get plenty of offers, but it's Gavin I want. I'll try your suggestion next Friday night when I'm out with my mates.' She then eyed Rhonnie fixedly. 'Be honest with me. You do like Dan, don't you?'

She responded dismissively, 'I might.' That was all she was willing to divulge on the subject. To change it she asked, 'It's my turn for a stroll around the camp today, I think, or is my memory playing me tricks?'

In Drina's endeavour to keep an eye on everyday goings on in the camp, she, Rhonnie or Jackie took it in turns to walk around the camp at no given time, just when work allowed, and to report back on anything they saw amiss. They also took the chance to have a chat with the campers en route, to check they were enjoying their stay.

Jackie told her, 'Yes, it is.'

'Then, if you're all right to hold the fort, I'll go now. After lunch we'll update the bookings board for next year.'

One of the girls from accounts came in, holding a folder full of cheques for Drina to sign. Leaving Jackie to deal with this, Rhonnie took her leave.

It was a very hot June day, the sun beating down from a cloudless sky, the temperature into the 80s. They had been lucky with the weather so far. Apart from the odd day of showers, and part of May when for over ten days it was like winter had suddenly descended, the weather had been glorious. According to the forecasters it looked set to remain that way for a good few weeks yet. Good news for the camp and campers.

Making her way down towards the pool, through a sea of colourful frocks and happy faces, Rhonnie couldn't help but remember the afternoon she had first arrived at the camp, back on that miserable rainy day in March. Its transformation was remarkable.

As she looked around Rhonnie was glad to see that all the shops were doing a roaring trade, which was good news for the camp's profits. She chuckled to herself as she watched children coming out of the sweet shops, licking their iced lollies or ice creams, some with faces sticky with candy floss, oblivious to anything else but the special treat they were eating. Then her eyes travelled along to the shop next door, the hairdresser's, at the expectant faces of those going in to be transformed by the talented stylists inside; the satisfied jaunty walks of those coming out.

Rhonnie's eyes travelled then to the next shop in the parade, the photographer's, and her smile faded when she saw Terry Jones deep in conversation with a young woman. Rhonnie watched them both searchingly. She didn't like the thought that she was spying, but then Terry had brought this on himself through his own errant ways.

Rhonnie saw the woman hand him something which he put into his pocket. They exchanged a few more words, then she went off in one direction, he the other. It all looked very suspicious to Rhonnie. She felt sure the woman had handed him money. She could only think it was a backhander to make sure the woman won whatever contest she was entering. Obviously the threat of losing his job had not been deterrent enough to put a stop to Terry's money-making scheme. But to bring him to task for his crime, first Rhonnie needed to have her suspicions confirmed.

She dashed her way through the throng of holidaymakers after the young woman. Catching up with her, Rhonnie said, 'Excuse me, but I need to ask you something.'

She was an attractive young woman of about eighteen. Not as pretty as some, perhaps, her nose was too big for a start and her figure wasn't curvy enough to outshine others in any of the pool competitions. Her best chance of winning would be to bribe a judge. But then it might be the talent contest she was after, knowing her particular skill wasn't quite good enough to put her above the other entrants without an added incentive.

She knew Rhonnie was a member of staff by the badge she wore pinned on her blouse announcing her position of office manager. Assuming she knew what Rhonnie was going to ask her, the girl told her with a smile, 'I'm having a great time, thanks, and so are my family. We're definitely coming back next year.'

'I'm really pleased to hear that. But that's not what I wanted to say. I just saw you with Terry, a stripey, and it looked to me like you were paying him for something?'

'Yes, that's right.'

Rhonnie's heart thumped. 'Can I ask what for?'

'Yeah, sure. I was in the Paradise last night with some other girls I met while I've been here. We were fed up as the music the band was playing was the old fuddy-duddy sort my parents like, so one of the girls suggested we went to the funfair. I'd spent the last of the money I'd taken out with me on a Coke, my mam and dad had gone to the cinema so I couldn't ask them for some, so I asked Terry to lend me a few shillings for the rides. He did and I promised to give it him back this morning, which was what I was just doing.' She looked concerned. 'He's not in trouble for helping me out, is he? He's really nice is Terry. He was so funny in the stripey show the other night. I think he should be on the telly, myself. He's as good as that Jimmy Tarbuck.'

Rhonnie was relieved that she hadn't after all caught Terry up to no good. She assured the young woman, 'No, he's not in trouble at all. I hope you enjoy the rest of your holiday.'

Arriving at the pool, she cast her eyes over the people sunbathing in deckchairs. Middle-aged men, the top button of their grey flannels undone, wore knotted handkerchiefs on their heads to protect their thinning crowns. While they snoozed, oblivious to what was going on around them, their wives in old-fashioned, dark, modestly cut dresses, straw hats on their heads, sat frowning in disapproval of the swimsuited and bikini-clad younger women frolicking with their beaux and friends in the pool under the watchful eyes of the two attendants. This same scene would be repeated down on the beach. In their own way everyone seemed to be having a good time, and Rhonnie was satisfied to see it. A couple of campers, recognising her as a member of staff, approached her to ask her what time the talent contest started tonight, not wanting to miss it as they'd mislaid their events programme for the week and missed this morning's Radio Jolly broadcast. Having told them and ascertained there was nothing else she could do to be of service, she went on her way.

Rhonnie was approaching the sports field, putting green and tennis courts when she saw Sam the donkey man hurrying towards her. The expression on his weather-beaten face was one of alarm. Sam Biggins was middle-aged and unmarried, not the brightest of people perhaps but a gentle soul nevertheless and possessed of a great tolerance towards children, which he needed in his line of work. He lived for his donkeys, cared for them like they were his own family. Each of them had a name and, according to Sam, an individual personality. He wouldn't think twice about sleeping in the stables alongside a sick animal, to nurse it through. His family had been in the donkey rides business since the turn of the century, Sam taking over when his widowed father had died several years ago. It was a joke amongst the staff that he'd never married as no woman would put up with coming eleventh in line to ten donkeys.

As they met up she asked him, 'Everything all right, Sam?'

It was apparent that he hadn't noticed Rhonnie. At the sound of her voice he jumped, looking at her blindly for a moment before he spoke. 'Oh, hello, Rhonnie love. No, everything ain't all right. I've had to leave the donkeys tied up as a young girl has spewed all down me trousers and I need to change 'em. It wasn't the young lass's fault, bless her. She said she didn't want a ride but her mam insisted, wanting a photograph of her to show the folks back home.'

A commotion down the path that Sam had just hurried along caught Rhonnie's attention then, and when she saw the cause she didn't know whether to laugh or cry. She said to him, 'Did you secure the donkeys before you left them?'

He eyed her strangely. ''Course I did. Why?'

'I hate to say this . . . but not tightly enough.'

She pointed over his shoulder and he turned to look, gawping in shock to see all ten donkeys following behind, stopping now and again to snatch juicy leaves from the hedge or the plants in a flowerbed.

In outrage Sam exclaimed, 'It was them pesky kids that let them loose, I know it was! They were mad at me for not giving them free rides. This is them getting their own back.'

Rhonnie knew which children he was referring to. She'd had to speak to their parents about them on several occasions since they had arrived at the camp four days ago. Their unruly behaviour was causing other campers grief, the parents being the sort to practise 'out of sight, out of mind'. Despite herself, Rhonnie couldn't help but giggle, though, along with the crowd that had now gathered to watch the donkeys' antics. A furious Sam, forgetting his ruined trousers and the awful smell emanating from him, went to round them up and take them back to the beach. Rhonnie wouldn't like to be on the receiving end of the ear-bashing the culprits were about to receive should they still be on the beach when he returned.

The rest of her walkaround went without mishap and by the time she got back to the top of the camp it was time for lunch.

The girls were already seated when she arrived, and Ginger, Shelly and Noreen were listening to one of the others regaling them all with an incident that had happened to her that morning. Shelly as usual was not able to stop herself from making a cutting comment. They all greeted Rhonnie, and the waitress arrived at the same time to put metal teapots on the table along with tongue salad for each of them.

As she ate, Rhonnie couldn't help but notice that there was something different about Noreen. She was unusually quiet today, seemed to be lost in her own thoughts. Whatever those were they were putting a smile on her lips and she seemed to have a strange inner glow about her. Come to think of it, she'd been acting this way over breakfast this morning too. Suddenly Rhonnie knew why. She said to her, 'Noreen, have you got yourself a boyfriend?'

With all eyes on her now, her round face immediately blushed scarlet.

'Have you then?' Ginger urged.

She gave a small shrug. 'I might have,' she said coyly.

Bren said, 'Well, yer either have or you haven't.'

'Well, yes then, I have.'

In disbelief one of the other girls demanded, 'Who is it?'

She anxiously gnawed her bottom lip. 'I . . . I can't tell you that.'

'Why not?" demanded Ginger.

'Well, it's just that he . . . we . . . want to keep it a secret for now.'

'Why? Oh, 'cos he's married, that's why,' one of the others said knowingly.

Noreen vigorously shook her head, declaring, 'No, he's not. It's just . . .'

Much to everyone's shock, Shelly snapped, 'Leave the girl be, for God's sake. If she wants to keep her boyfriend's name to herself, then that's her choice.'

Looking at Shelly in shock, Ginger said, 'Well, that's a turn up for the books, you being nice for a change.'

She gave a nonchalant shrug. 'Well, I can be sometimes. Does anyone want my tongue? I hate tongue.'

The subject was changed, and for the time being that was the end of it.

Returning back to the office to man the switchboard while Jackie had her lunch, Rhonnie was looking forward to seeing her face when she relayed the donkey incident to her, but before she had a chance, Jackie told her, 'Oh, good, you're back. You've a visitor, Rhonnie.'

She looked at Jackie, taken aback. 'A visitor! Who?'

'I dunno. I was in the accounts department returning some cheques so wasn't in the office when Mrs Jolly returned and your visitor arrived. When I did get back, she popped her head out of the office and asked me to tell you to go straight in as soon as you got back.'

Having no idea who her mystery visitor could be Rhonnie went over to the door, tapped on it and went inside. When she clapped eyes on who it was sitting beside Drina on the red velvet sofa in the corner of the room, Rhonnie stared at them in utter shock.

CHAPTER FOURTEEN

Finally finding her voice, she uttered, 'Dad!' Rhonnie was about to ask what he was doing here but then, overriding the shock of his unexpected appearance, the terrible state of him registered with her. Her normally happy-go-lucky, rotund father looked wretched and unshaven, his clothes crumpled, a good couple of stone lighter than when she'd last seen him. She knew without asking just what had brought about this dramatic transformation in him.

Drina was by her side now, resting one hand on her arm, a look of deep sympathy on her face. 'Take as long as you need, Rhonnie. I'll be working at your desk. Give your father another brandy. By the looks of him, he needs it.'

As soon as Drina had closed the door behind her, she went over to the sofa, sitting down beside her father and taking his hand in hers, to squeeze it tightly. Looking into his pained eyes, tears of distress filling her own, she choked, 'You know, don't you, Dad?'

He nodded miserably. 'The real reason you left home? Yes, I know.' He looked at her anxiously. 'I'm sorry, love, if my coming here causes you any trouble, but I needed to . . .'

She interjected, 'You did the right thing, Dad. I'm just sorry you had to come here under these circumstances.'

He whispered, 'So am I, love.' With his free hand he picked up the tumbler of brandy Drina had already given him. He then gave his daughter a wan smile 'She seems a very nice woman, your boss. Made me feel very welcome.' He took another swig before saying, 'You should have told me, Rhonnie.'

'I'm sorry, Dad, I couldn't.'

He eyed her imploringly. 'But why couldn't you, love? You've always been able to talk to me about anything before this.'

'I know, Dad, I know, but apart from the fact I just couldn't bring myself to break your heart again and risk you sinking back into the same state you did after Mum died, that woman threatened that if I breathed a word she would make you believe I was telling lies. She'd have told you I didn't like the fact she'd taken Mum's place, and turned you against me.'

'Mavis would never have turned me against you, love,' Artie Fleming told her with conviction.

'I know, Dad, but at the time I was frightened she would manage to. How did you find out the truth about her?'

It greatly distressed Rhonnie to see the sheer pain in his eyes then. He was visibly shaking as he began to relay the events that had brought him here.

'Nearly three weeks ago Ralf Duggins broke his leg, which meant the boss had to do a shift around so the rest of us drivers could pull in his loads until they got a temporary driver in to cover. It ended up that instead of me being away five days on a trip to Aberdeen, it was only three nights down to Devon. I thought it would be a nice surprise for Mavis, having me home sooner than she thought, so I decided I'd treat her and Tracy to a meal at the Berni Inn.'

He paused for a moment to draw a deep breath. His voice barely audible, he continued, 'It was me who got the surprise. I arrived home at just before seven to find the house in a right state, Tracy lolling on the settee watching some teenage music show on the television and no sign at all of Mavis. Tracy told me her mother had been called urgently to a friend who needed her help. She didn't know when she'd be back. She told me that Mrs Trimble was looking after her, and was down the yard in the toilet. Thinking that Mavis would be back soon so I could still surprise her by taking her out, I went for a wash and change. But she wasn't back, so I thought I'd go for a pint down the Nelson for a change instead of at my usual place. The beer there is better and a penny a pint cheaper.

'I wonder now if I hadn't gone to the Nelson whether I'd still be in the dark about Mavis. Anyway, I saw her as soon as I walked in. It was her laugh that alerted me. It was barely eight o'clock and she was the worse for drink, draped all over a bloke, obviously more than just friends with him. I was so shocked I stood in the middle of the pub staring at her, couldn't believe what I was seeing. This couldn't be my Mavis. It was her twin sister, it had to be. I believed Mavis was a good woman, not the sort to fornicate behind her husband's back while he was away working. You can't imagine how devastated I was feeling then and how stupid for being blind to the real her, just accepting the one she showed me as the genuine article. I dragged her home. After sending Mrs Trimble home and Tracy to her room, as I didn't want her hearing what her mother was up to, I demanded Mavis tell me what she thought she was playing at.'

Artie paused for a moment, to wipe tears from his eyes with the back of one hand, before he continued in a voice choked with emotion. 'Can you believe she laughed at me, love? Told me I was a fat, boring old fart that she'd only hooked up with because she was desperate for someone to take care of her and her daughter. She said some other thing to me too, not nice at all, that I don't wish to repeat. I told her to pack her and her daughter's bags and get out. She flatly refused, told me she wasn't going anywhere and was glad I'd found out when I had as it meant she hadn't got to play the dutiful wife any longer. If I wanted to leave that was up to me, she said. She didn't care if I did as she'd already got someone lined up to take my place. If I didn't choose to go then at least I now knew what the score was. She didn't intend to change.

'I couldn't stay in that house a moment longer. It didn't feel like my home, she had seen to that. All I could think of was that I was glad your mother wasn't around to witness with her own eyes how stupid I'd been. That wicked woman had tainted the house and everything in it that me and your mother had scrimped and saved for. I went upstairs to pack up my stuff and when I came back down Mavis had gone out again, obviously to find her bloke and say the coast was clear for him to move in. I couldn't face anyone, Rhonnie . . . workmates, neighbours, friends, no one, not even you then. I felt terrible for bringing her into your life and making it so miserable that you had to leave. I was worried you might hate me for it.'

She erupted, 'Never, Dad. I could never hate you for anything. I love you too much. I couldn't have wished for a better dad than you. I don't blame you for falling for Mavis. When you met her you were a sad and lonely man, who thought you'd be on your own for the rest of your life and couldn't see past your luck after she made a beeline for you. When all's said and done, I can't deny Mavis is a good-looking woman.'

He sniffed back tears and whispered, 'Thanks for understanding, love.'

'So where have you been for the last three weeks?'

'To be honest, the first few days are a blur. I just remember waking up one morning in a cheap bed and breakfast place, not having been out for days, because I was worried I might bump into Mavis and terrified I might do something to her I'd live to regret. I don't remember whether it was a bus I caught or a train, but I ended up in Nottingham in a cheap bed and breakfast. I think the landlady was starting to get a bit worried as I hardly left my room. Anyway, a couple of days ago, it hit me that you might decide to pay a visit home, and I couldn't bear for you to walk in and find out what had happened. I knew I had to come and tell you everything.'

'But how did you know where I was? When I wrote to you I deliberately didn't include my address. Only because I was frightened of you turning up because you suspected I hadn't been honest about why I'd left home. I didn't want to have to lie to your face,' she explained.

He gave a wan smile. 'I knew if no one else then you'd tell Carol where you were. I went to see her. You'd obviously taken her into your confidence about Mavis, and judging by the state of me when I turned up at her door, Carol knew why I had to see you urgently. She told me to tell you that she hopes you'll forgive her for breaking her word, in the circumstances.'

Rhonnie affectionately patted his hand. 'Of course I do, Dad. I'll write to Carol and put her mind at rest.' She looked searchingly at him for a moment, the sadness she was feeling for him hardly bearable. 'Right, first things first. Let's get you a bed for the night and something to eat. And after you've had a good night's sleep, tomorrow we'll make some plans for your future.'

She could tell by the expression on his face that he felt he hadn't got one. There was also a look of relief that she was taking control of his dire situation, relieving him of the burden.

As soon as she walked out of the inner office, Drina held out a chalet key to Rhonnie, saying, 'Go and get your father settled in. Take as long as you need. I've spoken to Chef Brown and he's having a tray made up with a hot meal which will be delivered to the chalet in an hour. Your poor father looks like he's not eaten properly for a while, let alone slept.' When Rhonnie started to cry, Drina was up out of her chair and beside her in an instant, a comforting arm around the young woman's shoulders. 'There, there, dear. It'll be all right, believe me. I don't know what exactly has happened to your father to bring him here, but I do know it was something that has affected him very badly. We'll look after him, though, get him through this. He's with friends now.'

Rhonnie's tears became a torrent. 'Oh, Mrs Jolly, you're so kind. I will pay for his stay . . .'

Drina cut in, 'I wouldn't hear of it. That chalet is lying empty for the rest of this week so your father might as well make use of it. If he decides to stay longer then we'll find him something more permanent. If he's looking for work, I'm sure Dan could use an extra pair of hands on the discotheque project, but that's for your father to decide when he's feeling more himself. So off you go. Oh, and take that bottle of brandy with you. A couple of shots of that after his dinner will help him sleep better. It does me when I'm feeling under par.'

At well after one in the morning, Rhonnie was lying in bed staring up at the ceiling unable to sleep. It wasn't the gentle snores of her chalet mate or the humid night air making her restless, but the emotions raging inside her. She felt murderous towards Mavis for selfishly causing Artie such heartbreak. Rhonnie desperately tried to push these thoughts aside by telling herself that someone, some day, would see that Mavis received her just deserts for the cruel way she used innocent people. With a lot of love and understanding, her father would be helped to recover and returned to his happy-go-lucky self, she knew, but regardless sleep still wouldn't come. Finally, she decided a walk in the night air might do the trick. As quietly as she could so as not to disturb her chalet mate Val, she rose, dressed in a pair of trousers and a woollen jumper, and let herself out.

The camp was deathly quiet, nothing stirring, as Rhonnie walked slowly down the dimly lit paths towards the beach. She intended to sit there for a while in the hope that the lulling sound of the waves breaking against the shore would help to soothe her turmoil. Arriving at the end of the duckboards, she slipped off her shoes and stepped on to the sand. The only light guiding her now was from a full moon shining down from a cloudless sky. Rhonnie was surprised to find the sand was still warm under her feet as she stepped over it towards a dune and made herself comfortable inside its crescent-shaped base.

Knees drawn up to her chin, she rested her arms on them and looked up at the moon. As a child her mother had told her that if she made a wish when the moon was full, looking straight at it and not through a window, then it would come true. She had made several in the past but her wishes hadn't come true. When she'd told her mother, she had just replied that Rhonnie obviously hadn't wished hard enough. She was an adult now and knew that what her mother had told her was just a fairy story, but the way she felt at the moment anything that would help her father was worth a try. Looking straight at the moon, Rhonnie said out loud, 'Dear moon, my wish is for my father to get over this awful time and return to his old happy self. Please, this one time, grant my wish?'

'They say that's a sign of madness.'

She was so engrossed in making her wish, she hadn't noticed someone sit down next to her. At the unexpected voice, Rhonnie almost jumped out of her skin. She gasped in surprise to find Dan close beside her. Composing herself, she asked in a casual manner, 'What is?'

'Talking to the moon.'

'In that case, are you sure you feel safe sitting so close to me?'

'I'll take the risk.'

'What are you doing here at this time of night?'

'Same as you, I expect. Couldn't sleep. There's a path by my cottage that leads down to the beach and on nights like this, when I can't drop off, I often take a walk hoping that will do the trick. I find it so peaceful on the beach when no one else is around.'

She smiled at him. 'Sorry if my chat with the moon disturbed your solitude.'

'I'm sure I can forgive you.'

They lapsed into silence for a moment before he asked her, 'What did you wish for?'

She turned her head to look at him. 'How did you know I was making a wish?'

'Because my mother used to tell me that if you made a wish on a full moon it would come true.'

'So did mine. And have you ever wished on a full moon?'

'Many times.'

'Has it come true?'

'No. My mother told me I obviously hadn't wished hard enough.' He shifted around to face her. 'Look, Rhonnie, I know what you were wishing for. Mrs J told me when I went for dinner at her house tonight . . . about your father turning up out of the blue, in a right state.'

She looked surprised. 'You had dinner with Mrs Jolly?' She suddenly realised she had made that sound as if she was surprised Drina would have dinner with the likes of him, and blurted out, 'Oh, not that I think it's odd she would have dinner with you, I didn't mean that at all. It's just that . . .' Her mind went blank and she sat staring at him like an idiot.

He chuckled. 'Got yourself into a hole there, haven't you, Rhonnie? And no idea how to get out of it. I understand what you were getting at. It's not the done thing, is it, for the boss, and a woman on her own at that, to invite one of her employees to eat at her home?' He paused for a moment, turning to face out towards the sea.

'Since my mum died, Drina has insisted I go over there at least once a month, to make sure I have a decent meal inside me as she puts it, despite the fact that I'm quite capable of cooking for myself. I don't know all the story as my mum wouldn't talk much about her past, but I know she was married to a relation of Mr Jolly's and when my father died – I don't remember him, I was very young when he did – he left her in dire straits and she turned to Joe for help. He had her moved up here, rented a cottage for her to live in and gave her a job at the camp. She was in charge of the cleaning staff. Mr Jolly became like a father figure to me. I worked for him during the school holidays and at weekends. I loved working at the camp, especially on the funfair which is in my blood. My mother was English but my father was a full-blown gypsy, you see.

'When I left school there was no question of where I would work. Mr Jolly had made it his business to see I learned how the camp was run from the bottom up. He was a hard taskmaster, but fair. I hated the office side, though. Paperwork of any type is not my forte. I like using my hands and getting them dirty. When Mr Jolly was happy I could learn no more, he put me in charge of the maintenance crew and of overseeing any new building projects. I have a lot to thank him for. I hate to think just where my mother and I would have ended up if he had turned her away.

'Mrs Jolly was always very kind to my mother and me, too, couldn't have made us more welcome when we first came here. Since Mother died she has kept a maternal eye on me. I think the world of Mrs Jolly, there's nothing I wouldn't do for her. She has asked me to look after your father should he take up the offer of working here with me. Rest assured that I will, Rhonnie.'

Dan abruptly stopped talking, feeling a bit shocked about revealing so much. He had never been the sort to open up about himself to anyone, believing his private life was his alone, yet he just had without hesitation, and to a woman he hardly knew. When he was younger he was certainly guilty of sleeping with any pretty girl who took his fancy, but he had come to learn that shallow one-night stands were not for him. He wanted a relationship that was far more than just physical. He wanted to be with a woman with a brain in her head, who was fun to be with and with whom he felt comfortable. He definitely did not want the needy sort, relentlessly chasing after him, demanding he spend every spare minute with her from the moment they met, which had been the case with the type of girl he had gone out with before he'd grown up sufficiently to realise what he wanted. Since he had come to that realisation he hadn't met any woman he felt would fulfil all his needs. Until recently, that was.

From the moment he had set eyes on Rhonnie – as she was going around the camps with Mr Jolly and Jackie the first day she had started work at the camp – he had sensed she was something special, felt inexplicably drawn to her. He'd not wanted to risk making a complete fool of himself, charging over to introduce himself to her in front of Jackie and Mrs Jolly. Then, as luck would have it, he had spotted her alone on the swings and had, without hesitation, seized the opportunity to aquaint himself with her. He'd certainly enjoyed his time with her, sensing that she returned his feelings. But despite keeping his eyes peeled for her when he was out and about around the camp, he hadn't seen sight of her again. He couldn't believe his luck when she had come into the Paradise while he was helping out the bar staff, and he certainly wasn't about to let that chance pass. He'd been thrilled when she'd agreed to accompany him to the fair. His enjoyable time with her there had made Dan determined to ask her out on a proper date before they parted. When the time came, though, his nerve had failed him, he had no idea why. He had come over all schoolboyish and shy, leaving without asking, and he'd been kicking himself ever since.

Now fate was giving him another opportunity to ask Rhonnie out. But since she knew he was aware of her father's predicament, did he really want to appear thoughtless by asking her to spend time with him while she had a crisis on her hands? No, he did not, he decided. He wanted to get this right. Which left him with no choice but to bide his time until her father's need wasn't so great and Rhonnie was free from worry.

She was saying to him now, 'Yes, Mrs Jolly is a lovely woman. I couldn't wish for a better boss. I don't know how I'm ever going to repay her for the kindness she has shown me and my father at this terrible time. I pray he will decide to stay here even if it's only until he's got over what . . . well, I'm sure you'll understand I don't feel it's right to divulge what caused him to get into the state he is? That's for him to do, if he chooses. I do hope he takes you up the job offer. It's good of you to say you'll keep an eye on him too.'

Dan thought, If only you knew I'd do anything for you, Rhonnie. He said, 'Well, I look out for all the men I'm in charge of so I wouldn't be treating your father any differently. Look, I'm no expert in these matters but it might help his recovery to know he's needed, if you understand me? Is he good with his hands?'

'He knows his way around an engine. Has to with his job as a long-distance lorry driver. Well, that *was* his job, but I should imagine with him disappearing off like he has, his firm will have replaced him by now. He always did any repairs around our house. Did a good job too. He built me a rabbit hutch once. It was still in one piece when the rabbit died.'

'He sounds like a good man to have around. When you decide to tell him about the offer of work, make sure he knows it's not charity. I could really do with a man like him helping me on the disco revamp.'

Rhonnie smiled. 'I will.' She rubbed her hands wearily over her face. 'I'd best get off and try and get some sleep.'

'Me too.' He stood up and extended one hand to help her to her feet.

As she grasped it Dan felt as if a bolt of lightning had shot through him, and had to fight with himself not to pull her into his arms and kiss her pain away, reminding himself that now was not the time to make his feelings known.

As Rhonnie grabbed his hand to help herself up and stared into his handsome face to thank him, she had to fight against a great urge to melt against him, feel his strong arms around her, giving her comfort. If ever she'd needed comfort, it was now. She sensed he liked her and enjoyed her company, judging by the way he'd reacted to her during their time at the fair, but he'd given no indication he thought any more of her than that. He couldn't do or he would have asked her out on a proper date by now. But then, even if he had, she wasn't in any position to embark on a relationship with a man while her father's need of her was so great.

CHAPTER FIFTEEN

At the beginning of August, alongside Drina and Jackie, Rhonnie looked around the transformed room under the Paradise. Gone were all the cobwebs and the dust, and the concrete floor had been covered with floorboards and varnished to a high shine. The bare brick walls were freshly painted in colourful tones, one of them sporting a modern psychedelic mural. At the far end of the dance floor was a small dais for the DJ to work from with turntables and two huge speakers, which were connected to several wall-mounted ones around the rest of the room. The ceiling was covered with glass stars that reflected the light from the rotating glass ball that hung at its centre.

Opposite the women, against the far wall, stood two dozen or so tables and chairs for those who wanted to watch not dance. The long well-stocked bar, serving alcohol to those who were of age and soft drinks to those who were not, was the other side of the room, faced with black vinyl intermittently embellished with cut-outs of records and musical notes. The bar staff here would be wearing their own trendy clothes.

In Rhonnie's opinion the younger generation of campers were going to love this place, and she was positive that being able to let their hair down and party to the kind of music they usually listened to was going to make a marked difference to their enjoyment of their holidays.

But this room's transformation could only take second place

to the one her father had undergone. At first she'd felt like she was directing words of encouragement to a brick wall, but finally she had seen signs that they were breaking through Artie's barrier of misery and taking effect. Now his old zest for life was beginning to return. He'd actually gone out socially for the first time last night, accompanying Rhonnie and Mrs Jolly for a drink at the Paradise. He'd stayed for just one but it was a definite start. She knew he had only accepted the offer of work because at heart he was a proud man, not the sort to expect his daughter to fund him no matter how low he was feeling. His job with the maintenance crew, five men in all including their boss Dan, had given him a reason to get up in the morning, and as the weeks went by, and he got to know the other men and feel like part of the team, seeing the fruits of their labours as the disco took shape, his confidence began to rise. Rhonnie felt she had a lot to thank Drina and Dan for, and even Jackie had done her best to make him feel welcome, bringing in gifts of her mother's homemade cakes and biscuits. He was still far from his old self yet but Rhonnie was certain that it was only a matter of time.

She turned to Drina now and said, 'I can see by your face that you are pleased with the result, Mrs Jolly. The youngsters are going to love it here. I can't believe what Dan and his men have done. Mr Jolly will be amazed when he finds out what you've done, won't he?'

Drina responded shortly, 'We'll see, dear.'

Rhonnie eyed her quizzically, wondering what she meant by that. Surely he couldn't fail to be pleased with the way his wife had risen to the challenge of running the camp during his recovery, and the changes for the better she had instigated there. She did wonder, though, if Drina's short remark had been because at the moment she was worried by the fact that several campers had reported thefts from their chalets while they were out.

It had started about a fortnight ago. In the first few instances both Drina and Rhonnie had felt the losses were down to the campers' own carelessness, though they had assured them that should anyone hand in their items, they would be informed immediately. But the total number of complaints had now risen to over a dozen, and there might even be more including campers who had returned home meantime and not yet discovered their property was missing. It could no longer be denied that there was a thief in the camp. And if that wasn't bad enough, it had to be one of the staff who was responsible because there were no campers who had stayed long enough to have carried out all the thefts. Rhonnie felt sure this was playing on her boss's mind, as it was on her own.

Dan came over then, his handsome face beaming, and Rhonnie immediately hoped she wasn't revealing the longing she felt for him.

He smiled a greeting at her before saying to Drina, 'Is the result to your satisfaction, Mrs J?'

She patted his arm. 'You've surpassed yourself, Dan dear. You and your men have obviously worked around the clock to get this done. I thought it might not be ready before the season ended. I'd like you to take the men for a drink on me.' She delved in her pocket and took out a five-pound note which she handed to him. 'That should be enough for a few drinks each.'

He waved it away. 'Already seen to, but I will extend your appreciation to them for their efforts. Excuse me, won't you, but there are still a couple of little jobs left to finish off so it's all ready for opening night tomorrow.'

Rhonnie said to Drina, 'We need to write out the announcement for the receptionist to relay over the radio, announcing the opening party tomorrow night, and confirm with Herman's Hermits' agent that the group is definitely coming. We are very fortunate to get them, they're a very popular band, have been on *Top of the Pops* several times.' She laughed. 'I doubt we would have got them at all if their agent hadn't jumped to the wrong conclusion when I said we were a holiday camp. Before I could tell him which one, he assumed I meant Butlin's and was delighted at the exposure this would give the band, playing at the top holiday camp in the country. By the time I did get a chance to point out his mistake it was too late. We'd agreed terms and he'd committed the band to the gig.'

Drina looked at her, taken aback. 'I don't understand half these words you youngsters come out with. Gig, fab, hip, swinging. It's like you're sending secret messages to each other about something you don't want us oldies to understand. And who in their right mind burdens their son with a name like Herman? Poor lad.'

Rhonnie laughed. 'That's not his real name, Mrs Jolly. He's called Peter Noone. That's just the name they've called the group.'

Drina said, 'It's all going way over my head, dear. We'd best get back upstairs, deal with what you've just mentioned and double check everything else to make sure that tomorrow's opening party goes with a swing.'

Rhonnie suddenly exclaimed, 'Oh, my goodness. There is one very important thing we haven't given any thought to at all.'

Drina looked worried. 'What's that?'

'A name for the discotheque.'

'Oh, we haven't, have we?' Drina looked pensive for a moment before she said, 'I think we've enough on our plates to deal with without that headache too. Let's give the job to Jackie.'

Rhonnie called over to the girl, who was on the dais miming into the mic, pretending she was the DJ. She was told to put the equipment down in case she broke anything and then to come with them back to the office as they had an important job for her to do.

Eager to know just what it was, Jackie replaced the mic carefully on its stand and bounded after them.

At just before eight-thirty the next evening, the opening speech welcoming everyone to the camp's latest addition, Groovy's, had been made. Drina had proposed saying a few words after being introduced by their now resident DJ. Looking around before she even began, she was very aware the crowd of teenagers and people in their early twenties were willing her to get on with it as they were desperate for Herman's Hermits to make their appearance, and to start dancing. In truth Drina was mortally relieved to get away with saying little more than welcome to them all as she had been shaking with nerves at the prospect of making an address to such a large audience anyway.

Glad that her part in the proceedings was over, she was now standing by the wall at the side of the room, feeling somewhat out of place amongst a sea of young women wearing the latest fashions. Drina herself had chosen to wear a pink satin evening gown she had bought last year from Liberty's in London for a ball Joe and she had been invited to. To one side of her stood Rhonnie, looking very attractive in a floaty, lime green-coloured granny-style dress. Beside her stood Artie, looking smart in a suit and tie but somewhat out of place at this venue specifically intended for those half his age. Standing the other side of Drina was Dan, who didn't own a suit but still looked immaculate in tight black trousers, white shirt worn with a thin black tie, and a black-and-white checked jacket with plain black lapels.

They stood with drinks in hand, watching the dancers, in particular Jackie who was busily dancing around a pile of handbags belonging to several other girls she was friendly with at Jolly's, flinging her arms about and wiggling her hips in time to the beat of the song Herman's Hermits were playing: their first hit 'I'm Into Something Good'.

Terry Jones was doing a first-rate job of acting as compère for the evening, having the audience in stitches with his comic way of announcing the next event in the special programe that had been put together to make sure Groovy's opening night was a special one. Rhonnie felt it was a shame that due to his greed in lining his own pockets with bribes he would not now advance within the company. The good thing was that it did seem as though he was no longer taking bribes to fix contests, as the management had no evidence to the contrary. Colin had obviously done a good job in letting it be known that such practices would not be tolerated.

Weaving her way through the crowd, Rhonnie saw Ginger heading towards her. A little the worse for drink, she slurred, 'This place is fab! I'm having a whale of a time, and so are the others.' She then leaned closer to Rhonnie and whispered, 'Going to introduce me to your friend?'

Rhonnie screwed up her face, telling Ginger she didn't know what friend she was referring to.

'Dan, you daft 'a'porth. I'm hoping he'll ask me to dance.'

Rhonnie liked Ginger very much but wasn't happy about introducing another woman to Dan considering the way she felt about him. Regardless, she said, 'Oh, of course I will.' She leaned forward, saying to Drina, 'Excuse me.' Then called to Dan, 'Dan, this is Ginger.'

He nodded and smiled at her and said, 'Pleased to meet you.' Then returned his attention to the dancers.

A disappointed Ginger said to Rhonnie, 'Oh, well, you can't blame a girl for trying. Coming for a dance, Rhonnie?'

'Wouldn't be right of me to abandon Mrs Jolly, but I will as soon as she leaves.'

'We're over there,' Ginger told her, pointing across the room. Then added, 'Or is it over there?' pointing in the opposite direction. 'Well, we're somewhere over there anyway. See you.'

'Yes, see you,' Rhonnie responded.

The volume of the music was getting too much for Drina who shouted out to the others, 'Well, I've done my bit. Best leave you youngsters to it.'

Artie was feeling exactly the same way. 'Yes, I'm going to call it a night too.'

'You're not going to bed yet, Artie, surely?' Drina said to him. 'I'm going to find somewhere a little quieter to sit down and enjoy the rest of my drink, if you'd care to join me?'

He responded without hesitation, 'I'd like that very much, Mrs Jolly.'

As she made to leave she looked at both Rhonnie and Dan, both looking awkward, not sure what to do now the others were leaving them on their own together. Drina shook her head at them and said, 'When are you two going to stop pussyfooting around each other? It's so apparent you both . . . how would you young ones say it? . . . have the hots for each other. For goodness' sake, ask Rhonnie to dance, Dan, you know you're itching to. Same as Rhonnie is itching for you to ask her.'

With that she walked off.

Rhonnie was wishing the ground would open and swallow her up. She was too mortified to look at Dan and see his reaction to Drina's outburst because as far as Rhonnie was aware her boss was wrong in her assumption. What had possessed her to put Dan in such a compromising situation? Rhonnie couldn't even put it down to drink as her boss had only had one. Rhonnie just wanted to put some distance between her and Dan and hope they never crossed paths again while she was feeling so embarrassed. What must he think of her? Spinning on her heel, she rushed away.

Dan was staring across the room, frozen with shock. It was as if Drina had read his mind. He did very much want to ask Rhonnie to dance with him, but knew one dance wouldn't be nearly enough for him. He would want to take matters further. But there was Artie to consider . . . Oh, what the hell? he thought. Was there ever be a right time to start a relationship?

Taking a steadying breath he turned to face Rhonnie, to ask her to dance, but to his dismay she was gone. He gazed frantically around in search of her, over to the bar hoping she had gone to get another drink but couldn't see her there, then all around the room. It was like looking for a needle in a haystack due to the number of dancers and those milling around the edges. Rhonnie seemed to have disappeared into thin air. Then his eyes fell on the stairs leading up to the entrance and he just caught sight of the bottom of her green dress before it disappeared from view.

Kicking up his heels, he dashed through the crowds, just managing to arrive at the bottom of the stairs as Rhonnie was about to pull open one of the doors at the top and make her way through it.

'Rhonnie,' he shouted to her. When she didn't respond, he bellowed out, 'RHONNIE.'

She did hear him that time and froze for a moment, aware it would be rude to ignore Dan's summons. He bolted up the stairs to join her, pulling her into the side so that people coming and going could get past them both. 'Where are you going?' he asked.

She fibbed, 'I did tell you I was leaving. You obviously didn't hear me. Well, the music is loud.'

'So where are you going exactly?'

Rhonnie couldn't understand why he wanted to know. 'I'm . . . er . . .' Her brain raced for a plausible excuse. 'The toilet.'

'What's wrong with the toilets downstairs?'

She feigned a laugh. 'Oh, I forgot about those. Well, I'm up here now, so I might as well use the one in the Paradise.'

'I'll wait for you.'

She looked surprised. 'What for?'

'Mrs J ordered us to have a dance, remember?'

She waved a dismissive hand. 'Oh, Mrs Jolly might be our boss but we don't have to do as she orders us in our own time.'

'But I want to dance with you, Rhonnie.'

She looked surprised. 'You do?'

Dan nodded. 'But there is something I want to do much more.'

'Oh! What's that then?'

'This.' Cupping her face in his hands, he bent his head and kissed her, long and with fervour. Finally releasing her, he looked searchingly at her and said, 'I'm not reading this wrong, am I, Rhonnie? You do like me, don't you?'

She was still reeling from his unexpected kiss. Finding her voice, she uttered, 'I might, just a bit.'

'Oh, just a bit! But hopefully enough to go out with me on a proper date?'

She gulped, wondering if she was dreaming this. 'You mean as a boyfriend and girlfriend proper date sort of thing?'

He nodded vehemently.

It felt to her like she had been waiting for aeons to hear him say those words to her and she couldn't help but blurt out, 'Oh, I think I like you a big enough bit to do that.'

Forgetting they were on the stairs, in his delight at her response he scooped her up in his arms, made to swing her around, lost his footing and they both tumbled down the stairs, to land in a heap at the bottom. Remarkably, neither of them had suffered any physical damage, but before they could untangle themselves and get up off the floor, an inebriated voice nearby was heard to quip, 'Now I know what they mean by *falling for someone*.'

Rhonnie and Dan looked at each other and burst into laughter.

Just after twelve, with Dan's arm slung protectively around Rhonnie's shoulders, they walked together towards her chalet. Neither of them actually wanted this evening to end but both were aware they had to work in the morning and needed to be bright and alert. Despite being exhausted from their evening of dancing together, both of them doubted they'd get much sleep from the sheer euphoria filling them as they realised they were entering a very important new phase in their lives.

Arriving outside her door, Dan enveloped Rhonnie in his arms, saying to her, 'It seems my mother wasn't spinning me a fairy story after all. If you wish hard enough on a full moon it will come true.'

She pulled away slightly to look up at him. 'My wish about my father certainly seems to have come true.'

'My wish too, that I made after you left me that night on the beach. You've agreed to go out with me, Rhonnie. Though it remains to be seen whether all I wish for will be granted.'

'Oh, what was the rest of your wish, then?'

'Oh, I can't tell you that. I will when it happens, though. So when are we going for this night out then?'

'Whenever you like.'

'Tomorrow night too soon?'

'Not for me, no.'

'Then I'll meet you at the entrance gates at eight.'

Their kiss goodnight could have gone on forever as far as they were concerned.

Neither of them managed much sleep that night, and neither of them cared.

CHAPTER SIXTEEN

The world looked a different place to Rhonnie the next morning as she left the chalet to make her way to the restaurant for breakfast. To her the colours of the flowers were far more vibrant, the shrubs and grass lusher, the morning air fresher, the sky a deeper blue, and she felt glad to be alive. Dan had left her in no doubt last night how he felt about her and she was still basking in the glow of discovering her feelings for him were reciprocated.

In all the time she had been dating him, Ivan had never made her feel so wanted, so cherished, as Dan did, and she realised now that what she had thought in her inexperience was love for Ivan was really no more than a sister would feel for a brother she was very fond of.

Of course Rhonnie knew it would be stupid to hope that her and Dan's budding relationship would stay their secret until they were ready to inform the world. There had been far too many staff partying at Groovy's last night for that. She knew many of them, but especially Ginger, would have seen how much fun Rhonnie and Dan had had dancing to the upbeat music, how close they'd held each other during the smooches, the fact that they'd left together at the end of the night. And so she was prepared for an inquisition from Ginger, Shelly, Noreen and the other girls over breakfast.

Good job too as their probing questions came one after the other and she had no choice but to admit to them that she and

Dan were dating. Ginger surprised her by expressing delight for Rhonnie, and made her laugh by telling her that this news was going to cause many broken hearts today when it got around that the best-looking man on the camp was now spoken for. They would all have to find another one to fantasize over.

Shelly, true to form, couldn't help but pass a nasty comment, telling Rhonnie that their romance wouldn't last and she'd be a fool to think it would after he'd got what he wanted from her, as men like him weren't the marrying kind. Rhonnie chose to ignore this.

The only one who didn't make any comment whatsoever on the matter was Noreen. She was in a world of her own, her mind obviously filled with thoughts of her own boyfriend. Rhonnie wondered just who this mystery man was? But she didn't blame Noreen or her new man for keeping each other secret.

Drina was beside herself, waiting eagerly to find out what had happened between Dan and Rhonnie after she'd left them the previous night. She called Rhonnie into her office immediately she heard her arrive, vehemently hoping her encouragement had done the trick and finally brought them together.

As soon as Rhonnie had shut the door, Drina said to her, 'So?'

Rhonnie looked at her quizzically. 'So what, Mrs Jolly?'

'Oh, for goodness' sake, put me out of my misery and tell me you two finally got it together?'

Rhonnie so wanted to throw her arms around the woman, thank her profusely for the part she had played in getting Dan to admit his feelings, but her mischievous side felt the need to have a little fun with her boss first.

'What I want to know is what you and my dad got up to after you both left to find a quieter place to finish your drinks? I haven't seen him this morning so can't ask him.'

Drina looked indignant. 'Got up to? I can assure you, Rhonnie dear, we didn't get up to anything other than enjoying each other's company over drinks in the Paradise lounge. He's a very nice man, is Artie. He made me laugh so much with some of the stories he told me of his life on the road. But if you're wondering if he told me anything about what brought him here, then he didn't mention a word. He's unburdened himself by telling you, and I believe he just wants to put the whole thing behind him now and get on with his future. Oh, and I asked him if he'd like to have a drink with me again.' Then she added hurriedly, 'Only because I think he needs to be amongst people, not sitting in his chalet brooding, and I can't deny it was nice for me to have company of my own age.'

Rhonnie was pleased to hear that their time together last night seemed to have evoked some of Artie's old self, if he was regaling her with his lorry-driving stories. But she hadn't failed to notice the glint in her boss's eyes when she had been talking about him. For a moment it crossed Rhonnie's mind that Mrs Jolly liked her father more than she was letting on but then she scolded herself for thinking that. Mrs Jolly was a married woman and from what Rhonnie knew of her, most definitely not the sort to fornicate with another man behind her sick husband's back.

Drina asked her, 'You don't mind if your father and I have a drink together now and again, do you, dear?'

'No, of course I don't,' Rhonnie assured her. 'I'm all for anything that aids his recovery.'

Drina was looking at her expectantly. 'So are you now ready to tell me what happened with you and Dan after I left, or do I have to go and ask him?'

A broad grin on her face, Rhonnie told her, 'I'm seeing him tonight. It's all down to you. Thank you.'

Drina responded, 'Thank God for that! Maybe now I'll get you both to concentrate on your work.'

Rhonnie knew she was only joking, and giggled.

Despite how busy the rest of the day was for Rhonnie, it seemed to pass slowly. She was desperate to see Dan again. Deep down she was a little worried that he might have changed his mind about her and not want a relationship after all. It never crossed her mind that Dan was worrying just as much as she was.

Their evening out together surpassed their expectations. Rhonnie arrived to meet Dan at the gates ten minutes before eight, to find him already waiting for her. She did a double take when she spotted him sitting astride his motor bike, his long legs firmly planted each side to keep it upright, grinning in delight to see her and obviously expecting her to get on the back. After her hair-raising trip courtesy of her kindly saviour in the sidecar of his motor bike the first day she had arrived, she had vowed never to have anything to do with them again. She was about to tell Dan that but then realised it was wrong to think of her saviour's reckless behaviour when she had no evidence Dan would act in any way that would put her life in danger. She suspected that while on his own on the bike he would certainly put it through its paces around the quiet country roads, but she needn't have worried that he would ride it at breakneck speed with her on the back. With Rhonnie's arms clinging around him, he rode the bike carefully at a leisurely pace and she thoroughly enjoyed the feeling of the warm evening breeze whipping through her hair, and the views of the beautiful countryside as it went past.

He took her to a quiet little pub seemingly in the middle of nowhere, informing her that he was very much looking forward to introducing her to his friends outside the camp but that for now he just wanted to have her to himself. Having bought their drinks and ordered chicken and chips in a basket, they fell into easy conversation which continued throughout their meal, only stopping during the ride back to the camp.

As Rhonnie got into bed that night she was in no doubt that Dan was the one she was going to spend the rest of her life with, and he'd left her in no doubt that he felt the same way about her.

CHAPTER SEVENTEEN

Two weeks later, mid-morning in Drina's office, she was looking extremely worried as she faced Rhonnie and Jackie. 'We can't ignore this any longer, girls. The woman this morning was adamant that she had left her rings on her chest of drawers before she went out last night. She couldn't wear them as the heat had swollen her fingers. She noticed they were missing when she went to try and put them back on this morning. Over the last month, that's more than a dozen complaints of missing property that seems to have been taken from the chalets during the evening while the campers were out. Individually there's been nothing of great value, but lumped together they would bring in a tidy sum. The right thing would be to call in the police and let them investigate, but unless they catch the thief red-handed I don't see what they can do about it. They could do a search of the staff quarters but I doubt the culprit is stupid enough to keep their spoils in their chalet. Oh, it really distresses me to think we have a thief amongst them.'

She rubbed her hands wearily over her face and issued a deep sigh. 'Up to now we've managed to keep the lid on this, only us three and the receptionists who have been sworn to secrecy know about this state of affairs, but I fear it's only a matter of time before it gets out that Jolly's has a thief in its midst. Thankfully, none of the campers is aware of the other incidents and I pray it stays that way. But if just one of them returns home not satisfied with the way we've handled their complaint, and starts spreading the story, all we need is for the newspapers to get wind and then we're really in trouble.

'Besides, now we're certain we have a thief amongst us it's not at all right we're fobbing off the campers like we are. I have no idea how, but I'm going to do something to put a stop to these thefts. I was hoping you two might have some ideas?'

Rhonnie and Jackie looked thoughtful for several moments before Jackie offered her suggestion. 'Well, all of them seem to have taken place in the evening, going by what the campers have told us. Most people who are out leave the chalet by seven-thirty and start coming back about eleven, so it's my belief that the thefts must be taking place during these hours. Maybe we should stake out the chalets, like the police do in those American cop shows.'

Drina looked at her quizzically. 'What on earth does that mean?'

'Well, on a stakeout you hide and keep a watch until the thief makes their move. Then you catch them red-handed.'

Drina scolded, 'This isn't a television programme, Jackie, this is . . .'

Rhonnie cut in then. 'Jackie has a point, Mrs Jolly. I was thinking along those lines myself.'

Jackie puffed out her chest, pleased to have pipped Rhonnie to the post.

Their boss frowned. 'How do you propose we . . . stake out . . . over two thousand chalets? There are only three of us.'

'We can rope in Dan and my dad and the receptionists. That would make nine of us,' Rhonnie told her.

Drina mused, 'It's still an awful lot of chalets to keep an eye on.'

'Well, it's the only thing I can think of. We obviously can't watch them all so we'll just have to pick a spot each where we have a good view of as many chalets as possible, and pray our thief happens to pick one to rob that is visible to us. We might have to go out for a few nights before we strike lucky, but it's better than doing nothing, isn't it?'

'Yes, it's got to be,' agreed Jackie, excited at the prospect of doing some sleuthing like she'd seen the cops on television carry out.

Drina looked as if she was going to cry. 'You're both prepared to give up your leisure time to help catch this thief?'

Rhonnie told her, 'Yes, of course. The camp's survival is important to me, and I know I speak for Dan and Dad and the receptionists too.'

'And me,' piped up Jackie.

Drina swallowed back a lump in her throat. 'Well, then, we'd better get the girls up here and locate Dan and your father, Rhonnie, and make some campaign plans.'

The nine of them had been out for ten nights on the trot, ten fruitless, laborious nights, each of them hidden in a strategic place and hardly daring to move a muscle for fear of discovery. While they'd been keeping watch, at least two further robberies had been conducted under their noses according to the campers who'd reported missing property the next day. By now everyone was beginning to think they were wasting their time and that there must be another way of catching this criminal, if they could only think of it.

Crouched behind a low hedge at the front of a chalet, dressed in black trousers and jumper, her honey-blonde hair covered by a dark scarf loaned to her by Drina, Rhonnie longed to stand up and stretch her cramped legs but daren't as it would be just her luck for the thief to happen along at the same time. She pulled back the sleeve of her jumper, straining her eyes in the darkness to read the time. She just managed to make out that it was coming up for nine, and heaved a fed-up sigh. Still two hours to go. Two whole hours before she and Dan could snatch an hour or two together.

They had barely had time for each other during the last ten days and she was missing him dreadfully, as he was her. It was particularly hard for Rhonnie knowing that he was not far away, crouched behind a hedge like her, several rows down from where she was. He might as well have been the other side of the world as she couldn't pop over and see him for a quick kiss and a cuddle, just as she couldn't stand up and stretch her legs for fear of breaking her cover.

She suddenly stiffened as the sound of footsteps reached her ears. They were coming from her right. With her heart thumping in anticipation, she peered hard in that direction. Then she sighed in frustration. The footsteps belonged to a man. He was visible to her as he was passing under one of the lamp-posts further down the path, apparently very drunk since he was lurching from one side to the other in his attempt to navigate his way.

Rhonnie's eyes then darted further back down the path as the sound of running footsteps reached her. Out of the darkness a middle-aged woman appeared. On spotting the drunken man, she called out to him, 'There yer are, yer drunken sot! I've been chasing all over the camp for you.'

At the sound of the woman's voice, he swayed round and held out his arms to her, slurring, 'Hello, love of my life. Come and give your hubby a kiss.'

When she reached him her response was to hit him across the head with her handbag, and shout, 'You'll get no kisses from me tonight, you big oaf. You had me so worried, going off like that without a word. When I couldn't find yer, I thought you'd fallen in the pool and drowned. By the time I've finished with yer, you'll wish you had! Making me look an idiot in front of those nice people we met at the Paradise. After your antics, they won't want to know us any more. What are yer doing down here anyway? You're nowhere near our chalet. It's back the other way.' She stepped behind him and gave him a shove. 'Now get a move on,' she ordered him. They began to retrace their steps, the man stumbling along trying to fend off the further blows his wife continued aiming at him with her handbag.

Rhonnie had to fight with herself to stifle a fit of the giggles at the comical scene. She had just managed to settle herself down again when another sound reached her ears. She nearly jumped out of her skin when a hand was clamped over her mouth, stifling her scream of fear. A familiar voice whispered in her ear, 'It's only me, Rhonnie.'

The hand was then dropped from her mouth, enabling her to swivel her head and ask the man crouching down behind her: 'Dan, what are you doing here? You're supposed to be keeping watch from your own vantage point?'

He had his arms around her now, pulling her into him, so that she was almost sitting on his knee. He whispered back, 'I was missing you, so I popped over for a quick kiss and a cuddle.'

How glad she was he had, but regardless Rhonnie scolded him. 'What will the others think if they find out you've deserted your post?'

'I'll tell them I was just having a quick tea break.'

She clamped a hand over her mouth, to mask a chuckle. 'Did you have to mention tea? I could murder a cup.'

'We should have brought a flask and some sandwiches along. We could have had a picnic.'

She playfully slapped his leg. 'Stop making me laugh, Dan.'

He pulled her even closer to him. 'Can I have my kiss and cuddle now?'

Rhonnie made to twist around and oblige him but then another sound reached her ears. She urgently whispered, 'Shush, what was that?'

She felt him shrug his shoulders. 'I never heard anything.'

'There it is again.' She raised herself high enough to see over the low hedge, peering up and down, at first seeing nothing. Then her eyes made out the shape of a figure creeping close to the hedge on the other side of the path to her left. The only reason someone would be creeping along like that was because they were trying not to be noticed. It had to be the thief.

'I'm sure that's them over there,' she hissed to Dan.

He peered in the direction she was pointing. 'I can't see any . . . Oh, yes, I can now. I can't make out if it's a man or a woman, though.'

'No, I can't either. Shush, they're getting closer and might hear us.'

Both tense with expectation, they watched the figure continue to creep its way forward. Then it stopped to look around at all the chalets, seeming to be searching for a particular one. Finding it, the figure slunk furtively towards the door. Before letting themself into the chalet using a key, they turned to check the coast was clear. Rhonnie and Dan automatically ducked their heads for fear of being spotted. But not before Rhonnie had caught a glimpse of the thief's face, enough to recognise them by.

On hearing the chalet door click shut she lifted her head, her face wreathed in shock, and whispered to Dan, 'Did you see who it was?'

'I did. Just a quick glance, but enough to recognise them.'

Her face was grim. 'Oh, God, Dan, I can't believe it. That's the last person I would have suspected. And all this time we thought it was Terry Jones.'

Dan said to her, 'Shall we get this over with?'

Rhonnie had thought it would bring her the greatest of pleasure to be the one to catch the thief, see their expression when they realised the game was up, but now she knew who it was, she felt only shock and bewilderment.

Dan insisted he go in first as he wasn't prepared to risk any harm coming to Rhonnie should the thief turn violent when they realised the game was up. They stole down the path to the chalet as far as the door. As he grabbed hold of the door knob Dan took a deep breath before he turned it, thrust the door open and stepped inside, Rhonnie following close behind.

The thief was in the process of rifling through a drawer, using the light from a small torch they carried. At the noise of the door banging open, they spun around, face turning ashen, to see Rhonnie and Dan looking at them accusingly.

Back in Drina's office a while later, the thief was sitting on a sofa, head bent, sobbing hysterically.

Rhonnie was sitting beside the culprit, a grim-faced Drina and Dan watching them. Jackie had been despatched to make tea, and the receptionists sent home with a stern warning to keep this development to themselves. It had been decided that Rhonnie would question the thief as she was better acquainted with them.

Still having difficulty accepting this turn of events, a completely mystified Rhonnie asked, 'Whatever possessed you to risk your job, your whole future, just to make a few extra quid for yourself? You aren't stupid. You knew what a gamble this was, risking a prison sentence to line your own pockets.'

Noreen's head jerked up, her swollen red eyes bulging in horror. She wailed, 'Prison? I can't go to prison! He promised me I'd never be caught. The plan was perfect, he said. He'd check people out, decide whether they might have stuff that was worth something, and find out their chalet number. On a night when they were out enjoying themselves down the Paradise, he'd alert me and I'd let myself into the chalet using a skeleton key he'd managed to get hold of. I'd to take whatever I thought would be worth a few bob, but no more than a couple of things at a time, so that when the campers couldn't find their stuff they'd more than likely think they'd lost it somewhere. When he thought we had enough, he was going to take it all to a pawn shop.'

Rhonnie could see it all now. Having had his contest-fixing scheme curtailed, Terry had come up with another plan to line his own pockets. He'd needed an accomplice, though, and who better to dupe than a girl like Noreen? Desperate for a man to show her affection, she wouldn't be able to believe her luck that a handsome, popular young stripey like Terry had noticed her, and would do anything to keep him.

She said to Noreen, 'How exactly did he get you to act as his accomplice? Did he tell you he loved you? That you were the woman of his dreams and he wanted the money to buy you nice things . . . to wine and dine you . . . do the things he couldn't afford to do on his wages?'

She uttered, 'It was for our wedding.'

Rhonnie declared, 'Oh, Noreen, you really believed he was going to marry you! Just how gullible are you? Terry had no intention of marrying you. He was just using you to make some money for himself – certainly not to spend on you. Were you so besotted with him that you couldn't see through his lies?'

Noreen was staring at her quizzically. 'Terry?'

Rhonnie frowned in bewilderment. 'Well, it's Terry that's got you into this mess, isn't it?'

The girl shook her head. 'No.'

They all looked shocked to hear that Terry wasn't behind the thefts, as they had assumed due to his past history.

Rhonnie asked, 'So who is it then?'

Before Noreen could respond there was a knock on the door. It opened and Jackie began to come through with a tray of tea. Like the rest of them, Drina was desperate now to discover just who had cajoled Noreen into being his accomplice so she waved Jackie away, signalling to her 'not now'. As soon as the girl had shut the door behind herself, Drina urged, 'Just who put you up to helping him, Noreen?'

She blurted out, 'Oh, I can't tell you that. I love him. And I don't care what you say, Rhonnie, he loves me too, I know he does. I won't get him into trouble,' she stubbornly declared.

Rhonnie grabbed her arm and shook it in annoyance, saying in no uncertain terms, 'Noreen, for God's sake, no man who really loves a woman will lure her into criminal activities, no matter what he proposes to use the money for.'

As Rhonnie's words sank in, Noreen visibly shrank before their eyes and uttered, distraught, 'No, he wouldn't betray me, would he?' Then she wailed miserably, 'Oh, Rhonnie, I really thought he loved me. He told me he had wanted to be with me for a long time but daren't say anything to me 'cos he was frightened I wouldn't feel the same about him.

'I couldn't believe a man like him felt that way about me. I wanted to tell everyone about my new fella. I was desperate to see Shelly's face when she heard, after all her nasty comments to me that I'd never land any man unless he was blind or desperate. But he didn't want me to have to put up with the ribbing we'd get from the other staff. He told me he was only trying to protect me, and that's why I promised him I wouldn't tell anyone we were together until after we were married. Oh, the wedding we'd planned was going to be like a fairy tale. We'd even decided what names we'd call our children.'

A fresh flood of tears filled her eyes then flooded down her face. She blubbered, 'I told him I didn't care if we could only afford a small wedding, but he said he wasn't prepared to marry me if he couldn't give me the type of ceremony he wanted me to have. That we'd have to save up, and it could take years on our wages. I couldn't bear the thought of waiting years to marry him, so that's why I agreed to do what Colin asked me.'

Rhonnie gawped at her, struck speechless by this unexpected announcement. 'Colin! You said Colin, Noreen?'

Drina exclaimed with conviction, 'She's got to be lying. Colin is one of the most honest people I have ever met. He'd never be involved in anything like this.'

Dan mirrored her feelings. 'The Colin I know is as straight as a die.'

Noreen cried out in a frenzy, 'I'm not lying, I'm not!'

Rhonnie looked over at Drina then and told her, 'Mrs Jolly, Noreen might be gullible but I know she's not a liar.'

Dan said, 'Well, there's only one way to find out. We get Colin up here and see what he has to say about all this.'

Drina and Rhonnie agreed. Under strict instructions she was only to inform Colin that Mrs Jolly would like a word with him in the office, Jackie was despatched to fetch him from the Paradise where he was on duty, along with several other stripeys, helping to keep the campers entertained. While they waited for him to arrive, Dan and Drina went into the general office to drink a cup of by now tepid tea, Rhonnie deciding to stay with Noreen and offer some support to the distraught girl. Her naïveté had landed her in bad trouble and she was going to pay heavily for it, for the rest of her life.

Drina and Dan returned to the office immediately they heard Colin's and Jackie's footsteps on the stairs.

Instructed to go straight into the office, Colin bounced in, a big grin on his face, saying, 'Jackie said you wanted me, Mrs . . .' He stopped short on seeing the others and greeted them all jocularly with, 'If I'd realised I was being summoned to a party, I'd have brought a bottle with me.' He looked at Noreen for a moment as though trying to recall who she was, before saying, 'Noreen, isn't it? You're one of the chalet maids, aren't you?'

She blurted out, 'You know very well who I am, Colin.'

He looked taken aback. 'I know of you, but I don't know you personally.' Then he asked Drina, quizzically, 'What's this all about, Mrs Jolly?'

As the sofas were occupied, she told him to take a seat on the chair already pulled forward for him. As soon as he was settled, she said to him, 'Colin, we've suspected for a while that we have a thief in the camp. Tonight we caught Noreen in a chalet, rifling through a camper's possessions. She's admitted she's the thief but has accused you of putting her up to it, telling us you two are in love and that you needed the money so as to get married and plan a future together.'

He sat staring back at Drina.

'What!' he exclaimed. Then he fixed his eyes on Noreen and said to her, 'Look, you're a nice girl and all that, and I don't want to hurt your feelings . . . but you're not my type. I've already got a girlfriend and she certainly wouldn't stand for me messing about with anyone else, for any reason, I can assure you.'

Hurt beaming from her eyes, Noreen cried out, 'You've got another girlfriend! Who is it? You told me I was the only one for you. You told me you loved me! Wanted to marry me. Why are you doing this to me, Colin?'

He looked helplessly at the others. 'You don't believe her, do you? Come on, you all know me well enough to realise I would never do such a thing. Noreen's obviously using me to cover up for the real villian in all this.'

A knowing expression settled on his face. 'I have a good idea who that is. I didn't want to have to tell you this, Mrs Jolly, but it was Terry Jones who was taking bribes to fix the competitions. When I confronted him with it, he begged me not to tell you and to give him another chance. I was worried about doing so as I know he's got a criminal record, but he wore me down and I agreed. Only so long as he understood there'd be no further chances.' Colin issued a deep sigh. 'I can't believe he's let me down so badly. Of course, he's bound to deny all this when you tackle him, but he's your man all right. Can I go now, Mrs Jolly? Only there's an old dear back at the Paradise waiting for me to dance with her.'

Rhonnie could tell the others thought the same thing as she did. That all the evidence pointed to Terry Jones and somehow he'd frightened Noreen into keeping his name out of it should she ever be caught.

Drina said to Colin, 'Yes, of course you can go. I'm only sorry you've been dragged into all this.' She gave a deep sigh and said to Dan, 'We'd best get Terry up here. Will you fetch him, please?'

As both men started to depart, Rhonnie's thoughts whirled. For all Noreen's faults, the girl wasn't the sort to make a good liar. Rhonnie's gut feeling was that Noreen was telling the truth. But then that would mean Colin had fooled them all, and it was he who was the liar. Either Noreen or Colin was. But which of them? Suddenly an idea flashed into her mind.

Dan and Colin were just about to walk out of the office when she stopped them by calling out, 'Oh, but we've forgotten something Noreen told us that is rather damning to you, Colin.'

Noreen was far too consumed in her own misery to have heard a word Rhonnie had said, but Dan and Drina were looking at her quizzically. As far as they were concerned Noreen hadn't told them anything of the sort, and they wondered what Rhonnie was up to. Colin was shrugging his shoulders, saying, 'She can't possibly have told you anything that could be damning to me. I've told you, I've never had anything to do with her personally.'

'Well, then, she was lying, was she, when she told us that she knows where you hide the stolen property and will show us?'

He scoffed, 'Damned right she was. She can't possibly know where I hide the goods because I always make sure . . .' He stopped talking abruptly, realising what he had just said, and quickly tried to cover himself by blurting, 'What I mean is . . .'

Dan already had a firm grip on his arm and was hissing furiously at him, 'Don't bother, Colin. There's no climbing out of the hole you've just landed yourself in. You've well and truly dug your own grave.'

Drina was looking at him aghast. 'Oh, Colin, you of all people. Was it not bad enough you were fleecing innocent people for your own ends? But to be prepared to make an innocent man pay for your crimes . . . It was you, not Terry, who was fixing the contests. Dan, please get him out of my sight. Ask Jackie to call the police.'

It hit him like a thunderbolt then that the game was up and he was in very serious trouble. Colin seemed to snap and shrieked out, 'If I'm going down, then so is Shelly. She wanted us to go travelling in Europe, pay our way around by fruit picking. We needed a car and we'd no money to buy one. It was all her idea how we could make some . . . her suggestion that that stupid cow Noreen would make a perfect stooge. Shelly's as much a part of this as I am. If I'm going to jail then so is she.'

With Colin still shouting frenziedly that Shelly was as guilty as he was, Dan grabbed him around the waist and carried him bodily out of the office.

Rhonnie meanwhile was rubbing her aching forehead. She was lost for words over this new revelation of Shelly's involvement. It now made sense to her why that morning a month or so ago at breakfast, when Noreen had first let on she had a boyfriend and was being probed by the rest of them to reveal who it was, Shelly had jumped to her defence, telling everyone to leave her alone. It was obvious now why she had: out of fear that Noreen, in her desperation to tell everyone just who her boyfriend was, would wreck Colin and Shelly's nasty plan before it had yielded the spoils they were after.

Drina said to Rhonnie, 'You look like you're in need of a brandy as much as I am, dear. I'll pour us both a large one.'

CHAPTER EIGHTEEN

The next evening Rhonnie walked into the crowded Paradise, saw Dan wasn't waiting for her where they'd agreed, and headed to the bar to join the queue for drinks.

It had been a long day, spent dealing with the aftermath of the previous evening. They were all still stunned by their discovery and the usual good-humoured banter that passed between them as they went about their work was replaced instead by a subdued mood. Fortunately, by the time the police had arrived last night and departed a while later with Colin, Shelly and Noreen in the back of a black van, most of the campers had retired for the night. The few who had witnessed the police arriving and enquired about it the next day at Reception were told that the girls there weren't at liberty to talk about it, but it was nothing for the holidaymakers to worry about. Thankfully they had all accepted this and gone off to enjoy their day. The staff were another matter. Rumours ran rife as to why Colin, Noreen and Shelly were now languishing in police cells.

Rhonnie felt that Ginger, having palled around with both Shelly and Noreen, should be told what had happened. With Drina's agreement, she broke the news. Ginger was mortified. She wasn't at all surprised that Shelly was involved in such a despicable scheme, felt she was going to get her just deserts and wouldn't miss her caustic tongue, but she was distressed over the way Noreen had been dragged down by her involvement. Drina had called a meeting of the camp supervisors where they were told what to say to their underlings, on strict instructions that if any of this got out to the campers, then their employment at Jolly's would be terminated with immediate effect.

There was only one person who benefited from Colin and Shelly's wicked plan: Terry Jones. His anger at the news that Colin had showed no remorse about trying to frame him for his own crimes quickly faded when he heard he was being rewarded with the job he had coverted for so long. Rhonnie felt she could actually see his head swelling when Drina told Terry of his promotion to head stripey. It didn't matter a jot to him that he'd only got the step up through default: he was top dog among the stripeys now, and weren't all the rest of them going to know it? He was, though, the best man for the job, Rhonnie had no doubt.

The last ten days of working in the office during the day then on surveillance by night had taken their toll. Had Rhonnie been meeting anyone else tonight she would not have hesitated to postpone their arrangement and go early to bed. But it was Dan she was meeting and, the way she felt about him, the only thing that would stop her doing so was if she were on her deathbed. When they had made the date before they parted last night, they were both in agreement that all they wanted to do was spend time together on their own, and so they'd planned on going down to the beach away from all the campers.

Rhonnie had arrived early at the Paradise as she had allowed herself time beforehand to call in on her father in his chalet, meaning to spend some time with him there. The last thing she wanted was for him to think that she was neglecting him now she had Dan, but as it turned out she spent hardly any time talking to him.

Artie was fortunate enough to have a chalet to himself, thanks to Drina who had realised that he needed to be on his own while he got over his trauma. When Rhonnie arrived at the chalet, though, she found Artie getting ready to go out. As she sat down on his bed, she quipped, 'Got a heavy date, Dad? You look very smart.'

He was looking into a small mirror, hung at head-height on the wall over the chest of drawers, and straightening his tie. 'I'm meeting Mrs Jolly. We're going to the cinema to see *Charade* with Cary Grant and Audrey Hepburn.'

Rhonnie eyed him worriedly. Her father and Drina had been out together several times to her knowledge since the opening night of Groovy's. She was pleased he was going out and about and had company, but concerned he might be heading for more trouble. 'Dad,' she ventured.

Now busily brushing his hair into place, he asked, 'Yes, love?'

'Er . . . you haven't forgotten Mrs Jolly is a married woman, have you?'

He turned to look at her indignantly. 'Of course I haven't. Look, love, I've told you before, Mrs Jolly and I are just friends who go out together occasionally, nothing more to it than that. It's no fun being on your own at our age. When her husband comes home, she'll have him to take her out and I'll have to find myself another friend, won't I? I can't deny I like Mrs Jolly very much, and if she weren't married . . . well, that might be a different story. Although I'm in no rush to get involved again when I'm still getting over what Mavis did to me. Now you go and meet that young man of yours and leave your old dad to spruce himself up properly.'

Mind at rest, Rhonnie leaped off the bed, threw her arms around him and kissed his cheek. To the sounds of him complaining that her hug had creased his shirt, she headed off to the Paradise.

After a long wait, she finally found herself at the front of the queue and ordered her drink from Tony Driver, a chubby young barman with a likeable personality. When he returned with her half of Woodpecker cider, Rhonnie giggled to see that for a bit of fun he had put in the top at least half a dozen glacé cherries each stabbed through with a colourful cocktail umbrella. Armed with her drink, she went off to stand by a pillar close to the bar where she had arranged to meet Dan. The resident band was playing Glenn Miller's 'Chattanooga Choo Choo' and several dozen or so older campers, who'd have been teenagers at the end of the forties, were treating the rest of the audience to their lindy hop dances. It was hilarious to see the now middle-aged men struggling to throw their much older and heavier wives through their legs, not even attempting to swing them up in the air.

Then Rhonnie's enjoyment of the scene was very rudely interrupted by a loud, raucous burst of laughter that erupted nearby. She didn't need to turn around to know who had been responsible. Sam Goodman's irritating boom of a laugh and voice to go with it, plus his overbearing ways, had been annoying them all for four days now. And it was set to go on for another ten yet as he and his long-suffering wife were at the camp for a fortnight.

At the moment, dressed in a loud black-and-white checked suit which strained over his huge stomach, his black hair greased back with Brylcreem, a fat cigar clamped between two fingers, Sam Goodman had his arm around a much younger woman. She wore a tight dress which barely covered her hourglass figure, and bleached-blonde hair curled around her attractive, heavily made up face. The rest of her group of friends looked on, as Sam entertained them with anecdotes about his life as a very successful used car dealer, and splashed his money about on drinks for them all, like there was plenty more where that came from. But it was his wife Rhonnie's attention was fixed on. A pleasant-faced, middle-aged woman, with a good figure for her age, dressed in a navy full-skirted belted dress, the princess neckline showing just a hint of still-firm breasts, she sat quietly on a stool at the bar, sipping a Babycham. Jane Goodman was doing her best to ignore her husband's flirtation with a woman almost half his age but Rhonnie could tell she was acutely embarrassed, fighting to hide her humiliation at the pitying looks she was receiving from other female campers.

Sam Goodman was so wrapped up in bragging about himself

to his captive audience that he didn't see his wife knock back the rest of her drink, slip off the bar stool and walk out.

As Rhonnie watched her leave, her excitement about her own imminent date with Dan was temporarily set aside. She had a feeling that woman needed a shoulder to cry on. Rhonnie felt the need to offer her own. First going over to the nearest table to put down her drink, she went after Sam's wife.

Outside the Paradise, looking around, she couldn't see Jane Goodman for a moment through a throng of people making their way towards the Paradise and the cinema, but then she spotted her heading towards the fountain. By the time she caught up with Jane, the other woman had already perched on the edge of it and was looking up at the amber-coloured sky. The sun was casting its last rays of the evening before disappearing below the horizon.

'Mind if I join you?' Rhonnie asked.

Her gaze still tilted skyward, Jane told her, 'Be my guest.'

Rhonnie perched beside her and they both sat there for a moment in silence before Rhonnie ventured, 'It's a lovely evening, isn't it? Up to now we've had a wonderful summer. Hopefully it will last well into the autumn.'

Jane mused distractedly, 'And then Christmas is on us, and another year has passed. We're a year older, and what then? Just another fifty-two weeks of the same old struggle to look forward to.'

Jane was clearly not a happy woman, judging by what she had just said, and Rhonnie's thoughts raced. She was wondering how to approach her with an offer of help . . . what in fact she could offer except for someone to listen if Jane wanted to unburden herself.

Before she could think of something, though, Jane said to her, 'You work here, don't you? I've seen you a couple of times around the camp. I know why you're here. I saw you watching me in the Paradise. I could see you were feeling sorry for me, for obvious reasons. You and dozens of others who saw my husband carrying on. You've no need to worry, though. I'm fine.' Jane lowered her gaze for a moment and asked, 'Are you married?'

Rhonnie shook her head. 'No. I have met someone that I wouldn't say no to, though, if he asked me.'

The other woman looked at her meaningfully. 'Bit of advice. Just make sure first that you're not seeing him through rose-coloured glasses. Make sure you know just what you're letting yourself in for with your intended before you tie yourself to him for life.'

Rhonnie eyed her quizzically. 'You're telling me this because you don't want me to make the same mistake that you did?'

Jane gave a reluctant laugh. 'You're very astute. Yes, I would hate any woman to have the kind of life I've had just because they were momentarily besotted.' She heaved a sigh and told Rhonnie, 'When I met Sam I was young and naïve. He was good-looking and funny, never short of a girlfriend, and I thought I was the luckiest girl alive when he asked me out. He swept me off my feet. I wouldn't listen to my parents, the rest of my family or my friends, who were all begging me not to marry him as they could see exactly the kind of man he was and what sort of life I'd have with him. By the time I realised I should have listened to them, I'd saddled myself with a know-it-all insufferable bore who was playing around behind my back any chance he got. I'd two children and a third on the way so there was no way out of the hell hole I was in. All I could do was bide my time, bite my tongue, turn a blind eye to his infidelities, and wait until the right time arrived for me to get him out of my life for good. My children have grown up and are making their own way in the world now so that time has finally arrived.'

'You're going to leave him?' Rhonnie asked.

'Oh, no. I'm forty-five, not a youngster any more ready to start all over again. The business my husband is bragging about in the Paradise is not the big successful used car firm he's making them believe it is. It's just a small backstreet affair, but it will support me well enough when I take it over. Then I can enjoy spending the profits doing things I've always wanted to do, and not have to scrimp and scrape while he spends most of them on wine, women and song. We've a nice little three-bedroomed semi, not in the best of areas but decent enough. With him out of the picture, hopefully I'll be able to rekindle my relationship with my family and friends. Yes, after twenty-five years of purgatory, life is going.'

Rhonnie didn't think for a minute a man like Sam Goodman was going to walk away from his marriage, house and business just because his wife had had enough of him. 'I can't see a man like him willingly surrendering his marriage, house and business?' she prompted.

Jane smiled at her. 'You're right, he wouldn't. His opinion is that everything we own has been solely provided by him. The doesn't consider for a minute that I made any contribution whatsoever by looking after the house, cooking, washing, raising the children. He gave me housekeeping and considered that my payment. If I asked him for a divorce, I think he'd be shocked at first, hurt even, but mostly he wouldn't be able to understand my reasons, because he believes I've got it made having him for a husband. He would tell me there was something wrong with me, that I wasn't right in the head, if I said it was over. Then he'd tell me to go and get a divorce if I wanted one but that he'd see me in hell before he'd hand over a penny more of what he'd worked hard for. He'd wave me off and immediately move one of his . . . lady friends in, and not give me a second thought.'

Rhonnie was looking at her, utterly confused. 'But then how are you going to end up with the business and the house?'

'Easy. I'm going to kill him.' Jane smiled warmly at her. 'Well, it's been lovely talking to you.' Then she stood up and made her way back into the Paradise, leaving Rhonnie gawping after her, trying to take in what she had just said.

Having parked his motor bike, Dan was hurrying over to the Paradise, eager to meet Rhonnie, when he spotted her perched on the edge of the fountain and changed course. He couldn't help but notice the stunned expression on her face. Perching himself beside her, he asked, 'What's the matter, Rhonnie? You look like someone's walked over your grave.'

She turned her head to look at him. 'Oh, hello, Dan.' Then she stared blankly for a moment, her thoughts back on what Jane Goodman had just shockingly announced. She was joking, surely? Trouble was, Rhonnie didn't think she had been. She gave Dan a smile. 'Nothing's wrong.' She cupped his face in her hands and kissed his lips. 'Let's get out of these crowds and somewhere more private. I want a proper kiss from you.'

He grinned at her as he stood up, took her arm and pulled her to her feet. 'More than happy to oblige,' he said. 'Lead the way.'

CHAPTER NINETEEN

Rhonnie was humming happily to herself as she sat on the bottom of her bed to style her hair in front of the small mirror propped on her chest of drawers. Dan had told her he was taking her somewhere special tonight. She hadn't been able to get out of him where exactly he meant, but felt sure he was going to introduce her to his friends. She wanted to look extra specially nice for him. This afternoon Drina had given her a few hours off in lieu of all the time she'd spent hunting the chalet thief. Since Ginger's shift was finished, splashing out on a taxi, they both went off to Skegness to look for a new outfit for Rhonnie. After scouring the shops and becoming convinced she would not find anything, in a little boutique up a side street she discovered just the thing: a short-sleeved, black-and-white dogtooth-check shift dress, its hemline ending an inch above her knees. She already had a pair of white plastic boots, a white butcher boy cap and a black shoulder bag that would go perfectly with it.

Her chalet mate, Val, was just leaving to start her shift. She said to Rhonnie, 'Hope you have a great time tonight. If any of Dan's mates are anywhere near as good-looking and nice as he is, put one in your handbag and bring him back for me.'

As she opened the door to leave, Rhonnie found Ginger about to knock.

Before she could say anything, Rhonnie pre-empted her with,

'Val has already asked me to bag one of Dan's mates for her. I suppose that's what you've come to ask me too?'

Ginger grinned. 'I thought that went without saying? I'm actually here on the cadge. I've just laddered my last pair of tights, put my hand straight through them as I was pulling them up, and wondered if you'd a spare pair.'

Rhonnie told Ginger to help herself out of her underwear drawer then said, 'I thought you weren't going out tonight?'

Ginger was sitting on the bed next to her now, pulling on the tights. 'I wasn't, but then the girls persuaded me to go and watch the stripeys' show tonight. I've seen it before but they said it was better that than moping around over Noreen. I know there's nothing I can do about it, but I can't help picturing her in a cell, waiting to hear how long a sentence she's going to be serving.'

Rhonnie heaved a sigh. 'Yes, I know. Let's hope the judge is lenient with her.'

'Mmm,' Ginger mused. 'I bloody hope he's not with Colin and Shelly though! That pair deserve to rot in hell, in my opinion.' She stood up and pulled down her bright orange minidress, not really the right colour to wear with her hair but Ginger obviously thought otherwise. 'Will I do?' she asked Rhonnie.

'You'll knock 'em dead.' She then looked at her friend knowingly. 'Am I right in thinking you're hoping a certain waiter who's just started at the camp is going to make an appearance tonight?'

Ginger gave a secretive smile. 'You might be. Shelly would have said he looks like the back end of a bus, but I think he's gorgeous.'

'Shelly hardly had a nice word to say about anyone, and thankfully she's no longer here to exercise her nasty tongue. If the new waiter doesn't think you're gorgeous too then he needs glasses,' Rhonnie told her friend.

After telling Rhonnie she hoped she had a good night, Ginger left her to finish getting ready for her date with Dan. As she put on her make-up Rhonnie was suddenly reminded that she wasn't the only one on a special date tonight. After taking on board Rhonnie's advice on how to play Gavin at his own game, the next time she had seen him at a dance hall Jackie had completely ignored him. Just as Rhonnie had prophesied, thinking Jackie was no longer interested in him and that someone else had caught her eye, Gavin immediately asked her out. Instead of being jubilant that Rhonnie's ploy had worked, Jackie though had decided she didn't want to go out with the likes of him any longer, a man who played silly childish games to make himself look good in front of his mates, and had turned him down.

Meanwhile another young man had been observing Jackie. As soon as Keith Watson saw that she wasn't interested in Gavin any longer, he'd wasted no time in asking her out. He was meeting her at the camp tonight, she having received special permission for him to come in as her guest, and they were going for a drink at the Paradise and to watch the stripeys' show. Rhonnie herself would be keen to hear tomorrow how Jackie's date had gone.

She had just finishing dressing and was pleased with her reflection – not that she could see all of it in one go in the small mirror, but pleased with what she could see anyway – when there was a tap on the door. Thinking it was like Paddy's Market in her chalet tonight, she called out, 'Come in.'

Rhonnie smiled with pleasure to see that the visitor was her father. 'Hello, Dad,' she greeted him, stepping over to kiss his cheek.

'I thought I'd pop in and say hello on my way to the Paradise. I didn't know whether you'd already have left to meet Dan, but I'm glad I caught you. I wanted to say I hope you have a nice evening.'

Everyone seemed to be going to watch the stripeys show tonight. Even Drina had mentioned in passing this afternoon that she was going to watch it too, excusing her attendance by saying she wanted to make sure the performances were still up to standard under Terry. Rhonnie suspected that the majority of the staff not on duty would be there tonight, just to see if the man who had bragged so blatantly that he would do a far better job than Colin ever had would be proved wrong or right. If he was right the show should be good – and if he was wrong it would be unmissable. Since Drina was going, should Rhonnie be surprised her father was too? Despite his assurances to her that he considered Mrs Jolly to be no more than a friend, Rhonnie couldn't shake the worry that he was going to end up with a broken heart.

'Thanks, Dad. It'll be nice to meet Dan's friends,' she said.

Artie made no response to that, which wasn't like him, but before she could ask him why he was saying, 'Well, best get off as I want to bag a good seat and you know how quickly the tables are taken.'

She nearly said, 'For you and Mrs Jolly?' but decided against it. 'Enjoy yourself, Dad,' she said instead.

He paused for a moment before departing, to say in a casual manner to her, 'Er . . . I shan't be going to bed early, if you fancy a chat when you get back.'

She eyed him as he took his leave, wondering why he would think she would need to talk to him after her date with Dan. Having put away her make-up, she decided to leave the chalet herself before anyone else turned up and made her late.

She'd heard Dan's wolf whistle of appreciation at her efforts before she actually saw him, waiting for her by the fountain, just visible through the throng of people making their way into the entertainment venues.

As he joined her Rhonnie said to him, 'Will I do?'

He looked her up and down admiringly. 'You'll do for anything.'

She beamed at his compliment, then her smile faded and she exclaimed, 'Oh, I'm not really wearing suitable clothes to be riding on the back of a motor bike though, am I?'

'Good job we're not travelling by bike tonight then, isn't it? I've ordered us a taxi. It should be here any time now.'

With her arm hooked through his, Rhonnie's mind filled with

hope that she would make a good impression on his friends. They made their way towards the gate then heard her name being shouted out. Turning around, they saw Terry Jones running hell for leather out of the entrance to the Paradise, waving frantically at Rhonnie.

As he breathlessly reached them, Rhonnie asked, 'Where's the fire, Terry?'

'Eh? Oh, very funny. You should be on the stage. In fact, that's what I need you for.'

Now Rhonnie was confused. 'You're not making sense.'

Dan said to him, 'No, you're not, Terry, mate. We've a taxi due in a minute so can you . . .'

Terry blurted, 'You'll have to cancel that.' He then demanded of Rhonnie, 'Have you had a drink tonight?'

'What! No, not yet, why?'

'I've not had a drink either,' Dan told him.

'Doesn't matter whether you have or not, Dan. It's a woman I'm after, and a sober one too. Rhonnie will do nicely.'

Dan's eyes blazed. 'Now you look here, Terry Jones. You've always bragged you could get any woman you wanted, but you can damned well keep your eyes off mine.'

Terry snapped, 'Calm down, man. I don't mean I need her like that.'

'What do you want her for then?'

'We've a crisis. We're two short. We can manage without one at a pinch but not two.'

'Two what?' Rhonnie asked him, more confused than ever.

'Women for the show's opening number. Gabby's sprained her ankle . . . fell down the steps backstage, wasn't watching where she was going. She's with the nurse now, having it strapped up. Then five minutes ago Ginny decides to have a dose of the trots and can't leave the toilet.'

Rhonnie was gawping at him. 'Hang on a minute, Terry. Are you asking me what I think you are?'

He looked imploringly at her. 'Please, Rhonnie? The curtain

goes up in five minutes and I haven't time to find anyone else who hasn't been drinking. Can't have a half-sozzled dancer on the stage, falling all over the place, can I?'

'You can't have someone who can't dance either,' she told him.

'Look, it's only the can-can. It's easy. Just follow the other girls, you'll be fine.'

The thought of being on stage in front of all those people filled her with enough dread, let alone unprepared as she would be. She'd never so much as been in a school play before, always opting to help backstage instead. She knew there was no point in asking Dan for his opinion on what she should do as he would tell her that the choice was hers to make. It seemed she had no option but to agree to help Terry out so as not to disappoint the campers who were all expecting a good show. She had seen the can-can performed on variety shows on the television and, like Terry said, it didn't look that hard. Just kicking up your legs while waving around the hem of a frilly frock. She looked at Dan. 'Will your friends mind if we're late meeting them?'

He looked bemused for a moment before he responded, 'Oh, no. They'll understand.'

Before she could waver any longer, Terry had grabbed Rhonnie's arm and was pulling her towards the entrance of the Paradise, urging, 'Come on, we haven't got time to mess around, we need to get you into your costume.'

Rhonnie called back to Dan, 'Wait here for me, please.'

He chuckled to himself. Not likely, he thought. I wouldn't miss this for the world.

Less than five minutes later, Rhonnie was standing in the middle of a line up of five other girls in the wings, waiting for the red stage curtains to draw back, heralding to the audience that the show was beginning. She was wearing Gabby's costume, which had had to be pulled together using safety pins as Rhonnie was a size bigger. She hardly dared to breathe in case they burst. As she waited, her nerves mounted. Beads of sweat were clinging to her brow, her heart thumping rhythmically, her legs jelly-like. She wondered how they were holding her up, in fact.

She heard a whisper in her ear coming from Sally behind her. 'Just remember what I told you, Rhonnie. Before you go on, take a deep breath, don't whatever you do look at the audience and then just follow what I tell you. The routine is only two minutes long, that's all.'

Two minutes too long as far as Rhonnie was concerned. She vehemently wished the band would strike up now so she could get this nightmare situation over with.

Then her wish was granted as she heard Terry say, 'Right, girls, here we go.'

Immediately the band struck up the introduction to the can-can, the curtains started to open and loud applause broke out in the ballroom, along with loud roars of 'Hooray'.

Rhonnie didn't have time to draw breath. The next thing she knew the girls in front of her ran on to the stage, swinging the hems of their colourful dresses from side to side, and Sally was pushing her in the back to make her follow them.

Now lined up near the front of the stage with the others, Rhonnie completely forgot Sally's advice not to look out into the audience, and for a moment she froze. There was a sea of faces out there, all looking fixedly at her it seemed. Sheer terror ran through her. She jumped as she heard Sally hiss urgently at her, 'Kick up your right leg, Rhonnie.'

Obediently she kicked up a leg, but not her right, her left.

Sally hissed, 'No, your right. No, too late now, your left. No, I said left! Now your right . . .'

Having started off out of sync with the other girls, Rhonnie couldn't seem to get back in time. But it didn't matter now as they were running around the stage in a line, shaking their skirts from side to side. She thought, This is easy. If the rest of the routine carried on like this then she'd be fine. Only it didn't. Now they were back in line at the front of the stage again, turning around and bending forward, to flick up the back of their skirts, showing the audience their frilly knickers and wiggling their backsides. Rhonnie did this only she was several seconds behind the other girls and still wiggling her backside at the audience when the rest of them had all straightened up and turned around and were kicking up their legs again. As she quickly spun around to kick up her legs too, the sound of laughter and clapping resounded. She couldn't understand why the audience was laughing and clapping as this was a dance not a comedy sketch. And it wasn't finished yet.

Once again Sally was hissing out of the side of her mouth at her. 'You're kicking up the wrong leg again, Rhonnie. Do two rights . . . no, I said right, not left!'

As she desperately tried to keep in step with the others, following their actions, all Rhonnie wanted was for the stage to open and swallow her up. She was going to be the laughing stock of the camp tomorrow, the butt of everyone's jokes, and needed to prepare herself.

When they'd all gone around the stage again, shaking their skirts, then back in a line at the front of the stage, shaking their bottoms at the audience, Rhonnie did manage to spin around in time with the other girls, but then, to her horror, they all collapsed on the stage in the splits, signalling the end of the routine. No one had mentioned she had to do the splits! She couldn't do them anyway. So she did the only thing she could think of, something she'd seen other performers do at the end of a routine on television. She flung wide her arms and gave a bow. As she did so, she heard a ripping sound as the safety pins tore away from the fabric and her dress fell down, pooling around her ankles, leaving her facing the audience in just her bra and frilly knickers.

Her face flushing the colour of beetroot with acute embarrassment, Rhonnie yanked up her dress to cover her modesty and fled the stage. Thankfully the other stripeys in the dressing room where she had left her clothes were too busy getting themselves ready for their imminent performances to have time to ask how the show was going. Not wanting to witness the other girls' wrath for ruining their spot, Rhonnie rushed off to the backstage toilets, locking herself in a cubicle where she proceeded to change back into her own clothes, then sitting on the closed lid of the toilet with her head in her hands, full of regret for agreeing to do what she had in the first place. She knew now she was never going to be allowed to forget it.

She could hear the muted sounds of cheers and clapping so at least the audience were enjoying the rest of the show. Hopefully this would mean they'd forget the dire opening routine.

Rhonnie decided she would wait where she was until the show was over, and all the staff involved changed back into their stripey uniforms and mingling with the campers as the dancing started. Then she would slip out unnoticed and re-join Dan, just mortally thankful he hadn't witnessed her making such an idiot of herself. She hoped he wasn't annoyed at having to wait so long, but facing his annoyance was preferable to that of Terry Jones, who'd had his first show ruined.

Suddenly she heard the main door being thrust open and Terry's voice calling out, 'Rhonnie, are you in here?' Then the door of the cubicle was being pounded. 'I know you're in there, Rhonnie. Come on, there's no time for stage fright, you should be in costume by now for the clown routine.'

Jumping up from her seat, she thrust back the bolt on the door, yanking it open, to stand on the threshold glaring at Terry. 'You only told me you needed me for the opening dance?'

He gave a shrug. 'Sorry, forgot to mention the other one. You'd better hurry and change because . . .'

She blurted out, 'Forget it, Terry. Nothing . . . repeat NOTHING . . . will get me back on that stage again. I have never felt such a fool in all my life. I've messed up the show once, surely you're not prepared to let me loose again?'

He grinned at her. 'But the audience . . .'

'Don't mention the audience to me. Have you any idea what

I'm going to have to put up with tomorrow, from campers and staff alike after that shambles? If they were paying for tickets, they'd all be demanding their money back. Now move aside, I'm leaving.'

'But you can't, Rhonnie,' he cried urgently. 'Les and Mick can't do the clown routine without the stooge. There's no one spare to do it. They're all getting changed for the grand finale. Listen, Rhonnie, all you have to do is sit on a chair and pretend to read a book. Nothing else, honest. Please, please, you have to do this . . . for the good of the camp!'

She shut her eyes and heaved a sigh. Opening them again, she demanded, 'That's all I have to do?'

He nodded.

She sighed again. Surely if that was all then even she couldn't get it wrong. 'All right,' she reluctantly agreed.

Then a look of panic filled Terry's face as a piece of music reached his ears. Grabbing her arm, he pulled her out of the cubicle, ordering, 'Quick! We've only got a minute before you're on. There's no time to change, you'll do as you are.'

Next thing she knew she was sitting on a chair on stage, a book in her hand, doing as she'd been told and pretending to read it. In front of her, Les and Mick, dressed as clowns, one of them holding a foam custard pie, the other a bucket filled with small squares of coloured foil which to the audience would appear to be water, were arguing about who was the best clown. As the sketch went on, the argument grew more heated, with the audience braying for one to throw the water, the other the custard pie. Finally it reached the stage where both clowns were about to do that when one of them tripped, falling into the other, and next thing Rhonnie knew the custard pie was in her face, the bucket of foil falling like rain all over her, and the audience roaring with laughter.

She was stunned by the unexpectedness of it but all she could think of was that the two clowns had ruined her appearance. Dan couldn't very well take her to meet his friends, looking like she was now, and would have to let them down. Without thinking, clearing her eyes and mouth of foam with her hands, she jumped up, shouting out, 'Look what you've done to me! Dan was taking me to meet his friends but he can't now, can he? With me looking like this.'

She suddenly realised where she was and that all the audience had been privy to her outburst. Kicking up her heels, she dashed off into the wings and hid behind a piece of scenery where she burst into tears, furious that she had made an idiot of herself and ruined the show for the second time that night. She just thanked God again that Dan hadn't witnessed her performance, as if he had she'd be even more embarrassed than she was now.

Next thing she knew a pair of arms was holding her tight and she was being swung around and Dan was saying to her, 'I'm so proud of you, Rhonnie.'

She was horrified to hear it. 'You watched the show! You saw me make an utter fool of myself and ruin the routines?'

He grinned down at her. 'I had a bird's eye view. And you didn't make an idiot of yourself. You did your best in difficult circumstances and I'm proud of you for that. Don't forget, the other stripeys have been performing that routine for weeks, whereas you had no practice at all.'

By now Drina and Artie had joined them.

Drina told her, 'The campers loved it, Rhonnie. They thought your messing up was part of the act. We all loved it. It was so funny.'

A twinkle in his eyes, Artie said, 'I think you should be in the show permanently, doing exactly what you did tonight.'

Rhonnie's glare told him exactly what she thought of that suggestion.

Just then Terry appeared. 'Thanks for saving the day, Rhonnie.'

She snapped at him. 'You never told me I'd end up with a custard pie all over me!'

He gave an innocent shrug. 'Forgot to mention it, sorry.'

She huffed at that, then turned back to Dan. 'Your friends

are not going to be happy with you for letting them down, are they? By the time I've changed, and you too since you now have sticky foam all over you after giving me that hug, the pub will be shut and they'll have gone home.'

He grinned at her. 'Good job we weren't meeting my friends then, wasn't it?'

Rhonnie frowned at him. 'But I thought that's where you were taking me?'

'Thought wrong, sweetheart. I was taking you somewhere special for a meal. Like you said, it's too late for that now, but not too late for me to do what I'd planned to after we'd eaten.'

To her shock, he bent down on one knee, looked up at her and said, 'I love you, Rhonnie. Marry me, please?'

She couldn't believe this was happening, that the man she adored was telling her he wanted to spend the rest of his life with her. She stared back at him like an idiot.

Artie spoke up. 'Put the poor lad out of his misery, love. He's been like a cat on a hot tin roof with nerves about asking you, ever since he asked me for your hand a couple of days ago and I gave him my blessing.'

'Yeah, come on, Rhonnie, 'cos we all want to know if we need new frocks for a wedding?'

At the sound of Ginger's voice Rhonnie's head jerked up. She saw her friend grinning back at her, and Jackie standing next to her with a very nice-looking young man who had his arm around her shoulders. Virtually all of the staff who'd taken part in the show had gathered around too, all anxiously awaiting her answer. Drina, standing next to Artie, was dabbing her wet eyes with a handkerchief, obviously overcome by the romance of it all.

Rhonnie looked down at Dan, and as she smiled could feel the drying foam on her face cracking. In a voice that was choked with emotion she told him, 'I'd be honoured to marry you.'

A euphoric Dan leaped to his feet and gathered her in his arms to kiss her long and passionately as a loud cheer erupted from the rest of the gathering.

A good while later, mellow from the drinks Artie and Drina had insisted they have in celebration, Rhonnie and Dan sat cocooned in each other's arms, in what was to them their special place in the sand dune on the beach. Neither of them cared about the chilly wind blowing in off the sea, both savouring these precious moments alone together.

Dan kissed the top of her head and said, 'It's got to be getting on for one. I ought to take you back for your beauty sleep.'

'Cheeky,' she responded, laughing. Then sighed. 'I don't want to go back. I want to stay like this with you for ever.'

'Yeah, me too. Happy, Rhonnie?'

She turned her head and kissed his cheek. 'For the hundredth time . . . happier than I've ever been.'

He chuckled. 'Just checking.' They sat in silence for a moment longer before he said, 'You do know that all we're going to get now is demands to know the date?'

'Yes, I do. Well, they'll have to be patient and wait.'

'They don't have to.'

'Don't have to what?'

'Wait. I don't want to wait either. I want to wake up next to you every morning as soon as I can, Rhonnie. We both have jobs, and thanks to Mr Jolly's generosity towards my mother, I have a house for us to live in.'

'Mrs Jolly's,' she said.

He frowned. 'Mrs Jolly's what?'

'Generosity that you have a house for us to live in. When it boils down to it, if it hadn't been for her father's legacy which enabled Mr Jolly to develop the campsite, then he wouldn't have been in any position to rent the house for you and your mother to live in.'

Astonished by this information Dan exclaimed, 'I didn't know that! Mr Jolly has never spoken of where he got the land and money to build the camp. My father might have been a distant cousin of his, but I'm just an employee when all's said and done. It's not my place to ask him questions like that. But he always gave me the impression, and everyone else come to that, that it was his hard work and head for business that built this place.'

'Well, now you know it wasn't. Anyway, I've said too much. What Mrs Jolly told me . . . although she never said as much . . . I should have treated as confidential.'

Dan assured her, 'It will stay that way, Rhonnie.' Then he mused, 'Seeing how she's got stuck in and run the camp successfully and so obviously enjoys it . . .' he paused to kiss the top of Rhonnie's head again '. . . with your help, my darling, while Mr Jolly's been recovering from his stroke, I'm surprised she's not shown any interest in being involved in the place before?'

'Mmm, well, from a couple of things she's let slip to me, I get the impression she wasn't allowed to.' Rhonnie felt it right to drop the subject then as second guessing why things were the way they were between the Jollys wasn't any of her business. 'But then, my impression could have been wrong,' she added.

Dan said, 'Well, anyway, the fact still remains that I have a house for us to live in. So unless you feel otherwise, I want us to get married as soon as possible.'

Rhonnie responded without hesitation, 'So do I.'

He hugged her tight. 'Shall we elope to Gretna Green right now?'

'Sounds wonderful to me, but do you really think my dad will be happy I've done him out of walking his only daughter up the aisle?'

'No, I suppose not. I'd be furious if any daughter of ours denied me that. I hope you want lots of children, Rhonnie. At least ten?'

'I might draw the line at that many. Two would be nice.'

'Yes, one of each. But then, as long as they're healthy, I don't care. So I gather from what you said about your father walking you up the aisle it's a church wedding you would like?'

'I'm not really worried where we get married, Dan. Who I'm marrying is what's important to me. My dad's last wife saw to it that he hasn't any money for a big affair, so a small do at a register office would be absolutely fine by me.'

'And me too. So, the future Mrs Daniel Buckland, I'll go to Skegness tomorrow and enquire what dates they have. Any particular date you want me to enquire after?'

'No, surprise me.'

'Then you'd better waste no time in deciding what you're going to wear because I shall settle for the first available slot.'

CHAPTER TWENTY

Next morning an excited Drina was ordering Jackie, 'Please telephone to ask Chef Brown if he can spare me a bit of time today to discuss food, then ring the local florist and ask her to come here and bring her books so we can choose the flowers – most importantly, Rhonnie's bouquet. We only need to book one car to take us to the register office as we can use the company car for Rhonnie and Artie. Better telephone the taxi companies and see who can do it. Then we need to decide how we're going to decorate Groovy's for the reception . . . the youngsters will have to do without the place for one evening. Now what else?'

While an equally excited Jackie was scribbling down all of Drina's instructions Rhonnie was perched on her desk, looking over at them both, trying to get a word in though up to now Drina hadn't paused for breath long enough for her to do that. Seeing her chance now, she spoke up. 'Look, Mrs Jolly . . .'

Drina looked across at her, interjecting, 'Can I have a word in my office, dear? Please excuse us for a moment, Jackie.'

Inside her office, with the door shut, Drina said, 'I know what you're going to say, dear, that it's just a small do for you both because I gather Artie's not in a position money-wise to give you the sort of wedding he would like to. But I am, Rhonnie. Call it my gift to you and Dan. I'm so happy about this wedding. You are so well suited. And call me selfish, but this is the nearest

I'm going to get to organising a wedding as I have no daughter, have I? And as for my son . . . So will you indulge me?'

Rhonnie wouldn't hurt this dear lady's feelings if she could help it, so if Drina was arranging sacking dresses and the marriage ceremony in a hut, she would go along with it. She knew she didn't need to ask Dan if he minded about this generous gift to them as he was as fond of their boss as Rhonnie was. Whether it was the done thing or not to act this way, she threw her arms around Drina, hugged her fiercely and said emotionally, 'Would you do us the honour of being a witness, along with my father?'

Tears pricked Drina's eyes and she replied, 'Oh, of course I will, dear.' Then she looked bothered. 'I've got carried away, ploughing ahead with all the plans. I must remember that this is your day, Rhonnie, so of course you have to be happy with the arrangements. I just hope Dan doesn't come back and tell us it's tomorrow!' Then she said excitedly, 'Let's go back and see how Jackie is getting on.'

She had already dealt with Drina's instructions so far and was eagerly awaiting more. Rhonnie reminded them that they did have camp work to do, to which Drina waved a dismissive hand, telling her that could wait as the wedding plans were far more important. She was just about to continue from where she'd left off when the door to the stairs burst open and Fran Monkton, a stripey usually on beach duty with her partner Geoff Black, came bursting in so out of breath she couldn't speak for a moment.

It was several long seconds before she managed to blurt out, 'There's been an accident. Geoff's sent me up to get an ambulance called.'

They were all staring at her, stunned.

Jackie immediately got on the telephone to call 999 while both Rhonnie and Drina demanded simultaneously, 'Who's had the accident? How bad is it?'

'One of the campers. I don't really know any details as I was over the other side of the beach with my first aid kit, dealing with a child who'd been stung by a wasp, when Geoff ran over to tell me to get up to the office and have an ambulance called urgently.'

Jackie told them, 'It's on its way.'

Grave-faced, Drina said to Rhonnie, 'We'd best get down to the beach and see what's happened.'

They both arrived at the end of the duckboards as breathless as Fran had been when she arrived in the office. They stood there for a moment to calm themselves before carrying on over the beach to where a large crowd of people were gathered.

Pushing their way through the crowd, they finally arrived to find a man lying flat out on the sand, naked except for a pair of gaudy swimming trucks. Geoff Black was kneeling by his side, giving him mouth-to-mouth resuscitation. Rhonnie had never seen a dead body before, but regardless knew by the deathly whiteness of the man's face and the blueness of his lips that Geoff was wasting his time. The man was dead. Then she gave a gasp of shock as she suddenly recognised who the man was. Sam Goodman.

Drina immediately went over to Geoff Black to enquire what had happened, but Rhonnie couldn't move. She was remembering what his wife had told her a couple of nights ago, that she was going to kill him, and her own thoughts were running wild. Jane Goodman hadn't been serious, surely? Her husband's demise had to be a horrible coincidence.

She flashed a look around searching for Jane and saw her a few feet away, sitting in a deckchair with her head in her hands, two other women campers doing their best to offer her comfort and support. She certainly wasn't acting like a woman who'd just killed her husband, nor was the crowd of onlookers behaving as if they'd just witnessed a murder. Sam Goodman didn't have a knife sticking out of his chest, no pools of blood were seeping into the sand. In fact, as far as she could see, there were no visible signs that he'd been attacked. The only thing Rhonnie could think was that he'd drowned. Jane Goodman couldn't possibly have caused that without anyone seeing her, could she?

Dan's voice broke into her thoughts. 'What's going on, Rhonnie? I'd just got back from Skegness when I heard there'd been an accident, so I came straight here.'

Under normal circumstances she would have been beside herself to learn what date he had booked for their wedding, but that was the last thing on her mind at the moment. She informed him, 'It looks like one of the campers has drowned.'

'Oh, that's terrible. Some of them don't take a blind bit of notice of our warnings not to go out too far, and the currents around here are unpredictable.'

'I'm worried that's not really what happened to him, though. I need to talk to you in private, Dan.' She grabbed his arm and pulled him out of earshot of the rest of the crowd. 'His wife told me she was going to kill him. It was the other night when I was waiting for you before we came down here to have some time together. They were both in the Paradise, and in front of her he was flirting with a crowd of younger women, spouting off to them about what a successful businessman he was and splashing his cash around, not seeming to care a jot that he was humiliating his wife with his behaviour. I saw her slip out and felt so sorry for her I went after her, to see if she wanted someone to talk to. And that's when she told me she planned to kill him.'

Dan was looking at her in disbelief. 'But all women at some time or other threaten their husbands with that.' He laughed. 'I'm sure you'll say the same to me when I do something you don't agree with. Like them, you won't mean it though.'

'Oh, but she did mean it, Dan. I tried to tell myself at the time it was a joke, but the way she said it, so matter-of-factly, like she'd been planning it for years and knew just how she was going to do it . . . I just know she wasn't joking.'

He frowned at her, bemused. 'But I don't see how she could have caused him to drown without someone from the crowd on the beach and in the water seeing her? I mean he's a big man and it'd take a hell of a strong woman to hold him underwater, wouldn't it? Look, we can't accuse people of murder with no evidence . . . someone telling you they're planning to murder someone else isn't proof that they did. Let's see what the ambulance men say was the cause of death. He might have had a heart attack or something.'

Looking very upset, Drina arrived next to them and gravely said, 'There was nothing we could do for the poor man. I can't imagine how his wife is feeling. My heart goes out to her.' A distant clanging of bells was heard. 'Ah, here's the ambulance now.' The clanging stopped, to be replaced by another sound. 'Seems the police have arrived too.' They all saw two ambulance men come running over the sands, between them carrying a stretcher and a medical bag.

Drina said, 'I'd better go and make myself known to the police.'

Dan and Rhonnie followed her back to where Jane Goodman was sitting, still being comforted by the two campers, a distraught Geoff nearby being consoled by Fran. There was another man in swimming things, middle-aged, his face ashen, sitting slumped in a deckchair while a woman crouching by his side tried to comfort him. It didn't look as if she was succeeding. An ambulance man was kneeling beside Sam Goodman, feeling for a pulse. Not finding one, he looked up at his colleague and shook his head. They then proceeded to lift the body on to the stretcher and cover it with a red blanket. Two uniformed policemen then arrived and spoke briefly to the ambulance men before making their way over to where Drina, Rhonnie and Dan stood, a few feet away from Jane Goodman.

Drina stepped forward to introduce herself to the more senior-looking of the two, who told her his name was Sergeant Downs. His younger, more fresh-faced colleague was Constable Childs. Drina told him she was in the office when the alarm went up and that as yet she had no information on just how Mr Goodman had met his death. While Constable Childs dispersed the crowd, Sergeant Downs spoke to Jane Goodman.

Rhonnie and Dan watched closely as the policeman

sympathetically asked for her version of events. He said if she wasn't ready yet he'd come to her chalet later. When she dropped her hands from her face and lifted her head, Jane Goodman looked to be every inch a woman deep in shock, having unexpectedly lost the love of her life. Her face was etched with pain, her eyes red and puffy from crying, and she was visibly shaking.

Dan whispered to Rhonnie, 'She doesn't look to me a woman who's just murdered her husband.'

Rhonnie had to agree. Dan must be right. What Jane Goodman had told her must only have been said in the heat of the moment.

In a choked voice Jane said she would help Sergeant Downs as best she could. She told him that she had been reading a book while Sam was dozing in his deckchair. He then decided to go for a swim. She told him to enjoy himself, and went back to reading her book. It was about ten minutes later when urgent shouting from other campers had disturbed her. She looked out to sea and saw what looked like a swimmer in trouble. They kept disappearing under the water. She didn't realise it was her husband as the person was too far out. Another swimmer was frantically swimming over to try and help them. She had actually thought it was her husband who was going to the rescue as he was a good swimmer.

By now Geoff the beach stripey had sent Fran to the office to call for an ambulance and was wading into the sea to assist with the rescue. Along with others who were now realising something was wrong, she had run down to the shore. It wasn't until a man's body was being pulled on to the beach that she saw it was her husband. She couldn't praise Geoff highly enough for what he had tried to do to resuscitate Sam, but it was apparent just by looking at him that it was already too late. At that Jane burst into tears again, burying her face in her hands.

Sergeant Downs then questioned a still very shaken Mr Green, who told him that, weather permitting, he always took a swim out to the buoy about half a mile offshore at eleven, and was heading back after that when he noticed people frantically waving on the beach, obviously trying to alert him to the fact that someone was in trouble. Treading water, he took a look around and saw a man behind him fighting to keep afloat over near the buoy, about a hundred yards away. By the time he'd swum back to reach him, the other swimmer was floating face down on the surface, beginning to sink. He was a bigger man than Mr Green and much heavier; pulling him back to shore wasn't easy. Thankfully the stripey had swum out to help him, and between them they'd finally managed it. Just from one look at the man lying on the beach however it was obvious to him that it was too late, though he couldn't fault Geoff's attempts at artificial respiration.

Thanking him, Sergeant Downs then questioned Geoff, getting the same story. He also spoke to a couple of the onlookers who corroborated this version of events.

After instructing the ambulance men to take Sam's body to the morgue in Skegness, he spoke to Jane again for a moment, obviously to tell her of his conclusions. He then informed Drina, who was standing with Rhonnie and Dan, that he was in no doubt that Sam Goodman's death was due to accidental drowning and felt sure that the local coroner would confirm this at an inquest in a couple of days' time.

Drina told him that she would escort Mrs Goodman back to her chalet and have the doctor called to give the distraught widow something to help calm her down. She then asked Dan and Rhonnie respectively to escort Geoff and Mr Green back to their chalets and said she would have the doctor pay a visit to them too, as a precaution.

Geoff willingly went with Dan. He'd dealt with lots of situations during his time as a stripey but had never been involved in a tragic death before. The thought of a sedative to knock him out for a while sounded rather welcome. Mr Green, though, was insistent that he was fine and didn't need the doctor. His wife signalled to Rhonnie that she knew better. Crouching on either side of his deckchair they did their best to coax him into agreeing, using the excuse it was just as a precaution. They had managed to persuade him and were standing up when Drina passed by with her arm around a still visibly upset Jane Goodman, head bent, sobbing into a handerchief. Her boss flashed Rhonnie a wan smile and said to her, 'I'll see you later back in the office, dear.'

Rhonnie nodded in response. It was then that Jane lifted her head and shot her a look before she bowed it again. Rhonnie gasped and momentarily froze. The look the other woman had shot her had spoken volumes, leaving Rhonnie in no doubt whatsoever that, however impossible it seemed from the evidence, she had most definitely been responsible for her husband's death.

CHAPTER TWENTY-ONE

Seven days later Drina looked at Rhonnie in concern. Together with Jackie they were seated on the sofas in Drina's office, looking through pattern books of wedding dresses. The local dressmaker would make one when Rhonnie had chosen her style. The bride-to-be was appearing to be keenly interested but Drina knew that her mind wasn't completely on the task in hand. She'd not been herself since the day of Sam Goodman's tragic drowning. Although Drina had asked her several times since then if she was all right, suggesting that maybe she needed a visit from the doctor, each time Rhonnie had replied that she was fine. Her insistence didn't fool Drina, though. The girl had something on her mind that was bothering her deeply, but whatever it was it didn't look like Rhonnie was going to spill the beans.

Jackie couldn't hide her own excitement. She was like a volcano ready to burst, as was Ginger once Rhonnie had asked them both to be bridesmaids. Ginger was coming to join them as soon as her shift was over and Jackie was now willing Rhonnie to settle on a dress because that meant they would be able to fix the bridesmaids' too. In one of the books she was looking at she came across a dress she thought would be perfect for Rhonnie.

Pushing it in front of her, she said enthusiastically, 'Oh, Rhonnie, look at this one. Isn't it beautiful? Not sure about the lacy wrap thing over the top, and it hasn't got a train . . . but what do you think?'

Rhonnie cast her eyes quickly over it. 'Mmm, it's very nice if it was for a church wedding but not what I had in mind for the register office.'

Drina asked her, 'So what do you have in mind, Rhonnie? Your wedding is in three weeks' time and if you don't decide soon the dressmaker won't have time to make it . . . and then you'll be getting married in your birthday suit!'

Rhonnie didn't even crack a smile at the picture Drina conjured up, just gave a sigh and said, 'I'm not sure.'

Drina thought, Enough is enough. Looking at Jackie she said to her, 'Would you be kind enough to give us a moment, dear?'

At the meaningful stare her boss was giving her, Jackie immediately rose to go and make tea for them all, but the switchboard started buzzing, anouncing an outside call, so she said instead, 'I'll go and get that.'

As soon as Jackie had shut the door behind her, Drina demanded, 'Right, I want to know what's going on with you, Rhonnie.' She laid one hand on her employee's arm and asked, 'Have you changed your mind about marrying Dan and don't know how to tell him? Is that it?'

Rhonnie vehemently shook her head. 'No, not at all. I love Dan. I can't wait to marry him. I'm . . . er . . . just overwhelmed by it all.'

Drina sighed. She was in no doubt that Rhonnie was being evasive. Maybe she was still upset over the death of Sam Goodman. After all, it was an awful thing to have happened, and had affected everyone who had been involved in one way or another. Despite his insistence that he was fine, Mr Green had not been able to go for his regular swim since that day and Geoff had been taken off beach duties for the time being, as he was so concerned that another camper was going to drown he interpreted anyone waving their arms in the air while having fun as being in trouble and immediately swam out to drag them back to shore, despite their protests.

Rhonnie meanwhile was thinking that she couldn't go on like

this. Despite all her best efforts she couldn't shake off the nagging belief that Jane Goodman had killed her husband. That look had said it all, surely. But there was absolutely no evidence to go on and Rhonnie had not dared to voice her suspicions to anyone. Jane Goodman was leaving for home first thing tomorrow morning. Rhonnie felt compelled to speak to her about her husband's death.

She said to Drina, 'I have something I need to do, Mrs Jolly. Would it be all right if I go out for a while?'

All Drina's instincts told her that whatever it was, it had something to do with what was troubling Rhonnie. She told her, 'Take all the time you need, dear.'

The door to the chalet was open when Rhonnie arrived. When she looked inside she saw Jane with her back to her, busy putting clothes into a suitcase. Rhonnie tapped on the door to announce her presence. 'Hello, Mrs Goodman,' she said.

Holding a folded dress in her hands, Jane turned and looked towards the door, saw who her caller was and smiled warmly at her. She didn't have the air of a grieving widow. In fact, she looked to be positively glowing. She returned Rhonnie's greeting pleasantly.

'Hello. Please come in. I decided to start packing, not leave it all to the last minute. I'm not sure what to do with Sam's clothes. I don't really want to lug them all home . . . well, there's no point, is there, when he's no longer going to wear them? Is there a Seamen's Mission or somewhere like that I could donate them to? The clothes are not to everyone's taste but they'd maybe do someone a good turn.'

As she stepped over the threshold, Rhonnie told her, 'I'm sure there are good causes we could donate them to on your behalf. I came to see how you are feeling? If we can do anything else for you please say. The offer of the company car to take you home instead of travelling on the coach is still open, should you change your mind?'

'Oh, I'm quite happy to travel back on the coach. Be nice to be able to hold a coversation with the other passengers without Sam dominating it. The camp has been more than kind to me as it is. I shall write a letter to Mrs Jolly when I get back, thanking her for all her support. It was very good of her to come with me to the inquest, and good of you and her too to come to the funeral.'

'It was the least we could do. I'm glad your children managed to attend.'

'Yes, so am I. They were upset, he was their father after all, but if I'm honest he'll not be much of a loss to them as none of them really had much time for him. It's a shame all three of them had to return to work as it would have been nice if they could have stayed and enjoyed the facilities here.' She turned her head and looked over at a container sitting on the chest of drawers. It was a round plain metal object with a lid. Like the funeral, the urn containing Sam Goodman's ashes was the cheapest his wife could arrange. 'We're going to scatter Sam's ashes all together when I get back to Doncaster. We haven't decided where yet. As far as I'm concerned, they can be flushed down the toilet.'

She then looked hard at Rhonnie. 'I know why you're really here. You want to find out if I did kill Sam or if it was just a coincidence. Well, I don't want you to be left wondering for the rest of your life so I'll tell you. His death was no accident. I meant it when I said that I was going to kill him.' She smiled at the expression on Rhonnie's face.

'You're wondering how I could possibly have caused him to drown when I wasn't even in the water at the time. In fact, doing that was the easy bit. It was getting him to go in the first place that was the real problem. Sam was an adequate swimmer but didn't like exerting himself. That was the only part of my plan I wasn't sure how I was going to manage before we arrived here. I was determined I was going home a widow, determined to find a way to get him into the sea. Then I met Mr Green. I really wish I could thank him for the help he's given me, but of course I can't.

'Anyway, while we were on the beach every morning, I observed that on the dot of eleven Mr Green would go for a swim out to the buoy and back. As you saw for yourself when you came across my husband during his stay here, he couldn't bear anyone to outshine him in anything, and especially not in front of women. That morning when Mr Green went off for his swim all I had to say to Sam was, "There goes Mr Green for his constitutional – and just look at all the women watching him. Women do love a man who's athletic, don't they?" That was enough to have Sam shaking off his need for sleep and stepping out of his chair, sucking in his flabby stomach as best he could, and strutting off down the beach to make a big display of doing a couple of stretching exercises before he waded into the water. He swam after Mr Green, convinced all the women now had their eyes on him. Never did see himself as the fat slob he really was but a Greek god instead, the stupid man.'

Rhonnie was looking at her quizzically. 'But even having got your husband into the water, you couldn't be sure he'd drown, Mrs Goodman?'

A slow satisfied smile spread across Jane's face. 'I could when I knew he'd had enough Mogadons to send a horse to sleep crushed up in the mug of tea I'd given him out of our Thermos half an hour before.'

She put the dress she was holding neatly folded into the case and picked up a jumper. 'You will excuse me, won't you? I'd like to finish most of my packing then I need to get myself ready. After lunch I'm going to the cinema to watch a showing of *Brief Encounter*.' She heaved a happy sigh. 'It's so wonderful being able to do whatever I want, instead of always being bossed about by Sam.'

Rhonnie was reeling from what she'd just been told and said distractedly, 'Yes, of course.' She was about to say that she hoped Mrs Goodman would spend her holiday at Jolly's Camp again next year, but under the circumstances really didn't want to encourage her there again. She left the chalet and slowly walked back up the path to the office. She didn't quite know how she felt. Part of her couldn't help but admire the woman for getting rid of the cause of her own misery, but then she couldn't condone the way she had done it. Taking another's life for whatever reason was wrong in Rhonnie's eyes. Jane Goodman had, though, been extremely clever in planning and executing the perfect murder. None of the events surrounding Sam's death had raised any suspicions of foul play whatsoever, and they never would. If Jane hadn't actually told Rhonnie she was going to kill her husband, she wouldn't have been any the wiser herself.

Her only consolation was that at least she wouldn't spend the rest of her days wondering whether or not Jane had killed her husband. Rhonnie felt it best to keep this knowledge to herself. Drina should never be made aware that the camp which gave hard-working people a break from their mundane lives had been seen by one unscrupulous individual as an ideal place to carry out a murder.

CHAPTER TWENTY-TWO

Rhonnie took a deep breath then slowly exhaled as she looked out across the deserted golden sands at the waves crashing against the shore. There was a definite hint of autumn in the air on this late-September morning and the heavy clouds above threatened rain. Not that she cared. Rain, wind or shine, she was marrying the love of her life in a few hours' time and nothing could mar the joy she was feeling.

On the verge of starting a new episode in her life, it was hard for her to comprehend how much it had changed in only seven months. She had first arrived here devastated over her father's plight and her own broken relationship, with not a clue what the future held for her. She'd had absolutely no idea as she had walked through the gates that her life was about to change so much for the better.

It was six-thirty in the morning and she was surprised by how fresh and alert she felt considering she hadn't gone to bed until after twelve last night. Ginger, Jackie and a few of the other female members of staff she was friendly with had insisted on giving her a send off. They were still partying in Groovy's when she had slipped away at just after twelve, leaving them to it, not wanting to look like death warmed up when she was making her vows. Rhonnie was very glad now that she had been careful how much alcohol she had consumed. Considering the amount the others had had, she doubted they'd be feeling as good as she did this morning without the help of a few aspirin. And they still had work to go to. The camp didn't grind to a halt just because two of its staff were tying the knot. The wedding was at four-thirty and Drina had insisted Rhonnie should take the whole day off, but Saturday was the camp's busiest day so she'd said she should at least work the morning. Dan had said the same and was working then too.

Over the last seven months Rhonnie had grown used to sharing the cramped conditions of the chalet. It would take a bit of getting used to, living in a proper house again, in particular having a bathroom just down the corridor and not having to traipse over to the staff shower block in all weathers. She'd had no preconceived ideas of Dan's house when he'd taken her to visit it for the first time the day after they had set the date for the wedding. If anything she had thought it would be a little two up, two down workman's cottage in a row of others, and probably in need of a woman's touch considering he had been living there on his own for several years since his mother had died. She was very pleasantly surprised therefore when Dan had stopped his motor bike outside a pretty little detached, slate-roofed cottage with roses round the door and, to either side of the central path, a well-stocked, neatly kept garden. A chocolate box cottage, in fact. Before she had even seen inside Rhonnie knew she was going to be happy living here with Dan.

Inside the decor and furniture were tasteful and comfortable, and Dan kept it neat and tidy, admittedly with the help of a lady from a nearby village who came in to 'do' for him three times a week. He intended to keep her on after the wedding as Rhonnie had made it clear she did not want to give up her job, and he did not want her having to tackle housework after a hard day at work, especially if her father came to live with them should he not be ready by then to get a place of his own. Dan had been so pleased with Artie's work that he had made his position permanent, so should he want to he could now afford to rent a place of his own.

Dan had made it clear to Rhonnie that the house was to be

her home and she was to feel free to make whatever changes she wanted to it. But as she'd told him, the place already felt like home to her and except for a few knick-knacks, new bedding and such like, bought as they went along, there was nothing Rhonnie would change. The previous day they had brought down her clothes and personal belongings, ready for her to move in later tonight.

She wondered how Dan was feeling this morning, his last as a bachelor, and if he was as excited as she was. She really didn't need to wonder, though, as last evening when they had snatched a few minutes together after work before they had to get ready for their hen and stag parties, just the way he had looked at her, held her, his lingering kiss, had told her that he couldn't wait until they were sharing their lives together.

She took another deep breath of the fresh morning air and, with a warm glow filling her at the thought of what lay ahead for her today, turned and began to make her way back to her chalet, ready for her last breakfast in the restaurant with Ginger and the other girls.

Despite the early hour, Rhonnie wasn't the only camp employee up and about. The early-morning maintenance and cleaning staff were going about emptying bins, picking up litter, sweeping paths, washing shop windows and performing numerous other tasks so the site was all spick and span for when the campers got up. On spotting her each and every one of them had waved and called over their best wishes for today, and Rhonnie waved back, thanking them. If it had been possible she and Dan would have invited all the staff to the wedding, but as it was not she meant to make sure they at least got a slice of the huge three-tier fruit cake that Chef Brown had made, laced with plenty of brandy donated by Drina and decorated with white royal icing and handmade sugar-icing pink-and-white roses.

She had just arrived at the path skirting the tennis courts when from the direction of the campers' chalets a woman came hurrying towards her. She was in her late thirties, her face creased with worry, and wearing a faded pink candlewick dressing gown over her long winceyette nightdress. Her mousy brown hair was tightly wound over rollers under a hairnet, and she had slippers on her feet.

'Have yer seen me son?' she demanded. 'Seven years old, he is. Blond hair, blue eyes, this tall.' She indicated by holding her hand at thigh height. 'He'd be wearing short trousers, a red jumper and blue anorak. We got up this morning and he wasn't in his bunk.'

Rhonnie shook her head. 'I've just come back from the beach and haven't seen any children up and about at all. Er . . . have you looked under the bunk bed and your own, to see if he's hiding?'

The woman sharply retorted, ''Course I have, I'm not stupid. The first place we looked.' She then added remorsefully, 'I'm sorry, I didn't mean to snap at you like that, only I'm so worried about my Lenny.'

Rhonnie gave her a sympathetic smile. 'It's all right, I understand.' Then she asked, 'Has your son made any friends while he's been here and maybe gone to their chalet, to see if they're up and coming out to play?'

The mother was distraught by now, wringing her hands together. 'Yes, with a couple of kids in a chalet further down from us. I've already been there . . . actually knocked them up as they were still sleeping . . . but they ain't seen hide nor hair of Lenny since he was playing with them in the little playground near us just before we went to dinner at seven last night. The parents are out looking for him now, along with some other neighbours who volunteered to help us when they heard he was gone. But we looked everywhere . . . in the little park near us to see if he was on the swings, the shower block . . . though he won't go in there voluntarily, yer know what boys are like . . . up the shops. I was just heading down to the beach when I saw you coming back from that direction. I don't know where else ter look.'

Tears of distress filled her eyes and began to flow down her face as she wailed, 'What if summat has happened to him? What if he's lying hurt somewhere . . . Oh, I can't bear it! I'll kill the little bugger when I get hold of him, putting me and his dad and sister through this when we should be packing up to go home.'

Despite being extremely concerned herself about the whereabouts of the child, Rhonnie told his mother, 'I'm sure he's absolutely fine. He's probably back at your chalet now, wondering what all the fuss is about. Let's go back and check. If he's not there then I'll organise a proper search party by the staff. Rest assured, we'll find Lenny.'

The woman seemed somewhat mollified by Rhonnie's words and led the way back to her chalet, praying her son had returned from wherever he'd been, safe and well.

As they walked down the row they could see a cluster of people, still dressed in their nightclothes, milling around outside the woman's chalet. Thinking that this meant Lenny had been found, they hurried up to join them.

As soon as they did, his mother demanded, 'Have yer found my boy?'

One of the women answered, 'No, love. We all had a good search around and we can't find any sign of him.'

Lenny's mother wailed again. 'Oh, God, my Lenny is lying dead somewhere, I feel it in me water.'

Just then a middle-aged woman and man, also dressed in their nightclothes, hurried up to them. Eyes sparkling keenly, the woman asked no one in particular, 'What's going on?'

She was told by one of the gathering, who pointed at the distraught mother. 'That lady's son has gone missing. We can't find him anywhere.'

At this news the other woman scowled grimly. Folding her arms under her ample bosom, she addressed her husband. 'I bet that bloke's got summat to do with this. I told you he had a shifty look about him, didn't I, Norman?'

He nodded. 'Yes, you did, Hilda. Said it wasn't right the way he was watching the kids playing like that.'

Overhearing this conversation, another woman demanded, 'What's this about a shifty-looking bloke watching the kids playing?'

Having heard the question, several other people all looked at Hilda. Puffing out her chest importantly, she told them, 'Well, it's just that as we've been going around the camp, several times we've seen this chap . . . tall, brown hair, not bad-looking, in his late thirties . . . and he's always been hanging around where the kids are playing. He ain't got any of his own, not that we've seen him with anyway, so it didn't seen right to us.'

Rhonnie said to her, 'Just because you've seen someone watching children playing, doesn't mean to say they're up to no good.'

'Well, no, I grant yer, but in light of this kiddy going missing, it makes yer think, don't it, that he's one of those funny types?'

Someone asked, 'What's she mean?'

Someone else commented, 'A bloke that likes kids, if yer know what I mean.'

Lenny's mother cried frenziedly, 'Oh, my God! And you think this shifty bloke has got my lad?'

Just then a big man pushed his way through the gathering and said to her, 'Did I hear right? Some shifty bloke has got our lad?'

Rhonnie was deeply worried about the way this conversation was heading. 'We've no evidence at all this man has your son,' she intervened. 'We need to call the police and let them deal with this.'

Lenny's father frenziedly shouted back, 'And while we're waiting for them to come that man could have done all sorts to my son . . . murdered and buried him.' He then addressed the crowd. 'Does anyone know where this bastard's chalet is?'

Someone spoke up. 'I know which bloke yer mean. I've seen him hanging around the kids' play area too. His chalet's a couple of rows back.'

Lenny's father's face darkened with rage. He bellowed, 'Show me! If he's harmed a hair of my lad's head, he'll wish he'd never been born after I've finished with him.'

As Rhonnie had feared might happen, the mood of the crowd turned ugly. Several men shouted, 'We'll come with yer, mate.' Led by the man who said he knew where the suspect was residing, they all hurriedly marched off.

Rhonnie felt panic-stricken. On the word of one woman, the crowd had decided a man was guilty of unspeakable acts, and there was no telling what they would do to him in the mood they were in. She needed to stop them before something regrettable occurred. How one lone woman was going to stop a horde of rampaging men and women she hadn't a clue, but regardless she kicked up her heels and sped after them.

She had almost caught up with the throng when she heard her name being called, and turned to see Dan and two of his maintenance crew heading towards her. She was always glad to see him but never so much as she was at this moment.

A few yards away from her still, he called out, 'Matt was sweeping a path when he saw a load of people gathered around a chalet and thought it looked like trouble brewing. He saw you there too. He came to fetch me, and I've brought him and Jim with me just in case.' Dan had drawn level with her now and was looking worried. 'What's going on, Rhonnie?'

She blurted out, 'A little boy has gone missing, and a woman told them all she felt that one of the campers had been acting strangely. That was enough to incite them into believing this man had kidnapped the child, done God knows what to him, then murdered and buried him!'

Dan thought about this and commented, 'And meanwhile the child is probably safe and sound somewhere, oblivious to the trouble he's caused by going off on his own like this.' Grim-faced, he added, 'We need to put a stop to that lynch mob before things get really out of hand.' He was about to ask Rhonnie to go up to the office and call the police, but he was too late. She'd already spun on her heel, resuming her pursuit of the crowd. He hurriedly sent Matt instead, then full of concern for the child and for his beloved Rhonnie, who was heading into a volatile situation, he raced after her with Jim in tow.

The chalet in question was situated in the middle of a long row. By the time Ronnie caught up with the crowd they were all gathered outside it, urging the missing child's father to break down the door and drag their quarry out. The father was hammering on it loudly. People from neighbouring chalets were spilling out, wondering what was going on.

Without a thought for her own safety, Rhonnie pushed and shoved her way unceremoniously through the crowd to reach the chalet door, just as the child's father was about to shoulder it open. Flattening herself against it, she cried to him, 'Stop this now, before things turn ugly and someone really gets hurt! You can't just decide a man is guilty of something and dish out your own punishment mob-handed.'

With the crowd still egging him on, he raged at her, 'What are you expecting me to do then to the man that's got my kid? Ask him politely what he's done to Lenny, over a cup of tea? The police can have him when I've finished with him. That's if there's anything left of him, that is.'

He made to grab her shoulders and heave her out of the way, but instead it was he who was bodily pushed aside and Dan's voice was telling him, 'Lay a finger on her and you'll be spending a long time in hospital.'

Dan was just heaving him away from the door, the child's father was struggling to stop him, when the chalet door opened and a man in a dressing gown appeared, rubbing sleep from his eyes. He looked totally bewildered to see an angry crowd gathered around his chalet. Before he could utter a word, the child's father, still struggling with Dan, cried out, 'Where's my son, you murdering bastard?'

Despite Jim, a tall beefy young man, single-handedly trying to hold them back, the men in the crowd then surged forward, intending to grab the suspect. Sheer panic racing through her, Rhonnie pushed him back inside the chalet, dived in after him and slammed shut the door. Then she pulled the small chest of drawers at the bottom of the bed in front of it, although she was aware that it would hardly prevent an angry mob from getting in.

She then turned to face the bewildered occupant of the chalet who was by now sitting on his bed, looking utterly confused. He asked, 'Who are you?'

'Rhonda Fleming. I work in the offices.'

'Oh, yes, I think I've seen you going around. I'm William Carver. Pleased to meet you. But why are you here? And what's going on with all those people outside?'

She flashed a look around her, searching for any proof of a child having been in the chalet recently, but then if this man was guilty it was unlikely he'd leave evidence lying around. She perched on the bed opposite his, clasping her hands tightly together, and over the angry shouting coming from outside, carefully told him, 'A young boy has gone missing and . . . well, the child's father thinks you might be responsible.'

He stared at her appalled for several moments before exclaiming, 'What! But why would he think such a thing?'

'Because other campers have seen you hanging around the children's playgrounds.'

William looked blank for a moment before his shoulders slumped, his head drooped and he muttered, 'Oh, I see.'

Rhonnie gasped, 'So you don't deny you've been watching children?'

His head jerked up, eyes filled with horror. 'No, I don't deny it – I was. But not for the reason those people outside think I was.'

'So why were you watching them? I mean, you're obviously here on your own, have no children who would have been playing there, so why were you?'

He heaved a sigh and Rhonnie saw tears glint in his eyes. 'No . . . I don't have children . . . not now I don't.'

'But you did?'

He nodded. 'A son. Eric.' He shut his eyes, tears escaping from under his lashes to run down his face. 'He died six weeks ago from leukaemia. He was only eight.' He wiped his face using the sleeve of his checked wool dressing gown before he went on, 'My son was the apple of my eye. I was left a widower when my wife died giving birth to Eric. I thought nothing could be more painful than losing her but, believe me, losing a child is far worse than anything you can imagine. I vowed to her on her deathbed that I would do my absolute best to make sure our child had a happy life. My mother helped me look after Eric when he was a baby while I went to work and he was a happy, healthy child, a joy to have. We were as close as any father and son could be. We did all the things fathers and sons do together. He helped me in the garden, we went fishing, flying kites in the park.

'Last year I brought him here for a holiday and he loved it, had a whale of a time, and so did I. Immediately we got home I booked for us to come back again this year. It was only a couple of weeks later that I took him to the doctor because I knew something wasn't right with him. He sent us to the hospital and that was where Eric's illness was diagnosed. I was told the type of leukaemia he'd got was not treatable, it was particularly aggressive and he'd be lucky to see the year out. Eric was not told his illness was life-threatening but he was a bright little chap and I think he sensed he hadn't got long left. A few weeks ago he took a turn for the worse and had to be hospitalised. It was dreadful seeing him with all those tubes sticking out of him, knowing that whatever it was that was being pumped into him was not going to cure him. It was very difficult for me to try and be positive and discuss what we were going to do when he came out of hospital, especially coming here to the camp for our holiday when I knew that was not going to happen.

'One night he was rapidly sinking into a coma and the doctor told me that this was it. I just broke down, couldn't stop crying.

Suddenly, to my shock, I felt Eric's hand gently squeeze mine. He was looking up at me from his bed. With great difficulty, he told me not to cry for him as he'd soon be with his mummy in heaven. I was to promise him, he said, that I wouldn't miss out on our holiday just because he wouldn't be with me. Coming here without him was unthinkable to me then, but how could I not promise him what he asked? I knew my time here would be very difficult but I tried to get through it by imagining Eric was with me. That's why I've been visiting the children's areas. He loved playing on the swings and roundabouts.'

Her heart breaking for this man, Rhonnie said softly, 'And it wasn't the other children there you were seeing, but your son enjoying himself as he would have done had he not died?'

'Yes. Sounds pathetic, ridiculous even, pretending my dead son was with me, doesn't it?' He eyed her searchingly. 'I would find it hard to believe that story if I were you. But I could give you my doctor's number, if you like? He'll confirm everything I've told you about my son and my wife. He's been our family doctor since I was a boy.'

Rhonnie didn't need to have William's story confirmed. This man's grief for the loss of his child was no act. She reached over and laid a hand on his. 'My mother passed away a few years back and at times I still talk to her and in my mind hear her talking back to me. Imagining your son is here with you is neither pathetic nor ridiculous if it helps you get through. I'm so very sorry for your loss, Mr Carver. It sounds as if your son was a lovely boy.'

He flashed her a weak smile. 'Yes, he was.' Then he heaved a deep sigh. 'I never thought about what I was doing but I can understand why people might think I was acting suspiciously.' He looked worried. 'That child who's missing . . . His parents must be frantic.' He made to get up, saying, 'I need to go and explain myself to everyone who thinks I've kidnapped him, and then help in the search.'

There were still angry altercations going on outside and Rhonnie didn't think it wise for him to go out as she doubted anyone would listen to him. But she'd make them listen to her. Telling the man to stay where he was, she went over to the door, moved aside the chest, and opened the door just enough for her to get out through it, pulling it to behind her. Dan was still struggling to stop the missing child's father from entering the chalet; Jim still trying his best to stop the crowd now threatening to storm the place and drag the monster out to deal with him themselves.

On spotting Rhonnie come out of the chalet alone, shutting the door behind her, the missing child's father cried out, 'That bastard too scared to show himself? And what does that make you, shielding him, you bitch? What if it was your son that was . . .'

Dan furiously snapped at him, 'I warned you about . . .'

In no uncertain terms, Rhonnie interjected. 'Shut up and listen to what I have to tell you.' Then she turned to the rest of the crowd and shouted the same thing at them. Miraculously they all fell quiet and stared at her expectantly. She told them that the man they suspected of being responsible for the missing child was no more guilty of harming him than they were, and she told them why, concluding: 'If someone has taken Lenny, it is not Mr Carver. He's just coping with the loss of his own son in the best way he can.'

At the end of the story she had told them, everyone but the father of the missing boy was subdued and remorseful for their unwarranted actions against an innocent man. It was the father who spoke up. 'Well, if this Carver chap hasn't got him, where is my son?'

Rhonnie couldn't answer that. Instead she said, 'We need to search the camp again, every inch of it.'

'She's right,' announced Dan, and released the father who had calmed down by now. 'Best we split into twos so each area can be thoroughly checked.' He scanned his eyes over the crowd of fifteen or so before him and asked, 'Are you all in?'

They nodded.

He thanked them for their help.

Just then Matt came running towards them, shouting, 'The police will be here as soon as they can.'

Dan thanked him for letting them know and then told him to go back to the office to wait for their arrival and bring them down to the missing child's chalet. He proceeded to assign each couple an area, making sure the whole campsite was covered, no mean feat considering the size of it. He and Rhonnie would go down to the beach and do a thorough search of that, then back towards the outside sports facilities, to overlap with another couple searching that area.

They all went their separate ways. They were so consumed with the need to find Lenny safe and well that the fact it was their wedding day had temporarily slipped both Rhonnie's and Dan's mind. They both rushed down to the beach, searching for any sign of a child resembling Lenny's description. They found the area still deserted at this time of the morning, except for a couple of people walking dogs down by the water's edge. When they were approached they said they'd not seen any children during their outing. Rhonnie and Dan separated to search the dunes for a good distance each way, arranging to meet back at the duckboards.

It was half an hour later when they did, each disappointed to see the other alone. In silence they hurried back to the start of the path back to camp. It took them past the entrance to the funfair. As they hurried by the high colourful wooden fence and gates that secured the fairground, their eyes still darting all ways, a thought struck Rhonnie and she pulled Dan to a halt, saying, 'Has anyone checked in the fairground?'

He looked at her nonplussed. 'A boy of seven couldn't scale that fence and get over the barbed wire running around the top. I doubt I could do it myself.'

She scanned her eyes up and down the fence and large metal gates. 'Mmm, yes, you're right.'

They made to set off again when another thought struck Rhonnie. 'Dan, wait. Your maintenance men would have swept out the place earlier, wouldn't they?'

He nodded. 'Yes. Greg and Brian were assigned to do it first thing this morning.'

'Well, that means the gate would have been open while they were doing it and the boy could have slipped inside then. Maybe we haven't been able to find him as he's locked in.'

Dan nodded again. 'That's a thought, Rhonnie. Let's find out.' He delved into his pocket, pulling out his set of camp keys, and together they ran over to the gate, which Dan unlocked and pushed open. Having arranged to meet at the bottom of the fair by the fun house, Rhonnie went one way, Dan the other.

No stall or ride, corner or crevice, was left unchecked by them. Neither of them having found any sign of the child, they were both despondent when they met up again by the fun house.

'I was really hopeful we'd find him here,' Rhonnie told Dan as he put his arms around her to give her a hug.

Kissing the top of her head, he murmured, 'Me too. Let's hope one of the other searchers did.'

She nodded. 'Better go and find out.' Then a thought struck her. 'Oh, did you search the fun house?'

He shook his head. 'I take it you didn't either?'

'No. We'd best check or we can't be honest and say we've searched everywhere, can we? I'll do upstairs if you do down.'

As she mounted the stairs she was reminded of the first time she had come into the house of fun, on the night when Dan had brought her to the fair. The whole place had been brightly lit with colourful bulbs. Now it seemed deathly quiet and gloomy. On her other visit the stairs she was climbing had been moving up and down and from side to side, and she'd laughed until she cried at both her own and Dan's stumbling attempts to keep themselves upright whilst negotiating them. That night would always remain a happy memory for her and she felt it a great pity that her second visit would not. Calling out Lenny's name, as she could hear Dan doing downstairs, she found the Barrel of Love room empty of human life, the same as she did the Maze room, the Crazy Floor and Airjet room, and the

Distorted Mirror room. That left only the one room, with a slide that went down to the floor below. That was empty too. Back outside in the corridor she was about to head off for the stairs when she abruptly stopped as she heard a soft shuffling sound, like someone's clothes brushing against the wooden floor. She stood for a moment, straining her ears. Hearing nothing, she made to head off back down the stairs when the sound came again. This time she knew it had come from the Slide room. Whether human or animal, some form of life was in there. Praying it was human, terrified that it was a rat that had managed to escape detection by the maintenance staff, she tentatively retraced her steps into the dark interior.

Apart from the slide which disappeared through a large hole in the wall and the several steps leading up to it, the room was empty. Rhonnie frowned, confused. She had definitely heard a noise coming from in here and something must have made it. She cast her eyes around again, peering more intently this time. As they scanned past the steps accessing the slide she saw a bit of blue poking out from the small space behind them. Lenny's mother had said her son was wearing a blue anorak. Rhonnie stepped closer and to her joy saw she was looking at an elbow. Lenny was hiding in the small space.

But why was he hiding? What was he frightened of?

She moved closer to the steps, stopping several feet away to squat down on her haunches. In a soft voice she said, 'Hello, Lenny. My name is Rhonnie. I work at the camp. You've had us all so worried, especially your mum and dad and sister. They're running around all over, looking for you. And not just them, lots of other people are.' She waited for a moment for some sort of response, but on getting none continued, 'It must be a bit of a tight squeeze in there. Are you going to come out and stretch your legs and talk to me?'

There was silence for a moment before Lenny responded with a definite, 'No. I want to stay here.'

Her heart thumped. The young boy was obviously too

frightened to come out. Of what or who, though? In a gentle, coaxing voice she asked him, 'Has someone upset you, Lenny?'

There was silence for a moment before the answer came again. 'No.'

'Hurt you then?'

'No.'

'So why are you hiding in here then, love?'

There was another long silence before Rhonnie realised the young boy was crying. On her knees, she shuffled over until she was at the side of the steps, then put her hand gently on his elbow. 'Please tell me, Lenny. I can't help you if you don't. I'd like to help you, I really would.'

He continued blubbering for a moment before he uttered, 'Can you make my mam and dad stay here? I don't want to go home.'

Relief flooded through her. She said to him, 'That's lovely to hear, as it means you've really enjoyed yourself.'

She heard him sniff and then start to sob, 'I . . . have. It's . . . great here. I never want to leave.'

And why would he? she realised. To a seven year old, this place must feel magical, full of fun and freedom, away from the hustle and bustle of the grimy city he heralded from, where his life was otherwise regimented by school and his parents' rules. 'Oh, I don't think you'd find it much fun in the winter, sweetheart,' she told him. 'The camp shuts down from November until March, when it's very cold. And that means you'd be here on your own.'

There was a pause before he said, 'Oh! But I could stay 'til the place shuts for the winter, couldn't I?'

'Without your family with you? You'd miss them, wouldn't you?'

'But they could stay too.'

'But your dad has to go to work, and you and your sister to school.'

'My dad could get a job here, couldn't he? And me and my sister don't like school much, so we won't mind not going.'

This young chap had it all figured out it seemed. 'Where would you all live if you stayed here?'

'In our chalet, silly.'

'Oh, but you see . . . you know the bus that's on its way to fetch you? Well, it's bringing another little boy here for a week. He'll be needing your chalet. And other buses are bringing other children to stay in all the chalets. If we have to tell the little boy that's going to be staying in your chalet that he can't because the boy that was here before him doesn't want to go home, then that boy is going to be very upset at not having his week of fun here, isn't he? How would you have felt, love, when you first arrived, if you had to go straight back home because you'd no chalet to stay in?'

There was silence for a moment before he muttered, 'Upset.'

She gave his elbow a gentle squeeze. 'You don't really want to upset that little boy, do you, Lenny?'

He thought about this for a moment before he whispered, 'Not really.'

'I didn't think you would. Lenny, there's always next year to look forward to.'

'Mam and Dad said we can come again if me and my sister behave ourselves, but next summer is such a long time away.'

'It might seem a long time right now, but it'll fly past, believe me. Christmas is not far away and I bet you have a lot of fun at Christmas time. Of course, if you stayed here, Father Christmas wouldn't know where to deliver your presents so you wouldn't get any, would you? Then after Christmas you've got the visit from the Easter Bunny to look forward to, and sometime you've a birthday, then before you know it the summer holidays will be here again.'

He thought about this for a moment. 'Mmm, I suppose,' he muttered.

'You must have lots of family and friends who'd miss you terribly and you them if you stayed here.' She let him think about this for a moment before she said, 'I have to go now,

Lenny, I'm very hungry, you see, as I haven't had my breakfast yet. What about you? I bet you're hungry too, aren't you?'

He responded without hesitation, 'Yes. I'm starving.'

'Well, why don't we find your mum and dad so they can take you in for breakfast before you miss it?'

The thought of food seemed to do the trick. He shuffled his way out from under the steps.

Having finished a fruitless search downstairs, Dan had wondered why Rhonnie was taking so long to search the upper floor so had come up to investigate. Standing in the doorway, he'd been privy to most of the conversation that had taken place between her and Lenny and was smiling over at his future wife adoringly. He'd never doubted that she'd prove to be a wonderful mother to their children when they decided to have them, and witnessing the way she had handled Lenny only served to confirm this.

Having reunited parents and son, and thanked the police who had just turned up, together with the rest of the campers who had helped in the search for Lenny, Rhonnie and Dan were soon saying their goodbyes before both heading off to their respective workplaces.

Dan noticed she was looking pensive and asked what was bothering her.

'Well, it's just that it's our wedding day, isn't it? And it's supposed to be bad luck for a bride and groom to see each other before the actual ceremony.'

He told her with conviction, 'That's just superstitious nonsense cooked up by some dried-up old spinster to excuse the fact that she wasn't married. Had to have been a stroke of bad luck, didn't it? We are getting married later this afternoon, and nothing is going to stop that, you hear?'

She grinned up at him. 'I hear.'

CHAPTER TWENTY-THREE

Standing nervously by the fireplace in Drina's lounge later that afternoon, looking smart in his suit and crisp new white shirt, black shoes polished to a high shine, Artie gasped as his eyes settled on his beloved daughter who had appeared in the doorway opposite him. In a voice choked with emotion he uttered, 'Oh, love, you look absolutely beautiful.'

Wearing an ivory satin shift dress that ended just above her knees, an open-fronted, long-sleeved lace coat over the top, a band of small ivory silk roses in her hair, matching coloured sling-backed court shoes on her feet, Rhonnie entered the room. She smiled happily as she went over to him, saying, 'I'll do then, will I?'

He nodded proudly. 'I'll say.' His eyes clouded then, bottom lip trembling. 'I just wish . . .'

Although he was too choked to finish what he had been going to say, Rhonnie instinctively knew. She tenderly kissed his cheek and said, 'I'd give anything to have her here in the flesh with us too, Dad. But Mum is always with us . . . in here,' she said, placing her hand on her own heart then holding it against his.

He sniffed back tears. 'Yes, she is. And she'd have been a proud woman today, I know that. I'm so proud to be your father, Rhonnie. You're a credit to me and your mum, that's for sure. I can't say as I'm happy about handing you over to another man, but if I had to make the choice, Dan is the one I'd have gone for. You two were meant for each other.'

She smiled at him, tears pricking her eyes. 'Thanks, Dad.'

Along with Ginger and Jackie, who were both dressed in just-above-the-knee midnight blue satin shift dresses with matching long-sleeved boleros over the top, Drina had been standing outside the door, not wanting to intrude on such an intimate conversation between father and daughter. When they had composed themselves, though, she breezed in with a bottle of champagne in one hand, five glasses in the other. Holding the bottle out to him, she said to Artie, 'If you'll do the honours, we'll make a toast to our beautiful bride.'

Rhonnie had already thanked her for allowing them all to get ready for the wedding in her house . . . it was a beautiful place, such as any of them could only ever dream of living in, and they were all in awe of being given the run of it . . . but felt the urge again.

'Thank you again for letting us get ready here, Mrs Jolly,' said Rhonnie. 'We really appreciate it. Don't we, Dad . . . girls?'

Ginger and Jackie both vehemently nodded.

Artie didn't hear her as he was concentrating hard on pushing a stubborn cork out of the bottle of champagne.

Had Joe been here, Drina would not have been allowed to offer her hospitality to the wedding party. As soon as he had been accepted by his peers as a successful businessman, much to Drina's distaste, he'd started to distance himself from those he perceived as below him. He appeared to have forgotten his own humble roots, and only those from his new exalted circle were entertained by him in his house. Drina, on the other hand, never forgot where she came from. She'd had a wonderful time herself, doing all the things the mother of the bride would usually do, and this had helped to lessen her heartache that a momentous occasion such as this would never happen for her again. But there was also another reason why she had insisted the wedding party use her house to get ready in . . . a selfish one. It gave her an excuse to spend more time in Artie's company.

She was well aware she was deliberately travelling down a road that would end in heartache for her. But her feelings for

Artie were turning serious. If she was sensible she would walk away from him now, but the trouble was that their innocent outings together had allowed her to get to know him better, and the more she got to know him the more Drina liked what she was seeing . . . how easy he was to be with; how respectful he was towards women in general, not just with her; how appreciative he was towards anyone who did something for him; how much of an effort he made to look smart on the resources he had; how comfortable she felt while she was with him. Her feelings for him were deepening by the day. He had made it very plain to her that he really enjoyed her company, too, but other than that he had never made an inappropriate move towards her. But how she wished he would! Drina knew, though, that Artie would never put her in a compromising situation. There had been times recently when she'd wished that she was free from her tie to Joe, and able to pursue a proper relationship with Artie. But she was tied to her husband, stuck with being his wife in name only while he sought satisfaction with other women. This was the price Drina was having to pay for allowing herself to be swept off her feet at a very vulnerable time in her life.

She cast a surreptitious glance at Artie, still fiddling to free the cork, noticing that his tie was slightly askew. She so wanted to go over to him and straighten it. A gesture of that sort, though, was far too intimate for a married woman to show towards a man who was not her husband, so she had to fight with herself not to.

In fact, had she but known it, Artie was finding it just as much of a struggle not to express to Drina how beautiful she looked to him. She was wearing a turquoise woollen costume, with an A-line knee-length skirt and short, fitted double-breasted jacket. He would give anything to go over to her now, take her hand, kiss her and tell her how lovely she was. He was glad he was otherwise engaged, uncorking the bottle. He was very aware he should have listened to his daughter when she'd tried to warn him a while ago that he could be heading for trouble. If he continued accompanying Drina, he was well aware that his feelings for her would progress beyond platonic. He defied any man of his age not to feel attracted to such a generous, easy-going woman, one who never flaunted her money to those not so well off as she, but was a delight to be around. He felt very guilty for wishing she was free so that he could take matters further with her, but she wasn't so he had to content himself with spending whatever time with her he could and prepare himself for their association to end on the return of her husband.

Chatting with the other women as they waited for her father to uncork the bottle, and excited as she was about her forthcoming nuptials, Rhonnie was still able to detect the sparks of emotion flying between Artie and Drina. There was more going on between them than either cared to admit. There was nothing she wanted more than for her father to find someone he could be as happy with as he had been with her mother. Rhonnie would be so thrilled for that woman to be Drina Jolly, but it was never going to happen while she was tied to someone else. They were both heading for heartache, it seemed. As soon as Joe Jolly recovered enough to return home their relationship would have to end. But they were both old enough and intelligent enough to know what was in store if they carried on the way they were. Rhonnie felt she knew Drina well enough to know that she couldn't be in love or happy with her husband if she allowed herself to develop feelings for another man. It was such a shame that she and Artie had to deny their feelings for each other. She felt extremely guilty for thinking it, but Joe Jolly was standing in the way of two people living a very happy and fulfilling life together, which was obviously not what he was providing for his wife. It was a great pity he couldn't just disappear somehow, allowing them to be together.

With laughter in her voice, Drina responded to Rhonnie. 'I think I've got the message by now as this is the umpteenth time you've mentioned it. As I keep telling you, it's been my pleasure to have you all here.' Then, tongue-in-cheek, she said to Artie, 'Do you want me to call the fire brigade to help get that cork out?'

He replied, 'I think it's been soldered in.' Then at last he felt it move and declared, 'Oh, here it goes!'

With a loud pop the cork exploded out of the bottle to fly across the room and Artie filled all their glasses. They just had time to toast the bride and drain their drinks before the company Daimler and a taxi arrived to ferry them all to Skegness register office.

The place itself was drab with walls painted in dull cream and brown, and shabby chairs. The only adornment apart from a picture of the Queen hanging on the back wall was a dusty vase of plastic flowers on a window ledge. The registrar was a dour little man in a brown shiny suit whose manner would have been better suited to the profession of undertaker than presiding over the joyous occasion of marriage. This, though, did nothing to dampen the high spirits of the small gathering witnessing the union of Rhonnie and Dan. Much to the disapproval of the registrar, they all loudly clapped when he announced the couple to be man and wife.

As the euphoric couple were driven back through the camp gates, neither of them could believe what their eyes were seeing. Filling the large area around the fountain stood a huge cheering crowd of campers along with Terry Jones and his team of stripeys, who had obviously rounded them up to give the newly weds a riotous welcome back.

And nor could they believe their eyes when they entered Groovy's. Rhonnie had discussed with Dan the fact that Drina would make the place look special somehow for their reception, but neither of them had believed she would go to so much trouble. She'd had the place decked out with strings of pink and white balloons and matching streamers, crisp white cloths on the tables together with pink serviettes and centrepieces of pink and white flowers. Above the low stage area was a banner welcoming Mr and Mrs Buckland in pink and white lettering. Against the far wall stood a long trestle table groaning with a buffet which included sausage rolls, Coronation chicken, vol-au-vents, ham and egg and cress sandwiches, pineapple, cheese and small silver onions on sticks stuck into a large melon, plus several sherry trifles and Black Forest gateau. Dominating the centre of the table was the three-tier wedding cake adorned with its pink-and-white sugar roses.

Two barmen waited to serve drinks. On the side of the bar were a dozen or so bottles of perry wine to toast the happy couple with. The DJ's equipment was all in place, ready for dancing later on after the tables had been removed. The maintenance staff, cleaning staff, stripeys and other members of staff had clubbed together to buy the popular couple wedding presents, which were arranged on a separate small table near the bar along with cards of good wishes from friends who were not able to come, including to Rhonnie's delight, when she opened it later, one from Carol with a five-pound voucher inside to buy whatever she wanted from a branch of Marks and Spencer.

At just coming up to eleven that night, Dan gathered his new wife up in his arms to carry her over the cottage threshold. Kicking shut the door behind them and putting her down, he tenderly cupped her face in his hands. Despite Rhonnie's whole manner telling him he didn't need to ask, he did so anyway. 'Happy?'

'Couldn't be happier,' she replied with conviction. 'There's nothing about today that I would change.'

'Me neither,' he agreed. 'It seems our mums were right that if you wish hard enough things do come true.'

She looked at him strangely before a memory stirred and she said, 'So, if the second part of your wish has come true now you can tell me what it was.'

'That you'd marry me.'

She smiled at him. 'Well, that was granted before you even wished for it. I knew you were the one for me the moment I clapped eyes on you on that swing.'

He chuckled. 'Me, too. I wonder if anyone has realised we've absconded yet?'

She laughed back. 'I doubt it. Far too busy enjoying themselves. Wasn't it nice of our workmates to band together and buy us some gifts? I was overwhelmed. And Mrs Jolly certainly pushed the boat out for us, didn't she? I knew about some of the things she was planning, but not all. I'm surprised Jackie managed to keep it a secret as she was helping with all the arrangements. I shall arrange for a bouquet of flowers to be sent to Mrs Jolly from us both as a thank you.'

'I'm sure she'll appreciate that. Oh, that reminds me, she slipped something into my pocket just as we were about to cut the cake. Until you mentioned her name, I forgot all about it.' Dan put his hand in his jacket pocket and pulled out a long white envelope. While Rhonnie looked on, he slit it open and pulled out a folded peice of paper. When he unfolded it, another piece fluttered out of it on to the floor, which he bent to pick up. Looking at it, he gasped. 'Oh, my God!'

'What is it?' Rhonnie demanded.

'A cheque for fifty pounds.'

She too gasped in shock. 'What! You've read it wrong surely, Dan?'

He handed the cheque to her. She looked at it then lifted her eyes to his. 'No, you're not mistaken. But this amount is ridiculous considering what she's already done for us. Mrs Jolly must have made a mistake when she wrote it out.'

He was reading the letter that had also been included in the envelope. 'It's no mistake, Rhonnie. In the letter she says she wants us to have it to give our marriage the best start, and that we're to use it for a honeymoon when the season is over, go somewhere warm.'

Rhonnie was staring at him, stupefied. 'I know she's fond of us both, Dan, and we're very fond of her. In fact, I'm more than fond of her. But even so, we can't accept this cheque.'

'No, I agree, we can't.' Dan took her hand. 'But this can wait until tomorrow, my darling,' he told her, pulling her towards the stairs.

The next day, though, when Rhonnie and Dan both went into Drina's office to speak to her about the amount she'd given them as a wedding present, she made it very apparent that the topic was not open for discussion and so they had no alternative but to accept her generosity with good grace and look forward to going away somewhere warm as soon as the season was over.

CHAPTER TWENTY-FOUR

A week later at eleven o'clock in the morning, humming happily to herself as she decided what to cook Dan and herself for dinner that night, Rhonnie was setting up the small manual printing machine, ready to run off a new batch of programmes to hand to the next intake of campers who were due to arrive in two days' time, replacing those who were leaving. It was a laborious and arm-aching job and Jackie was going to share the work with her when she returned from taking her tour of the camp. Drina was in her office with the door closed, concentrating on her monthly check of the accounts books with Mr Holder, the accounts manager, a job she didn't particularly enjoy but which had to be done. Mr Holder had slipped out of the office for a moment to look for a missing invoice.

Hands covered in ink as she slid the blocks of letters into place, Rhonnie's attention was drawn to the door when she heard it open. She saw a good-looking silver-haired man enter and begin to make his way towards the boss's office, limping slightly on the stick he carried in one hand. He was casually dressed in an expensive pair of summer-weight cream-coloured trousers, black polo-neck jumper and matching double-breasted blazer with large gold buttons on the front and sleeves. He had an authoritative air about him. She was positive she had never met him before but he seemed vaguely familiar to her.

'Can I help you, sir?' Rhonnie called over to him, smiling a greeting.

He had obviously thought the office was empty. At the sound of this unexpected voice, he stopped to look over at her. 'Ah, you must be Dan's new wife.'

Now that he was facing her Rhonnie knew why he was familiar to her: through the array of photographs hanging in the boss's office, although he was a little thinner now than the latest pictures showed him. The newcomer was Joe Jolly. Her thoughts began to race with questions, but the most prominent one was what would happen to herself and Drina if his return to work was imminent?

He was smiling as he appraised Rhonnie openly. 'The lad has done well for himself. You're a good-looking woman.' He gave a dry laugh. 'Lucky for Dan I was out of the picture when you came along or he wouldn't have got a look in, would he, eh?'

She certainly didn't like the way he was looking at her, and whether he was making a joke or not she didn't appreciate his flirting with her, considering he knew she was a newly married woman, and too, one of his employees. Joe Jolly was a man with a big ego who obviously considered himself irresistible to women of all ages, it seemed to Rhonnie.

She didn't like what he said to her next either. Still looking at her in a way that made her feel most uncomfortable, he said, 'I appreciate what you've done in helping Mrs Jolly keep the camp functioning in my absence.'

She didn't at all like the way he implied by this that his wife hadn't the brains to run a business by herself, when in fact Drina had proved she was more than capable of it. Rhonnie had to stop herself from pointing this out, because he could well take extreme offence at an employee voicing such an opinion and instantly dismiss her. She had taken a dislike to Joe Jolly but regardless addressed him with the same respect as she would any employer. 'I'll let Mrs Jolly know you're here, Mr Jolly.'

She made to hurry across to the boss's office but he stopped her, saying, 'I wouldn't wish to disrupt your work. I'll announce myself.'

When the door to the office opened, Drina was fully expecting it to be Mr Holder returning with the missing invoice. When she saw who it actually was, she stared speechless at him as he limped towards her.

He said to her, 'Well, I expected a bit more of a welcome. You're looking at me like I've grown another head.'

Drina gave herself a mental shake. 'Yes, of course I'm pleased to see you, Joe. I wasn't expecting you, that's all. What are you doing here? You never mentioned the doctor was considering discharging you when I came to see you yesterday.'

'Thought I'd surprise you,' he told her.

Yes, she thought. You've certainly done that.

'Well, are you going to allow me to sit down?'

Drina was about to tell him that she wasn't stopping him, then realised he was referring to the fact that she was sitting in what he considered to be his chair. She wanted to tell him how pedantic he was being. He knew she had been standing in for him during his absence so where on earth did he expect to find her sitting when he'd decided to surprise her? She began to worry what this might mean for her and Rhonnie. She rose and walked around the desk while he limped over to ease himself awkwardly down into his chair. She took a seat in the one at the front of the desk.

'Would you like tea, Joe?' she asked him.

He lit a cigarette that he'd taken out of a gold case from his pocket along with a gold cigarette lighter, drawing deep on the smoke before saying to her, 'I've had enough tea to sink a battleship over the last few months. It's a stiff whisky I need. A Famous Grouse. Make it a large one.'

She eyed him, worried. 'I don't think . . .'

He interjected, 'Please stop fussing, Drina. I've had enough of nurses and doctors fussing over me, telling me what I can and can't do, to last me a lifetime.'

She got up and went over to the drinks cabinet to see to his request, not feeling happy about it as she knew the doctors had warned him that drinking alcohol, smoking and certain foods were off the menu for him from now on if he wanted to live to be a very old man. It didn't look like Joe was listening to them.

After taking a large mouthful of whisky and swilling it around his mouth to savour the taste before he swallowed it, he said, 'I trust Michael hasn't been stupid enough to pay another visit since the one after I took ill?'

She hadn't told him of their son's attempt to take advantage of his illness, abiding by the doctor's instructions not to do or say anything that would cause him the slightest distress and bring on another stroke, or worse a heart attack. It could only be one person who had: his mistress Fiona Hickson. She would have gained admittance to the convalescent home under the guise of being a member of the family. No doubt she had been desperate to see her lover, but also to tell him of the humiliation she had suffered at his son's hands. No doubt he'd promised that as soon as he was back at the helm, she would be reinstated.

Drina had known of their affair virtually from the time it had begun, the same as she had all the others Joe had had over the years they had been married. He had first appeared in her life at a very vulnerable time for her, telling her he'd been sent by the family to help her through her loss. She had been surprised at this because as far as she was aware the family had turned their back on her father once he'd left to make a life for himself and his daughter outside the community. She'd been very young and naïve, far too devastated by the unexpected loss of her father to question why the family had had such a change of heart or why such a handsome man as Joe could find the likes of her, a small, dumpy, ordinary-looking woman, attractive when he could have got himself someone far more glamorous. By the time she had realised that all his vows of undying love for her, his attentiveness and protectiveness, were just an act on his part, that all she was to him was a means to win a far better life for himself, thanks to her father's legacy, than the hand-to-mouth one he was living, being paid a pittance helping his uncle run his fairground rides, she was married to him and had unwittingly handed over control of all her assets.

In the big scheme of things, he hadn't been a bad husband to her. She knew he did care for her, not in the way she would have liked but more as a brother for a sister. He'd not kept her short of money, nor been short of compliments for her care of him and their son despite the way Michael had turned out. He'd made love to her just enough for her not to become suspicious that he was seeking sexual gratification with other women. So good was he at keeping part of his life to himself that Drina might never have suspected that his feelings towards her weren't genuine, had it not been for the fact that his love for another woman became so all-consuming. He was completely unable to disguise it. Drina couldn't help but see the way they stole looks at each other, the way their hands briefly touched when passing, his total devastation when she'd suddenly disappeared from his life and the fact that he was never quite the same after that, as if a light had gone out inside him.

She couldn't blame that woman or any others for falling for Joe. He was a charismatic man, and when he turned on his charm not many women could fail to be flattered. She had fallen for him herself when he'd focused his attention on her. She wondered if Fiona Hickson, like his previous dalliances, was astute enough not to harbour any illusions that her lover would leave his wife. Joe would never damage his reputation for being a devoted family man; the holiday camp could suffer from the stigma of a divorce, and he'd run the risk of losing friends and business associates who didn't agree with his behaviour. Drina had lost count of the number of times she had thought of leaving him, but she had nowhere to go. As Joe controlled their finances she'd no money either to fund a new life with, so whether she liked it or not she was stuck with him.

Now that his return to work was imminent, Drina knew he

would be expecting her to return to the role of dutiful wife while he picked up his life where he'd left it off. The thought sent a chill down Drina's spine. She'd had a taste of a far more fulfilling existence than being a housewife. Since stepping into Joe's shoes, on getting up in the morning her first thought was, I wonder what the day will bring today. It was a far cry from, What will I do to fill my day? She had discovered that she possessed skills she hadn't realised existed and had used them to keep the camp running, been instrumental in adding new facilities to improve it, dealt with those fleecing the company for their own ends, rewarded those who were committed and loyal to it. She had made new friends, especially Rhonnie, seeing them on a day-to-day basis and feeling that she was part of their lives. And for the first time she was experiencing what it felt like to be wanted by a man for herself, not for what she could bring him.

Her friendship with Artie would have to end now. This greatly saddened her as she really liked him, knew he liked her, and they got on so well together, like a pair of comfortable old slippers. Had things been different in her case . . . well, who knew? Drina also knew that her desire to play some sort of role in the company was just a dream that was not going to happen. Most husbands would be delighted that their wives wanted to be part of the family business, but Joe wasn't one of them. Should she even mention her desire, he would in his manipulative way make her feel guilty by accusing her of undermining his role of provider, reminding her that it was her job in return to care for him and their home – anything to protect his own freedom to carry on behind her back as he'd always done. She felt wicked to be thinking it, but how she wished that Joe's recovery hadn't been enough to permit him to return to work, so that she could continue working here and enjoy all the benefits it brought her. She could only hope he wasn't thinking of returning immediately and that she'd have a little time yet to get used to the idea.

'No, Michael hasn't been here since,' she answered her husband's question.

Joe pulled a face. 'Well, I doubt even he'd be stupid enough to attempt to rob me like that again, after being thwarted at the third time of trying.'

Drina bit her tongue. No matter that she had brought everything they'd had when starting the company, Joe still considered it his and not theirs. She looked at him searchingly, seeing the tiredness in his eyes, the pallor of his skin, and her annoyance at his self-absorption was replaced by compassion. 'You're looking tired, Joe. Hadn't you better be thinking of getting home and having a rest?'

He gave an irritated sigh. 'I asked you not to fuss, Drina.' Then he conceded, 'I am tired, but only because I'm not used to doing anything but sitting around all day, except when the physios are working on me. I'll soon get back into the swing of things, though. While I'm here I might as well take a look at the books, then I'll get Jimmy to run us home.'

His use of the word 'us' resounded in her head. 'You mean, you want me to come home with you?'

He eyed her strangely. 'You're my wife, aren't you? Your place is by my side, isn't it?'

'Yes . . . yes, of course. It's just that I've things to do.'

'Nothing I can't see to tomorrow.'

Her heart thumped painfully in her chest and she tried to sound as though she was just a concerned wife, when in truth she needed time to come to terms with returning to her old mundane life. 'You're not thinking of coming back to work so soon, Joe, surely?'

He snapped irritably, 'Drina, I asked you to stop fussing. I'm not a stupid man. I will ease myself back in gently. For the first week, I plan to work just the mornings and be contacted at home after that if necessary.' He looked at her searchingly and told her, 'You can't have any idea what it's been like for me in that convalescent home, with nothing to do but worry about you struggling to keep the business running. It's my job to look after you, Drina. It really distressed me seeing you when you visited me, looking so tired and worried . . . after all, you're not equipped to run this place so it must have kept you awake at night, having the welfare of the whole firm on your shoulders.' He gave her one of his disarming smiles. 'I'm back now to take all that burden off you.'

He swallowed the remainder of the whisky and held out the tumbler to her. 'Please get me another drink, then go and get your hair done in the salon or relax in the reading lounge and I'll have someone come and fetch you when I'm ready to go home. Oh, I know something that will occupy you while you're waiting for me. We'll have a dinner party on Friday night to celebrate my homecoming. Ask the Wintertons and the Harrises.'

She inwardly groaned. Both couples were the most insufferable bores. While the men talked about business and golf, she would be stuck trying to appear fascinated by the women's inane prattle over trivial matters while willing the time to hurry past. As the obedient wife Joe expected her to be, she took the tumbler, rose and replenished it. 'I'll be in the lounge,' she told him as she walked out, shutting the door behind her.

Hearing someone come out, Rhonnie stopped what she was doing and looked over. She knew Drina well enough to realise she was deeply upset. Seeing her like this really bothered Rhonnie. Hurrying across, she asked, 'Are you all right, Mrs Jolly?'

With forced lightness Drina replied, 'Yes, of course I am, dear. Couldn't be better. Mr Jolly is well enough to take back the reins starting tomorrow morning.'

Rhonnie gawped at her. 'You're not going to be working here any longer, you mean?'

'There won't be any need. This was only ever temporary until my husband returned. My place is at home, looking after him and his house.'

Even without seeing the tears sparkling in the older woman's eyes all Rhonnie's instincts were screaming at her that Drina wasn't happy about her husband reclaiming his role as head of the business, and her going back to being a housewife. Rhonnie had so enjoyed working with her, along with Jackie, that as time had gone by all thoughts of Mr Jolly returning and splitting up their team up had faded into the background. To have it thrust on her now so unexpectedly felt like someone had died. She wanted to curl up and cry for her monumental loss. She considered this lovely woman to be far more than just her employer, she was a true friend, almost a substitute mother figure, and the thought that Drina was going to disappear from her life was unbearable. Rhonnie implored her, 'But I will still see you, won't I, Mrs Jolly? I mean, I . . . I . . . well, you're more than just an employer. You've come to mean a lot to me.'

Drina fought to swallow the huge lump that had formed in her throat at Rhonnie's declaration. She so wanted to say that Rhonnie had come to mean a lot to her too, was the daughter she had never had, but to continue their friendship would only mean Drina herself being constantly reminded of a time when she had been happy, and she wasn't sure she could bear that.

Drina knew she had to get out of here before she broke down completely and made a fool of herself. As she patted her arm, she told Rhonnie, 'You take care, dear.'

With that she walked out of the office, leaving a distressed Rhonnie staring after her. How was her father going to react when he heard about this? He could try to hide it, but she dreaded Artie finding out. She knew he was going to be as devastated as she herself was.

Several moments later Jackie came in, a look of confusion on her pretty face. She said to Rhonnie, 'Mrs Jolly has just walked past me in Reception. She looked . . . well, like someone had died. I spoke to her but she ignored me. That's not like her at all.' Her face clouded over. 'Something awful happened while I was out, didn't it, Rhonnie?'

She took a deep breath and revealed, 'I think she's a little upset that she won't be working here any longer. Mr Jolly is back. He's in the office.'

Jackie's feelings were written all over her face. 'Oh!' she exclaimed. She took a deep breath. 'I should be happy that he's back fit and well but I'm not, Rhonnie. Mrs Jolly is a much better boss than he is. She made working here fun. She made me feel like I matter.' Then a terrible thought struck her. Alarmed, she said, 'Oh, but what will this mean for you, Rhonnie? Will Mr Jolly be bringing Miss Hickson back, do you think? I could cope with having him for a boss if you were still my manager, but I don't think I could go back to how things were before.'

Rhonnie shrugged. 'I don't know what Mr Jolly has in mind. Like you, I'll just have to wait and see. In the meantime we carry on as before, doing as good a job as we can.'

Jackie nodded in agreement. Rhonnie, though, was silently praying that should Mr Jolly wish to reinstate Miss Hickson she would have another job by now and coming back to Jolly's would not be on her agenda. Rhonnie didn't want to leave.

CHAPTER TWENTY-FIVE

While his mother was trying to come to terms with the return of his father and all its implications, in the damp dilapidated bedroom of a flat overlooking a builder's yard in a rundown area of Skegness, sitting on the edge of his unmade bed, Michael Jolly struck a match and lit the cigarette in his mouth, drawing the smoke deep into his lungs before blowing it slowly out.

A husky voice behind him snapped, 'I hope you're sitting there planning a way to make us some money as I'm telling yer for the last time, I ain't subbing you any longer. Apart from what you already owe me, the rent's due Friday and if you don't cough up your share this time, I mean it, yer out.'

He turned his head and looked scathingly at the hard-faced woman, ten years older than he was, lying sprawled behind him, naked except for a shabby underskirt. One of the straps had slipped down, exposing a large breast which she made no attempt to cover. They had just finished having rampant sex but if Michael never saw her again it wouldn't bother him in the slightest. To him she was a dirty slut. He was only using her and would leave as soon as he found something better. When he came into his inheritance, she would be old history.

He took another drag on his cigarette as he cast a look around the room; at the faded wallpaper peeling away in places through rising damp; at the several traps set by holes in the skirting board to catch the steady army of mice that came out in search of food. He shuddered in the cold draught that seeped in under the ill-fitting door and through the rotting window frames. A blinding anger rose within him as he surveyed the shabby furniture. As the only son of a wealthy man he shouldn't be living one step up from the gutter, ducking and diving for every penny, but in comfort. He should be mixing with his own sort not the scum he lived with. He should have a roll of notes in his pocket to spend as he liked, and more to fill it when it was empty.

He blamed his parents for his situation. What type of people threw their only son into the street, without a bean to his name, just because he did things they didn't agree with? The money he had helped himself to was going to be his one day anyway, so what was their problem? If they had cared one iota for him he wouldn't have had to resort to taking it off them as they would have given it to him, like other well-off fathers and mothers did. Did his parents not realise how humiliating it had been for him, being made to work with common council-estate lowlifes, only being given the same pittance a week that they received, being given all the dirty jobs to do and mocked behind his back? The campers had all thought he was just another worker and he'd never been given the respect he deserved as the son of the owner. His father should have given him a place by his side. But Michael would get his own back on them, when he got his hands on his inheritance and led the life he deserved to have.

That was the only reason he stayed in this godforsaken hole of a place – so that he was on the spot to claim his inheritance immediately the time came. His father was a respected member of the comunity in Mablethorpe and surrounding villages, providing jobs for the locals and contributing to the local economy via the goods and services he bought from firms in the vicinity. Any news of him, either good or bad, would be reported in the local newspapers. That was the way Michael had found out about his father's stroke, and hopefully would soon hear of his death.

Turning to look at the woman, he snarled at her, 'Lay off,

will you, Gloria? How many times do I have to tell you that you'll get the fucking money for the rent, and the rest I owe you.'

She gave a disparaging snort. 'Yeah, well, if this promise is as good as all the others you've made me, I won't hold me breath.' She raised herself up on the grubby pillow, reaching over to the small table at the side of the bed for a packet of Woodbine cigarettes and a box of matches. Extracting a cigarette, she lit it and blew out smoke, then gave a hacking cough before drawing on it again. Lying back on her pillow, she looked at the spotty, hairy back of the flabby, unattractive man she'd met in a back-street pub five months ago. He'd been homeless at the time, having just been thrown out by his previous squeeze. Her face screwed up in a look of disdain. For all Gloria's worldly wisdom, gained through years of selling her body for money, Michael Jolly had still managed to fool her into believing his tale that one day he'd be rich as the only son of the owner of Jolly's Holiday Camp further up the coast. He'd insisted that day was not far away as his father was in poor health, having just suffered a major stroke. It was only a matter of time before another finished him off, and if Gloria stuck by him now he would handsomely repay her with marriage, a big house to live in, plus a daily to do for her, money no object.

The lure of a way out of the hell of a life she led was all that had kept her going along with Michael, as nothing else about him appealed to her. As time had passed, though, and there'd been no sign of these supposed riches materialising, she was beginning to think that he was just taking her for a mug. She was finding herself faced with a dilemma. She could tell him to sling his hook before he fleeced her out of any more money, free herself to find someone else to bankroll her instead of the other way around, but then what if his future did turn out well and she missed out on a chance to vastly improve her lot, through not sticking with him a while longer? She thought about this for a moment and decided to put up with him for another few weeks. If nothing had changed for the better by then, Michael Jolly was past history as far as she was concerned.

Gloria had no idea that Michael was making enough to pay his share of the rent and food, even sometimes for a few drinks each down the local, but as the selfish man he was he chose to keep what he made for himself, only giving her a few shillings when it could not be avoided.

Michael wasn't stupid and only targeted the vulnerable, children and old folks. They couldn't take out their anger on him, and the threat of one of his meaty fists was enough to put the fear of God in them should they threaten to expose him.

At the moment he had no money for cigarettes or beer, and this was not a good time for him to try to coax some out of Gloria. As he stabbed out his last cigarette into the overflowing ashtray on the bedside table he thought it was time to pay one of his old dears a visit. He hadn't seen Mrs Frazer for a couple of weeks. By now she would have a few bob tucked away from her pension and her job minding neighbours' children. Having already helped himself to all her half-decent china and trinkets when he'd last been there and had sent her off into the kitchen to make him a cup of tea, he'd slipped up to her bedroom and helped himself to her dead husband's war medals, which had brought him in a nice few quid from the pawn. That had kept him going for the last two weeks. He'd also noticed a collection of silver and gold cufflinks gathering dust in a dish on her dressing table. He would have taken them as well but had thought he'd heard someone knocking on the old lady's door and hurried back down so as to appear like just another visitor who'd popped in to check on the old lady. After he'd paid a visit to Mrs Frazer today, he might go on and see if there were any visitors on the prom to fleece with his betting tricks. After that he'd spend the rest of today in the pub, drinking away his ill-gotten gains.

A while later, dressed for the off, telling Gloria that he was going to try to make some money to pay the rent, he went out, heading straight for Mrs Frazer's house where he let himself in through her back door.

He found her sitting in her well-worn armchair by the fire, having a doze. When he roughly shook her awake, she stared at him sleep-fuddled for several moments through rheumy eyes. Normally the old woman wouldn't be at all pleased to see Michael for obvious reasons, but much to his surprise she appeared glad to see him now, telling him as she struggled out of her chair that she would make him a cup of tea. While she was busy he would be checking her purse and looking round for anything of value he'd not yet come across.

Wishing the other half-dozen lonely souls he regularly visited made him feel so welcome, he went straight up the stairs to take another look at the cufflinks, hoping they were worth as much as his quick glance before had indicated. He was miffed to find they weren't. Only gold- and silver-plated, not solid. Still, better than nothing. Putting the six pairs in his pocket, he decided to have a look through the old dear's dressing-table drawers. He found a jewellery box but it yielded nothing of great value. Regardless he pocketed a cheap cameo brooch and a silver pendant. Hopefully what she had in her purse, added to what was in his pocket, would still make his visit worthwhile.

Going back down the stairs he arrived in the back room ready to look in her handbag when, to his utter shock, sitting comfortably in the shabby chair opposite Mrs Frazer, drinking a cup of tea, he saw a middle-aged man, smartly dressed in an expensive blue-and-white pinstripe double-breasted suit and black shirt and tie, with handmade black shoes on his feet. Every finger on both hands sported a big solid gold ring, some plain, some ornate with large gems set in them.

Michael immediately recognised the man but only knew him by his nickname of Cut Throat Charlie. He was the owner of a slot-machine arcade on the sea front. Rumour was, though, that the arcade was just a legitimate cover for his very profitable illicit sidelines of fencing stolen goods and money laundering for the local criminal fraternity. Allegedly, he had earned his nickname as a youth when in a temper he had slit another man's throat with a penknife for taking a more than passing interest in Charlie's then girlfriend, only escaping a murder charge when the police couldn't break the alibi other 'friends' gave him, after threats that if they didn't he would do the same to them. Michael was aware he would make himself a much better living offering his services to men like Charlie, but a term in jail held no appeal for him and neither did ending up maimed or dead in a back alley should anything go wrong on a job. He hadn't a clue what had brought a man like this into Mrs Frazer's back room and, as a coward, he wasn't about to wait around to find out.

He addressed Mrs Frazer. 'Well, I've . . . er . . . checked that little problem you asked me to look at and I'll come back with my toolbox to fix it for you as soon as I can. I'll be off then and leave you to entertain your visitor.'

He made to head off for the back door but the newcomer stopped him, saying, 'No need to leave on my account. Stay and have a cup of tea. Any friend of this dear lady is a friend of mine.'

Michael made an excuse and turned to go, nearly jumping out of his skin when a firm hand gripped his shoulder and he spun his head to see that a mean-looking bear of a man had stepped out of the kitchen and was looking at him in a way that told him if he had been asked to sit down and have a cup of tea, it was in his own best interests to do so. Michael was a big man himself but the heavy dwarfed him in all ways. He immediately perched himself on the edge of the sofa, all his instincts screaming at him that Charlie wasn't here to visit Mrs Frazer. It was Michael himself he'd come to see. His thoughts whirled frantically. But what could a man like him, who dealt with hardened criminals not petty ones, want to see him about? And how had he known Michael was here? Had Charlie had him followed? There was no way of knowing, he concluded fearfully. Accepting the cup of tea Mrs Frazer handed him and politely thanking her, he fought to stop his hands from shaking and rattling the cup in the saucer, trying to hide the fact that he was terrified.

Charlie took a sip of his tea, rested the cup back in its saucer, smiled over at Michael and said to him, 'It's nice to meet you at long last. I've heard quite a bit about you. How helpful you are to old people in particular.' His eyes narrowed. 'Though it's not them you're helping, is it? You're helping yourself to whatever they have that's worth something.' His smile faded and his eyes darkened thunderously. 'Well, you fucking lowlife, no one steals off my mother and gets away with it.'

Michael froze rigid, his face turning ashen, as the significance of what Charlie had just said hit him like a thunderbolt. It was several long moments before he uttered, '*Mother!* Mrs . . . Mrs Frazer is your mother? But . . . but she told me she hasn't any living relatives.'

Charlie gave him a look as though he was stupid, and picked an invisible speck of dust off his own lapel. 'You should never believe everything old ladies tell you. Mother has denied my existence for years because she doesn't approve of the way I earn my living. I've tried to persuade her to leave this slum of a place for a house I'll buy her with all mod cons, but she's a stubborn old bugger and won't hear of it. Insists she doesn't want to risk eternity in purgatory for enjoying the proceeds of crime. I never would have known what you were doing to her in the normal course of events – and not because she was afraid for your safety, she thinks you'll deserve all you get. But she can't bear the thought of me doing time in jail for sorting out a toe rag like you. Mother might not approve of what I do, but I'm still her son and she loves me.

'But, you see, even people with strong beliefs like Mother has have to climb down off their high horse in certain circumstances and resort to doing things they otherwise wouldn't dream of. That time came for Mother when you helped yourself to my father's war medals. He risked his life for king and country earning them, in fact he lost a leg for his trouble, and Mother treasured them more than anything, like I was going to when they passed down to me. When my mother went to polish them, as she did every week on a Sunday morning, and found them gone it broke her heart. That's when she finally came to tell me what was going on.'

Eyes blinking wildly, Michael was gazing at him in terror, not daring to think just what Charlie had in mind by way of retribution. In desperation, he blurted out, 'I'll . . . I'll get the medals back for you, I promise.'

Charlie smiled and shook his head. 'Too late, I've already done that.' He eyed his henchman, saying, 'Get him out of my sight. Make sure that afterwards you empty his pockets of whatever he's taken from Mother this time. Oh, and I don't need to tell you not to leave any incriminating evidence behind when you've finished.'

Before Michael could move a muscle he was grabbed by the scruff of his neck and hauled upright. As he was roughly manhandled towards the kitchen door he knew without a doubt that it was most unlikely he was going to be alive to see another dawn. Frenziedly trying to free himself, he screamed out, 'Please, I beg you! I'll do anything you ask . . . anything. Just please, don't hurt me.' They were at the back door by now and, having received no response, Michael knew that if he didn't come up with a bribe tempting enough to reverse Charlie's decision, and damned quick, then it was all over for him. He had been bodily dragged to the back door before he realised what might sway the man. 'Money!' he cried out. 'I can get you plenty. My father's a rich man. He's the owner of Jolly's Holiday Camp.'

Several long seconds passed and Michael had been dragged halfway down the yard before, much to his relief, a shout was heard from inside. 'Hold on. Bring him back in.'

Seconds later he was unceremoniously dumped back on the sofa.

Charlie looked at him for a moment before he snarled harshly,

'If you're lying to me, you'll suffer more pain than you ever imagined possible before you're put out of your misery. You understand?'

'I'm not lying . . . I'm not!' Michael shot back at him hysterically. 'My father is who I say he is. We just don't see eye to eye so we're estranged at the moment.'

Charlie thought about this then nodded slowly. 'All right, five thousand in cash and we'll call it quits.'

Michael gasped. How much! He doubted the safe would carry that amount in cash at any one time. He daren't tell Charlie that, though. Instead he stammered that Friday night was the best time to empty the safe as Saturday morning was when the weekly banking was done, praying that routine hadn't changed.

Telling Michael that he'd better not even think of doing a runner, Charlie arranged for him to bring the cash to the arcade on Friday night after the job was done. If he told the man behind the change counter he was expected, he'd be directed to the office where Charlie would be waiting for him.

The henchman then grabbed Michael by the scuff of his neck, dragged him to the back door and threw him out bodily. He landed heavily on the hard paving. Scrambling up painfully, Michael raced off as fast as his legs would carry him.

CHAPTER TWENTY-SIX

That evening Joe Jolly stood naked in front of his full-length dressing mirror surveying his reflection. No one could deny he was still a good-looking man. While most men in their fifties were beginning to acquire a paunch and sagging skin, he was still as lithe and firm as a man half his age, with well-defined muscles which he'd never hesitated to show off in all their glory to any good-looking woman who took his fancy.

When he had first been informed that he'd suffered a stroke, and that it was far too early to tell whether he would regain the use of the left side of his body or be able to speak properly again, he had been absolutely devastated. As far as he was concerned losing his faculties would be the worst possible thing that could ever happen to him, far worse than the business failing and going back to living the way he was before he'd improved his lot through marriage to Drina. The thought of no longer being the object of women's desires, but of their pity instead, was not an option he'd consider. With steely determination along with the skills of the best physiotherapists he could find, after a lot of pain and frustration he had managed to walk out of the home – albeit with a slight limp, but he could live with that – not be wheeled out in a chair, dribbling down his chin. He was ready to pick up his life where he'd left off.

It was a damned good life too, one that a man of his lowly origins could never have expected to have himself. He'd been just a fairground lackey, working for his uncle for a pittance, operating his four rides up and down the country, when word had reached him through the gypsy community that a distant cousin of his dead father had died a wealthy man. His eighteen-year-old daughter had now inherited the money. Joe immediately saw a chance to better his lot. When he set his mind to it, no woman was safe. He would sweep the girl off her feet, marry her, then what she had would be his. Simple. It did, though, mean that he was faced with making a huge personal sacrifice, but by using his persuasive charms on the other party involved, saying that what he proposed to do would benefit them both, he was given their blessing, albeit not without tears being shed.

He did not feel at all guilty for using Drina to better himself. He might not love her, and had to force himself to do his marital duty towards her often enough to prevent her becoming suspicious that he was seeking sexual gratification elsewhere, but otherwise he felt he'd been a good husband to her. He'd never kept her short of money, had allowed her free rein in their home, took her along to all the big functions that wives were invited to – and she in turn had got herself the kind of husband a homely, dumpy, unremarkable-looking woman like her would never normally expect to have. He couldn't fault her as a wife. She didn't nag, kept their home smart, was an excellent cook and a good hostess when he entertained friends at lunches and dinner parties. She'd been a good mother to their son . . . albeit Michael was far from a child either of them could be proud of, just a thoroughly bad lot. She had never quizzed Joe when he'd told her he'd be home for dinner then got a better offer and didn't arrive back until the early hours of the morning. Over the years he had actually grown quite fond of her. For a man like him, Drina was the perfect wife.

She had, though, both surprised and shocked him today when he had taken a look at the books to see how the company had fared during his absence, fully expecting to find Drina had just about managed to keep it ticking over due to her lack of experience, and that there would be many mistakes to rectify. Instead he had found takings in the shops and bars up, and that she had initiated a very lucrative new source of revenue by opening Groovy's. He could kick himself for not coming up with the idea himself. Of course the youngsters needed a place of their own in which to let their hair down away from the watchful eyes of their parents. It had taken his inexperienced wife to come up with it. He wouldn't dream of praising her for the upturn in business, though, for fear that she could then have a good argument to justify working at the camp for good, putting a stop to him carrying on as he pleased there. He wasn't going to risk that.

Now all he needed to do was to get Fiona back on board. Apart from the woman who had been the great love of his life, out of all the others he'd had affairs with over the years, Fiona was his ideal match. That was why she had lasted so long. She was not only very good-looking with a shapely figure, and enjoyed sex as much as he did, she was an independent woman who enjoyed living on her own in the flat in Mablethorpe overlooking the sea that he had bought her. With only herself to consider, marriage and children were of no interest to her. She had never made any demands on him to leave his wife, unlike other women with whom he had had dalliances. He knew she had tried to visit him in hospital and at the convalescent home but his male pride had precluded anyone seeing him in a vulnerable state so she had been refused admission. She had written to him regularly, though, and that was how Joe had learned of his son's rampage into the office a couple of days after his stroke, and Michael's subsequent humiliating dismissal of Fiona. She said she had taken a job temporarily with a firm in Skegness so as to pay her way and was patiently waiting for Joe to recover so that he could reinstate her in the job at the camp and they could resume their relationship. She couldn't wait to make up for lost time with him, she'd said. He couldn't wait either. He would stay late at the office and telephone her at her flat tomorrow evening, to tell her the good news.

He heard Drina call to say that dinner was ready. Taking another look at himself in the mirror and smiling conceitedly at the near-perfect specimen of manhood that looked back at him, he pulled on his clothes and went down to enjoy his meal.

A while later Drina was sitting at the long dining table opposite her husband. They were eating in silence, apart from a cursory word or two such as when Joe asked her to pass him the mint sauce. Drina hated eating in silence. To her mealtimes should be opportunities to share the events of the day. In her case there wasn't much to discuss, but she was very keen to hear of the latest goings on at the camp. Joe, though, preferred to concentrate on eating, so that's how it was.

Despite fighting with herself not to, knowing she was only causing herself more grief than she was already feeling over the ending of her relationship with Artie, Drina could not help but wonder what it would be like to be eating with him instead of with her husband. They wouldn't be in virtual silence now, that she did know, as Artie and she had always liked chatting amicably away over nothing in particular and laughing at each other's jokey comments. She knew he'd sincerely thank her for her culinary efforts too, unlike the cursory 'That was nice, dear' she knew Joe would give her when he'd finished. And neither would she be wondering whether Artie would be spending the evening with her whereas with Joe there was usually some excuse to go out, usually that he was needed back at the camp, when she knew very well he was going to visit his mistress. He'd not return until long after she'd retired to bed, creeping in so as not to wake her and risk her questioning the lateness of the hour, which she had in fact long ago stopped doing when she had realised what he was really up to. She wondered how long it would take him to get Fiona Hickson back on board or whether he would be looking around for someone new. She wondered too if Artie had heard the news of her husband's return, and if he had how he was feeling. If he was as upset as she was then she felt sorry for him. Although it would cause her deep distress to hear of it, she did sincerely hope he found a woman who was free to offer him the kind of life that a lovely man like him deserved, far removed from the miserable one Drina herself was stuck in.

Over in the cottage, Rhonnie was standing at the cooker stirring gravy to go with the liver, fried onions, mashed potatoes and tinned peas she had prepared ready for when Dan got home any time now, unless a critical maintenance problem occurred to keep him back in which case she would keep it hot for him. It would have been a bonus for them to travel back and forth to work together on Dan's motor bike but as his shift ran from six until six, and hers eight until five-thirty, it wasn't practical. At the moment she was walking the mile or so to and from work, which she rather enjoyed. Whether she would as much in winter was another matter.

Tonight she had cooked the meal automatically as all her thoughts were centred on Joe Jolly's return and its possible repercussions for her. She unaware of Dan arriving home until he called out, 'Have you got enough to feed a waif and stray I came across on the road home, sweetheart?'

She jumped and spun around, smiling happily to know that Dan was home and even more broadly to see that the waif and stray he was referring to was in fact her father. 'Of course I have,' she told them, even though there wasn't really enough. But she was more than willing for Artie to have the majority of her portion as her healthy appetite had deserted her after today's developments.

Artie said, 'I don't want to impose. You two are only just married, love. I was taking a walk when Dan came across me and insisted he brought me to see you.'

Just as Artie had been hoping would happen, she thought. Judging by his downcast expression he'd obviously heard the rumour about Joe Jolly and was anxious to find out whether it was true or not. She shook her head at him. 'You're not imposing at all, Dad. I'm glad to see you. I miss having a catch up with you at breakfast and in the restaurant at the end of the day. We've already asked you to come and live with us, and if that doesn't tell you how welcome you are then nothing will.' Setting another place at the table, she told them both to sit down as she was about to dish up. Then, conscious that it wasn't fair of her to be keeping information from her father when he was desperate to hear it, she said, 'I suppose you've both heard that Mr Jolly is back?'

Artie's face sagged with disappointment. 'So it's no rumour then?' he couldn't help but say.

She shook her head. 'No, it's not.'

Dan looked stunned to hear this. He took the top off two bottles of beer from the pantry, handing Artie one before he sat down at the table. 'I hadn't heard, but then I've been working all day down by the beach, fixing some holes in the fence around the funfair.' He wanted to express his relief that the man he held in such high esteem, and would for ever be indebted to for taking him under his wing and equipping him with the skills to provide a good living for himself, had recovered from his potentially life-threatening stroke. But he realised that what was good news for him wasn't necessarily so for his father-in-law or his wife, for their own individual reasons, so thought it best to keep his feelings on the matter to himself.

Rhonnie was watching her father pushing his food around distractedly. Her heart went out to him. Careful not to tell him I told you so, she said, 'I'm sorry, Dad.'

He lifted his head and looked at her in bewilderment. 'What are you sorry for, love?'

'Well . . . the fact that now Mr Jolly is back, your friendship with Mrs Jolly can't very well continue, can it? You both enjoyed each other's company, I know, and you'll miss her. I suspect she'll miss you too.'

His daughter was no fool. Artie knew she was well aware that despite his denials Drina Jolly had come to mean a lot to him. He would even go so far as to admit, but only to himself, that he had fallen in love with her. Rhonnie had tried to warn him that he was heading for trouble but he had chosen to ignore her, just wanted to enjoy the time he spent with Drina and not let what might happen in the future cloud that. Had he known just how devastated he would feel, he might have paid more heed to his daughter's warning.

Wanting to get off this subject, he pushed away his plate. Patting his stomach, he told Rhonnie, 'That was lovely. You're as good a cook as your mother was, God rest her soul.'

She couldn't blame her father for not wanting to pursue a topic that was painful to him. She stood up and collected the plates together just as the front door knocker resounded. As she was already standing, she told Dan that she would answer it. Most people were having their dinner at this hour, but maybe it was a neighbour from the row of terraced houses nearby. Rhonnie was surprised instead to find that the caller was Ginger. Her smile of welcome to her friend quickly evaporated when she saw the girl's tear-streaked face and realised she was in search of a shoulder to cry on.

Pulling Ginger inside and shutting the door against the cold night, Rhonnie demanded, 'What's happened?'

She blubbered, 'My boyfriend has dumped me for Geraldine Thomas. It was out of the blue. I found out he'd been seeing her behind my back for the last week. I really liked him, Rhonnie. I thought he was the one!'

She pulled the other girl inside and told her, 'Go and sit down at the table and I'll get you a cuppa, then you can tell me all about it.'

It seemed that her and Dan's night was going to be spent consoling two people whose lives had been turned upside down today through the actions of another. Little did Rhonnie know that before long she herself would need a shoulder to cry on.

CHAPTER TWENTY-SEVEN

Joe Jolly had been back at the helm for four days, and these had been four days of misery for Rhonnie and Jackie. They were not the only ones who did not welcome his return. The staff in general were showing signs of discontent. They did not appreciate Joe's vastly different style of management now they'd had a taster of his wife's. Drina wouldn't have expected anyone to drop what they were doing immediately, no matter how critical the task was, to attend to something she wanted doing. Nor was she intolerant of the slightest mistake on an employee's part, which in Joe's case could easily be down to his own poor communication when giving them the job in the first place. He felt that any talking that was not work-related meant no work was being done, so conversation between the staff was forbidden; she would never dismiss out of hand any employee's suggestion as to how to better the camp or their working conditions, but Joe saw it as insubordination when any member of staff queried the way he had ordained that things should be done. And Drina certainly didn't demand that every employee at all times show respect for their boss and the owner of the company.

Since Joe's return the atmosphere in the office had become subdued and watchful as opposed to the jovial, light-hearted hive of activity it had been under Drina. Jackie didn't at all appreciate going back to being treated like a naïve junior member of staff again by her boss, and Rhonnie was finding it very hard being treated so formally by him. Joe would only share with her what she needed to know to do her job, unlike his wife who'd involved Rhonnie in everything, in her easygoing way. Their taking turns to tour the camp on a daily basis had come to an abrupt halt as any checking on the camp was done by Joe himself, who gave them both the distinct impression he didn't trust their judgement. Tea was drunk at set times only, eleven in the morning and three in the afternoon. The time dragged by.

At the moment Joe Jolly was alone in his office with the door shut. From the bursts of laughter filtering through, Rhonnie suspecting he was making calls to his business associates informing them he was back in fine fettle and ready to join in with the usual social activities, such as rounds of golf and business lunches.

Having just finished putting a call through to Reception for them to take a message for a camper, Jackie heaved a deep fed-up sigh, looked across at Rhonnie and whispered, 'God, it's only ten-thirty and I feel like I've been here all day.'

The time was dragging for Rhonnie too. It wouldn't have been so bad had they been at liberty to chat while they worked. She was typing a pile of letters to campers confirming their bookings for next year. Since Joe's return work seemed like drudgery rather than a pleasure. He'd made it plain he thought her incapable of doing anything other than taking down a letter in shorthand and typing it out, plus clerical tasks like this that anyone with half a brain could deal with. He was certainly a very egotistical and self-important man.

Jackie was saying to her now, 'I wonder how Mrs Jolly is? She enjoyed working with us here. I bet she's feeling very lonely back at home, just being a housewife again.'

Rhonnie had wondered the same thing many times over the last four days. She responded, 'Well, I expect she's busy catching up with all her friends and enjoying her freedom to visit them or to put her feet up in the afternoon. Now, best get back to work in case Mr Jolly suddenly comes out of his office and catches us chatting.'

Jackie thought this was as good a time as any to tell Rhonnie what was on her mind. 'I saw a job advertised in the local paper last night. It's for a clerk typist in the back office of a furniture shop in Mablethorpe. I'm thinking of applying for it. It's a pity they don't want an office manager too or we could have applied together, couldn't we?'

Rhonnie looked at her sharply. The possibility of Jackie leaving had crossed her mind, but if the other girl went then she really didn't think she would be able to stand working here by herself 'Yes, it is a pity. I do . . .'

She was interrupted by the door to the stairs opening. To their shock they saw that the visitor was Fiona Hickson.

Looking extremely smart in a navy blue fitted jacket and pencil skirt which hugged her shapely hips, and with a broad smile on her face, she said breezily, 'Good morning, girls.' She made straight for Rhonnie's desk. 'Thank you so much for keeping the office ticking over during my absence,' she said. 'I shall be starting back here first thing Monday morning. Whatever you haven't been able to finish off by Sunday evening . . . I trust you will be working Sunday unless it's your day off this week? . . . leave it in a current pile with a note attached informing me where you've got to. I shall make sure a suitable reference is posted off to you. Mr Jolly in his office?'

Reeling from this news, Rhonnie mutely nodded. Then, finding her voice, she started to rise, saying, 'I'll inform Mr Jolly you're here, Miss Hickson.'

She smiled. 'He is expecting me. I don't need announcing.'

Rhonnie made to remind Fiona Hickson that Mr Jolly was emphatic that no one should enter his office unannounced when instinct suddenly told her that Mr Jolly and Miss Hickson were not just boss and office manager, but far more than that. They had been very discreet about it as she had never heard a word of gossip from any of the staff, not even a hint that they suspected the boss and his secretary of fooling around with each other during her time here. There'd been no such remark from the usually astute Jackie. Now Rhonnie realised that no matter how good a job she was doing, even if she was better at it than Miss Hickson, she was never going to be kept on once Mr Jolly returned. But at the moment her thoughts weren't for herself, but for Drina Jolly. How could Mr Jolly be cheating on such a lovely wife? She just hoped that Mrs Jolly never found out, and was spared the pain this knowledge would cause her.

As Fiona Hickson marched purposefully over to the boss's office she ordered Jackie, 'Tea, Miss Sims. Earl Grey for Mr Jolly, English Breakfast for me.' As though Jackie hadn't made it enough times before not to have it imprinted in her mind.

As soon as she had entered the office and closed the door firmly behind her, Jackie told Rhonnie decisively, 'That's it, I'm definitely applying for that job now. I can't go back to the way things were after working for you and Mrs Jolly.'

Rhonnie heaved a deep sigh. She hadn't mentioned to Dan her growing discontent with her job since Mr Jolly's return to the office because she knew he hero-worshipped the man and felt he owed him a debt of gratitude for what Joe had done for him and his mother when she had been alive. Rhonnie couldn't tell him either of her suspicions that the man he set such great store by was having an affair behind his wife's back.

That night she just told him that she had lost her job because Miss Hickson had been reinstated. Dan was mortally sorry for his wife, believing that she'd loved the job just as much under Joe Jolly as she had under Drina, but he told her he supposed this situation had always been on the cards. She'd get something else, he assured her, something she'd love just as much. Though maybe she didn't need to? He was quite happy to support her should she decide to stay at home, and they could think about starting a family. But Rhonnie wasn't ready to be a mother yet. She wanted to have more time with Dan first before they took on the role of parents so she meant to start looking for a new job first thing on Monday. She sadly doubted, though, that whatever job was offered her would be half as much fun as working for Mrs Jolly had been.

CHAPTER TWENTY-EIGHT

On Friday evening at just coming up to seven Joe Jolly replaced the receiver in its cradle after a conversation with Fiona. Well over an hour it had lasted, and by now the darkness had closed in. He was too busy thinking, though, to reach over and switch his desk lamp on. He was deeply regretting asking Drina to arrange a dinner party for this evening to celebrate his homecoming as he would far sooner have enjoyed a night in bed with Fiona. But then, he only had to wait until tomorrow night. Still, it was seven months now since he'd had sex, which for a man with his sexual appetite was seven months too long. For him to contain his need for another twenty-four hours would be impossible. It seemed he had no choice but to give Drina a treat tonight. When he was in dire need of sexual gratification, it wasn't important to him who satisfied it.

He swivelled around in his chair so that it faced the window, rested his feet on the sill, leaned his head against the back of his chair and gazed out into the night. From this position he couldn't see campers making their way towards the entertainment facilities but he could hear their excited voices. He smiled to himself. There had been times over the last few months when he had despaired of ever getting his life back on track, but now here he was, fully restored but for a slight limp. He could live with that. Life was great, he thought. He should really be setting off for home to get ready to receive his guests, but without warning tiredness overwhelmed him and he fell asleep.

From out of the hairdresser's unlit doorway a black-clad figure emerged, balaclava pulled down to hide his face. He was carrying a small black holdall. He stole across to Reception, swiftly unlocking the door with the aid of his well-used picklock, and slipped inside, shutting the door behind him. Michael paused for a moment, taking a deep breath to calm his jangling nerves. The first part of his plan had succeeded. Now he just had to hope the rest of it passed without mishap. He couldn't fail in this task. Cut Throat Charlie had not been uttering idle threats, he knew.

He deftly opened the door to the stairs and made his way up them. There was no light on in the office so he knew no one was in there, but all the same he paused at the door at the top of the stairs and put his ear against it, to satisfy himself there was no movement inside. Hearing nothing, he opened the door and stepped into the general office. He immediately made his way over to the secretary's desk, knelt down, opened the bottom drawer with his picklock, took out the metal cash box, prayed the safe key was still kept inside it and not now hidden somewhere else, and prised it open with the aid of a penknife. To his tremendous relief, under the petty cash which he pocketed, there was the safe key. That in hand, he got up and went over to his father's office. He let himself inside, going immediately to the safe and kneeling down before it to insert the key in the lock. He prayed it held what he was after or else he would have no choice but to forge a cheque in his father's name and beg Charlie to wait until he could cash it on Monday as soon as the banks opened and hope it wasn't noticed.

Joe woke with a start, just in time to hear the scraping of a key in a lock along with the click of it releasing. Spinning his chair around, only a foot or so away from him he saw a shadowy figure dressed all in black, face hidden under a balaclava, crouched before the safe, pulling open the door. Outrage flooded through him. Before he could stop himself Joe furiously exclaimed, 'What the hell . . .'

At the sound of his father's voice, a startled Michael jumped up to pull a crowbar out of his jacket. He had brought it with him in case he couldn't get his picklock to work and had to jemmy the office door open instead. He brandished it in a threatening manner at his father, growling in an attempt to disguise his voice, 'Don't dare move . . . I'm not afraid to use this.' Backing away from the safe a little, he ordered, 'Now get over here. Pass me the cash and you won't get hurt.'

Joe didn't need to hear the intruder's voice to know his identity. He would recognise his own son anywhere, no matter how he tried to disguise his voice. Temper rising, he snarled, 'Still up to your old tricks, I see, Michael. Well, this time I'm not going to turn a blind eye. I'm reporting you to the police. Let's hope a spell in jail will make you realise the error of your ways. Robbing anyone is bad enough, but your own family . . . You disgust me. I'm ashamed to admit that you're my son.'

Joe reached over for the telephone but, frantic to stop him, Michael whacked the crowbar hard down on it, badly cracking the Bakelite receiver. 'Next time it'll be your head,' he warned.

Through the slits in his balaclava, Michael glared with pure hatred at the man who had fathered him. The prospect of a jail sentence, closeted with hardened criminals for whom he would be no match, was unthinkable, and Charlie had made it clear to him that if he welshed in any way on their deal he wouldn't be safe from retaliation anywhere he chose to hide. Charlie's reach was long, he had been warned, and Michael didn't doubt it at all. But above even these fears his father's words had struck a nerve with him. Incensed, he shouted back, 'So you didn't rob your own family then, to get where you are today? What a hypocrite you are, Father. You married Mother just to get your hands on her inheritance, and if that's not stealing off your own family then I don't know what is. Fine example you've set me. If you can do it, so can I.'

Joe stared at him. He had never told anyone it was his wife's inheritance that had given him the means to start his business. 'Who's been spreading such a malicious rumour? I want to know. Tell me now.'

Still brandishing the crowbar warningly at him, Michael issued a scathing laugh. 'I've never heard anyone talk about it, Father. You are a master at keeping your private life secret from others, I'll give you that. I found out for myself.

'It was the school holidays. I'd sneaked off down the prom while Mother had gone to the shop in Threddlethorpe and left me mowing the grass. As soon as she walked through the gate I was off. I was showing some of my tricks to a group of kids when I saw coppers heading my way, so I scarpered quick and decided it was best I come home. Mother had obviously returned from the shops while I was gone as the bags were on the kitchen table. She must have found me gone, thought I was up at the camp and gone there to drag me back.

'Thanks to the cops I'd lost out on earning myself some money so I decided to have a rummage around in your bedroom, to see if I could compensate myself. In one of Mother's dressing-table drawers I found a wooden box and in it some papers: my birth certificate, Grandfather's death certificate, a few other bits, but also a letter from a bloke called Ackers who had sold my grandfather his land and presumably a load of money. It had never crossed my mind before how you got the land and enough cash to start the camp. That made it clear to me. Mother had inherited from her father when he died. That was how you got your hands on it when you married her. Why would a man like you marry a woman like my mother unless she had something you badly wanted? I mean, she's far from your usual type, isn't she? It doesn't take a genuis to work that out.'

His eyes darkened maliciously. 'Does Mother know the truth of why you married her or have you managed to keep her convinced all these years that it was for love? I wonder what she'd say if I told her about all the affairs you've had over the years? You might have thought you'd been clever enough to hide what you were up to, but I know about them all, Father. I've lost count of the number of times I followed you as a kid to a meeting with one of your *ladies*, in what you thought was a secluded place. You had no idea anyone was spying on you, let alone your own son, did you?'

Joe's face was dark as thunder. He snarled, 'You always were a sneaky kid.'

'Well, look on it as the only way I got to spend time with you. You never showed any interest in me, but you made time to spend with that cleaning woman's son, didn't you?'

Joe roared, 'That's because, unlike you, Dan badgered me to give him a job so that he could earn some pocket money. If you'd showed even just a hint of the pride he took in any task I gave him, then you would be helping me run this place now. But being the bone-idle type that you are, you found easier ways to make yourself money, didn't you? Like conning other kids out of their pocket money. I have no doubt that's how you survive now, by conning people or outright robbing them.'

They both jumped and stared at the telephone as it shrilled out. Joe automatically went to pick up the receiver but Michael stopped him by banging the crowbar down on top of it again, just missing his father's hand which he quickly withdrew.

'Leave it,' Michael spat at him. 'It'll only be that bitch Hickson wanting to know when she's next going to see you. I take it you're still shagging her? To my knowledge she's lasted much longer than any of your other floozies. She must have something the others hadn't got. Or is it because you're losing your touch, Father? Worried that if you get rid of her you won't get anyone else? After all, you're not getting any younger, are you, old man. She lives in a flat in Mablethorpe, doesn't she? Nice place it looks. A bit pricey, I'd say, for a secretary to afford. But then, she didn't buy it, did she? You did.

'When I worked in the accounts department I liked to have a snoop around. I found out the company owned a flat in

Mablethorpe which just happened to have the same address as the one I've seen you going into upteen times . . . the one where that bitch just happens to live. I can't tell you how much pleasure I got from having her marched off these premises with no by your leave when I paid a visit here after you first took ill. Telling her what a filthy tramp she was, carrying on with a man she knew was married. I couldn't give a damn what you got up to, of course. Didn't give a damn about Mother either after she stood by and did nothing when you threw me out. No, I did it for the sheer fun of it.'

Joe snarled at him, 'That call would have been from your mother, wondering where I am. We're having a dinner party and I'm late. I wouldn't be surprised if she sent security up to check when she got no reply. If I were you I'd . . .'

Michael cut in, 'Think I'm stupid, don't you, Father? As you didn't answer the telephone she'll automatically think you're on your way home. Now you listen to me. I can tell Mother all about your dirty little secrets and give her a few names so she can check I'm telling the truth . . . or I can keep my mouth shut, if you hand me the money from the safe and say nothing about it. What's it to be?'

Joe was staring at his son stupefied. If his own indiscretions came to his wife's notice and she had them confirmed – since after all some of his women hadn't been at all happy when he'd decided he was bored and had ended matters with them – then she'd have more than enough grounds for divorce. It could end up with the sale of the business and Joe losing all he'd worked hard for. He'd be too old to start again with what his share of the settlement would be after all outstanding loans on the business had been paid, and he'd not a hope of ever achieving anything comparable again plus the status that being owner of Jolly's brought with it. And there was the fact that if all this became common knowledge then his friends and business associates would drop him like a ton of bricks at their own wives' insistence, as they'd be bound to sympathise with Drina.

And he couldn't expect a woman like Fiona to stand by him, not when she was turfed out of the flat they called their 'love nest', when it was discovered by lawyers that he'd bought it through the business to make sure Drina never found out about it. But then, should he give in now to his son's demands there would be nothing to stop him being blackmailed again in the future. Joe was in such a dilemma, he didn't know what to do.

Michael was aware that his deadline with Charlie was approaching. He demanded, 'Make your mind up, Father, I haven't got all day.'

To stall for time while he tried to decide what to do for the best, Joe asked, 'I take it you owe the wrong sort of people money and that's why you've resorted to robbing your own parents again?'

Waving the crowbar at him menacingly, Michael snapped, 'Just tell me what it's to be, Father. After all, I'm only collecting some of my inheritance early, that's all.'

Joe shook his head at him. 'People leave their possessions to those they feel are deserving of them. You seem to think that just because you're my son, you can sit back and wait for me to die and then everything will be handed to you without your having to lift a finger to earn it. Well, I've got news for you. I've made sure you get nothing when I die, because that's what you deserve.'

Michael sniggered. 'So what have you done? Willed the lot to Mother? Because if you're not leaving anything to me, then you've no one else to leave it to except for distant cousins. I know you've no other close family left alive. If you leave everything to Mother then you can count on the fact that I will make it my business to take every penny off her. Leave it to distant cousins and I'll contest the will and win because I'm your only son. There's nothing you can do to change that fact. Now, I've had enough of this. Do I tell Mother your dirty secrets or what?'

Joe knew he had no choice but to agree to let his son help himself to the cash in the safe. He wasn't prepared to risk losing all he'd worked hard for or the position in life he'd forged himself. He was about to speak when instead he slumped back in his chair as a vice-like grip clamped his heart, followed by pain so excruciating it took his breath away. He knew immediately what was happening. The shock and stress of Michael's visit had brought on a heart attack, something the consultant had warned him could happen if he didn't take things much easier from now on and avoid situations such as the one he was now caught up in.

Gasping for breath, he croaked, 'Call an ambulance. I'm having a heart attack.'

Michael stared at his father blindly, unsure whether he really was ill or merely acting in an attempt to foil the robbery. It then struck him that even the most gifted actor couldn't put on a performance of the calibre his father was. The fact that he could be dying didn't bother Michael in the slightest; he merely saw it as his chance to get his hands on what he'd come for and get the hell out while his father was in any position to stop him.

Writhing in agony in his chair, all Joe could do was watch his son crouch down in front of the safe, frenziedly scooping out all the bundles of notes and bags of coins, roughly counting as he did. He was mortally relieved to find more than the five thousand pounds he needed, putting it all into the black holdall.

Having locked the safe again, Michael stood up, slung the holdall over his shoulder, and with one sweep of his beefy hand knocked the telephone off the desk so that his father couldn't reach it. Then he smirked at Joe before walking out of the office, shutting the door firmly behind him. After replacing the safe key where he had found it, he left the building without a backward glance.

CHAPTER TWENTY-NINE

Drina sat nursing a cup of tea at the kitchen table. Her face was grey from lack of sleep, eyes red and swollen from crying. Joe's appalling behaviour last night was the final straw. She had never felt so humiliated in all her life. She had worked hard to make the dinner party a success, throwing herself into cooking home-made potato and leek soup, Beef Wellington and a fancy gateau for dessert, followed by a board of various cheeses, grapes and sliced apple, and percolated coffee with cream. She'd polished the silver cutlery until it shone; set the table with her best linen cloth and china; checked they had enough spirits and mixers . . . all to do Joe proud, but also to help take Drina's own mind off how dreadfully she was missing working at the camp, all the friends she had made there, but most of all Artie's company.

When there was no sign of her husband at seven-thirty and the guests were due at eight, she had called his private line in the office and, receiving no reply, had assumed he was on his way home. But he still hadn't appeared by the time the guests arrived nor had he by the time they left, full of food and drink and not one of believing her excuses for Joe's absence. She'd said he'd had to work late at the camp after a major problem had occurred that only he could deal with. Where they thought he really was, she didn't want to guess.

Drina knew, though. Where else would he have spent the night but with his mistress, Fiona Hickson? Or, if not with her, then with some other woman who had caught his roving eye. In the past Joe had always let her know when he was going to be late home, covering his philanderings with the pretence that he was working, but he'd never not returned home before she had woken up in the morning. Last night, though, he couldn't even be bothered to do her the courtesy of telephoning with a lame excuse for his absence. Drina wondered what excuse he'd try to palm her off with when he did finally show up, which she suspected now would be after work tonight. But if this behaviour was a sign of things to come then enough was enough as far as Drina was concerned. She was no longer prepared to stay in a marriage that was growing ever more miserable for her, and especially since she had recently had a taste of what it was like to have someone show her care and respect.

She was going to leave Joe and seek a divorce. She knew he was having affairs but had no concrete proof to offer a lawyer. Saying you didn't love someone any longer was not enough of a reason in law to end a marriage with a share of the assets, so chances were she'd end up with nothing. Whereas she had worried before that if she left Joe she risked ending up walking the streets, with no skills to her name to help her get a job, now thanks to his stroke she knew she did possess skills that someone would pay for. As long as that pay brought her a roof over her head and food in her stomach, that was enough for Drina.

She was going to leave today. She'd no idea where she would go. She wished she had the confidence to see Artie, ask him if he wanted to take a chance on her like she was more than prepared to do on him, but although in some respects she had more confidence in her own abilities now, she still had none in her attractions as a woman. She decided she would follow her father's lead. He had embarked on a journey in the hope of gaining a better life for himself and his daughter without having a clue where he was heading, just seeing where the road led him. That's what she would do. She would catch a bus into Lincoln and see then where the road took her.

But first she would go to the office and tell Joe that she was leaving him. Despite how badly he'd treated her, she didn't feel it was right for him eventually to return home and find her gone with no explanation.

A while later, her cases packed with as many of her personal belongings as she was able to carry and standing by the door for her to collect later by taxi, Drina put on her coat, hooked her handbag on her arm, and set off to walk the mile to the camp.

When she arrived in the general office she was left in absolutely no doubt how much she had been missed and just how pleased the two young women there were to see her.

Jackie was clapping her hands in delight. She blurted out, 'Are you coming back to work, Mrs Jolly?'

At the same time Rhonnie told her with great sincerity, 'Oh, it's so good to see you, Mrs Jolly. I've been worried about you.'

Drina said, 'Well, you can see for yourself, dear, I'm fine. To answer your question, Jackie, no, I'm not coming back to work. But I have called in to see Mr Jolly. Will you tell him I'd like a few minutes of his time, please, Rhonnie?'

'I can't, Mrs Jolly. Well what I mean is, Mr Jolly hasn't arrived for work yet. Well, his door isn't open and he always usually has it open until Jackie and myself arrive so that he can check we're not late.'

Drina declined to say out loud what she thought of him for doing such a thing to loyal staff members.

Rhonnie was saying, 'Because time was wearing on, we were beginning to wonder if Mr Jolly had been taken ill again . . . er . . . not that we wished anything had happened to him, but when you walked in, well, we thought that you were coming back to work.'

Drina knew she would cry if she heard any more about how much the girls missed her, considering that when she left today it was doubtful she would ever see them again. She briskly said to Rhonnie, 'Mr Jolly must have had an errand to do before he came to work. I do need to see him, though, so I'll wait in my . . . his office for him.'

'Can I make you some tea, Mrs Jolly?' Jackie offered.

Drina thought she may as well have some while she waited. 'Yes, please, that would be lovely.'

Rhonnie had hardly positioned her fingers on the keys to her typewriter and Jackie had not reached the tea-making table at the back of the room when a frantic cry of 'Oh, my God!' was heard coming from the boss's office.

Rhonnie told Jackie to stay where she was and shot around her own desk and into the next room. She arrived to find Drina standing before the body of Joe Jolly, slumped in his office chair. His mouth gaped wide open; sightless eyes still held a reflection of the agony he had been in when he'd drawn his last breath. His skin was the colour of alabaster, his lips tinged blue.

Rhonnie called to Jackie to fetch the duty nurse quickly before she herself returned to Mrs Jolly. She put one arm protectively around Drina's shoulders and gently coaxed her away from the traumatic sight, leading her back into the outer office to await the nurse.

CHAPTER THIRTY

Positive that his father could not possibly have survived the severe heart attack he had seen him suffering the previous night, on Saturday morning bright and early Michael was waiting anxiously outside the local newsagent's for a copy of the local daily newspaper. He was desperate to read news of his father's death, and so was disappointed when he finally scanned his eyes over every page, even the sports ones, and found nothing at all. He supposed, though, depending on when Joe's body was discovered, it would have been a bit fast for the Saturday edition to report the death. This meant he had to wait until Monday for the next local paper to come out.

To Michael, Monday seemed an age away. He felt his temper rise. He wanted it confirmed that he was going to be collecting his dues very shortly and then he could start making definite plans for what he was going to do with the money, not just fantasize about it any longer. Other than waiting for news in the paper he had no way of having his father's death confirmed. He couldn't go and make enquiries up at the camp as his face was too well known by many of the staff there. He could hardly telephone the camp anonymously as that would awaken suspicions that there was more to his father's death than there appeared to be. And there was the money missing from the safe. He was glad now that he had taken the time to lock it up and return the key where he had found it, as hopefully it would now be thought that someone inside the office had helped themselves to the money, or even that Joe had had it himself as he was at liberty to do.

It was hard to stay patient but at least, Michael thought smugly, he had honoured his agreement with Cut Throat Charlie and his own life was no longer in danger, so that was one worry lifted. And his escapade last night had reaped him an added bonus. After he'd settled with Charlie he'd been left with nearly a hundred pounds, together with the fiver he'd swiped from the petty cash, more money than he'd been able to muster since he'd last been successful in robbing his parents. It would come in very handy indeed for helping him pass the time between now and Monday morning.

On Saturday afternoon, lying to Gloria that he was off to seek out holidaymakers to con and would take her out tonight if successful, he caught a train to Lincoln, deciding to give himself a taste of the sort of life he was shortly expecting to live. On arrival he made his way straight to Burton's the men's outfitters and bought himself an expensive off-the-peg suit with all the accessories. His new clothes neatly packed into bags, his next stop was at a shoe shop, then a barber's for a haircut and shave. Then he booked himself into the best hotel Lincoln offered, ordered himself a large breakfast from room service, and, after greedily clearing the plate, took a long soak in the bath while drinking the bottle of champagne he'd also had delivered.

Dressed smartly in his brand new clothes, he went out, spent a while in a bookie's, losing ten pounds in the process, then took himself off to a bar frequented by types he intended to be mixing with in future. He met what he considered to be a classy hooker and took her back to his hotel room, where he meant to spend the rest of the weekend with her having rampant sex and eating good food along with more champagne, before he was back in Skegness waiting outside the newsagent's for the papers to arrive on Monday.

But to his fury he awoke in the early hours of Monday morning to find that she had absconded with all the rest of the money he had left from his father's safe, but for the loose change in his trouser pockets amounting to just under three pounds. This left him with no choice but to steal his way out of the hotel through the back corridors, slinking in the shadows to avoid detection by the staff as he was unable to settle his bill. Thankfully he hadn't given his real name when booking in, but they'd still be able to give a description to the police so it would be a long time before he'd dare show his face here again. But then, he didn't plan to remain in England anyway so it was of no consequence to him.

Catching the first bus back to Mablethorpe at a quarter to six, he arrived at the newsagent's just as the papers were delivered. Unable to contain himself, he forcefully pushed his way to the head of the queue and was reading the headlines before he'd paid for the paper. And, joy of joys, there it was on the front page, the very story he'd been desperate to read. According to the report, his father had been found dead on Saturday morning in his office . . . it didn't say by whom. The doctor who'd attended believed he had died from a massive heart attack the evening before. From the broken telephone found nearby him on the floor, it appeared that Joe Jolly had tried to phone for help when he realised what was happening to him, but had knocked it off the table and out of reach before he could. There was no mention of the money missing from the safe, so probably when the paper went to press it hadn't yet been discovered. The report then went on to describe Joe Jolly as a well-respected member of the community, praised his abilities as a businessman, and ended with commiserations to his family and friends for their sad loss. At those last words, Michael snorted with amusement. Like hell was Joe Jolly's death a sad loss to him! In jubilation he punched the air with one fist and cried out, 'Eureka!' much to the bemusement of an old gentleman standing close by him reading the same page of the newspaper. For the life of him he could not figure out what the young man could be so happy about at the sudden death of such a prominent local figure.

The funeral, the newspaper reported, would take place on Thursday at Threddington Church at two o'clock. Michael had no intention of attending to pay his last respects to the man he had come to despise, father or not, but he certainly meant to be present at the reading of the will in order to take immediate possession of his inheritance.

CHAPTER THIRTY-ONE

Drina checked her appearance in the dressing mirror, the same one in which her husband had conceitedly admired himself only a few days ago. She, though, wasn't pleased in any way with her reflection. Black had never suited her. Whereas on other women it hid their lumps and bumps, making them look slinky and sexy, all the colour did for her was make her appear shorter and dumpier than she actually was. But today wasn't about what she looked like. Today was about laying her husband to rest.

She wearily shut her eyes as a surge of guilt returned. It had been plaguing her ever since she had discovered Joe's body. While he was dying she'd believed him to be with his mistress and was herself planning to leave him. This was something she would have to learn to live with, though, as she couldn't change the past. She might have been planning to free herself from her tie to Joe but never for a moment had she wished it to be in this way. Although any romantic feelings for him had dwindled long ago, his untimely death had left her devastated.

She heard a tap on the door and turned to see Rhonnie come in. 'The car is here, Mrs Jolly.'

Drina gave her a wan smile. 'Thank you, dear. I'll be down in a moment.'

Drina had no idea how she would have coped over the last few days without the support of Rhonnie and Dan, who had taken over the running of the camp, kept up staff morale, and helped her make the funeral arrangements. She would never be able to thank either of them enough for the care they'd shown her in her hour of need. It had been apparent to Drina that Rhonnie herself was indifferent to Joe's death as her short association with him hadn't been particularly happy, but Dan was extremely upset by the loss of the man he'd held in such high esteem.

Knowing without doubt what Michael was planning to do with the camp and the house once they were put in his name – sell them both and live the good life on the proceeds, for however long they lasted – Drina had not bothered to unpack her suitcases, only taking from them her toiletries and the clothes she'd needed over the last five days. She had no doubt whatsoever that her son would take great delight in turfing her out with immediate effect, just for the spite of it. With no other options open to her she still planned to see where the road led her and, wherever she landed up, work hard to make the best future she could for herself. She was, though, very much concerned for Jolly's employees, in particular the four she considered her friends, Rhonnie, Dan, Artie and Jackie, hoping that for all Michael's selfishness he did have a shred of decency lurking somewhere and would sort out a buyer for the camp who intended to keep it running so that their jobs were safe, and not sell to a developer or such like to build houses on.

Knowing her son as she did, Drina realised Michael wouldn't bother attending the funeral and pretending to be a grieving son, but he would be there on the dot for the reading of the will. Out of respect for Joe she'd have to sit and watch Michael gloat as Mr Grimbold, Joe's solicitor, proclaimed him sole beneficiary to his father's estate. That Joe would not leave 'his' wealth to Drina was understood between them. Because of their Romany traditions, no matter that it had originated from her family, Joe believed the marital assets to be entirely his to dispose of as he chose – and that meant they'd go to his male heir, she knew. She could contest this, but that would take time and money – and Drina had no stomach for the fight.

She knew that she would need to prepare herself to come face to face with Joe's current mistress at the funeral. Although she did not condone the woman's behaviour in having an affair with a married man, she did feel some sympathy for Fiona's loss of her lover. It was going to be difficult for her, having to hide her devastation so that none of the other mourners had an inkling that her relationship with Joe had been anything more than that between boss and employee. She'd need to keep her reputation as a respectable woman intact. Drina could have taken this opportunity to let Fiona Hickson know she was aware of her illicit carryings on with Joe and to give her a piece of her mind, but felt the woman was suffering enough already. Added to her heartache was the fact that she knew she no longer had a job with Jolly's.

When Rhonnie had been consoling Drina after the shock of finding Joe, she had let her know that she would be there for her night and day if necessary, as Fiona Hickson had been reinstated and was resuming her job in the camp on Monday. Drina was a tolerant person but not tolerant enough to let the woman who had caused her so much hurt over the years keep her job at the camp by shoving Rhonnie out of her way. As matters stood, until Michael was officially handed his inheritance, Drina herself was technically in charge of the business, so who stayed and who went was her decision. She thought it only fair and morally right that Fiona Hickson be told personally of her lover's death, and not through reading about it in the local paper or when she arrived to commence work again on Monday morning. So on Saturday afternoon, when she had disturbed Mr Grimbold at home to inform him of Joe's demise, Drina also asked him if he would be kind enough to telephone Fiona and break the news to her. All he was aware of was that he was informing Joe's office manager of the sudden death – and, at the same time, that unfortunately her services would not now be required.

On Monday morning a reluctant Mr Holder, the accountant,

who had not wanted to bother her at such a time but felt compelled to due to the seriousness of the situation, informed Drina that he'd belatedly gone to do the banking of the week's takings only to discover a large amount of cash missing, over five thousand pounds. Mr Jolly had left no record informing him what had been done with the money and Mr Holder could not account for it in the books. He'd also discovered the petty cash was five pounds short too.

She didn't tell Mr Holder so but Drina immediately assumed she knew what Joe had done with the money. He must have gifted it to Fiona Hickson, to compensate her for the wages she'd lost out on while she had been temporarily relieved of her post at Jolly's courtesy of Michael. His spiteful actions in ordering the woman out could only have resulted from his discovery of her affair with his father. He had exceeded his authority there, of course, but at least it had brought Rhonnie back into the fold. Why Joe had decided to add the five pounds from the petty cash as well, as if he wasn't already giving her enough, would always remain a mystery.

Rhonnie had been over the moon to know that she had her job back and Drina just prayed that she wasn't about to lose it again very shortly, along with the rest of the employees.

Collecting her dark coat from the bed, she put it on, slipped on her black court shoes and picked up the matching bag, and went to take her place as chief mourner in the funeral procession.

Meanwhile in the dingy flat in Skegness, after a long hard night spent selling her body to anyone who would pay for it, Gloria finally roused herself at one o'clock to see Michael had finally returned after being absent all weekend. He was dressed very smartly in a suit she'd never seen before along with a new shirt and shoes, combing his recently cut hair before a cracked shaving mirror on top of the shabby chest of drawers. Reclining on one elbow she demanded, 'Where did you get the money from to tog yourself up all posh like?'

Still teasing his hair into place, Michael blandly answered her, 'Found it in a gutter.'

Gloria tutted to let him know she didn't believe him. 'So hand over my share, for the rent and food you owe me?'

'Can't, I'm wearing it,' he said.

'You bastard!' she screamed at him. 'Well, enough is enough. I want you out. Wherever it is yer off to, yer can take yer stuff with yer.'

He turned to face her then, grinning wickedly. 'Be my pleasure. Only I've no need for that old tat any longer, so do what you like with it.' He took great delight in adding, 'I've come into my inheritance, you see. So I no longer have need of you either.'

Her eyes bulged. 'What! But . . . but you promised me . . .'

Laughing, he cut her short. 'Then more fool you, for believing my promises.' He scathingly ran his eyes over her and said sardonically, 'Come on, Gloria, look at you. Do you really think I want a slut like you on my arm, mixing with the people that I will be meeting in future?'

In blind rage she launched herself up and at him. Before she could wreak any damage he had caught hold of her wrists, digging his fingernails in as hard as he could until she cried out in pain. Throwing her forcefully back on the bed, he snarled menacingly, 'Try that again and I'll break your fucking neck. Well, I can't say it's been a pleasure, Gloria.'

With that Michael turned and walked out, his taunting laughter the last she heard of him.

Drina had expected a lot of people to come and pay their respects to Joe, but was surprised by the number who did. The church was packed with his friends and business associates, all seeming genuinely grieved by his sudden demise. She was very gratified to see that the cleaning supervisor, head stripey Terry Jones, the off duty nurse, chief receptionist, and several other employees, including Artie, had used their spare time to come and pay their respects too. When she came face to face with Artie, neither of them said a word to each other but he sought her hand and squeezed it to let her know his thoughts were with her. She wished she could tell him how much her thoughts were with him too, but this was neither the time nor the place, and besides, her lack of self-confidence still prevented her from telling him how she felt.

If anyone noticed the absence of Michael, then out of respect no comment was made in her presence, but during the wake at the house she did overhear several mourners expressing their disgust that Joe's only son hadn't bothered to show up and pay his respects.

Drina didn't see her son finally arrive, only knew he had when all the mourners had departed and Mr Grimbold, a slight, grey-haired man in his sixties discreetly asked her if she was ready now for the will reading.

Dan had been most surprised that morning to receive a letter from the solicitor requesting his presence at the reading, but then had realised the reason why he'd been asked. When his mother died, he had naturally been worried where that left him legally and Joe had assured him that the cottage was his to live in for life should he want to, and had said furthermore he would make provision in his will to that effect. Joe had obviously been true to his word and the solicitor's request for Dan's presence was so that he could be informed officially that he was now the owner of the cottage. He was thrilled to be a house owner but still extremely upset by the way it had come about. He knew he'd find the experience overwhelming so asked Rhonnie to accompany him to the reading for support.

Drina suspected that her son would be waiting for them in his father's study, having slipped into the house unnoticed so as not to come face to face with any genuine mourners. She was right. When she showed Mr Grimbold into the study Michael was already sitting in his father's chair behind the desk, feet up on top of it, a look of smug satisfaction on his face. Drina fought to avoid his gaze. She felt wicked that the child to whom she had given life, the one she had loved with every fibre of her being when he was born and had vowed to care for to the best of her ability, she now couldn't bear to look at. She could sense his eyes boring into her, telling her silently that these were the last minutes she was ever going to spend in this house.

Much to Drina's embarrassment, Michael made no attempt to offer the solicitor the place behind the desk, but remained sitting there himself so that the other man had no choice but to take a seat on the visitor's side.

As soon as Dan and Rhonnie walked in a moment or two later, Michael erupted, 'What are they doing in here? This is family business and they aren't family.'

Mr Grimbold gave a discreet cough and evenly informed him that Mr Buckland was here at the solicitor's request as he was a beneficiary of Mr Jolly's will. If Mr Buckland wanted his wife with him during the reading then that was his right.

Michael was not at all happy to learn that he was not his father's sole beneficiary but supposed that after all Buckland had worked for Joe since he was a young boy, and was probably his longest-serving member of staff. If he'd been left a pair of cufflinks or such like by way of thanking him for his loyalty, then Michael could afford to be gracious about that.

With everyone seated now, holding Joe Jolly's last Will and Testament in his hand, Mr Grimbold cleared his throat and began. 'I . . .'

He got no further before he was rudely interrupted by Michael who commanded him, 'Cut the crap, old man, and get to the nitty-gritty. I want this over with so I can start celebrating.'

Drina cringed in shame for her son's lack of respect. Rhonnie and Dan just stared at him in disbelief.

Not a muscle of the old solicitor's face moved but he looked to Drina for guidance. She nodded to tell him it was all right with her if he did as her son demanded, wanting to get this over with so she could escape from Michael as quickly as possible.

Mr Grimbold cleared his throat and began again. 'I leave my entire estate to my eldest son and heir . . .'

At this juncture, Michael leaned his head back in the chair and closed his eyes, meaning to savour every bit of what he'd waited so long to hear.

'. . . Daniel Buckland,' Mr Grimbold concluded.

Everyone in the room stared at him in total shock.

Michael's eyes opened wide and he roared, '*What!* You stupid man, you've read out the wrong name.'

Mr Grimbold said calmly, 'I can assure you I haven't, sir. Mr Buckland is Mr Jolly's son from his relationship with a Miss Sadie Buckland, although she styled herself Mrs. Although Mr Joseph Jolly is not named on Mr Buckland's birth certificate, I do have in my possession a letter in Mr Jolly's own hand admitting he is Mr Buckland's father.' He delved into his briefcase, pulled out a white envelope which he held for Michael to take while continuing, 'I should tell you, sir, that in Mr Jolly's original will, made just after you were born, he made provision to divide his estate equally between yourself and Mr Buckland, his wish being that both his sons, as the half-brothers they are, would work together to run the business. But ten years ago, you having proved by then to be . . . well . . . something of a disappointment to Mr Jolly, and showing no sign of ever changing for the better, he instructed me to write the new will, leaving his entire estate to Mr Buckland.'

Everyone but Michael was still stunned speechless by these revelations. He was on his feet now, his face wreathed in fury, ignoring the envelope Mr Grimbold was offering him. He banged one fat fist on the desk top, frenziedly yelling out, 'That letter is a forgery! My mother's bribed you to fake it, to stop me getting my rights.' He wagged one finger at Dan then. 'He's got to be in on it too. You're all in on it! This is fraud. I'll have you all jailed for this. That man is not my father's son . . .'

Unconcerned by Michael's rantings and threats, Mr Grimbold quietly said to him, 'I can assure you, sir, that the letter is no forgery. Mr Jolly had witnesses present at the time of writing it to avoid a situation such as this arising. Those witnesses were my two business partners, solicitors in their own right, who would never risk being barred from practising or losing their good reputation by putting their name to anything that wasn't lawful.'

Michael froze then, staring wildly at the solicitor. His father had warned him he was leaving him nothing but Michael had firmly believed he'd been bluffing at the time, with no idea then that he wasn't Joe's only offspring. Hatred escalated inside him. To be disinherited in favour of a bastard . . . all his hopes and dreams for the future he planned himself faded and died. What the hell was he going to do now? All he possessed was what he was wearing; the only money he had was the loose change in his pocket. He'd not even enough for a bed for the night in a cheap lodging house. After his parting words to Gloria and the way he'd treated her there was no hope that she'd ever take him back, even just for one night out of pity for his situation. But above all these worries, a flame of resolve flared in him.

Stepping over to his mother, he bent and whispered in her ear, 'The newspaper report on Father's death wasn't accurate, Mother dearest. He did not knock the telephone off the desk, trying to pick it up and call for help. It was I who knocked it off, to stop him from receiving any.' Then, at his mother's gasp of shock, righting himself he reared back his head and furiously announced to the rest of the gathering, 'Be warned. I will find a way to get what is mine, you see if I don't.'

With that he stormed from the house and out into the darkening, chilly afternoon.

CHAPTER THIRTY-TWO

Despite reeling herself from the shocking news that Dan was in fact Joe Jolly's son, Rhonnie wondered how his widow was feeling now that it had been announced. While Dan was sitting stiffly beside Rhonnie, staring blindly into space, Drina Jolly sat with her head bowed and her hands clasped tightly together in her lap. Each of them needed her support, but it was impossible for Rhonnie to offer it to them both simultaneously and she wondered which was most in need.

She was still trying to make the difficult decision when Drina politely thanked Mr Grimbold and asked them all to excuse her. She left the room in silence. Rhonnie heard her footsteps going upstairs. She turned to Dan. 'Darling . . .' she ventured.

He slowly turned his head to look at her, eyes filled with hurt and bewilderment. 'Rhonnie, I need to be on my own for a while,' he said.

She patted his hand by way of telling him she perfectly understood, then hurried after Drina.

She found her friend upstairs, sitting on her bed with her head in her hands, quietly sobbing. Rhonnie went over and sat down beside her, putting one arm protectively around her shoulders. 'I am so sorry about all this, Mrs Jolly. I can see you had no idea that Dan was Mr Jolly's son. I know Dan had no idea either. It must have come as a terrible shock to both of you.'

In fact, as shocking as it had been to Drina to learn of this, it was not the full reason why she was now so distressed.

Michael's confession had shocked her to the core. He'd been there in the office at the time his father was having a heart attack; had more than likely been the cause of it too as it was obvious to Drina now that it was Michael who had taken the money from the safe, not Joe who had given it to Fiona Hickson. And not only that but her son had prevented his father from summoning help which could have resulted in his life being saved. Drina couldn't bear to think that such a despicable human being was her own flesh and blood. She could never tell another living soul how low he had actually sunk and just what he was capable of.

She lifted her head. With tears still streaming down her face, she sobbed to Rhonnie, 'I don't know who I feel most sorry for. Poor Dan for finding out this way who his father really was – or myself for being so naïve I did not realise the extent of Joe's deceit.' She paused and gave a violent shudder, as if someone was walking over her grave, before quietly continuing, 'I should have known. Dan obviously meant far more to Joe than he admitted. The son of a dead cousin, he said. But the way he was with Dan, people often used to joke that if they didn't know better, they would have believed them to be father and son. Little did any of us but Joe himself know how true that was! Even when our own son came along, Joe's relationship with Dan never changed. But then at the time, you see, I was having to come to terms with the fact that it was apparent to me that Dan's mother, Sadie, was far more to Joe than just a distant relative's widow. But I never thought beyond that.

'It took me a while to realise that something was going on between Joe and Sadie. I first began to suspect from little things . . . the way they looked at each other when they thought no one else was watching them; the way their hands would touch when they passed each other. Joe making any excuse he could to visit her in the cottage, and his eyes lighting up when she walked into a room. I realised then they were besotted with each other and were having an affair.

'When she first arrived on our doorstep, only months after we'd married in fact, as far as I was aware it was out of the blue. I realise now it must all have been planned very carefully by them both. She appeared and told my husband his cousin had died, leaving her with their toddler to care for and no way to earn a living for them both. She said she'd no family to turn to because they had been so disappointed and disgusted when they learned she was having a relationship with a no-good gypsy fairground worker, warning her they would never give her their permission to marry him, even for the sake of the child she was then carrying. She loved Joe's cousin, she said, far too much ever to contemplate giving him up, so she went ahead and married him. Joe's cousin had told her about him, said that they were good friends and Joe would help if she was ever in trouble. That's why she had come to us when she was widowed.

'Sadie was a very pretty young woman, the same age as I was, and I can't deny that I took an instant liking to her, really welcomed the idea of having someone my own age around to be friends with. I felt so sad for her, though. I had not long since lost my father and knew how painful that was, so couldn't imagine what she was going through, losing her beloved husband in a fairground accident, leaving her with a two-year-old child to care for and no one but us to turn to. I told Joe that we must help her, and of course I realise now why he readily agreed. Joe insisted that the least he could do in memory of his dead cousin was to find his wife and son somewhere to live and give her a decent job so that she was able to support them both properly. He said he knew his cousin would have done the same for me had the tables been turned.'

Drina paused long enough to heave a miserable sigh before going on, 'Now I realise that story was only partially true. Sadie's parents *had* disowned her for getting romantically involved with a gypsy fairground worker and refused to give her their blessing or permission to marry him, but the cousin didn't exist. It was Joe himself who had fathered her child. When he heard through the gypsy grapevine that my father had died, leaving me a relatively wealthy woman, Sadie and he were obviously living a hand-to-mouth existence. Fairground workers don't make much money and unless they somehow manage to buy their own rides they never improve their lot. Joe obviously saw this as a golden opportunity for him to improve both their lives and their son's. Whether he was in fact a distant cousin of my father's sent up by the family to help me, I'm now beginning to doubt very much. Knowing Joe as I do, even if Sadie had been absolutely against the idea of him marrying another woman to get his hands on her assets, by the time he'd worked his charms on her, she would have been putty in his hands. Joe always got his own way.

'When Sadie first showed up, the camp was still just a tent and caravan site, the development of the chalets only in the planning stages, so Joe gave her a job in the little shop in a hut where we sold essentials to the campers, like wood for the campfires, bread, milk, that kind of thing, and as I then believed secured the tenancy on the cottage you now live in for her and Dan to live in. By the time she died, Sadie was in charge of all the chalet maids and general cleaning staff. It wasn't until after that that I learned from Dan that he thought Mr Jolly very kind to be letting him stay on in the house rent-free, and of Joe's promise to him that he'd never need to worry about his living arrangements because the house would be made over to him in my husband's will. Joe had obviously lied to me about renting the cottage and had bought it for them using some of my inheritance, hiding the cost in the business somehow so I wouldn't ever find out.

'Until Sadie died so tragically and unexpectedly when Dan had only just turned fifteen, I'd only suspected them of having a passing affair. But Joe's reaction to her death left me in no doubt of his total devastation. It was as if a light had gone out behind his eyes. Life had lost its meaning for him. Sadie had in fact been the love of his life. Joe had many affairs after that, probably with more women than I know of, but I know none of them ever meant as much to him as Sadie had done.'

She flashed a wan smile at Rhonnie then. 'You must be wondering why I never left my husband, knowing how badly he was betraying me and that he'd never actually loved me but married me for my inheritance? Well, just as Sadie pretended was the case for her, I had no one to turn to and nowhere to go. No money of my own to start again with, my inheritance being all tied up in the business. And besides, Joe would never have divorced me because of the damage it would have done to the business and his own reputation.'

Drina couldn't admit she had actually made the decision finally to leave Joe and her last visit to the office had been to tell him so. She was overwhelmed with guilt that she had believed him to be with another woman when in fact he was innocent for once and, worse still, dying at the time.

She heaved another sigh then and affectionately patted Rhonnie's hand, telling her in all sincerity, 'I'm very fond of Dan. Have lost count of the number of times I wished my own son was just like him . . . that he was my son, in fact. If I could pick anyone to inherit Joe's estate, Dan would be my first choice. The camp, for obvious reasons, is very close to my heart. It gives me great comfort to know that you and Dan together will make the perfect team to keep the place operating successfully. People will be coming here on holidays to remember for many years to come.' She rose to her feet then, telling Rhonnie, 'I have to be going. It's getting late and I don't want to miss the last bus into Mablethorpe tonight. I wish you and Dan all the best, my dear.'

Rhonnie watched her prepare to go, feeling consumed by sadness for the loveless life a wonderful woman like Drina Jolly had endured, simply because she had fallen for the charms of a deceitful man. She'd watched Drina put on her coat, hook her handbag over her arm and begin to walk out before what she'd just said fully registered. Rhonnie jumped up off the bed, calling,

'Where are you going, Mrs Jolly? You can't leave . . . you belong here.'

Dan walked in then, still looking ashen and drawn from the shock of what he'd discovered today. Nevertheless there was something important that he must do. He said to Drina, 'Rhonnie's right. You can't leave, you belong here.'

Drina smiled at him. 'I appreciate your saying that, but I need to start my new life. The business and this house are yours now.'

He shook his head. 'No, they're not.' He looked over at Rhonnie apologetically. 'I should have discussed it with you first but I needed to do what I knew was right, and couldn't let Mr Grimbold leave without instructing him.'

Rhonnie smiled back at him. 'Darling, I will stand by you no matter what you've done. Besides, whatever it is, it will have been the right thing for you – and that's all that matters for me.'

Drina was looking at him, puzzled. 'Just what have you done, Dan?'

'Handed back what is not rightfully mine . . . not yet, at least. Without that inheritance from your father, there would have been no business or house for me to inherit. Yes, I do know all about that. Please don't think badly of her but Rhonnie told me. With no disrespect to Mr Jolly, when you were running the place while he was recovering from his stroke, the staff were far happier with your way of doing things than they were under him. You were born to run the camp, Mrs Jolly, and Rhonnie and I will be more than happy just to help you do that, until you're ready to hand it over to me. And we're happy living in our little cottage. This house is your home. Mr Grimbold is going to have the legal papers drawn up as fast as he can.'

Rhonnie was looking over at her husband with such pride and love that she felt she would burst.

Drina was speechless.

CHAPTER THIRTY-THREE

Several weeks later Rhonnie and Dan stood by the entrance gates to the camp, waving off the coach containing the last of the seasonal staff. Not Ginger, though. Much to Rhonnie's delight, her friend and a couple of other chalet maids were sharing a small flat in Mablethorpe during the winter months and all of them had secured jobs to tide them over until they returned next March to get the camp ready for the start of the season, which meant Rhonnie would still see her regularly. Unbeknown to Ginger, Rhonnie had had a long chat with her supervisor yesterday and received the distinct impression that the woman was holding back from praising Ginger's work too highly because she didn't want to lose a good worker. Rhonnie supposed she couldn't blame her. But come next spring Rhonnie meant to recommend to Drina, as she and Dan now called her, that they give Ginger a chance to fulfil her long-term dream of becoming a receptionist. Rhonnie desperately wanted to tell her friend her plan, knowing she would be beside herself with excitement, but until it was definite she would just have to keep it to herself so as not to risk disappointing Ginger.

Dan said to her, 'Where's Drina, by the way? I thought she'd have been here to see the last of the staff away.'

'Oh, she said her goodbyes last night at the staff leaving party. She's gone out . . . wouldn't say where. Funny, but my father has gone out too and *he* wouldn't tell me where he was off to either. Those two can deny it as much as they like but I know that after a suitable time has passed there will be the announcement of an engagement. I'd bet my last penny on that.'

'And you'd be happy with that, love?' he asked her.

'You know very well I'd be absolutely delighted. Drina would become proper family to us both then, wouldn't she? And I know you'd like that as much as I would.'

'You're right, I would.' Dan then walked around to stand behind one of the two tall wrought-iron gates. 'Come on then, Rhonnie,' he called over to her. 'Let's get these main gates shut. You may be winding down to take it a lot easier over the winter, but my job keeping the camp ship-shape and in perfect working order is certainly not seasonal. I'm as busy as I always am, and don't forget I have to organise men to cover me while we're away on honeymoon in Spain next week, thanks to Drina's wedding present.'

That was something Rhonnie was very much looking forward to. A whole week in a Spanish hotel with no crises at the camp disrupting their time together. She smiled back at him as together they heaved the gates shut.

While Dan chained and padlocked them, Rhonnie leaned back against the railings and heaved a sigh.

Dan immediately looked over at her in concern. 'What's the matter, Rhonnie?'

'Oh, absolutely nothing. There's not a happier woman alive than me. I was just remembering the first time I walked through these gates into what felt to me then like a ghost town. It seems incredible that it was only just coming up for nine months ago. Such a lot has happened to me since then. I'm married now to the most wonderful man in the world. My father has got himself away from his awful wife and stepdaughter and has a permanent job with the maintenance crew, thanks to you. I'm helping to run the place with the most perfect boss I could ever wish for. Together we've dealt with staff fleecing the campers, and rampaging holidaymakers hell-bent on lynching an innocent man. I've walked in on a man dressed in women's underwear . . . all that as well as the normal day-to-day dramas that crop up working in a place like this.' She didn't mention the fact that they had also had a murder committed in the camp as she had nothing to substantiate this, bar the widow's confession. She finished off, 'And you've had to deal with discovering that your father was nearby all the time you were growing up, and you never knew.' Her face clouded over. 'Oh, Dan, do you think Michael meant his threat never to give up on finding a way to claim what he feels is rightfully his?'

Dan pulled a grim face. 'Knowing what he's like, I have no doubt he's working on it right now. And if anyone will find a way, he will.'

'Mmm,' Rhonnie agreed worriedly, then said more brightly, 'Well, we'll just have to face that if and when the time comes.'

As she caught Dan's hand and they walked back together towards Reception, she wondered what next season would bring with it, considering the roller-coaster ride they had faced this year. Rhonnie decided that it would be wisest to prepare herself for absolutely anything.